"If we're living in a golden age for the historical novel, then one of the genre's most gifted practitioners is American writer John Vernon . . . Vernon's description is extraordinary." — *Seattle Times*

"Too good a piece of fiction to be called a novelization . . . The fate of the Powell expedition is known, and so, to a certain extent, are the characters of the men who were on it. They live and breathe, grow lean, brown, and disputatious in this novel."
— *New York Times Book Review*

"Richly imagined . . . Vernon injects the sage of the Powell expedition with an even stronger dose of irony, tension, and tragedy than history itself provides, and thus does *The Last Canyon* leave us with both a plausible explanation of an old mystery and an augury of what will follow in the wake of Powell's famous river-boats." — *Los Angeles Times*

"A good read . . . Vernon's best fictional creations are the everyday conversations — complaining, sniping, gossiping — of Powell and his cantankerous crew." — *Denver Post*

"An adventure that rivals the life and times of explorers Lewis and Clark . . . Vernon attacks his subject with uncanny detail and enthusiasm . . . a powerful story." — *Binghamton Press and Sun-Bulletin*

"Blending fact and fiction, Vernon provides an illuminating perspective on a less familiar moment in American history . . . The research is sound and the story well written." — *Library Journal*

"When historical novels are produced by writers whose expertise in the field is matched by vivid storytelling skills, the results — as in this novel — are generally outstanding." — *Publishers Weekly*

"A rousing story of adventure and exploration . . . the many voices Vernon weaves into his tale remind the reader of the price of those discoveries for the men who made them." — *BookPage*

"Vernon's best yet." — *Kirkus Reviews*

BOOKS BY JOHN VERNON

The Last Canyon
A Book of Reasons
All for Love
Peter Doyle
Lindbergh's Son
La Salle
Money and Fiction
Poetry and the Body
Ann
The Garden and the Map

The Last Canyon

John Vernon

A Mariner Book
HOUGHTON MIFFLIN COMPANY
Boston   New York

First Mariner Books edition 2002

Visit our Web site: www.houghtonmifflinbooks.com.

Library of Congress Cataloging-in-Publication Data
Vernon, John, date.
The last canyon / John Vernon.
   p.   cm.
   ISBN 0-618-10940-4
   ISBN 0-618-25774-8 (pbk.)
   1. Powell, John Wesley, 1834–1902 — Fiction. 2. Colorado
River (Colo.–Mexico) — Fiction. 3. Grand Canyon (Ariz.) —
Fiction. 4. Conservationists — Fiction. 5. Paiute Indians —
Fiction. 6. Naturalists — Fiction. 7. Explorers — Fiction. I. Title.
PS3572.E76 G74   2001
813'.54 — dc21   2001024546

Printed in the United States of America

QUM 10 9 8 7 6 5 4 3 2 1

Book design by Melissa Lotfy
Typefaces: Adobe Caslon, Rockwell

Map by Jacques Chazaud

For Ann

Author's Note

The name "Grand Canyon" had been used before Powell's 1869 expedition, but wasn't yet common; Powell in fact helped fix that name in the imagination of Americans with his 1874 account of the expedition. When the trip took place, however, "Big Canyon" and "Great Canyon" were also frequently employed. I've chosen "Great Canyon" as the operable name in this novel to emphasize the lack of familiarity in 1869 with what has since become an American icon.

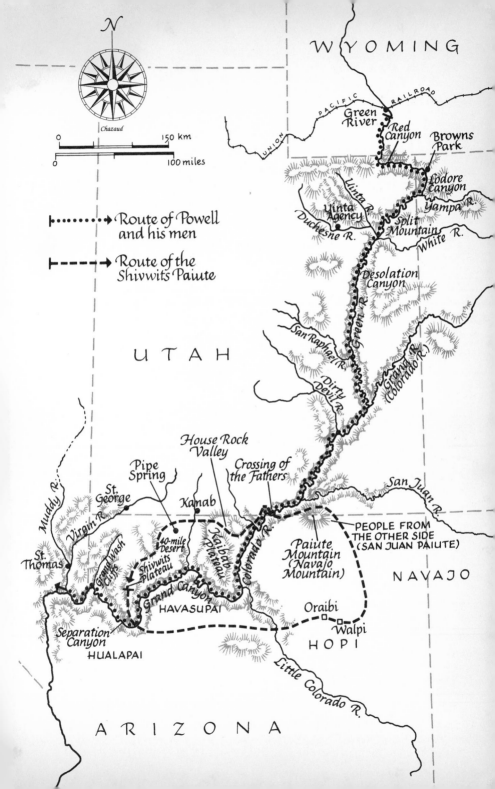

Characters

The *Emma Dean:* Major Powell, Bill Dunn, Jack Sumner

The *Kitty Clyde's Sister:* Walter Powell, George Bradley

The *No Name:* Oramel Howland, Seneca Howland, Frank Goodman

The *Maid of the Canyon:* William Hawkins (a.k.a. Missouri Rhodes), Andy Hall

SHIVWITS PAIUTE CHARACTERS — TOAB'S FAMILY

NAME	RELATION	ENGLISH MEANING
Onchok	—	Wink
Pooeechuts	Onchok's wife	Mouse
Mara	Pooeechuts's sister	Metate (grinding stone)
Toab	Onchok's cousin	Rabbit Tick
Kwits		Left-handed
Soxor	Children of Onchok and Pooeechuts	Moist
Chookwadum		Skinny One

Note: For the historical Paiute, cousins were equivalent to siblings and were often referred to as "brother" or "sister."

OTHER CHARACTERS

Teskimalauwa	Havasupai seer
Pangwits	San Juan Paiute shaman, brother of Mara and Pooeechuts
Hoskininni	Leader of a Navajo band
Nankapeea	Kaibab Paiute
Jacob Hamblin	Mormon leader
Paantung	Shivwits Paiute

Part One

May 23—June 15, 1869

1

Dearest Emma,

Rec'd yours of the 13th inst. and trust no more will follow, as we launch tomorrow, consequently further letters to me will lie unopened in their dusty pigeonholes. I will, as we discussed, write to you from the Uinta Agency, tho' knowing precisely when is impossible. We could take as much as a month to arrive there, depending upon the hazards on the river. After that our course is all unknown territory, for a thousand miles, and we shan't be again among civilized people until we reach the southern settlements in Utah Territory.

"Civilized"? "Again"? I say these with a wink. Green River City is a wicked place; and the Mormon towns too in the southern wilds of Utah are said to be full of wastrels and laggards who engage in shameful orgies. That is slander and calumny, one Latter Day Saint passing through here informed me last week. I assured him I would judge for myself. And you may too, Emma my love. If Detroit becomes weary, jump on a train and join us regardless of where we wash up — on whatever lurid shore — once our Odyssey is finished.

No, I'll join you. I'll come to you in Detroit. You'll be easier to find.

Don't tell your father that I've called this place wicked — he'll send an angel to destroy it. And wicked's a mild sketch. It's changed in three months. Now the line is completed, the pashas of the Union Pacific have chosen Bryan, not Green River City, as the base for their

3

terminal buildings, much to the chagrin of the locals, who promptly fled, leaving only the riffraff. The line completed! You must have seen it in the papers, Em—the final spike hammered at Promontory Summit, the Atlantic and Pacific coasts at last linked—they played it up to beat the band. The consequence is, half this town is boarded up. Of the several thousand who lived here in March, perhaps a hundred remain. Remember what I said before leaving?—these Hell on Wheels towns are as transitory as soap bubbles. And they hold human life as cheaply as at Gettysburg. One nymph du pave among our soiled doves inhaled charcoal fumes in her crib a week ago and was found dead the following morning.

There's not a tree, shrub, flower, or patch of grass anywhere about except along the river. The hills are scorched daily by the unrelenting sun. Little wonder the people have bolted!

Our camp is by the river, and most of us keep as much as possible away from the town, except, as you might imagine, your friend Bill Dunn, who struts along the main street every inch the oleaginous desperado. He may look ferocious, with that raven-black hair falling to his shoulders, and the fat and blood of countless slaughtered beasts adding luster to his buckskin, but looks are deceiving. Those who sputter and grouse and behave with surly bluster are often mild as kittens, I've learned. His principal fault is his speech—blunt, frank, and harsh—but men such as that often prove the most loyal. When I gently reprimanded his surliness last week he turned away and said, "I don't wish to be happy."

"Why is that?" I asked.

"Afraid it won't last."

I trust him more than some softer-spoken men, for instance Oramel Howland. Dearest, don't exult—I should have listened to you. The knowledge he claimed of elementary surveying and map-making and the like when we met him last year made a happy impression. But when I unpacked the instruments this week—the sextant, the barometers, the precious chronometer—he showed no interest whatsoever. I begin to suspect he is less than meets the eye. He fusses and scolds and every now and then gives me that prophet-of-the-Bible stare, which I counter with my own, though my beard is shorter. (His, now long and white, curls back in the wind.) I bloat my eyes enough to burn a hole through him, but he seldom wilts. Since we're both of the Wesleyan body—and because he is my senior, tho' only by a year—he may think he has as much right as I to preach to the men, but so far (in my presence, at least) he suppresses the urge. I've learned he's already sent a dispatch to his paper, the *Rocky Mountain News*, which violates my agreement with the *Tribune* in Chicago, but I've decided there's no sense in kicking up a row. Each man on this voyage has his interests and inducements—or his own madness, to use your word—and I have mine. Ora did relinquish his position on the *News* to join our corps, so I'm loath to begrudge him the occasional dispatch, and besides, once beyond the Uinta Agency all is unexplored territory, and dispatches won't be possible then, as we'll be incommunicado.

We've all given up something. Jack Sumner gave up his trading post, and William Hawkins, like Dunn, gave up his trapping, tho' that's little sacrifice, since beaver are scarcer than hen's teeth these days. Sumner, Dunn, and Oramel Howland are bringing their gold pans, and I'm not blind to that especial madness, indeed I encouraged it. I told them I knew quite a bit about rocks, having lectured on the subject, and that's what I gave up, the comforts of the classroom, for the duration of this voyage. But didn't their eyes light up when I described the rivers we'll descend, and the gorges they've carved deep into the earth, and who knew what sort of veins would be exposed or what a man might find if he brought along his gold pan?

As for my madness, as you know—and I made this clear to them —it is geological knowledge. I informed the gold hunters that our voyage will be no ordinary junket but a scientific exploring expedition, the first to venture through all the canyons on the Green and Colorado Rivers, culminating in the greatest canyon of all, rumored to be 300 miles long—and they ought not to mind if their one-armed commander measures and weighs and takes samples and describes *all* we come across in the rock and mineral department, not just gold. I said I needed their help not only with physical work but with a profusion of scientific observations, and to their credit they give the instruments a fling, but sometimes I must rescue them (the instruments, that is). Each man is charged with making independent estimates of the distances between compass bearings, and Ora shall take said compass bearings at every river bend. Bill Dunn seems adept with the barometers, and Ora pretends to have mastered the sextant, but I shan't let him handle it. His task will be to write down my observations for latitude and longitude and use them for his maps. Dunn wished to know why we needed maps, since the river would take us where it would regardless, and I told him that was not the proper attitude. What sort of nation, I asked—turning my head to include all the others—can build a transcontinental railroad yet be ignorant so long of what its borders contain? Maps are more precious than gold, I said, and Dunn wrinkled his nose. Between you and me, Emma, I'm afraid we'll be a little raw at first in the business of surveying and mapping the country, but I've educated roughnecks before, and most of these men were in the war—they've the habit of obedience. All are bronzed, hardy bucks in the vigor of life, and I've no real regrets in the choices I made, not even dear Ora, whose labors will be under my watchful eye, not yours, I ought to add—he resented your orders this winter past.

You should have seen our corps hail the new men as one by one they arrived. A dunking was the usual salutation, but George Bradley glowered and backed off his greeting party, including Bill Dunn, and George is even shorter than I (tho' only by a finger). Until a few weeks ago, he was orderly sergeant at Fort Bridger, but General Grant—excuse me, President—obtained his release at my request, that he might go on this expedition. George will be useful; he comes from a family of Massachusetts boatmen and is skilled in the repair and the management of vessels. Little misfortunes work him into a passion, but he is made of good gum and has a ready hand and a powerful arm and appears brave and generous, if something of a lone wolf.

Andy Hall, another newcomer, I spotted rowing in circles in a homemade boat not far from our camp, and I enlisted him at once. He is a Scotch boy and only eighteen years old, even younger than Ora's brother Seneca, but a good deal stronger. When we stand side by side he is the tallest of our crew. Young as he is, he has had considerable experience with adversity, having worked as a bullwhacker for the railroad. A merchant in town described him as a skilled Indian fighter. If I know my wife as well as the back of my hand—and you must admit I do—I am satisfied that, confronted with Andy, your first reaction would be to sketch his massive head, surmounted by a beaked nose, surrounded by ears, and beset with blue eyes as deep as forest pools. He will serve as cook's assistant—Hawkins as cook.

Finally, not counting myself, there is a ninth, added yesterday, an Englishman named Frank Goodman. I confess he is a stranger. His face is florid, so is his speech, and at the last moment he showed up in our camp and asked if I was the famous Major John Wesley Powell, having read about our expedition in the papers. I said I was indeed the person he sought, minus that part about the fame. You'll be famous enough after this voyage, he vowed, and then he begged to come along, even offered me money—and I capitulated, but refused the money. I thought we could use another stout, willing hand, but now I have my doubts. He seems somewhat namby-pamby.

All have been practicing handling the boats and learning the signals I'll make with my flags. Their antics extend to roughhousing on the water, and I've been pleased to observe that my oversized bulkheads are splendidly watertight and prevent the boats from sinking when capsized. The men are quite amazed.

Of course they've heard all the stories. They've listened to preposterous descriptions of thousand-foot waterfalls, of suckholes that can swallow an iron-plated *Monitor*, of stretches of river that run so fast they go uphill for several miles at a time. A man in this town described our goal, the "Great Canyon," as the most stupendous gorge known on the globe. He hasn't seen it, of course; no one has, except in fleeting glimpses from the rim. That doesn't prevent authoritative declarations of the sort this dabster made: that the height of the walls causes birds to exhaust themselves before they can fly out, with the result that they drop back senseless into the canyon; or that powerful waves of the Colorado River can knock a large hawk out of the sky. I told the men such stories are ant paste, and they agreed to come along with my solemn assurances—but who really knows?

You asked in your last about hostile Indians. Bill Dunn assures me that once beyond the Uinta Agency we will meet none, and the agency Utes, as you know from the winter, are warm and open-hearted, if somewhat unsavory. Those Indians in the country south toward which we go—Paiute and Navajo and Apache, principally—never venture into the canyons, Bill has learned. They are too deep, and the river too swift.

Yes, I wish you could have stayed and come with us. Not just for my comfort; you have all the requirements—hardiness, vigor, and practical wisdom—but I could not do this to your father, subject his precious daughter for who knows how many more months to the crudity of mountain men. Note that I say your father, not you. I know your strengths, and they are steadfast yet patient, strengths of heart above all.

We have rations for ten months, and our boats are as soundly constructed as I could wish: three built of oak, staunch and firm, double-ribbed, with double stem- and sternposts, and further strengthened by the bulkheads. As we discussed, I made the fourth boat smaller, and of pine, though cut to the same pattern. And, surprise—I've named her for you. She is called the *Emma Dean* and has a sharp cutwater. She is in every way built for speed and flexibility, and shall be our lead boat, with me in command.

We feel quite proud of our little fleet as it lies in the river waiting for us to embark: the Stars and Stripes, spread by a stiff breeze, over the *Emma Dean;* the waves rocking the little vessels; and the current of the Green, swollen, mad, and seeming eager to bear us down through its mysterious canyons.

The good people of Green River City, such as they are—all one hundred of the merchants, miners, gamblers, Mexicans, Indians, mulewhackers, saloonkeepers, soiled doves, and infernal wretches left in the town—plan to see us off in the morning, but I suspect the only ones who actually appear will be those who manage to drink until dawn. We leave as early as possible; at midday the heat becomes intolerable, enough to boil the fish in the water.

My brother sends his regards. He grows more melancholy the longer we delay, and today when I told him we launch tomorrow he launched himself—into song, of course—and you've heard his booming voice. Walter is strong and can row like the devil and will go mad again if he stands around idle, as I mentioned in my last. Lord, send him peace of mind.

And now, my dear, I have one more thing to say. After eight years of marriage, declarations of affection between husband and wife are like a coin effaced from use, or I should say overuse. You already know my feelings on this matter—my shameful discomfort. I can think of you and a fountain of tears starts from my eyes, but in speaking of love, or putting pen to paper, my too great measure of irksome discomfort often robs me of words. Actions speak louder than words, dearest Emma. My love will be expressed in the caution with which I face dangers on this voyage, in my management of hazard and want, in my continual vigilance, and in my safe return. What perils there are, what breakers and torrents lie in wait on the river, what precipices will suddenly appear beneath our boats, who can truly say? My grim determination to see you again and embrace you will bring me back whole. It need not be said that anyone in my position would be hard pressed to peer into the future, to anticipate dangers unsuspected and unbegotten, whether of the river or of hostile Indians. No one knows what waits ahead, tho' on the score of Indians I suspect Dunn is right—that either from fear or superstition our dusky brethren stay away from the river and its steep and gloomy canyons. The land is too harsh and the hazards too great even for feathered men. And as for the waters, they may be high now, but that is just the spring flood. For the first 200 miles the Green is free of rapids save the occasional meager ripple. It will carry me safely, and I'll end where I began—in your arms again.

Your Loving Husband,
Wes

2

Wes looked around him: all hell was breaking loose. His boat had nosed down, got gripped by the river, and wind had turned to water. The *Emma Dean* shot forward in a blink and Wes was shouting and Jack Sumner rowing air and Bill Dunn pulling so hard on his oars that a tholepin popped out and clattered to his feet. He dropped down to pick it up. Between Bill in the bow and Jack in the stern, Wes waved his stump and bellowed out orders lost to the roar and hiss. "Left, boys, left! Man your oars, Bill!" Shouts reduced to bird squeal. Bill leaned over the gunnel now and was fumbling with the tholepin. Wes bent down and shouted in his ear, "What the devil are you doing?"

"Major Powell, sir, I can't make the fucker fit!"

Just moments ago they'd been drifting in a dream on a placid tilt of river, a bubble's downward sag. Below and beyond it, peaks of waves and gouts of foam had leapt like little demons trying to find the doomed men. Prominent in the rapids ahead was a monstrous boulder stacking up the river—neck folds on a bull.

Now they raced toward it. "Left," Wes screamed, then looked back to spot, a hundred feet behind them, the *Kitty Clyde's Sister* sliding into the rapids, with George Bradley and Wes's brother attempting to row, the latter's mouth wide open in song. Even George couldn't hear Walter's voice, Wes thought. The roar of the rapids, more like fire than water, drowned all other sounds. But Wes knew what his brother was singing: "John Anderson, My Jo." He could tell by the satisfied warp of Walter's mouth.

He turned back to face upriver, clinging to his rope tied around a strut, which he used for busting rapids. His inflated life preserver wrapped snug around his neck felt like a horse collar and took away some dignity, since no one else wore one. The *Emma Dean* climbed waves then dropped then climbed again, and above her the canyon walls rose in red bluffs and the noontime sun flamed off the sandstone and the river caught its light and spread it like a rash.

The *No Name* entered the rapids now, and twisting around Wes saw it jumping like a deer jumping logs, and the grown men inside bouncing up and down—the two Howland brothers and the helpless Frank Goodman, clinging to his seat. Wes shouted again—he wasn't sure why or at whom or even what—then a wave cuffed his boat, nearly knocking him over, and something in his spine broke into blossom and he righted himself in the act of turning back, and all this happened in a moment. The unceasing roar filled the air and the river rose before him. "Left, boys!" he screamed, stressing that direction with his head and upper torso. The right stump helped too, straining left across his chest, with nerve ends sprouting a frantic phantom arm. He watched Bill in front of him rowing with one oar and felt like clubbing the oaf. They weren't going left, they were broadsiding toward the huge rock ahead and he screamed, "Both oars, Bill!" Furrows of water rocked the boat left and right, sending columns and streamers ten or more feet high toward Wes, half standing, and bucked him like a mustang. From his height above the men he could see the fatal boulder, obscured by a left-moving sheer wall of water. "We're lost, boys, we're lost!" He stood to full height—five foot four—and shaking his head, laughed like a madman.

A shard of his attention sensed the *Maid* back there shooting into the rapids, and detected as though from an inner distance the howls and execrations of Andy Hall and William Hawkins.

The *Emma Dean* reached its crisis. Wes had to sit when his boat rose and hung suspended in time, remitted from gravity, but shaking like a peak about to blow. She seemed to keep rising while water crashed through her, her forward momentum still jerking her up. At last she paused. Out of nowhere he pictured the real Emma Dean, safe in Detroit. And the water carved open, or so it seemed—it positively parted to receive them.

They shot straight ahead through two walls of water, and now it was just a never-ending breathless race. Wes stood again. Below him, Bill Dunn with the tholepin in his hand looked startled as a baby laid on his back. Wes turned to signal the others left, as far left as possible, but he had to hang on and couldn't use his flag. It was all body language—head butts, stump flaps. The *Emma Dean* didn't race, she flew through the air, then slammed down so hard he was airborne for an instant. She spun around madly, pinning Wes to his seat, but the boys worked the oars—this was water they could bite—and the boat swung downriver, slowing to full steam. Amazingly, Bill still rowed with one oar. It mattered less now. A perfectly flat slide of water had found them and they rode it down the wind toward the next hanging avalanche of river, then rode that around a bend—these rapids were endless—past shawls of foam pouring over boulders left and right of their boat. The river slowed as it curved.

"Ain't you done with that yet?" Jack Sumner barked. Bill Dunn fumbling with the tholepin again.

"Can't get it back in."

"We rode all that way with it out?"

"I suppose."

As the rapids diminished, the sound of Walter's song broke across the water.

Now we maun totter down, John,
But hand in hand we'll go,
And sleep thegither at the foot,
John Anderson, my jo.

Wes pulled off his rubber life preserver. He wore it as a favor to Emma, since with his one arm, swimming would be tricky if her namesake capsized. You needed every crutch, he thought, every human expedient—gadgets, prayer, quick wit, charms, and spells—when the unknown lay around every corner.

They'd herded together, the *Emma,* the *Sister,* the *No Name,* and the *Maid,* in a gentle eddy near a beach at a bend. Here the river looped right. The men began to bail, all except Frank Goodman in the *No Name*—sitting up smartly now—and Bill Dunn in the *Emma Dean,* still working on the tholepin. Wes asked too, "That's not done, Bill?" at which Seneca Howland looked up from his boat, bailing like mad, and said, "Bill, are you Dunn?"

"Shut your damn piehole."

A snarl, a stare. The games men play with each other, thought Wes.

They anchored the boats, climbed onto shore, and sprawled in the sand at a bend in the river eating biscuits and dried apples passed out by Hawkins. First willows then box elders and cottonwoods grew on the rocky soil behind them, then the broken ground rose to high red cliffs seamed into blocks. The river had quieted down at this bend, and their boats hardly tugged at the deadman anchors.

Wes checked the four boats for damage then sat on the *Emma*'s bow deck by himself and observed his men: Andy Hall of the big head and nose and powerful arms, the former mule driver. He walked as if another Andy Hall, made of buckets and poles, were pitching forward inside him while trying not to spill.

Hawkins the cook with his dark eyes, enormous shag mustache, and small wisp of beard on a dinky chin. Hawkins's face was singular, fixed as cement, but his name a buzzing crowd—sometimes Missouri Rhodes, sometimes William Rhodes Hawkins, sometimes

Billy, sometimes Cook—and Wes hadn't managed to learn about his past, no one had. Or if they had they weren't saying.

Jack Sumner's mustache had bleached in the sun, and like Hawkins Jack was short though round-shouldered, a human cannonball. He'd given up his store in Hot Sulphur Springs to come on this trip and often reminded others of this fact in Wes's presence. Otherwise, Jack kept his own counsel. Wes had made him his Peter, his rock, but seldom really knew what he was thinking.

Bill Dunn's stringy black hair brushed his shoulders, and his beard held as much grease, it appeared, as his filthy breeches. Bill sat in the sand. Had he fixed the tholepin at last, the big lunk? He'd better have, thought Wes, he couldn't row without it. Next to Bill, Ora Howland, head resting on his arms, seemed to be sleeping. He often slept, but when baby brother Seneca, to his right, commenced idly digging in the sand with a stick, Ora lifted his head. "Leave the sand be."

Seneca stood and tossed the stick away. Last night he'd told Wes he'd come along for the adventure.

George Bradley was off sitting by himself but within earshot. Quiet, thought Wes, but quiet men sometimes made fewer mistakes. And George knew boats — their one experienced boatman. Since the first few days after their launch, George had camped alone every night. Quiet, and a loner. Wes instinctively trusted him.

Between George and the rest of the men bunched together, Wes's brother Walter reached for the sky, stretching prodigiously, then paced in a circle, peered up at the cliffs, inspected the river. At last he walked back and rejoined the group, sitting next to Frank Goodman. "How come you didn't bail?" he asked the Englishman.

"Afraid I couldn't."

"What'd you do to yourself?"

"Sandbar crumbled beneath me last night. I was—discharging my burden in the dark."

"I suppose that'll do it."

"Can't yawn, can't sneeze. Speaking causes discomfort." Frank seemed to be smiling, but Wes wasn't sure—his nose did all the talking. The loose mouth just hung there. "If I feel the need to sneeze, the sensation is like being stabbed in the back. Then I can't. It's cut off before the crisis."

"Need yourself a woman," said Walter, who turned to his brother and winked. Wes nodded. Walter's moods ranged from distracted bonhomie to rage to self-torture, and who knew when they'd shift? Surprise me, Wes thought. Most of the others had fought in the war too. They knew the damage of combat and the Icarian falls suffered by some, and ought to indulge his brother, he'd decided. Still, every time Walter opened his mouth Wes felt alarmed, ready to jump in.

Walter folded his arms across his knees and lowered his head.

Wes ate a biscuit and let the sun warm him. This was his hastily assembled crew, his disciples, the men Emma had said wouldn't last the first week. As of yesterday she was wrong. Still, they'd just begun. And Wes knew from the war that first skirmishes weren't always predictive of a battle's outcome, and this would be a battle, but of the oddest sort. For one thing, their enemy—the river—was also their lifeline. In one week he'd glimpsed the river's fitful moods: it lulled you like a dream, then shocked you awake with the same looming anxiety war made you feel, as though even at rest you were always approaching the edge of a cliff.

Andy Hall waded in the river to his calves and pissed upstream. Like spitting into the wind, Wes thought. Andy shook his member at the rapids, now diminished in the distance. "Best ride so far, Major Powell," he said walking back. He brushed sand off his drawers, and Wes noted the union suit—too small. The boy was still growing. No one had changed clothes, all still wore the standard uniform for rapids: flannel shirts and drawers, kerchief tied around the neck.

"It was fun, I'll say that." Hawkins spit in the sand.

"Fun? Christ almighty," Andy said. "It wasn't fun, it was exciting."

"Same difference."

"No sir," said Andy. "Fun's a good time, but exciting is different. Exciting's the kind of good time you know you had only after it's over. It's like being shot at by a drunk."

"I wouldn't have thought being shot at was exciting."

"When it's over, I said."

"I'll tell you about exciting," said Jack Sumner. "Exciting has to be a little dangerous, like a black-eyed whore."

"Exciting gets old," George Bradley said. He was twenty feet away, sitting in the sand, but didn't raise his voice; Wes strained to listen. "We been gone a week, we got a thousand miles to go, and we'll be sick to death of getting dunked like this by the time we get through. Sick of each other too."

"Sick of you already, George."

"Sick of this canyon."

"Don't the sun feel good, though?"

"First you freeze, then you burn."

"I thought it was over," said the Englishman. "Thought we'd gone to meet our Maker."

Walter Powell raised his head. "Then how come you're smiling?"

"Something amusing just occurred to me."

Walter's lips thinned. "You're one of those boys which your nose points up and your chin points down and there's what I call a saddle between your nose pits and your mouth."

"So?"

"So wipe that stupid grin off your face."

Wes jumped up, guided Walter aside, and said, "Let's get to work. Walter, help Hawkins reload the *Maid*. Ora—compass bearing." Acting for two, Wes's one arm swung wildly as he walked, and the walking was labored—he stomped through sand. Short as a fence-post, shirtsleeve pinned up, he fought the inclination to list.

He stopped to watch Ora take a bearing and scribble on his sketchpad. Wes had been teaching him the meander system for mapping their course: compass bearings at every bend, the distance between bends approximated, approximations compared and averaged. Those figures in turn were corrected by astronomical stations taken with a sextant fifty miles apart and linked by the river estimates. Only trouble was, you could not take bearings and cling to a runaway boat at the same time. If they'd gone around a bend in those last rapids, would Ora's map even show it? Wading to shore, Ora asked his brother how far he made it from their last bearing.

"Forgot to keep track," Seneca said.

"Hawkins?"

"Eight miles."

"George?"

"Eleven."

"Six," said Wes.

Ora settled on nine.

Meanwhile, Bill Dunn had unpacked the barometers and, having loosened the screw beneath the cistern case, stood in the sand holding one up, waiting for the mercury to reach its level in the tube. The wooden box with the other two barometers stood open in the sand, and when Wes walked up the first thing he did was close the lid and latch it tight. "You have your tables?" he asked.

"In the boat."

Bill's usual expression when he tried to concentrate was startled dismay, or confused irritation. His long hair looked black as an Indian's, and his smell was burnished, carrion, and old, a copper bowl filled with chopped meat gone bad. His beard appeared to be a solid thing, whereas Wes's muttonchops felt made of sparse lamb's wool. Standing there, Wes looked him squarely in the face while Bill glanced around like a boy at the blackboard. He'd been teaching Bill to keep careful track of their ever-falling base line, but it took a lot of patience.

"Thermometer?"

"In the boat."

"Watch?"

"In my breeches."

"Where are they?"

"In the boat."

"I'll hold that. Get the tables, the thermometer, and the watch."

Bill handed the barometer to Wes and stumbled over mudflats to unlatch the *Emma Dean*'s bow compartment. He rooted around and pulled out a thermometer, pocket watch, and leather case, then slogged back to his commander.

"I think it's settled on a reading." Wes held up the barometer. Its long glass tube, cased in brass, showed no moisture in the sun — a good sign. Bill placed his nose two inches from the thing and squinted at the scale. "Twenty-four point six."

"What does that give you?"

Bill opened the case and pulled out the little notebook with the tables in the back. He flipped through the pages. "Five thousand four hundred feet?"

"Write it down."

Bill licked his thumb and turned the pages, then licked the pencil and wrote down the numbers. Before Wes could prompt him, he screwed one eye up and consulted the temperature and referred to the tables, then plugged in the correction. It took him several minutes to multiply the figures, and while he did Wes returned the barometer to its box, and the box to the *No Name*'s stern compartment.

Bill entered the corrected altitude in the notebook, slipped the notebook into the case, and started for the boat. Seneca Howland whispered as he passed, "Bill, are you Dunn?"

"You're forgetting something," said Wes.

"*What?*" Bill spun around, slapped his forehead. With watch in hand and pencil in teeth, he took out the notebook again and jotted down the time. And the weather conditions.

A raven flew by. Wes heard the wooden croak and the soft *whoop whoop* of its wings above his head. "Let's get started," he called to the men.

They climbed into the boats while Wes watched the raven, whose head hung down, yellow eye watching him. The bird crossed the canyon rising on thermals toward the opposite rim. For no apparent reason he folded his wings and bulleted through the air a few feet, rolling on his shaggy neck. Then he opened his wings and with another croak wheeled up toward the cliffs looming over the canyon. The croak was a thick piece of air wedging open.

He landed on a tree and stabbed at his tail—plagued by lice, no doubt. But Wes could barely make him out now. From the raven's lofty perch the tiny boats below gliding down the river would hardly seem to be moving, Wes thought. The raven was one thing rooted in the world, while the little men below rode on ten separate rivers, none quite the same.

3

The next day the rapids worsened and they had to portage. Wes had named this place Red Canyon; an Adam in his garden, he spent names like coins. Red Canyon ran east, parallel to mountains to the south, and seemed to be endless, but at least it gave them sun from early morning to late evening. Around a bend, the river pinched, lashed by eddies and crosscurrents and filled with boulders in the main channel, each of which uttered its own dull roar. They landed on the right and Wes jumped out and stormed up the bank to see the way ahead.

The sun beat down. Two humping slopes of earth massed with fallen rock descended to the river, which hung between them like a flume. It was not only fast but filled with rocks. "We could run it," said Andy.

"Go ahead. Have a party."

They spent the next hour clearing a path along the bank, ripping up scrub oak and levering boulders, then had to unload all the supplies—the rifles, saws, barometers, and compasses, the sextants, thermometers, mess kit and clothes, the hundred-pound sacks of dried apples, the salt pork and bacon, the sugar, beans and coffee, the endless sacks of flour—and haul them through the talus. They stripped to their waists and left their shirts upriver, then on return trips jumped in the rocky eddies near the bank to cool off. Once the boats were emptied out, they ran a long rope through the ring on the stern post of the *Emma Dean* and doubled it back. George Bradley tied another rope to the bow, and Walter and Andy, the two largest men, clambered over talus downstream carrying the bow rope. Wes pointed out a boulder on shore where they could see upstream. Then he ran back upriver to the boats and they began.

The rest of the men except George Bradley held on to the doubled-back stern rope on the bank while George and Wes shoved and kicked the *Emma Dean* through shallows and eddies to the edge of the rapids. They threaded it around rocks and clung to the boat until the rapids caught it, then the six men on the bank, holding on for dear life, slowly lowered it inches at a time.

The sun was merciless. Sweat greased the hands of the men on the bank. The *Emma Dean* strained, pulling on its rope past the worst of the rapids, and when it ran out of rope Wes climbed a rock and raised his flag. He made sure they were ready—the six men upstream hanging on to the stern rope, and the two downstream. He swung the flag down in a wide arc and the men upstream released one end of the doubled stern rope and it whipped through the ring and the boat cut through water, slashing left and right past Walter and Andy until, slowing, it reached the end of their bow line and they hauled it in.

Wes paced the bank, anxious and distracted, until the next boat was ready. Lining down the boats took all morning, then they had to reload them. He began to grow alarmed about the water in the supposedly watertight compartment of the *Emma Dean*. A picture raided his mind: water clouding one of their pocket watches—or worse, the chronometer—and fouling its works. He checked the other boats and found the *Sister* leaking too, so he moved the chronometer from its bow to the drier stern compartment. It took another day to find a place to spread their clothes and rations to dry, and another after that to reach Browns Park, where the canyon walls shrank and the mountains fell away and they could caulk their battered boats with oakum and pitch and preserve their equipment from their enemy, the river.

Browns Park was a place where fur trappers once had held their rendezvous, and Wes knew that made it hallowed ground for Sumner, Dunn, and Hawkins; with Wes and Emma, they'd been here last winter for a few cold days. It was rimmed by steep slopes, red and green in the distance, and broken by hills and mesas in the valley and by terraces and bluffs along the banks of the river. He sent Bill and George out to hunt and they came back with fish. Bill explained they'd hiked to a creek where he spotted trout and tried to shoot them with his pistol, but it didn't work. George caught some whitefish with his fishing rod instead.

The next day being Sunday, George and Oramel suggested the men observe it, but Wes wanted to see the canyon up ahead. "Fasten your belts and gird up your loins," he told the two men, the stumpy George Bradley and the prophet Ora Howland. Those two rowed like Christian slaves doing the minimum, but the others pulled hard, bucking winds all the way through a broad valley.

It rained off and on. Clouds were still massing to the east when they landed, so they pitched the tents. They camped in sandy soil on a ledge above the river near the end of Browns Park, with gambel oaks around them and cottonwoods overhead and willows nearby with which they made mattresses. Downstream the river entered the mountains between two cliffs with a tinny distant roar, and Wes stared at those gates, having spotted them last year when snow lay on the ground. Massive and high, the sandstone cliffs were broken with seams but just about perpendicular. And the left one flamed up when a cloud unleashed the sun.

Bill Dunn took their elevation and discovered they'd fallen about a hundred feet since the Red Canyon rapids. Oramel plotted their recent course and worked on his maps, but they were water-stained and damp. Jack Sumner and Hawkins tried panning the river—no color showed.

Wes walked downstream to stare at the canyon's gates because something felt wrong, some thought half formed when he'd stood here last winter. This was the voyage he'd begun planning then. This was the scientific exploration he'd dreamed of for a year, the one that would carry him deep into unknown country, through canyons and mountains and past looming landforms whose secrets had locked up millennia of history. He'd studied erosion, analyzed rocks, read about uplifts, and rejected the notion that earth's scarred and knotted surface was the product of catastrophe, as Professor Whitney claimed. In its elephantine mass the earth's surface delimited its own capacity for change. Change was logical, slow, persistent, and was written in river and rock and their characters, inscribed in landforms born of their friction. Yet here, and in similar sites they'd come across last winter, the river cut directly into a ridge of mountains. It didn't have to do that; it could have stayed in this valley. Across the river from this spot the valley curled east and its obstacles were fewer and lower, he observed. But to the south—solid rock. It looked as if someone had struck a meaty hand through the heart of the mountains and plowed that narrow furrow. It was even more awful to behold in this light, he imagined telling Emma. This late afternoon pre–summer solstice light. The sun couldn't strike the canyon's inner walls, which grew darker as they plunged, answering the brilliance in this valley with gloom. Standing here, it felt impossible to resist the sepia theology, the allegory of the chromos, the familiar parables of light and dark.

Although Emma could resist them. She was a better skeptic than he. Just yesterday, Ora had compared the twists and snares of the river to the Christian's earthly voyage, and Wes couldn't help it—for a moment he thought the man was right. After all, unless perversely inspired, why would a river choose to cleave a massive block of mountains? First the crafty river seemed to run without design, then it made for the highest point in sight, as though ordinary valleys weren't worthy of its notice.

Ordinary valleys, of course, were ancient; they'd been worn down by time. Here the river cut gorges, stark and high, without the rounded walls of eastern river valleys. From everything he'd learned about the Great Canyon, a thousand miles south, the same held true there: high walls, massive and chiseled—profound, gloomy depths— precipitous spires, towering pinnacles, labyrinthine chasms. It overwhelmed conception. How his heart ached to see what the inner eye could only feebly sketch!

A glacier could have carved the canyon before him. Maybe that was the answer. Or maybe the answer was an underground river whose roof of earth collapsed and got washed away. No, long ago he'd rejected that idea. The ability of water to carry off soil seemed incontrovertible, but common sense and Ockham's razor made short work of the fantasy of underground rivers. The river itself had sliced through this mountain, but how?

4

"Plunder! Plunder! Come and get it!" That evening Hawkins had cooked the bacon on sticks, catching its grease in a cup for dipping biscuits. Made from flour, water, salt, and saleratus, the biscuits usually baked up golden brown and took suggestive shapes not ordinarily appetizing. But the men were always hungry. On a rock at the fire's edge sat a pot of beans.

"Where's the plunder?" asked the Englishman.

"I said that plunder to make you come quick. Tell the boys to go out and shoot us some game, then I'll say plunder truly."

"Shot some yesterday," said George.

"Skinny ducks and bony fish. Where's the meat?"

"Move it over just a skoshy bit, would you please, Lime Juicer?"

At the end of the log, Jack Sumner tried to sit next to Frank Goodman. The left-handed Englishman seemed to need a lot of room, since he always ate with his right elbow cocked.

"Come now, Major, won't you take a bit of Simon?" Hawkins handed Wes's plate to his brother, then nodded at the bucket. From a tin he scooped soap and plunged his hand into the water. Wes plunged his in too, and Hawkins's hand remedied the deficiency of limb, enabling Wes to wash his own. Meanwhile, Walter cut up his brother's bacon.

Tin plates on knees, they sat on logs around the fire in huddled postures of protection. Wes had read Darwin and understood the suggestion of animals in a pack. Now and then someone stood and dipped his biscuit in the grease cup, which sat on a flat rock. The wind was still testy and blew the smoke around, but that at least kept the mosquitoes away.

Downriver, dying sunlight caught the canyon's gates and turned the cliffs to flaming gold. A convulsion of light in the gray clouds behind them contracted and a rainbow showed its stump.

Mockingbirds sang. Frogs had started croaking. In a pool on the mudflat below their little camp, trematode larvae formed cysts on tadpole limbs, assuring that some would grow deformed legs. Routine signs of slaughter lay around. Beneath the cottonwood sheltering their camp, a few feet away from a blossoming balsamroot whose yellow had pooled in the deep light of dusk, an ant dislodged some dirt at the edge of a crater and the ant lion beneath it exploded in jerks, showering sand to force the ant down. The ant lion destroyed his perfect little crater with these fitful landslides, but he could always dig another. During the war, in prison camp, Walter Powell had seen centipedes and millipedes large as water snakes in a boot, and next to the boot he'd seen his own shadow bleeding on the floor. But if he could see what that ant saw, or feel what it felt, he'd go mad again and stay mad forever. Oval and flat, grayish brown, with toothed mandibles, studded all over with warts and bristles, the ant lion seized the ant with his pincers, punctured its body, and sucked out the juices.

He hurled the drained carcass out beyond his pit.

This monster was not the dragon by the roadside watching for a sinner to pass. He was only the size of a watermelon seed and the ant hadn't even screamed.

And on a ridge above their camp, a sodden mass of fur and quills lay in bunchgrass. Late that winter, a porcupine crossing a deep bank of snow had been surrounded by coyotes, one of which tunneled underneath his body and ripped his belly open—the only unprotected part. With care, the whole pack excavated his flesh. Now the quills lay scattered in clumps of fur and skin, and the same coyote who'd tunneled through the snow trotted past them and sniffed. Then he walked into their camp. "Coyote!" shouted Andy.

Bill Dunn shot to his tent for a pistol, but the coyote turned back, looking over his shoulder. He'd loped off briskly the same way he'd come before Bill could fire. "Smart as whips," he declared.

"Taste like skunk, though," said Wes.

He watched Bill walk off in the coyote's direction. Across the fire, Hawkins asked Frank Goodman what part of England he was from.

"Plymouth."

"Where's that?"

"Shipping town. South coast. You of all people should know about Plymouth. Your ancestors came from that town to Massachusetts."

"Not mine," said Andy.

"Nor mine neither."

"Mine came from the coal mines."

"From the fiery depths."

"From Missouri."

Frank Goodman threw up his hands. "Your lives are so circumscribed! You have no sense of history."

"That's enough of your gassing," said Walter Powell, chasing a bean down his plate with his biscuit. "We got a sense of history good as anybody's. It just don't go far back."

"No further than your backsides."

"Don't give me that sass. Shut your damn mouth." Walter stood up and dipped his plate in the washbucket.

"By God," said the Englishman.

"Don't 'by God' me."

"Well."

"That's right. Well."

Wes stood up, took his brother by the arm, and whispered in his ear to leave Goodman alone.

"He's just a brass button," said Walter, looking down.

Hawkins rang the bean pot with his spoon. "Roll out! Roll out! Pigs in the peachery! Who's for more silage?"

Andy Hall held out his tin plate. Bill Dunn came back and announced that the coyote had killed a porcupine and been visiting the scene.

"How do you know?"

"He pissed next to these. Ground still wet." Bill passed out some porcupine quills.

"What's this for?" said Seneca.

"Pick your teeth. Spear a mouse."

"Where'd you find them?"

"Up the ridge."

When everyone was finished and the plates were dipped and stacked, Seneca cried out in pain. "Porcupine quills don't make good toothpicks on Sunday, June 6," he exclaimed. Mouth stretched open, he probed wounded gums with his finger.

"You mean you actually used them?" asked Bill. "You're greener than I thought."

The young man's face bloomed in red and white blotches.

Seated on the log, his brother Ora had removed the sketches for his map from their well-oiled leather case and spread them on the ground. Wes watched as he lay his arms on his knees, lowered his head, and promptly fell asleep.

The day began pulling its light from the valley. To Wes's disappointment the clouds had not blown out, so he couldn't use the sextant. But he footed up their estimated distance to be a hundred and forty river miles, fifty as the crow flies from their point of departure back at Green River City. He willed himself to wake up later that night and see how the sky looked.

As usual, George Bradley slept apart from the others. He declined the tent and lay under a wagon sheet on a shelf above their camp. Everyone else slept with their boatmates, three to a tent, except for Walter Powell, who joined Andy Hall and Hawkins. From that tent Walter sang "Old Shady," which meant he'd calmed down. No one told him to stow it.

In the middle of the night, when Wes woke to the sound of someone hawking, he reached for his boots with his right arm before realizing it was missing. He'd been listening to Emma play a Schubert impromptu—no, he'd been searching the forests of his Wisconsin boyhood for an enormous yellow pine bent over in an arch. The search was full of sadness from hearing Emma at the piano, and besides, he was lost. When he woke in his tent, the ravines and gorges of his dreaming mind began their process of vanishing like folds in rising dough, and he checked the sky outside the tent and found it drunk with stars. He couldn't hear the river but sensed its weight below them, sliding through the earth with a deep steady pressure.

He pulled on his boots and exited the tent, careful not to wake Bill Dunn or Jack Sumner. Stars flooded the valley. He woke Ora Howland, who retrieved the sextant from the *Maid of the Canyon* and the heavy chronometer—it looked like a giant pocket watch—from the *Kitty Clyde's Sister*. Meanwhile, Wes raked out the fire's banked coals and fed them with branches and pieces of oak. They worked together in silence. The air was still and cool, the wind depleted, but the stars were slowly moving, circling the earth. With his compass, Wes located north and set up his sextant on its tripod. He sighted through the eyepiece and moved the index arm until Polaris sat squarely on the wire. "Ora," he whispered. "I need a candle."

Oramel rummaged in the *No Name* for a candle while Wes looked up at the quicksand of stars and tried to resist being pulled in. He flinched when Ora lit a match beside him. With the candle they scrutinized the calibrated scale and found the altitude, and Wes jotted it down, then pulled out his pocket almanac. He consulted his table of mean refractions and calculated their latitude as 45°25′.

He took observations for time and distance on the moon's edge in relation to Polaris. As the moon reached the wire, the Major whispered "now" and Ora, holding his candle to the chronometer, noted the time. Wes consulted his nautical almanac and together he and Ora performed the subtraction from Greenwich Mean Time. Ora wrote down the hour, minutes, and seconds. Then every few minutes for the next hour they took a new reading.

When Ora yawned, his entire skinny body hung down from the empty crater of his mouth. Wes held the candle to Ora's list of readings. He computed a mean from their twelve observations and calculated their longitude. Ora shrugged. "Just where I thought we were."

They packed up the instruments. Why didn't Ora sit down then and there to plot their location and make corrections to his map, Wes wished to know. But he kept the question to himself. Yawning, Ora crept back into his tent.

Still, it was remarkable—to locate themselves amid a floodtide of stars who knew how many million miles away. But everything was connected, Wes thought. He sat there all night, drifting off then waking. Stirring the fire, watching the sky sponge up the stars as it turned from ashen gray to sifted blue at dawn, he thought of their little seed of a planet racing across the universe, just like their seed pods racing down the river. And what lay ahead?

5

They loaded up the boats and floated out of Browns Park, passing those enormous gates of red sandstone. Inside, the canyon walls were higher than any they'd seen—and consequently darker—and the water, cold and fast and relentless, prompted Andy to shout, "How does the water come down at Lodore?" to which Wes, who knew Southey's poem by heart, boomed out, "Collecting, projecting, receding and speeding, and shocking and rocking, and darting and parting, and threading and spreading, and whizzing and hissing, and dripping and skipping . . ." until the rushing waters drowned him out. But they had a name for this canyon now—Lodore—much to the disgust of Jack Sumner, who announced that the idea of using limey trash to find names for new discoveries was un-American.

They struck a chain of rapids, but none they couldn't run. They turned it into a race. The oarsmen rowed hard to skim the river like birds, and the ruddermen in the rear steered with their long oars, facing forward and shouting directions. Every now and then Wes in the pilot boat ran ahead to scout the river, then signaled for the others.

On terraces from which enormous cliffs leaped, the rock was a deep brownish red lichened over, but slanted walls of sun made it crimson on top. In some places slopes of piñons hung in shadows by the shore, in others the walls plunged straight into the river, suggesting a new source of worry to the Major: where on earth would they land if they couldn't run a rapid? Squeezed by the canyon, the river was deep, but deep did not mean free of obstacles, and who knew how many boulders lay just beneath the surface?

They camped on a little platform of rocks with no room for George to go off by himself.

Next day they started early and the rapids persisted. High cliffs obstructed the early morning sunlight, and in their drawers and shirts the men grew wet and cold. As always in the *Emma,* Bill sat in the bow and Jack in the stern, and Bill, facing Wes, lay his strong upper torso across both oars. He was rowing for the body heat, Wes figured, since in most stretches the river ran swiftly. Bill pulled and they flew, like whipping a fast horse. A hawk shrieked overhead and Bill looked up, but Wes didn't bother. He was watching Bill row, feeling vaguely envious—watching him strain with each lunge of the oars like a man granted parturition by the gods. The high faint scream came from overhead again. "I'd like to see this from a hawk's perspective," said Wes.

Bill pulled on the oars. "Give me the worm's-eye view any day."

"My father would say we sit in God's palm. Yet we pygmies strive against it."

"I'll buy that. Thou knowest, Lord. My daddy said to me, 'I brought you in, Bill, I can take you out again. I can make another one looks just the same.'"

"What religion was he, Bill?"

"What religion? Whiskey."

"What was he raised as?"

"Raised as a drunk."

"Still living?"

"Not to my knowledge."

"Did he teach you to trap?"

"He was a worthless piece of furniture. He taught me how to curse."

Each talked while looking up at canyon walls, Wes to the east, Dunn to the west.

"Well, you're your own man now."

"That I am."

"Make it easy on yourself."

"I will."

"I've estimated these walls as two thousand feet high."

Bill's head, tilted back, confronted the sky. "Make your hair curl, don't it?"

"Suppose you were the Creator," said Wes. "What better way to impress the human mind with a foretaste of eternity?"

"You mean, 'Chasms like this could smash you to a grease stain if you step off the rim, so mend your sinful ways'?"

Wes smiled. He couldn't help it—with infidels such as Bill he'd talk religion like his father, whereas with believers like Oramel Howland, always grousing about how we ought to stop on the Sabbath and maybe a prayer now and then wouldn't hurt, he talked geology instead, as though everything he did followed laws of compensation.

A roar ahead grew louder—Wes hadn't been watching. They were crossing, he realized, a flat apron of water toward a line beyond which the pot had started boiling. Behind him he heard a hollow rubber hiss—Jack Sumner inflating the Major's life preserver. Bill raised his oars and the *Emma Dean* gently revolved in the water, slow and peaceful. Wes found his flag, crawled past Jack, and climbed on top of the stern deck to see.

"How's she look?"

"Ferocious."

Bill Dunn pivoted the boat and started rowing toward the cauldron.

"You'll want to slow up," said Wes.

"It's just another repetition only more of it."

"I've decided we should land."

"No and hell no."

Wes raised his voice. "Ease up, Bill. Row to shore. Row to shore!"

Bill shook his head in disgust and held his oars. Jack tossed the

Major's life preserver aside and started rowing to shore, but the boat slid downriver.

"Faster!" Wes signaled the other boats with his flag—left and right and down. The roar from the rapids grew deafening, monstrous. They pulled right hard, both men rowing now, watching the line where the cauldron began. Like a tent made of silk, the river stretched taut to a flowing apex before dropping off its horizon, beyond which churned a series of ten-foot waves surrounded by rocks, impossible to run. The sliding plane of water pulling them closer was surprisingly unruffled, their lack of progress toward the riverbank that much more alarming.

But they made it to shore, first the *Emma Dean*, then the *Sister*. Wes disembarked and scrambled up the bank to see the rapids better. The brown and gray river poured over rock, or the rock raked the water—hard to tell which. It is to be observed, he told himself, practicing for his account of this voyage, that the water on the ocean merely rises and falls. A wave, if there are waves, is a form passing through. But here on the river the form remains and the water charges through it, and multiply that by a thousand waves which impede and lash the water yet whip it ever faster—

A shout came from the river. To his horror, the *No Name* with Ora, Seneca, and the Englishman was perched at the apex, then shot forward. She went completely under, fountained up and flew, blasted through a wave and hung there on its hip. Purple-brown blocks of rock stood all around her. Wes waved the flag madly, as though that would help. He hurried back to intercept the *Maid*, leaping as he ran with great sweeps of the flag, relieved when the final boat made it to shore.

But the *No Name* was in trouble. In her, Frank Goodman found himself in Ora's arms and saw oars fly through the air. Both men were screaming, but even inches from each other neither could hear. A series of splintering crashes ensued like successive doors slamming, and Frank spotted Seneca bobbing in the river twenty feet behind, then saw half the boat was with him. They were spinning in their own half of namelessness, he and Ora Howland—like a whirligig in pond scum—crushed by walls of water. They slowed down and clung to each other like babies being rocked, but the motion was the boat's, or the boat's bow. Then the river erupted and, ripped from Ora's arms, Frank flew down the rapids behind Ora in the bow. It was odd: facing Frank, Ora looked sheathed like a body in a coffin, which skidded and dipped, bucking hard, rising up. Now the coffin exploded. Something pummeled Frank, water pried his mouth open, he caromed from rock to rock, although packed folds of water cushioned these collisions. All he could think was what a stupid way to die. He'd lost sight of Ora. He found a rhythm, though—pin to pin, as in skittles—and timed his feeble lunge for the next rock. By sheer miracle it worked, he thought he'd busted his jaw, but now at least he had a rock to cling to. The river poured over the rock and over him, but he wouldn't let go. And now he had something, the utmost, to say to Walter Powell when he saw him. His bowels loosened, a wire of fear shot through his heart. The river was draining him, giving him the shivers, and the water felt as hard as this rock he hugged. The unrelenting roar may have been the worst part—as bad as the force of constant pressure trying to pry him from the rock.

He'd say something to Walter—call *me* a brass button—something that would knock that bastard from his perch, and if he, Frank, died, so much the better. He'd die with that lunatic's name on his lips.

Something poked his shoulder. He twisted his head, and beside him lay a long piece of root. He saw Ora lying flat across the water gripping the far end of the root, and for the rest of his life Frank never wondered why it didn't seem odd that Ora should be lying on the water like that, like some legless Christ.

It turned out to be a sandbank. Ora pulled Frank through a nest of river tendons and he lay on the sand exhausted for a minute, then Ora kicked him and they went to help Seneca. The latter clung to rocks at the sandbank's lower end, but by the time they arrived he'd made it onto their island. "ANYTHING BROKE?" Ora shouted at his brother.

"NOT THAT I CAN FEEL!"

This long, narrow sandbank was surrounded by river. Below it, the rapids began to diminish. How far down the river they'd gone they couldn't tell—it all happened in a blink—but the others on shore were out of sight now. Oramel had some matches in his shirt as a caution against just such a catastrophe, and they blew on them, spread them on a rock, and gathered some driftwood. From a large pine trunk washed up on the sand he scraped some pitch and they started a fire. It seemed the water was rising—Frank was the first to notice. Frank was also shivering and his lips had turned blue. The breeze from the rapids smelled like gunpowder.

Soon the others ran up on the shore across the way, making meaningless signals. The three signaled back that the water was rising, and those on shore jumped up and down as though comprehending—or not. Frank Goodman's shirt nearly caught fire, but at least he felt warmer once their pile of wood was burning. He stopped shaking and sat there peacefully awaiting his demise from rising water.

Moments later, it seemed, the *Emma Dean* shot onto the sand beside them and they grabbed it instinctively, as if it wouldn't stop. Jack Sumner had rowed out alone to rescue them.

They pulled the boat up to the head of the island, waded as far as they could into the river, and Seneca sat on a rock and held the gunnel while the others climbed in. He gave them a push and jumped into the boat. Jack rowed to shore singlehanded, not trusting them with oars after what they'd been through.

The others ran up, hollered in relief, and embraced the three men. Andy Hall slapped their backs. Frank Goodman, however, held off from Walter Powell. And Wes scowled and issued orders. The men lined down the remaining two boats and walked them through shallows to a spot downstream where a bonfire could be started.

Farther downstream the stern of the *No Name* lay wrecked against a rock in the middle of the river, and Wes descended the bank to take a look. The deck compartment seemed intact amid a pile of splintered wood, but the river was a mess of water, rocks, and spray. Was it worth the risk to salvage it? They'd lost, Wes calculated, nearly two thousand pounds of food and equipment—flour, bacon, rifles, ammunition, bedding, thermometers, barometers, knives, axes, trade beads, some cook gear—and Ora's maps.

He walked back. Frank Goodman announced that the wreck had carried off every stitch of his clothes except the shirt and drawers he wore. Also his tintypes, knife and gun, books, extra boots, belt, rubber poncho, blankets, thread and needles, pocket watch, and cash he wouldn't specify the amount of—all gone.

He was closest in size to Walter Powell, so the latter shrugged and rummaged through his clothes and gave him some breeches and shirts, also blankets and a hat. As Wes watched, Frank looked away and wept. Wes could see that Walter hardly noticed. Yet, after that day he left the Englishman alone. And for the next several weeks Wes sensed his brother's volatile nature floating, unable to decide whom to single out next.

The worst loss of all was the barometers. Wes had distributed essential instruments among the four boats in case one got wrecked—but not the barometers. All three had lain in the single box they came in, designed to protect them; now, for all he knew, they'd been smashed. He could delay their trip a month and walk to Salt Lake City and purchase new ones. That seemed out of the question. They still had the sextant, chronometer, compasses, and two thermometers. Together, from memory, they could redraw Ora's maps. The barometers, however, were their only means of taking altitudes, and just as important, of measuring geological strata. Wes blamed himself, but that wasn't good enough. Their trip was spoiled and his sole relief was to make himself hard. He walked up to Oramel. "You had to have seen my signal," he said.

"What signal was that?"

"You old fool. To land."

Ora borrowed a page from the Major and gave him a look that said, Bend down and tie my shoes. It didn't work. His long gray-white beard made it seem comical. He was in fact the oldest in their group—thirty-five to Wes's thirty-four—but that didn't make him *old*. Still, Wes treated him like some ancient general who'd held his post beyond his time. Wes was short and his muttonchops sparse, but his dark eyes and glowering brow lay Ora under siege.

"What's the signal to land?"

"Don't get your feathers up."

"Had you fallen asleep again?"

"By God, I won't be catechized!"

"Did you even see the signal?"

"We'd shipped a lot of water. I can't say I saw the signal. I saw it too late."

Wes abruptly turned and walked away but heard Bill Dunn observe to his departing back: "It's the fucking war all over again."

The rest of the men surrounded the bonfire. "When rage fills *me*," said the Englishman, "I gently balance my cup on my knee whilst pulling on my breeches and shaving simultaneously."

"That don't answer for me."

Frank the Englishman was giddy, filled with bliss at having survived and equally with despair at having lost all he owned. "Well. I chatter." He sat on the sand.

Oramel Howland asked George Bradley if Major Powell had truly signaled. "Signaled us," said George. "Were you still around the bend?"

"Must have been."

"When them big boats fill with water, not much you can do as far as directing them."

"You can bail," said Bill.

"There you go," said Seneca. "We were bailing for sure. And looking out for signals."

The bonfire at least seemed to warm the canyon walls. Hawkins started a meal while everyone else spread equipment out to dry—all except Seneca. He'd had enough that day and sat down before the fire and heaved a big sigh. He lay back on the sand and announced to the sky: "I am possessed of an irresistible inclination to flop."

Andy Hall threw some blankets on a bush to dry and declared of his boat, "She won't gee nor haw nor whoa worth a damn—as if she wasn't broke."

"Needs a good kick."

After they'd eaten their hardtack and salt pork and drunk their coffee and rinsed their dishes in the river, Jack Sumner pulled Wes aside and talked *sotto voce* about rowing to the wreck. The stern compartment looked intact. Some things called for desperate measures.

Wes said he'd see.

That night, for the first time on their voyage, his stump hurt. The nerve endings felt on fire, the same old problem since his amputation. A blunt stone was jammed into his ribs, but he didn't change position because who needed sleep? Sleep was just a way for ordinary men to postpone decisions and hide from their problems.

In the middle of the night he crawled out of his blankets, sat on a rock, and stared at the river, listening to it roar. Solid black water, white highlights of foam. He thought of his wound in the war, of how Walter had stanched the bleeding right away and dragged him to a tree, and of the amputation two days later. At least it wasn't a leg. He imagined himself walking to Salt Lake now, searching shops for a barometer, then having to wait for a shipment from Chicago. One by one the men left behind would desert, and who could blame them? By his estimate, Salt Lake City was a hundred and fifty miles away.

The next morning he took another look at the wreck. It lay against a rock where the current, if anything, seemed to accelerate. More rocks sat between the shore and the wreck but not all in fast water.

Jack Sumner walked up. "What think you, Major Powell?"

"I'm thinking without those barometers we might just as well pack up and go home."

"You needed them for your observations, right?"

"I can't do without them."

"And if you got them back—why, then it's smooth sailing?"

"I can't say it's smooth sailing. This won't be our last setback."

"My sentiments exactly. Them instruments were packed in shavings, I believe. It's likely they're in good order. Me and Bill Dunn could row out and see."

Wes looked at Jack. "Take the little boat."

"I was planning to, Major."

"Tell the men to unload it."

"I was planning to."

"Fine."

He watched them push off and row between rocks, heading for the main channel. Where the current picked up they found the running edge between fast and slow water and rode it downriver, threading outsized boulders. They pulled hard for the taut blanket of water wrapped around the rock and broadsided in. The bump hardly seemed to shake the *Emma Dean*. The river split here and ran off to either side. Its ever-healing fabric upwelled in calm, or so it seemed to Wes on shore. His heart began to lighten. Bill wrapped the bow line around a jutting rock, of which there were several. The stern of the *No Name* was wedged in those rocks, protected by the largest one.

The deck looked half submerged. With one foot in the *Emma*

and one on a rock, Jack axed the stern deck and Bill, leaning out, ripped off the boards. They shouted and waved and pulled out a box, and from the shore Wes recognized it right away. They cheered again and pulled something else out and Wes felt his burden lift and sunlight struck the shore—or perhaps he just noticed it then. The sun had begun its five- or six-hour journey from one canyon rim to the other.

The barometers were salvaged, even the box was dry. When the boat returned Wes inspected them with care, and the wet flour as well—they dumped it in the river—and the two thermometers and some candles. How could the flour receive such a dunking but the box of instruments stay dry? You'd think the gods were helping them. But in only three weeks he'd learned that water found its own course regardless of gods or careful precautions, including frequent caulking. "What's that?" he asked, nodding at Bill.

"A jug."

"Give it here."

Bill Dunn, slumped, handed the jug to Major Powell, who uncorked it, smelled the whiskey, looked at Bill. "I'll take charge of this," he said.

No one said a thing.

Later, lining down, Jack Sumner approached him. "Do we got to portage every time the river squeals?"

"I'm not taking any chances."

"I make it we've gone four miles since this morning."

"Four and a half."

They stood in the sun on a huge talus slope next to the river. Tumbled down from cliffs above, the broken rocks and boulders had swept into the current, making it impassable. A tree lizard lay on a rock and watched the two, its soft throat beating.

"So we found the barometers," Jack said.

"I'm extremely grateful."

"Now that jug."

"What jug?"

"With the whiskey inside it."

"What about it?" asked Wes.

"The men, well, they smuggled it onto the *No Name* way back there in Wyoming."

"And you let them?"

"Where's the harm?"

"It hampers judgment. How do I know that jug wasn't the cause of Ora missing my signals?"

"You don't. That's what I mean. What I propose is I could take charge of it, as second-in-command. Make sure it's shared around, but only once the day is over. We could use it for medicinal."

Wes shrugged. He'd been through this before. At Shiloh, at Vicksburg . . . He supposed the men could use a little whiskey, what with sand in sopping clothes, being drenched then burned then drenched, and endless portages, rancid bacon, grit in their coffee, and now a boat wrecked. And they'd barely begun. "It's your responsibility then."

"Well. I'm sure the men are grateful."

"I trust your discretion."

"Well. I'm no more an officer than a dude. But it's muddy going. They need . . . a little lift."

The next night in camp all the men were drunk except Major Powell, his brother, and George Bradley, camped off by himself again. It had come around to Sunday, and this Sabbath they'd kept. But that didn't stop the exhausted crew from passing the jug until it was empty. Now they sat on logs before the fire, and Walter sat apart, perched on a boulder. He wasn't sure where Wes was—out somewhere in the darkness adding up the stars. Wes had spent most of the day away from the camp taking geological sections and collecting fossils. If he happened to be within hearing distance, a good song might reassure him that all was well in camp, even if it wasn't, and that flesh and blood was near. But Walter couldn't summon up the will to sing. Legs folded underneath him, he felt himself sinking into despair. Seneca Howland lay on a blanket beside him, and past Seneca was the fire with the remaining men on logs reflected in its light and circled by darkness.

"Thought I'd made my last bow," said Oramel Howland.

"Thought I'd come to a tragic end," said his brother.

Ora stood up and waved his finger at Frank. "You. You were clinging to me for dear life."

"Quite the other way around. It was you, my dear friend, who clung to me like a monkey to a coconut tree."

"Both of you was clinging to each other."

"I never saw the boat break up."

Ora sat. "Dashed to pieces."

"The river just burst it away on every side."

"It seemed to transpire as in a dream—very slowly."

"Nothing slow about the way you screamed."

"Alls I could see from shore was a smashed boat and two heads like squashes racing through the haystacks."

"Only two?"

"Did you hear me shouting?" Frank Goodman asked. "I was shouting 'Goodbye, boys!' Did anyone hear it?"

Bill Dunn slapped his knee. "How long you going to talk about this? It don't bear repeating."

"If *you* almost died, you'd talk about it too."

"I almost died a hundred times."

"Ain't you glad we found them barometers, Bill?"

"Pleased as punch. Like to crack them over your head right now and pour the damn mercury down your ear, Jack."

"The Major says they'll have to be repaired."

"I don't doubt it. Fix this, fix that. A whole catalogue of shoulds. Maybe you don't like your thumb the way it sits? God made it wrong? Think I'll fix it, by Christ!"

"Least we don't have to hike to Salt Lake City."

"More damned nonsense."

"Bill, is it true a scorpion once bit you on the ass?"

"It's true."

"What happened?"

"He died is what happened," said Jack Sumner.

"Which one?"

"The scorpion."

"That's one of the hundred times Bill almost died."

Andy turned to William Hawkins. "Where you from, Hawkins?"

"That ain't my name."

"What is it?"

"Missouri Rhodes."

"How come you changed it?"

"I didn't. Okay, it's William Rhodes Hawkins. Missouri for short."

"So where you from?"

"Just think for a minute."

"I'm thinking. There."

"What's my name?"

"Missouri?" Andy thought again. "You're from Missouri?"

Hawkins looked away in disgust.

"You said that was your name, not that you was *from* there."

"It don't take a scholar."

"I'm from Scotland," said Andy.

"You don't talk like no Scotchman."

" 'Tis a brough bracht moonlicht nicht."

"That's more like it."

"Came here when I was six."

"Where's here?"

"Illinois."

"Same state as Major Powell. You know him there?"

"It's a big place."

Andy stood up and started pacing back and forth, looking at Hawkins. "How come you got all those names?"

"None of your beeswax."

"You don't look as old as you look."

"That makes a lot of sense."

"You ever shoot a flying fish?"

"What kind of question is that?"

"I did once."

"I never even seen the ocean."

"No! You don't say. That why you come on this trip, Hawkins?"

"Come to work like a galley slave. Come to hunt game and cook."

"But we're going all the way to the ocean," said Andy. "I am at least."

"Well, bully for you."

Andy spotted Walter Powell. "Hey Walter! Does the Major have any more whiskey cached away? Some for medicinal?"

Walter Powell didn't answer.

"I swallowed a bee today!"

"How'd you do that?" Hawkins asked.

"Struggling through some piñons and cedars looking for firewood. Scared up a swarm of bees. One flew right in my mouth. Felt him buzzing around in there all day."

"Open your mouth. Lie on your back and stay real still. Don't breathe a fucking word."

"Goddamn! He just stung me."

"Sounds like a bad case."

"Stung me again!"

"Bees only sting once."

"Mr. Powell, sir, gimme some of your whiskey," Andy said.

Walter said nothing.

"Drink some water. Drown him dead," said Hawkins.

"I tried that already. Mr. Powell, sir, he's still flying around above the water I drunk and stinging my heart out!"

"Got to drink a whole gallon."

"Of whiskey?"

"Get him drunk."

Walter Powell wasn't listening. He was thinking of Camp Sorghum in South Carolina, his prison in the war. Every morning the men washed in a creek behind their shanties, except those who were dying inch by inch. The creek was where the Union prisoners fought amongst themselves—where those with long faces and those who whined and groused went after each other—so Walter washed upstream. But they didn't like that. They accused him of spreading disease and filth, and how come he always carried that cold cream around, and what kind of gal was he anyway? So he took the pot of cream and threw it in a rage, barely missing Jink Lewis's head. It smashed against a rock and after that Walter drew a blank. He woke in the prison hospital with an ache in both ears and climbed out of bed and simply walked away. They found him in the woods and carried him back. *Something* had broken, some link between events. It was the cold cream, he thought. Not his brother's bloody arm or a Reb's exploded belly or the dismembered limbs in a pile outside the hospital tent at Shiloh, no, those didn't haunt him—instead, the cold cream did. It seemed to be some kind of limit or screen—the limit of the finite—waste, grease, disease. He never touched the stuff again. The revenge of the unctuous. A wet thing that won't come off. Smashed against a rock like the white star of death.

"Hey Walter, sing a song."

Walter kept mum.

"Don't ask him, you miscreant, he might just do it."

"Sing 'Old Shady,' Walter."

"I'll sing it," said Hawkins.

"No you won't."

"I'll sing it if he don't."

"Hey, where's my medal?" Andy Hall was on his knees behind the log, feeling around with his palms in the dirt.

"What medal is that?"

"My Saint Christopher."

"I didn't know you was a Roman."

"I always take it off if I'm going to imbibe."

"I thought everyone in Scotland was a hard-shell Presbyterian."

"Not me." Andy stood up. "All right, nobody move."

Hawkins launched into "Old Shady" in a bad church voice, one apt to crack any stray graven images.

> Won't dey laugh when dey see old Shady a-coming, coming,
>   Hail! mighty day
> Den away, away, I can't wait any longer,
>   Hooray, hooray, I'm going home.

Walter climbed off his rock and stood there. He would slap that man hard, the one who was singing. But first he had to wait for the needles in his legs to hatch and rise in swarms and let him know he was standing, not afloat on stubs. He found himself making an odd sort of gesture: dipping the first three fingers of his right hand into the palm of the left, then bringing them to his face and rubbing his cheeks with soft, patient strokes. He was still doing that when his brother came back, when Hawkins's song had stopped, when the men had all turned in.

6

Next morning, Hawkins's call of "Roll out" woke exactly no one except Wes. He'd seen the empty jug, he'd allowed it to happen, now it was over and done with, good. One more day here and they'd be off again. After a while George Bradley showed up and poured himself some coffee, then Andy Hall appeared and asked if anyone had found his medal.

He'd never see it again. A pack rat had taken it.

Cracks had opened up in the inch-thick oak of the *Sister* and the *Maid*, so Bradley and Seneca Howland spent the day caulking them with hot pitch from nearby pine trees. They caulked the *Emma*'s deck too, since water was entering the watertight compartment not from the river but from the cockpit, as Wes had discovered, when they couldn't bail fast enough.

Oramel Howland worked on his map once he'd drunk enough coffee. He staked some wagon sheets up on oars for shade and with Major Powell's help restored the compass bearings they'd lost: from Green River City to Henry's Fork, 25° east of south; from there to the lower end of Browns Park, 25° south of east; from Browns Park to this spot, 25° west of south. They consulted the Major's sextant readings and decided that Oramel's last remembered estimates exceeded the distance on a straight line from the end of Browns Park to their present point in a ratio of about five to three, and from that they concluded the river distance from launch to this place was about—pretty close to—near as they could tell—a hundred and eighty miles.

That is, Wes concluded these things. Ora went along. With the log Wes had kept of their latitude and longitude at selected points they were able to grid a presentable map that seemed to make sense. It ended in nowhere, of course, like a half-tied pendant noose. But that's where they were, he'd determined, and could take some comfort from it—suspended in nowhere.

Bill Dunn took elevations. Frank Goodman borrowed Seneca's sewing kit and tried making some of Walter's clothes fit. Walter bounced around from one group to another, helping where he could and singing "Laura Lee," as happy as a clam, with no memory of the interior abyss he'd fallen into last night, nor of crawling out. Even when Hawkins declared there was something queer about the taste of the coffee and reached into the pot with his bowie knife and pulled out one of Walter's black and dripping socks, Walter didn't snap. He laughed with the rest.

Wes and George Bradley, between other tasks, copied entries into their diaries from the little slips of paper on which they kept notes.

Andy Hall approached Wes and asked about Hawkins. Was he right with the law? Running from something?

"Why do you ask?"

"His name ain't William Hawkins. It's Missouri Rhodes."

Jack Sumner walked up. "William Rhodes Hawkins," he said. "Missouri's a sobriquet."

"What's that?"

"A moniker," said Jack.

"Another name bestowed along the way," Wes patiently explained.

"See, that's what I mean. It's like a gunman on a poster."

"You think he's running from the law?" asked Jack. "He wouldn't run if his pants was on fire."

But Andy looked worried.

Wes came up with new assignments for the boats: himself, Jack Sumner, and Bill Dunn in the *Emma,* as before; Walter, Seneca, George Bradley, and Frank Goodman in the *Sister;* and Hawkins, Andy Hall, and Oramel in the *Maid.* The chief question had been, with only three boats, who would get the Englishman? Wes decided the best boatman in the group would have to take the extra weight.

George didn't like it. Sputtering like a sausage, the young salt from New England—with round face, brown eyes, and a nasty cut above the left eye, from having fallen in his boat—approached Wes before they launched and worked himself into a passion at the prospect of transporting burdensome passengers whose space was better used for something practical, like fish hooks. He'd gone, in his boat, from a crew of two, himself and Walter, all the way to four, thus doubling his duties and headaches and chores. George often referred to the *Sister* as his boat, and whenever they landed he pulled her on shore to upend and examine her. Wes had observed his frequent loss of patience at the slightest irritant. Mishaps frustrated him—they had to be corrected. Frank Goodman, he told the Major now, was a walking mishap, and he said so in the Englishman's earshot, but that didn't seem to matter. Everyone talked about Frank in front of Frank, and someone had to take him.

It took Wes most of the next few days to put the loss of the *No Name* behind him. The river helped; it kept plowing ahead. Lodore Canyon would take them to the confluence of the Green and Yampa Rivers, their first major landmark. A fourth of their food and equipment had been lost, there was one less boat, but here they were on their way. They'd managed to survive. Out of nowhere a gust of rage blew through his heart, yet it left him feeling violently alive, impelled to shout hosannas. He looked back at Jack, turned to face Bill, smiled to himself, and wisely kept silent.

The rage was for Ora. Ora existed to correct the lives of others, not his own. Schoolmaster, parson—his vigilance when it came to Wes Powell must have exhausted him, for when it came to himself, to his own duties, he'd proven lax so far. Wes thought back to Ora's behavior during the winter, when they'd first met. Ora seemed a born leader, thoughtful and determined. He intimidated Wes. They'd been camped east of here, living in cabins on the White River above its confluence with the Green, and the first winter thaw had just flooded their camp with knee-high water. So they moved to higher ground and built a new cabin and Emma moved in the moment it was finished. The others slept on the ground—Ora, Seneca, Hawkins, Bill Dunn, and Wes's student Sam Garman. The next day Ora requested that Major Powell keep his wife away from the men. She bossed them too much, in case he hadn't noticed. Garman was leaving, Ora announced, because he couldn't take being bossed by a woman anymore.

It was true. Garman left. And without mentioning Ora's complaint, Wes did take pains to keep Emma from the men for the rest of the winter—early spring, really, just four months ago. He asked for her help on extended pack trips to collect rocks and fossils. Ora's request had taken him aback, and his instinct had been to guard her, not the men.

Maybe he wouldn't shout hosannas, maybe just breathe an enormous sigh of relief. He glanced at the cliffs and the sparse rash of trees and the water gliding by. The high broken walls of the canyon drifted past, and when the sun struck the water it sent red and yellow columns clear to the bottom, which caught them and broke them and toppled them back. His account of this voyage, what would it be, monograph or narrative? *Geological Notes Pertaining to . . .* It would depend, of course, on the specimens he found, the observations he made, the character of the country. The world lay ahead and they were cleaving it in two and his mind was the edge, his solitary mind. Wes could almost taste the promise of knowledge, the conversion into words. They'd survived a calamity—bad luck lay behind. Still, all at once, his heart gulped air—

"What's that?" said Bill Dunn. Wes turned to look: a coyote staring at them from the bank. Bill said, "Him again."

"Who?" said Jack Sumner.

"That coyote," said Bill.

Jack feathered his oars and held them suspended. As he and Wes watched, the coyote loped off, glancing over his shoulder. Jack turned around. "It ain't the same one, you lackbrain." He smiled and winked at Wes. "That other one before was fifteen miles ago."

"It's the same," said Bill.

Part Two

1

A thousand miles south of Powell and his crew. On the Great Canyon's rim. Two women, two children, two men: a family. Past junipers and pines, into clearings of bunchgrass, over ruts fanning out to staggering canyons—on foot, slow, too poor for horses, crossing the earth step by step in a line, transporting all they own in baskets on their backs. Blue sky above, red earth beneath, and always the distant roar of wind, whose gusts are like ghosts swinging blankets of seeds. The wind pours everywhere through the great trees, back and forth, down and up, at their heels, in their faces.

Toab came last and watched the others ahead: Onchok, his cousin, in a limp, soiled breechclout. Overnight, he'd become careless, fretful. He'd changed since it happened—everything had.

Pooeechuts, wife of Onchok. Her conical basket hung on her back from a tumpline pulling tight across her collarbone. The women carried the baskets, that was their job. Mara, her sister, reached back to feel hers—just checking, Toab guessed. Still there. Still intact. Its bottom point worn smooth and she seemed to be caressing it. Both women wore dresses made of stretched deerskin with large sleeveless holes. As Mara reached back, Toab noticed the curl of black hair pinching out between her arm and breast.

Baskets on the women's heads, smaller of course. Also woven from yucca, also conical, to block the burning sun.

Soxor, like her father, wore a breechclout. But it wouldn't be long before her blood came, Toab thought, and she'd have to wear a dress. Kwits, her small brother, wore nothing but black hair hanging to his shoulders. Between them, their mother had made them leave room for their absent sister: a hollow in the air shaped like Chookwadum. Toab could picture her taking long strides, loping along like a bundle of sticks. He saw that upward bounce when she lifted her heels.

They hardly seemed to move at all. The earth swallowed their progress. Tied to one another by a scrawny string of time, they patiently marched across their winding plateau. That was it, patience: they'd need patience to find her, good luck and patience, Toab told himself. But did the others know that? Did Onchok, with his prating —or his sudden gloom? For this dangerous hunt they'd left their daily lives behind, their home, their friends. They'd hung pieces of sage on their summer shelters so their relatives could tell how long they'd been gone. If the sage turned brown they'd be gone a long time. If it dried completely and fell to the ground they were never coming back.

Every now and then they stopped and sat and waited for bits of themselves to catch up. Some pieces were back there, slower than the rest.

They walked all morning on mostly level ground that snaked around encroaching canyons. Tall ponderosas gave way to stunted trees, to cholla armed with sharp spines, to lizards pumping up and down. When Toab looked back there he was, still behind them. Would he follow them all the way down? Or would he see that jackrabbit beneath the manzanita and chase him through brush, sending dust in swirling walls up behind their paths? Toab understood coyotes; they'd helped him before. He knew what would happen later in the day when this one grew tired and returned to his den: he'd pass into the earth, which would seal up behind him like the water in a lake, and once inside he would shed his fur and snout, throw them off like cloak and mask, and stand on two legs and walk on two feet. And he'd eat and mill around and talk with other people who, like him, were animals outside in the visible world, but people inside.

They watch the outsiders: frogs watch from their ponds, birds from their bushes, coyotes from their dens. They watch us poor humans, Toab thought, without fur, beaks, or tails. They take pity on our helplessness, naked and alone, and give us their fur, their meat, their feathers—give us their eyes, their sense of smell, their knowledge of the world, their songs for the dead. And when they go outside again they put their animal bodies back on, to feel more at home, more comfortable probably. And to be seen by us, he thought, by men without eyes except those they'd given us.

As the plateau narrowed, Onchok turned right and headed toward its sudden edge, through cactus and sage and thick sprawling junipers, some obscuring the trail. Kwits stopped and waited for Toab to catch up. Pinch him! cried his sister. Instead, he offered Toab a juniper berry, held it to his mouth. Toab snapped it up.

Then down: down rocks to a narrow ledge, down through fissures in the cliff face, down a steep slope and across an esplanade barren and red—down through canyons cleft from the air itself, their great spaces pouring into each other, to a world inside the world. It took them all day. Coyote didn't follow. They crossed one more terrace and descended some talus and entered a canyon winding through earth, which led to the deepest canyon of all and their gardens on a ridge beside the Pawhaw—the Colorado River—but nothing was ripe yet. The days were getting longer but still weren't long enough. Their corn, squash, and melons sat hard on the ground, irrigated by springs pulled like threads from a cliff. To one side stood their arbors —shade houses covered with brush and cornstalks; they needed repair. Rabbitskin robes hung inside the arbors for use on cold nights.

The river was high. Toab watched it slide past hardly making a sound.

After patching the arbors with fresh juniper boughs they sharpened sticks and gathered agave. Some were so high their stalks had bent completely over. This was the season when the agave shot up, and most had grown a foot a day for the past few weeks, driving the last sweetness into the plants' fibers. Some were in flower and smelled like rotten meat, but Toab trimmed off the flowers. He asked the plants to be good food and thanked them in advance and picked up a heavy rock and drove his sharpened stick into their juicy hearts and wrenched them from the ground, then trimmed off the bayonet leaves and stringy roots. The others followed his lead. With one or two hearts gathered on each stick, they brought them into camp and started fires with driftwood in deep stone-lined pits that had been there as long as Toab could remember—or his father or grandfather.

The fires burned all night, fed by Toab and Onchok, until the pits filled to the top with hot coals.

At dawn they all painted their cheeks and brows red. They raked coals aside to form a deep crater and placed the agave in, trying not to burn themselves. Then they raked the coals back and piled hot stones on top, then bunchgrass, then dirt, and sang songs and ate seedcakes while the agave roasted. The boy, Kwits, sang his song about being left-handed, and they did a round dance in which everyone looked to the left as they moved:

> *Ya ya, look around to the left,*
> *Around to the left take a good look,*
> *Around to the left, around to the left.*

Only a man born during the summer could watch over the agave while it baked after dark, that's the way they'd always done it. Onchok and Toab were born in winter, and Kwits was too young. But Mara was born in summer, Toab knew, so he bent the rule and let her tend the agave. Three pits were burning, and she vented them from time to time by thrusting her stick into the coals and jerking it.

The next day at daybreak they danced the yant dance and sang yant songs:

> *The wind blows through*
> *The stalks he used to have*
> *Standing on the mountains.*

They pulled some roasted agave from still hot coals, put it on basket trays, and sucked out the juice, sweeter and more full of heavy musk than a valley crammed with peaches. Most of it they mashed and pressed flat and spread out on rocks to dry. Later, they would roll the dried agave into cakes.

Toab found corn husks inside their shade houses to wrap the cakes in when they were ready.

For the next several days the women wove baskets, especially trays. Pooeechuts and her sister Mara worked fast; Soxor helped too but left the hard parts to them. Meanwhile, Onchok went hunting and would be gone a few days. Toab lingered at the camp and watched the women weave.

They boiled yucca spears and trimmed willow shoots and split them in three. They soaked devil's-claw seedpods and peeled off the black strips to highlight the trays, working circles of points, squash blossoms, and cog wheels into their designs. The baskets were for trading. They'd also taken buckskins to trade, and antelope skins and nets for catching rabbits.

Onchok returned from his hunt empty-handed—as usual, thought Toab.

When the baskets were finished, Toab and Onchok built a raft to cross the river. With cords made from yucca, they lashed driftwood logs together.

Toab, Onchok, and Mara crossed first. They loaded a half-full basket on the raft, pushed the raft into the river, and clinging to its edge were carried downstream in the warm, quick water. On the other side they left the basket on the shore and Toab looked openly at Mara's wet breasts and the dripping black hair that fell forked between her thighs, but she turned away. He glanced at Onchok, also staring at Mara. Then the three formed a line, walking on shore, and with a cord pulled the raft upstream. At a bend they jumped in and hung on to the raft and shot back across the river, taken by the current.

After they'd ferried the supplies, all the baskets, and the two children they returned for Pooeechuts, the slight one—the mouse. When she had crossed over she stepped calmly off the raft in her deerskin dress while Onchok labored out of the river and collapsed on the sand.

Leaving the canyon, they climbed up slowly—the baskets were heavy, the agave weighed them down. Now Toab set the pace and Onchok lagged behind. As they climbed the air grew a little cooler and the women stronger. Toab watched Onchok, his cousin—his brother. Toab's job was to help his brother grow better, help him get right with the world again. But Onchok slowed down. He sat on a rock. Toab stopped the others.

They rested and ate seedcakes and Toab thought back to when Onchok had first met Pooeechuts and married her, the time when all of them were younger. He hadn't heard of her band, the Kwaiantuk-watsing—the People from the Other Side—but they were Newe like themselves. Their language and the way they did things were the same, but their baskets were stronger, more tightly woven. They lived across the Pawhaw up near Paiute Mountain, a place so far away that no one Toab knew had ever been there.

As for Toab and his band, they were She-bits. They'd never called themselves Paiute. Mostly they were simply Newe, the People, but their band was She-bits, White Earth People. When the Mormons arrived they pronounced it "Shivwits," and over time that's what it became.

That day years ago when Onchok met Pooeechuts, the People from the Other Side were coming to trade near Kwaganti's camp east of Shivwits country, bringing not only their baskets but Navajo blankets. Toab and Onchok took some of their buckskins and went to this trade to see what they could get.

What Onchok got was a wife. The basket makers, it turned out, brought lots of women, those who in fact had made the baskets. All the other Paiute were desperate for women, especially the Shivwits. In the Paiute bands women had been kidnapped and sold over the years, and now the bands were mostly men and a few older wives and babies. It was just the Ute at first, who stole Paiute children and used them as slaves, but over time a market developed and the Ute started selling the Paiute they'd kidnapped, first to the Spanish, then to Americans and Mormons. The Navajo also stole Paiute children and sold them to the Spanish, but not as much as the Ute. And the Mormons too, being nearby, got themselves some Paiute women and children, not by theft but in trade. When the Mormons came they brought sheep and cattle, which ate the Paiute's grass and drove away the deer. They took over the springs. And when the Paiute got poor and hungry enough, the Mormons offered rifles and sheep for Paiute children, especially the girls.

What could young men do without women to marry? The Shivwits lived farther from the Mormon settlements than the other Paiute bands, but because the Kaibab and Uinkarets had lost so many women, they courted and married Shivwits girls. So the stream of life running through the Shivwits threatened to dry up.

When Onchok spotted Pooeechuts at the trade, the small, brisk woman had baskets within baskets: dozens of trays inside a burden basket she'd carried all the way from the Other Side. She'd come with her father, who'd brought Navajo blankets. Later, she told her Shivwits husband that her father regretted coming there to trade because the people were so poor. Onchok traded one dressed buckskin for three of her basket trays, each woven with circles of points. Her baskets of red, white, and black were delicate and flawless, he told Toab—like the person who made them.

But Onchok was worried. He'd heard rumors about those women from the east, the ones from the Other Side. They were said to have a row of holes around their cunts through which they threaded cords. And if a woman turned out not to like a man, while they were fucking she could pull the strings from behind her anus and his prick would be caught. Eventually he would wither and die.

He learned it wasn't true. They all had a round dance, and Onchok asked Toab to arrange with Pooeechuts to meet him in the brush at a certain signal. Her father saw it all. He was hesitant about the marriage—the Shivwits were poor and lived too far away—but he let her decide, that was her privilege. Pooeechuts moved with Onchok to Shivwits country, two hundred miles from her home.

That was more than ten years ago. And though the world had since started to change, Toab thought their isolated plateau was safer than most places. The Shivwits lived farther west and south than any other Paiute, surrounded by canyons and close to the greatest canyon of all, the Pawhaw-oowipi. Its remoteness protected them. And Pooeechuts fit right in. Her name meant Mouse, and she could live anywhere, even in a hole. Over ten years she'd borne seven children, three of whom survived. Halfway through that time, her father died —her mother had died a long time before—and her younger sister, Mara, came from the Other Side to live with Pooeechuts and her band of Shivwits.

During those years a Ute named Blackhawk began a war against the Mormons, and as a result the tribes kept to themselves. So both Ute and Mormons found fewer opportunities to steal or buy Paiute children. The Navajo took advantage of the Mormons' preoccupation with the Ute to steal their sheep and cattle, crossing the river far to the east where most people crossed it, up near Paiute Mountain, then crossing back with their stolen stock.

The Shivwits didn't cross there. They had their own crossing closer to home, the one they'd used today.

Because of Blackhawk's war against the Mormons, the relations between the Paiute on the one hand and Ute and Navajo on the other seemed to shift. Still, the Navajo were ancient enemies of both the Paiute and the Ute. And the Ute had always stolen Paiute children, yet they were the Paiute's wealthy relatives. So some Paiute helped the Ute and Navajo and raided nearby towns.

But Toab and the other Shivwits didn't join them.

Other Paiute helped the Mormons, because they'd grown destitute and relied on them for food. Strange things happened: when some Paiute stole Mormon cattle, other Paiute returned them, and when some Paiute killed Mormons, other Paiute were tortured and murdered for the killings. Meanwhile, the Paiute, Ute, and Navajo seemed to have formed an uneasy alliance. Nothing made sense, and it was safest for the Shivwits just to stay where they were. Once some Mormons baptized a group of Shivwits and gave them special shirts. But Toab and Onchok's family didn't go; they distrusted the Mormons. The Mormons had cut down and taken a lot of trees from Shivwits land without asking permission. Maybe they thought the place was unoccupied, since when they ventured out onto the plateau most Shivwits hid. Onchok and his family could disappear easily into the cracks and depths of a land that always baffled strangers. And later they didn't come down with the diseases their relatives caught, like smallpox and cholera. So they'd done something right by not mixing with the Mormons. Those diseases were punishment.

Still, Onchok grew curious. He fingered the new shirts his relatives wore. They weren't buckskin or bark; they were soft against flesh. He thought he'd like to meet a few Mormons, to ask them for shirts. But now they weren't around.

Then, just a few weeks ago, things went crazy. A bearded Mormon looking for clearings to run his sheep came out on the plateau and saw Pooeechuts and her three children digging sego lilies. The man found Onchok, pulled him aside, and, speaking Paiute, gave him some tobacco and took him riding in his wagon. No other Mormon Onchok had heard of could speak the Newe's language.

They stopped by a spring. The Mormon's long beard split at the bottom, curling left and right. In the back of the wagon he unwrapped a burlap bundle and showed Onchok two rifles. He let Onchok hold one while explaining his proposal to trade these guns for Onchok's two youngest children.

Onchok grew confused. He'd always wanted a gun, and this heavy Springfield felt alive in his hands. Guns made it easier to kill bighorn and deer, which were harder to hunt thanks to the Mormons and their stock. And the man wanted his two youngest children, not the older Soxor, his favorite. He and Pooeechuts could always make more children — that was something they were good at. He agreed to the deal without consulting his wife or his brother Toab. Pooeechuts said nothing; she had to go along with it. And no one asked the children, Chookwadum and Kwits, who wound up spending one night in the Mormon camp and running off the next day.

The Mormon was enraged. He wanted his rifles back, and when Onchok refused he boxed his ear and knocked him down, demanding the children. But no one knew where they were. The Mormon threatened to hang Onchok by his filthy heels and twist off his crooked thumbs. Then he noticed Toab next to a tree, pointing one of the rifles at him. How could he know that Toab, so composed, had never fired a rifle and had no ammunition?

The Mormon left but promised to return with his friends. He would show them no mercy, get back his children or his guns or both, or die trying, he said.

Two days later Kwits returned by himself and said that after running from the Mormon, he and Chookwadum had been kidnapped up near Pigeon Canyon.

Kidnapped by whom? asked Toab.

Navajo. They separated him from his sister. On the second night he managed to escape, but she was still tied by the wrist to her captor.

What sort of Navajo?

Braves, on horses. They called each other by name but their language was incomprehensible to Kwits. One name stuck out: Hashkay.

Hashkay?

Or Hoshkey. Something like that. He seemed to be the leader.

So the family went off to find Chookwadum, which meant looking for the Navajo Hashkay. They left flushed with anger: Toab scolded Onchok for selling his children and being so greedy. Thinking of it now made him bitter again. Onchok didn't care about getting Chookwadum back, he only cared about his guns. And he knew no more about how to use them than his brother.

Toab hadn't lived with Onchok's family until this trouble started. He'd joined them to help his brother, but now he was taking charge, it seemed, though Onchok was nominally the family's head. It was as if Toab shook out his brother's bones, climbed into his skin, and acted for him now, as Coyote once had done for Wolf.

The night before they left, they built a big fire and Toab climbed inside it. While he stood in the flames his hair flew straight up and brown owls of smoke peeled off his body. He wasn't hurt, he wouldn't jump out. I'm fireproof, he screamed. They all felt his power.

The Navajo went east on horses, Onchok's family went south on foot. But once across the river they were nearer the Navajo, whose territory was immense. And Toab knew whom to ask about finding Hashkay. When he was a boy, every spring his father had taken him across the river and up the other side, the way they'd come today. Here, in Hualapai country, his father had rights to a cave where he'd always obtained his red paint. More recently, two years ago, Toab and a few other Shivwits had helped the Hualapai, who were fighting the Americans. American troops had tried to stop the Hualapai from driving miners from their land, but by the time Toab got there the fighting was over. Since then he'd been back three or four times to trade with and visit both the Hualapai and Havasupai, picking up more of their language each time. So it was here he'd start asking about Hashkay, with his friends on this side of the river. After that they'd go on to Oraibi, where Toab had also spent time. He'd explained to his brother that the Oraibi and the other Moqui traded with, fought with, and sometimes married the Navajo.

Havasupai, Hualapai, Moqui—these were names Toab had recently learned. The whites not only changed the Paiute world, they replaced all their names. Now his band was called Shivwits and his tribe Paiute. Now what had been the Oaw-duhpaiuts were the Hualapai, now the Ko-inina were the Havasupai and the Pu-hawng-weets—the Cane Knife People—the Navajo, and the Mookweech from Oraibi had become the Moqui. The Pawhaw had become the Colorado River and the Pawhaw-oowipi the Great Canyon. Paiute Mountain wasn't yet Navajo Mountain, but it was by the time Toab told this story to his grandchildren. Navajo Mountain, broad, round, and gray, alone on the horizon far to the east. The Paiute were there before the Navajo, but the other name won because the Navajo moved in and were more plentiful. And that name, "Navajo," wasn't even Navajo. The Navajo called themselves the Diné.

Often, he and his band of Shivwits were just "Indians" to the Americans and "Lamanites" to the Mormons, usually when they were being discussed as though they weren't present. When good became bad, when the Shivwits killed the cattle and sheep that were ruining their grass—the grass they'd always depended on for food—they became simply redskins, red devils, red niggers.

They were redskins now, having cheated a Mormon out of his rifles. They were Payuche to the Mookweech and Navajo—troublesome pests who ate grass seeds and roots. And those were the people whose help they would need to find Chookwadum.

It took some persuading to get Onchok to come. The Mormon had humiliated him by boxing his ear, and Onchok wanted revenge. He wanted his guns and he wanted his daughter and he didn't want to go on this trip because of the Navajo, who were ruthless and strong. But Toab convinced him: a father should rescue his child, he said. When they left, Onchok gamely led. Now, across the river, Toab was their guide.

Below them, the canyon fell into another canyon and Toab couldn't see the river. He saw bands of color leaping cliff to cliff, distances hidden inside the distance, and, drenched in light, an unflinching world that shrank yet sustained them. They were presences within a larger presence.

He asked Onchok if he was ready to go.

Onchok stood up and stretched and looked down. Let's get going, he said.

2

They climbed to the top of a wooded plateau, found a group of Hualapai, and stayed with them a few days, feasting and trading. The Hualapai didn't have much contact with the Navajo; they hadn't heard of Hashkay.

With three Hualapai men they made their way east, across broken ridges and through snaking canyons where Toab dreamed he'd have good hunting. The next morning he stood on a rise above their camp with a bighorn ram slung across his shoulders.

They ate the liver raw, gorged on roasted meat, and cracked and sucked the bones, but Toab said they should put some bones aside to make grease for paint. Then they hiked another day and found the cliff with the paint cave high out of reach, but he knew where his father had hidden the pole. He dug it out of the sand, leaned it against the cliff, and with a piece of bread and Mara's burden basket climbed up the pole's notched teeth to the cave. He left the offering of bread at its entrance, then bent down to go in and gather all the red ocher he could carry in the burden basket.

That night they made paint, by mixing ocher with the grease boiled out of the bighorn's bones, and packed it in a bag made from the ram's scrotum. They put a spot of paint on Kwits's and Soxor's brows to keep ghosts away. They didn't say one could be Chookwadum's ghost, that was unthinkable. But Toab sometimes thought it.

They hiked farther east and at last descended into Havasu Canyon where Toab found his Havasupai friends tending their fields. It wouldn't be polite just to blurt out why they'd come; the proper way to do things was to visit awhile, to eat and swap gifts and talk and hold dances. All took sweats together, four at a time, and cooled off in the waterfall afterward. Onchok had never tried a sweat before—the Shivwits didn't have sweat lodges—and he liked it, he said.

Sweats induced dreams, and Toab had a strange one. He dreamed of three white men, one with a black beard as thick as bear's fur, another whose beard curled back in the wind, the third one beardless. The one with the black beard picked up a rock and ate it.

The dream puzzled him, made him apprehensive and eager to get going, to find the story coming toward them. His Havasupai friend Teskimalauwa said no white men were anywhere in the vicinity.

The Havasupai liked the basket trays they'd made, so Mara and Pooeechuts gave some as presents to the leaders. The recipients praised the beauty of the baskets and gave the Shivwits buckskins. For several days the women made more baskets, then traded for blankets. Onchok made arrows from serviceberry branches, heating the black points in the fire until they glowed red. Everyone knew Paiute arrows were the best. They traded them for sandals, since theirs were wearing out.

Toab asked about Hashkay. Teskimalauwa said he'd never heard of him, but he dreamed how to find the Navajo who'd taken Chookwadum—he said they ought to ask in Oraibi. That was Toab's plan anyway; the Mookweech, in their own secretive way, knew the Navajo best.

They held a round dance and sang songs about Chookwadum in which they always found her with the Navajo Hashkay. They found Chookwadum and went back home and everything became the same. But Toab knew, if no one else did, that the story rolling toward them like a broken wheel would bring unexpected things. They might find Chookwadum, they might go back home, but nothing, he knew, would be the same again.

At last they set out for Oraibi with a group of Havasupai, who often traded there, but they didn't get far. To Teskimalauwa's surprise, a party of Americans in the Mookweech Trail Canyon had set up camp with their burros and tents. They'd dug holes in the dry wash and had metal tools and pans. Right away Sinyella, another Havasupai, recognized the mining implements. He was furious—no miners had ever come in here before. The Shivwits and Havasupai looked down from a slope above the miners' camp, unsure of what to do.

Soxor slipped and dislodged some rocks. The miners looked up, ran into their tents, and came out with rifles. The Shivwits scrambled up toward a rock shelter, but the Havasupai decided to stand their ground. The miners laughed and shouted. They set their rifles on a rock, one held up a steaming pot and another a spoon, and they waved down the Indians. The Havasupai went.

It took the miners a while to coax Onchok's family down, and to be safe Toab told the children to stay inside the rock shelter with the burden baskets. These were the first American miners the Shivwits had seen. The four adults descended and shook hands with the white men, who smelled like wet dogs. They all shared a mush of beans and burnt biscuits served up on filthy metal plates. The miners jabbered away in the incomprehensible tongue the Mormons also used, and pointed at the women. The way they dragged their voices through beds of gravel gave Toab an insight into their world—unguarded, full of need, coarse and brash, strong and weak.

The canyon grew cool. Light began to leak out, bats jerked across the sky, frogs croaked, crickets sawed. In the cottonwood trees there must have been more than fifty mockingbirds singing. A miner with a squint and a gash of black hair invited Onchok to his tent. He showed him some mirrors. He gave him tobacco, needles, a mirror, then leaned into his ear and mumbled prayers and incantations while Onchok just stared at the presents in his hands. He'd never seen a mirror before. Already, the miner was outside the tent, pulling Pooeechuts up by one hand. He started back with her. As Onchok emerged through the flap, the miner leered and gestured him away.

One of Onchok's eyes squinted—he'd been named accordingly. But facing this miner was like peering into the mirror in his hand: his left eye squinted and fluttered nearly shut just like Onchok's right one. His black beard looked foul. He pushed Onchok aside and bent into the tent leading Pooeechuts.

Another miner walked toward Toab while Teskimalauwa took this opportunity to fumble his prick out of his breechclout and piss into the fire. When the miner turned at the hissing sound, Toab jumped up and smashed his head with a rock. The third white man ran for the rifles but Toab got there first. He ran to the campfire and threw them on the hissing flames.

By this time Pooeechuts had escaped from the tent and was running up the cliff and the others quickly followed. One rifle went off in the fire, but the miner who'd purchased Pooeechuts's favors kicked at the other one and pulled it out. Squinting over the barrel through his black hair, he fired up the slope and hit Pooeechuts's arm. Opening the rifle, he ran for his tent. He came out shooting, but now only Toab was standing on the rocks. He shouted Ya ya, waved his arms, and turned around and slapped his buttocks at the miner, who fired again but missed. Toab threw rocks and the two miners ducked and reloaded their guns. The one whose head he'd bashed sat on the ground, touching the wound and examining his fingers.

Toab scrambled up the slope. Pretty soon night came. The Paiute and Havasupai slipped away in the darkness and followed the trail back to Havasu Canyon. There, they dressed and poulticed

Pooeechuts's arm, smashed beneath the elbow. Bits of bone bled from her skin. The Havasupai healer medicined Pooeechuts while several braves with bows and arrows went back for the miners but couldn't find them.

The arm looked bad and they waited a week before resuming their walk to Oraibi. Toab told his family what he knew about Oraibi and the other Mookweech towns. Everyone went to Oraibi to trade —Navajo, Paiute, Havasupai, Hualapai—because the Mookweech had things no one else had, including metal tools and needles from the Spanish. They lived in stone houses with doors in the roofs from which they climbed on long poles and ladders. Then how did they hunt? Onchok asked. If their homes weren't movable, how could they travel with the game or with the seasons for seeds or pine nuts or agave?

They didn't move around, Toab said. Their gardens were right below their villages. Oraibi was a village, but there were others too, he told them.

Onchok had seen plenty of stone houses in the Great Canyon, and Mara and Pooeechuts had seen them on the Other Side, near Paiute Mountain, some high in cliffs tucked into alcoves. Had the Mookweech built them?

Yes, said Toab. Then, long ago, abandoned them.

The Mookweech and the Paiute had never gotten along. Now Toab explained why. He'd been with the Mookweech and the Havasupai, he'd met plenty of people, seen lots of places. He'd learned about the Mookweech; it made trading with them easier. They called themselves not Mookweech but Hopi-shinunu—Peaceful Ones—Hopi for short. A long time ago they lived in the Great Canyon and on the Other Side, some even lived on the Shivwits' plateau. But they couldn't grow anything in those places, so they moved east and south to where they are now.

They were born in the canyons. At first they were short, with pointy ears and bowed legs, even though like the Paiute they never rode horses. When the land was young it was changing all the time, trying to change into a story—that's how it all started. Deep in a canyon the earth turned and cracked and an eye opened up. That got things going. In a mound of yellow clay at the bottom of a canyon beside a turquoise river a little crater appeared, an inverted cone of sand. The eye appeared in that. Then something under-ground scratched. Grains of sand slid. With yellow crusted nails, a finger emerged. Two fingers, three, seamed with mud and dirt. The hole opened wider—Toab demonstrated by spreading his fingers. A hand broke the surface and felt for the edge. It scratched and clawed and dug its way out, gripped plates of dried mud, broke them off and pulled them down. The arm widened the hole and a head squeezed through mashed against the arm, dirt breaking off and pouring down —Toab stood and raised his clawing hands describing this laborious emergence.

The Shivwits and Havasupai sat around a fire. The healer had squeezed what blood he could from Pooeechuts's wounded arm, then plastered it with piñon pitch and rabbit fur. Now Pooeechuts lay be-side the fire with the arm in a trench covered with wet sand and hot ashes. From a cliff not far away came the sound of water falling, the hollow protest of a stream forced to stand. Around them, the cotton-woods made figures in moonlight: people rising from earth. Clouds raced across the moon, and when it emerged, filling the darkness, mockingbirds low in the trees began singing.

Toab described the first naked man reaching down to help the next one, a woman. Mud and dirt clotted her hair and secret folds, but she brushed herself off, drying in the air.

More people crawled out. With each the hole widened, and grew wider for the fat ones. They too climbed up the bamboo shoot that jutted from the hole, emerging naked and caked with dried mud.

What's this place? one of them asked.

The fourth world, said Masauwu, who'd been waiting there for them.

They looked at him. They'd been insects in the first world, ani-mals in the second, and people in the third, but nowhere had they seen anybody like him. His hair was burned off and his face streaked with blood. His black eyes were cratered deep in his head, his skin scarred with burn marks. A painted line crossed his weak upper nose that spread toward his cheekbones. Around his head he wore a neck-lace of bones.

He was the one they'd heard from the third world, walking back and forth across the sky above their heads.

A hummingbird flew from one person to the next, sorting them out, herding them like sheep. Some hung back and peered down into the hole to the world they'd just left, which darkened as they watched it. Others washed in the river while behind them the hole began to spew water. A greenish mound formed with the hole in its roof, and it's still there today, Toab said, inside the Great Canyon. The Mookweech know how to get there.

They waited in the canyon that had given birth to them. Above, high cliffs. Two rivers met downstream: one's soft blue brushed ledges and dams, the other's red mud churned in heavy rapids. The only way out of the canyon was to climb up the cliffs. They couldn't see how, but Hummingbird helped. He led them up footpaths and across narrow ledges with nothing but air and clouds underneath them. People clung to the rock face. Some refused to move. You'd better get used to it, Hummingbird said. You'll live high on cliffs yourselves someday.

On the plateau above they walked east beneath a completely empty sky. They were heading toward mesas out on the horizon, which fell beyond the mesas.

There, they moved into caves and a few of them remembered from the third world how to build a fire. They made arrowheads from flint and held wild knapping parties up on the mesas, leaving piles of slivered stone. They made sticks to throw darts that could penetrate a deer's body and come out the other side.

They made clothes from buckskin and sandals from yucca and figurines from split twigs — toys used to teach the children how to hunt. Young boys showered these figures with twigs, pretending they were spears. Masauwu brought them corn and taught them how to grind it. They dug pits for houses and over the pits built walls of rocks, chinking the gaps with mud smoothed by corn cobs rolled back and forth across them. On their walls they hung fox skins, weapons, and masks, and below them made fires to cast light on what they'd hung. They sat on benches they'd made and looked at the walls.

They invented ladders to climb out of their houses. They made bows and arrows out of serviceberry branches with deer sinew strings. A lump of clay slipped out of somebody's hand into a fire too hot to pluck it out. Next morning when the fire had died to coals they picked up the lump and saw how hard it was. So they found more clay and made plates and bowls and cups, setting aside the smelly sheep horns they'd used before for drinking.

They multiplied. They built houses on mesa tops with plazas to dance in, and kivas for the men. They performed ceremonies in which dancing men wore helmets decorated with feathers and held woven yucca shields and shook rattles made from gourds. During lulls in the ceremonies, clowns painted white with topknots on their heads and bloody deer hooves tied to their wrists dragged each other through the dirt, or mimicked fucking each other, or groveled in the plaza eating dirt and trash and gnawing their own arms like dogs gnawing bones. The clowns formed two lines back to back in the plaza and grabbed their own pricks and held a mock tug of war.

These people became the Mookweech's ancestors. Then one day something happened. A creature ran across a nearby playa with a sack on his back.

Toab paused. He knew he shouldn't continue now. This part of the story belonged to the Newe, and the Newe told their own stories in the winter. One punishment for telling stories in the summer was that rattlesnakes would bite the teller; in the winter there weren't any rattlesnakes around. But Toab was wearing bundles of carrot leaves around his ankles to ward off snakes, and they were sitting by a fire, and Pooeechuts was hurt—what else could they do while she healed but tell stories? And this piece of the story, though belonging to the Newe, still pertained to the Mookweech, he knew. It had taken him a while to understand that their stories were tangled together.

The creature ran on two legs with a sack on his back. He looked like a coyote but his nose was too short. He stopped, held up the sack, listened, and opened it. Then he ran off to defecate, ran back, and shut the sack, but now he saw the tracks that ran in all directions, because the sack had emptied out and all the tribes had scattered.

Except for the scraps. Coyote shook them out. They changed into people, naked and filthy, who ran into the caves where the Mookweech used to live.

Right away the two groups mistrusted each other. The new people begged for food, but the Mookweech scorned them. The new people raided their gardens and fields, and the Mookweech ran out and bashed their heads with axes. But some survived to form armies.

Ants and beetles screamed. Blood watered the crops. Both sides made armor from deer ribs and shoulder blades, formed armies that advanced behind shields and fending sticks. Soon caves filled with severed limbs. People ate their enemies. A woman walked around with the skin of a head stuffed with pebbles and wood chips on a string tied to her wrist.

Seated on a rock watching this slaughter, Masauwu held his head. They didn't understand him, didn't understand Death, who was caretaker of the world. At last he went away. That was their punishment.

The new people ran off but kept returning and fighting. The Mookweech abandoned their houses on mesas that were so vulnerable to attack and built new ones in cliffs. In fields of canyons running through the countryside, in every high cliff and alcove they could find, they built houses and towers, storage rooms and kivas, and cut steps in steep rock to climb into these villages. They constructed watchtowers and dug reservoirs for water and farmed in the valleys, but the rain became extinct.

The valleys grew dry, the cottonwoods and aspens shriveled up and disappeared, and worms ate the corn. Each time something died someone said: Whose fault was that? Who can we blame? A man in a mask came to one of their cliff towns. He had burn marks on his arms and wore a necklace of bones. He told the people they were stupid—they'd been fighting themselves. Did they ever wonder, he asked the Mookweech, why their enemies spoke the same language as they did?

They turned on each other. Some killed their own leaders, burned their own kivas, and walked away from their cliff houses leaving axes on the floor and food in bowls and sick people in the corners. These people walked south and found new mesas and built new villages. They haven't moved since, having found the best place. The others stayed away, crossed the river to live. Toab waved north toward the Great Canyon.

The story was over. Onchok said, The best place? They don't live in the best place. We do, not them.

The Havasupai said nothing. Toab had been speaking in the language of the Newe and his hosts hadn't understood a word. But they'd enjoyed the telling. They'd laughed with the Shivwits and held their breath at the same time.

After a week Pooeechuts felt better and they started again for Oraibi, along and through canyons, over plateaus, and across a painted desert. Still weak, she couldn't carry her basket; Soxor did. And one day of walking weakened her again. When they stopped and spent a fitful night beneath a rock overhang, she vomited, trembling by a fire. But they were almost there. They couldn't turn back.

Teskimalauwa and Sinyella came along again to trade at Oraibi. Toab had followed this path with them before, so the three men led the way. Out of concern for Pooeechuts, they took their time and rested often. They crossed a brown desert, and at first their destination, the mesa ahead, was just a rise on the horizon. But as they drew closer they saw houses on top and the people on their roofs and other people on rocks at the edge of the mesa or halfway down a path—all looking down at the approaching visitors.

Once there, the Havasupai were welcomed by the villagers with exclamations of joy. Don't go away! Stay here a long time! Help us harvest the corn! But Onchok and his family were politely ignored because, thanks to Coyote, the Paiute long ago had become the enemies the Mookweech had to fight. Even though their language sounded almost the same.

3

At their camp below Oraibi, Pooeechuts lay inside an arbor. They'd made brush shelters near a dried-up spring at the base of the mesa, with melon patches and cornfields in the valley beyond. This late in the day the long shadow of the mesa stretched to the east. Kneeling beside her, Onchok applied a ragweed poultice to his wife's arm.

Soxor and Kwits were getting water. Toab had singed a rabbit on the fire. As he was pulling off the fur, Mara sat down beside him and he handed her the rabbit. Is this a good one? she asked.

Looks like it.

He'd already opened and emptied it of innards. She wrinkled her nose, pulling at the fur. Where did you get it?

From a Mookweech.

For what?

Some biscuits.

That's all?

She continued plucking fur.

Toab told her that tomorrow when the ceremonies were over they'd begin trading. The dancing in the plaza had been going on all day. Mara knew that; she'd just come from there, the only Paiute in a world of Mookweech. They'd ignored her, she told him.

Were you wearing your basket hat?

No, I took it off. She told him she'd seen the kachinas dressed like trees, with slit-eyed helmets, ruffs of spruce around their necks, and chests blackened with corn soot. She'd heard the turtleshell rattles that made hollow sounds when they stomped their feet together in the dance. She'd seen the eagles to be sacrificed chained to the roofs; one old man watching a boy tease one of the eagles called him a little Payuche. And she'd seen the new brides; their white wedding robes and white deerskin boots were finer than any clothes she could imagine. But when the kachinas gave out presents, including baskets of pine nuts, the baskets were not as well made as hers. Telling this to Toab, she leaned back smiling.

The Mookweech won't like your baskets, he teased.

They'll like them fine.

Toab squatted at the fire and pushed aside the burning wood. Mara gave him the rabbit to lay on the coals. From a conical basket she pulled a plucked swallow and a porcupine head and put them next to the rabbit; their eyeballs popped and hissed. She poured cornmeal from a pouch into a boiling basket lined with pitch and clay, and when Soxor and Kwits arrived with the water, she added some to the cornmeal, dropped in a hot rock, stirred it with a stick, then threw in dumplings—balls of mashed crickets mixed with grass seed flour.

With their forefingers wrapped across the tops of their thumbs, they scooped the food from bowls. Mara encouraged her sister to sit up, and fed her with her own hand, making sure she got some meat.

The shadows were long but the day was even longer. Toab looked at Mara, remembering her nakedness when they crossed the river. He touched her hair behind her neck and spotted the small seed of a bug running down beneath her ear then running back. Let me louse you, he said.

Mara hissed. We're not married!

A small man with a shadow the length of a tree approached their encampment wearing only a breechclout: the healer from Oraibi, come to medicine Pooeechuts. Teskimalauwa had sent him, he announced. The two Havasupai men were staying in the village with their Mookweech trading partners. On the healer's forehead, a curtain of black hair hung to his eyes. His dark skin appeared covered with dust. He entered the arbor and examined Pooeechuts's arm, squatting in the dirt, and she turned her head away. He didn't seem to mind healing a Paiute, but they'd have to pay a lot: two baskets, he said.

He leaned forward, spat on his fingers, and gently massaged her arm around the wound. He blew on the arm, wet his fingers again, and massaged the raw edges, cleaning off Onchok's ragweed poultice. He stroked the wound and breathed on his right hand every four strokes and Pooeechuts never winced. He prayed and sucked her wound and prayed some more. Then he sucked and came up with something squirming in his mouth—a centipede—and spat it into the fire, where it sizzled and curled. From a pouch he pulled a handful of leaves and handed them to Mara to put on the wound.

She paid him with the baskets. He walked off, heading toward the steps up the mesa leading to the village. The others bedded down in the arbor while Mara boiled the leaves and lay them on her sister's arm.

4

The next day Toab made sure the others were awake before first light so they could organize their things for the trade.

Pooeechuts seemed better. She wasn't facing west, where the dead people live, so the healer must have been a good one. As the first birds woke up and darkness decayed, Toab felt the power from Oraibi on the mesa above them. He heard in the distance the turtle-shell rattles, the last part of the ceremony taking place this morning. You had to be careful among the Mookweech—their power could split the air above your head. In most ways, though, the Oraibi and the Paiute weren't that different from each other. A lot of their words for things were the same, he could almost understand them. And like the Paiute, Oraibi men had long shadows in the evening, and their women were crafty, and their children often hungry.

He watched Mara boil leaves and put them on her sister's arm. Death was just like stepping over a line, his father used to say. There's really little difference between life and death, and you can cross the line or not as you choose.

Everyone in the family went to the trade, even Pooeechuts. Soxor and Mara wore the burden baskets. They climbed the steep steps cut into ledges up to the mesa top and made their way through alleys amid piles of garbage, past stray dogs and burros, some with clipped ears—punished for raiding farmers' gardens. The village was just waking up, it appeared. Stone houses rose in tiers from either side of the plaza, each succeeding story set back from the first, like cliffs in the Great Canyon, thought Toab. They heard the turtle shells again and, looking up, spotted on a hill just beyond the village a long green and black line of departing kachinas, a row of walking trees against the morning sky.

A caller appeared on a roof above the plaza. Toab found he understood the shrill high voice telling someone his corn was getting ripe and someone else to fetch wood for a certain kiva. The caller named a family whose goats were getting into his cousin's melon patch and said they should pen them. At the end he announced a day of trading today, a holiday now that the ceremony was finished.

Men and women climbed out of houses onto the roofs with bowls of water, and the men filled their mouths and sprayed water on their hands. They washed their faces and soaped their hair, and the women washed their long black hair in suds made from yucca roots, and combed it out with Spanish combs.

The women dressed each other's hair, the young ones with coiled whorls, the older ones with a great roll on the back.

Teskimalauwa and Sinyella entered the plaza and greeted their Paiute friends. More people came, and soon the trading began. The Oraibi lay their wares out on blankets, the Havasupai on the dirt, the Shivwits on buckskin. Hundreds came and people talked loudly in an effort to confuse each other, and dogs fought over garbage and children raced around and donkeys fouled the plaza. Kwits joined some boys running up and down the ladders searching for eagle feathers. They danced around the plaza stomping their feet, and Kwits shouted to his mother, I'm a kachina!

Out past the plaza, beyond the stone houses and the chimney pots and ladders jutting through roofs, the yellow-gray desert spread to the horizon, crossed by passing shadows. When the sun emerged from the rushing clouds the desert came closer.

People from other villages had come and seemed to know exactly where to set up. Some crowded the Shivwits, and Toab realized they owned that spot but were too polite to tell them. When some Oraibi invited the Shivwits out into the middle of the plaza, the real trading started. Mara pulled out their basket trays and Toab cautioned her: Just a few at first.

The agave cakes went fast. The Oraibi loved them, and the Paiute made the best ones. Two Mookweech women from another village, leading a burro, looked at the basket trays, picked them up, turned them over, inspected them thoroughly, and loudly criticized their color and design. They appeared to be wealthy. Their lined faces were handsome, and one had something Toab hadn't seen before, a solid streak of white in her black hair, which was pulled into a roll. At last they offered some cornmeal for a tray, and Toab asked how much. They pulled out a parfleche and indicated half. He shook his head. They walked off with their burro.

A crowd had formed around the Shivwits. Behind them, outside the wall of a house, four women ground corn with metates and manos, doing it here instead of on the roof so they wouldn't miss anything. Mara and Pooeechuts kneeled behind the agave cakes, Onchok squatted beside his bows and arrows, and Toab stood waving and talking to the people, inviting them over. Soxor sat with the burden baskets, and when someone tugged the buckskin underneath their wares, she pulled another buckskin out of a basket and handed it to Toab. He traded it for a Navajo blanket.

They traded some agave for pine nuts and one of Onchok's bows with a handful of arrows for blue cornmeal, and some red paint for a lot of jerked deer meat the Mookweech had gotten in trade from the Navajo. The two women with the burro had circled the plaza and come back to offer all the cornmeal in their parfleche for that basket tray. Toab said he'd give it to them if they threw in the parfleche. Expressionless, they nodded.

He told Mara these Mookweech were hard customers—they wanted a buckskin for a handful of nuts. Yes, but they like the trays, she said. Toab nodded: Just keep two or three out.

Pooeechuts, tired, had reclined on the ground behind their buckskin and was falling asleep.

It was still early morning but clouds had filled the sky, the darkest Toab had seen since leaving home. It didn't rain, however, and Teskimalauwa told Toab the reason—a certain clan leader from Oraibi was preventing rain. Someone had caught this man in the act. They thought he was a two-heart, since he was stingy with food at the ceremonies and a lot of his children had died in infancy. Their deaths, it was said, had fed his power. Still, this man's accusers couldn't be trusted—they were friendly with the Navajo at Walpi.

The Navajo at Walpi? asked Toab.

These people had told Teskimalauwa that some Navajo men had married Walpi women and that men from Walpi once fought in disguise with the Navajo against the Oraibi. It didn't matter that the Walpi were Mookweech too. The Mookweech had so many clans and societies, so many taboos and plenty of sneakers—men who slept with other men's wives—that they often found it hard to get along with each other.

Toab knew Walpi was somewhere to the east, but he'd never been there.

The two women with the burro stood against a wall not far from the Paiute. Toab watched them. Their burro's parfleches were bulging with goods—they must have done a lot of trading. Toab asked Teskimalauwa to ask them if they'd like to trade their burro. The women weren't interested, but a few minutes later one wandered over and picked up another basket tray. She pointed out that the border wasn't done correctly, the black and red lines shouldn't slant like that. She turned the basket in her hands and spoke to the other Mookweech gathered there, who laughed at what she said.

Toab approached the other woman by the wall and, speaking slowly and using his hands, asked if he could look at the burro. She nodded and glanced away. He walked around the animal and suddenly dropped his mouth in astonishment: the creature's tail was chopped off. He cleared a path through the people milling around and led the burro by its nose while shaking his head, stumbling as he led it, imitating its lame walk, to their great amusement. The Mookweech woman standing by the wall asked him why he wanted it, then.

He didn't want it, he said.

Fine, she said, they couldn't trade it anyway, it belonged to their brother.

If you could trade it, he asked, how many baskets would you take?

Both women laughed. *Those* baskets? they said.

After a while the woman by the wall joined her companion at the buckskin and picked up a basket. She declared for all to hear that twenty-five of these poorly made baskets wouldn't compensate for the loss of their burro.

That was Toab's cue to laugh.

Meanwhile, Mara was still trading basket trays. She traded a rabbit net for a sack of beans, some agave for some corn, basket trays for flour and colored shells and needles—and Toab watched the women watch as the number of baskets dwindled. Three Oraibi women handed out bowls of melon to everyone standing there, including the Paiute, and Toab and his family tossed the chunks into their mouths with their fingers. Into the empty bowls the Oraibi spooned pikami, a steamed pudding made of cornmeal and wheat sprouts, which the Shivwits scooped up with forefingers curled across the tops of their thumbs.

The women with the burro walked away and came back twice before offering a deal: the rest of the basket trays for the burro. Only the burro; they'd keep the parfleches. But just twelve trays remained and they'd thought there were more, so Toab had to throw in the buckskin on the ground and the remaining agave rolls and some red paint, but they shook their heads. As a last resort he dropped two lightning stones into their hands from a rabbitskin pouch. These were pieces of quartz crystal that produced light when rubbed together—the products of lightning plowing the ground. The crystals held a memory of the lightning. Some people feared the stones, he knew—for some they were taboo—but not the Paiute or Mookweech, who prized them highly. The women looked at each other and agreed to the trade.

The next day Toab and his family said goodbye to their Havasupai friends and walked to Walpi. They hung the baskets on either side of the burro, who was indeed lame but walked with care. Though the baskets were heavy, he didn't balk.

Toab walked behind Mara. He pinched her arm, and she shook him off. Back in Shivwits country, they hadn't always kept company. They'd never spent so much time together as during this past week, since Pooeechuts had been shot.

Pooeechuts seemed better and walked with a lilt, relieved of her basket.

The burro knew all the trails in Mookweech country. They crossed a desert dazed with yellow light in the hot sun. The clouds had moved off to pile up in the east, but the huge sky dwarfed them. In this country you might see three or four different thunderstorms at once and never feel a drop. They trooped past Second Mesa, circling east. Walpi was out on the end of First Mesa, on its narrow top, thin as a knife edge—it took another hour to get there. At the base of the mesa stone corrals had been built to hold the people's burros.

They made their way up past enormous boulders along a broken path like a bull lizard's back. Walpi used to be called the Seven Walpi People, because that was the number of Mookweech who lived there when it was founded, Toab had learned. Reaching the top, they crossed a ridge just wide enough for a wagon. Walpi itself, built on naked rock, consisted of a single road whose end was a plaza surrounded by houses perched on the mesa's edge. The desert lay four hundred feet below them.

Here, the people weren't friendly. Men came out to watch them unload and gazed with unconcealed suspicion at their burro. Others stood in doorways. No one asked them in, and if some of them were Navajo Toab couldn't tell. One man approached and Toab pulled him aside and held a long conversation with single words and hand signs while the rest of the Shivwits squatted in the dirt, resting.

Mara noticed an old man sitting on a pile of rubble. Grinning, he waved a knife at a boy walking by with his mother, then grabbed his own crotch, and the boy clutched the mother, but she just laughed.

The Walpi did relent—they let the Shivwits sleep crowded together in a little stone shed. They brought them mutton stew with parched corn. That night, Toab heard sounds from the kiva. The Walpi having a meeting.

The next morning Toab and Onchok met with the village elders. Toab gave them their last basket tray, one he'd kept hidden from the women with the burro. They properly thanked him but said they couldn't provide any information about a Navajo called Hashkay. What kind of name was that? Squatting in a circle with the Paiute men, the Mookweech wore hairknots tied up with red cloth. They were barefoot, in breechclouts.

Are there Navajo living with you? Toab asked.

One man nodded faintly. He looked the same as the others.

And you've never heard of Hashkay? It could be Hoshkey.

He shrugged and glanced away. Direct questions weren't polite, but what could Toab do? Then the man said, Maybe he's one of those people who went north to live, up there—he gestured vaguely. Maybe he hid up near Tokonave when the American Kit Carson was killing all the Navajo. Maybe his name sounds like someone up there.

Tokonave? asked Toab.

They misunderstood each other and resorted to hand signs. Eventually Toab realized Tokonave was their name for Paiute Mountain. How could he find it from here? he asked. And did they know the Paiute living near there, the Kwaiantukwatsing?

This Walpi Navajo knew them by a different name, the Bayoh'tseen. They'd helped the Navajo who hid from Kit Carson. But Hashkay, he said, that name sounded funny.

Toab looked over at Kwits across the plaza. He was sitting on a wall next to his sister, the desert beyond them. Their mother and aunt had unloaded the burro and were trading with some Walpi in the dirt before the wall.

By noon, they'd reloaded the burro for their trip. Toab told Mara where they were going, and she told her sister and their faces lit up. The way there would take them through unknown country, but the closer they got to Paiute Mountain the more Mara and Pooeechuts would recognize where they were. When they got there they'd find the very canyon where they were born and their relatives still lived — the People from the Other Side.

Part Three

July 3—July 13, 1869

1

Dearest Emma,

I write this not far from the very spot where you and I huddled
'neath buffalo robes amid the Utes last winter; it seems centuries ago.
I would be more pleased to say we've come safely this distance, nearly
one fourth the length of our voyage, had we not met with some seri-
ous mishaps. Do not upset yourself. No one has been lost or gravely
injured, but one boat is destroyed along with all its cargo. Here is
how it happened.

From Green River City to Henry's Fork, sixty miles by river, took
us ten hours, for the river propelled us with the speed of the wind.
We then ran down through Flaming Gorge in flaming style, and
came to Red Canyon and Browns Park in little more than a week. At
the end of this park begins a deep canyon which I decided to name
Lodore, with Andy Hall's help. The gloomy depths of this canyon,
its towering cliffs and crags of granite, may be more readily imagined
than expressed. Here we met with disaster, owing to the inattention
of Oramel Howland, who ignored my signal to land just before a
ghastly stretch of river. Ora has furnished me with more proofs of his
incompetence than I ever thought possible. I saw his like in the war
pretty often; some muddled through, some were destroyed, and for a
precious few hardship actually annealed their character.

The result of Ora's laxity was that his boat, the *No Name,* was
wrecked in the worst rapids we've seen. Details will appear in the
Tribune, whose dispatches I send on the same pack train with this

letter. We lost 2,000 lbs of provisions, the bedding and clothing of three men, as well as Ora's topographical work, some instruments, three rifles, much ammunition, and several pistols, knives, belts, and scabbards. Frank Goodman, the Englishman who begged to come along, lost everything he owned except a shirt and pair of drawers. Thanks to some brave and skillful rowing from Jack Sumner and Bill Dunn, we did manage to recover our barometers from the wreck, although I soon discovered the reason for their courage: along with the barometers they retrieved a jug of whiskey, smuggled onto the *No Name* at Green River City.

If I ever undertake such an expedition again, I will bring with me scientists and educated men, not fur trappers and tipplers — nor Sunday School teachers.

Ora and I had words about his negligence, but I've decided not to lose my temper with him, nor with any of the men. He reminds me of my father. There are times I feel compelled to approach him for advice, only to be doused with a sermon. Did you know that he not only taught Sunday School but was business agent for the *Sunday School Casket?* Not to mention trustee for a mining company and editor for Mr. Byers' newspaper in Denver. It is not safe to engage him in chin music; his own kudos becomes the principal theme.

Sorrows come in battalions. Several days after our wreck, a heavy wind swept down the river, fanning Hawkins' cook fire into a conflagration fed by the dead thickets of willows on the little beach we'd chosen for a camp. I was on the cliffs above searching for fossils when this occurred. There was scarcely any room on the small bench of land for the men to retreat, so they made for the boats, each crew member with something on fire, Bradley his kerchief, Walter his mustache, Oramel his drawers. Hawkins filled his arms with kitchen implements while the others cut the boats free, and in jumping for a boat he landed in the water, quenching the flames on his buckskins but dropping nearly all our pots, pans, and dishes. They managed to pull poor Hawkins into the boat, but those implements were lost to violent currents, as we'd unfortunately camped at the head of a series of nasty-looking rapids. Man is born unto trouble! The crew had to man the oars and find the best channel in a rough stretch of river that hadn't been scouted, while concurrently engaged in dousing little fires on their clothes with bailing cups. By "luck and pluck" they made it.

And speaking of bailing cups, they are now the only dishes we have, and we use them for drinking coffee and soup, eating beans and rice, and dipping Hawkins' gritty biscuits. Two of the gold pans closed over each other now serve as our oven for baking those biscuits. The camp shovel stirs our beans as they cook, and a forefinger curled over the top of a thumb takes the place of a spoon.

We were not unpleased to leave the Canyon of Lodore and arrive at the confluence of the Yampa River. Despite these misadventures, the men are still full of snap and spirit, and I've discovered the spring has not left my step in any deplorable manner. Lodore was a chapter of disaster and toil, notwithstanding which it held considerable scenic interest. Stately pines and furs, rock cliffs set in deep shadows, pools of water embosomed in the crags, profound chasms, plunging cataracts and cascades.

At the Yampa River we rested several days and explored the environs. Here we found a rock, 700 feet high and a mile or more in length, whose echo ricocheted back and forth against the cliffs across the river, as many as ten times by Hawkins' count. I am profoundly satisfied that the name Echo Rock will cling to it. The Green sweeps around this massive fin of stone, and the Yampa comes in from the east at this point, through a labyrinth of canyons; it greatly increases the volume of the Green.

Some of us climbed up above this confluence, through pines and junipers, across a series of gulches, and over bare stretches of naked sandstone, to a place where I could see the Uinta Mountains to the west, the Wind River range to the north, the towering Rockies far to the east. South, however, was terra incognita, an utter mystery. I made out plateaus and canyons, and imagined I could see where the river sawed through them, and thought that if I persevered, that if all our bad fortune was now behind us, that if I remained fertile in expedients, then the whole extent of my pride and ambition would satisfy itself in exploring that immensity.

Across hills and mountains, we saw the wind pull clouds of pollen out of the pine trees. The gorges swirling around the mouth of the Yampa were a Daedalean maze, honeycombed with deep yellow canyons. South of the Yampa was a bowl-shaped valley positively swarming with colors and landforms; it ran into red hills, rose to sloping terraces, continued toward broken benches and outcrops white as winter snow, and eventually by way of wrinkled red mesas and hogbacks and cliffs reached a line of mountains. Often on this voyage I've wished you were with me, but never more than at this place. The grandeur of it truly beggars language and palls imagination. Yet what was I doing while gazing upon it but attempting to describe it to you in my mind?

Below us the Green swung around Echo Rock. Between that cliff's western side and the new canyon we entered the next day, a perfect plume of earth sprung from the riverbank along upcurving ridges of red and yellow rock. Inside its gullies green pines grew; the cliff rose above the river like an overturned rainbow hung with rags of rock. It was either a fold or a fault; Professor Dana would know. His theories on monoclines seemed to fit it to a T. It had been exposed over centuries and eons as the river carved out this canyon—in other words, erosion and the powerful scouring force of water had uncovered this mystery, as they had uncovered others. Here is one of the others: near the eminence upon which we stood were purple-red rocks strewn on the dirt and dust. They looked identical to the lowest strata of the cliffs in Lodore Canyon, but there the formation was 3,000 feet lower! And the sandstone cliffs at the mouth of the Yampa were above it there, whereas here they were below it.

This matter of landforms and their relation to rivers, as you know, dearest Emma, has occupied my attention greatly in the past. Here, it positively preys upon my mind. You are aware, since we've discussed it, of John Strong Newberry's idea that the land sculptures and canyons of the West are the products of erosion, and owe their topographical features entirely to the action of water. But how? Newberry doesn't address that issue, but it fairly bellows from these mountains. After Browns Park, at the Gates of Lodore, the Green River turns south and cuts a path through a spine of the Uintas, tho' it could have more easily continued east through the same valley it was in. The Uintas, as you know, are unique in that their axis runs east and west instead of north and south, unlike most mountain ranges in North America. Regardless, all mountains are watersheds. They are sources of rivers. From mountains creeks gather, running down their sides as they gouge out their courses. At their source these creeks run through mere gullies, tho' of course they deepen the further down they go. "Down" is the key. A creek such as that, or the river it becomes, cannot saw through a mountain. The real cutting only happens when the river has volume, in the valley below, and by then the mountain looms high above its channel.

I have not been able to solve this problem, but continue daily to apply my mind to it. This mystery, by the way, mocked me again as we continued downstream from the mouth of the Yampa. At the end of the gorge we named Whirlpool Canyon, the Green swings south and then, as if alive, seems to probe about for something, indecisive of its course. What it finds is a mountain off by itself, and with a flourish of perversity it goes directly through it. We decided to call this place Split Mountain. It is a great and isolated mound opened up through its center and eroded to such a considerable degree that the river canyon's walls are surmounted by pinnacles, and the yellow cliffs contain numberless deep gullies and crevices and springs.

Well, I haven't solved the puzzle but I won't let it go, as it gives me no satisfaction to allow it to linger. River erosion is the force that excavates canyons, that much is clear; but since a river cannot flow uphill, how can it cut a mountain in half as if the latter were soft as a melon? Perhaps the "Great Canyon" will furnish an answer—if we experience no more disasters.

After Split Mountain we debouched into a valley, and I recognized it at once as the place where we would eventually meet the White River from the east and the Uinta from the west. You know this country yourself from last year. But what a telling contrast! No more looming canyons and torrents of water—rather, one enormous valley open to the sky, and the river so sluggish we were forced to row. In two more days we came to the Uinta, and after obtaining the local time, taking observations for latitude and longitude, and making excursions into the adjacent country, I invited the men to write letters to loved ones. Write your final letters, I joked; they did not appreciate the ghastly humor. I sent Andy Hall and my brother to the Ute Agency twenty-five miles up the Uinta with the first yield of letters.

Two days later, Hawkins, Frank Goodman, and I followed them, leaving Sumner, Dunn, Bradley, and the Howlands behind, and here

I've renewed my acquaintance with the Ute, a handsome race of people, and here we've attempted to replenish our supplies. We lost considerable provisions in the *No Name*'s wreck, and our hunters have not been especially successful, tho' Hawkins did manage to shoot a deer in Whirlpool Canyon.

Yesterday I visited with the old chief Tsaúwiat, who, by the way, asks after you. I took some more vocabularies to supplement those we collected last year, and have progressed in my knowledge of the Ute language. Tsaúwiat is, even more than last winter, shrunken, wrinkled, and dry, the wreck of a man, and the agent's assistant, Mr. Lake, tells me he no longer has influence.

The agent, I should add, is away on business. I suspect his business is seeing the newly completed railroad, as government employees receive generous discounts — payback no doubt for the generous land grants the railroad received in building the line. How long will such discounts last? No doubt they'll be a distant memory by the time the government chooses to employ *me*.

At any rate, the ancient Ute chief is said to be over 100 years old. Still, he and his wife, "the Bishop" (remember?), are garrulous old fossils, and they asked me what became of the sketches you made of them. I told them the truth: they hang on the wall above your bed at your father's house in Detroit for the duration of my absence. Naturally, "Detroit" held no meaning for them.

The Ute still occupy their elkskin lodges and refuse to build houses. They have taken as best they can to farming, but prefer running horses to cultivating turnips. One aboriginal philosopher recounted some stories of his people that I found instructive. These people have practically anticipated Darwin by centuries, Emma. They hold that the whole animal world once existed on the same plane as man. We were all, they say, one family together. Furthermore, in some mysterious manner, the coyote came first; he preceded all other living beings, and from him they spring, and so do you and I. All living creatures, this man seemed to say, including humans beings, once existed exclusively in the form of coyotes; at other times he appeared to maintain that the coyote created all creatures and humans, or served as a sort of conduit for their birth. Moreover, unlike our Almighty, the coyote is no epitome of virtue and perfection; he did both foolish and wicked things and made a lot of mistakes and still bedevils our fortunes. This man told of the coyote racing over a desert with a sack containing all the races of humans—where he obtained it wasn't clear. Coyote stopped to do something and the humans escaped and scattered over the earth, which does as well in my view to account for the babble of languages and nations in the world as the biblical story of the tower.

I asked about the tribes we would encounter further south. He warned us against the perfidious Navajo, but laughed at his cousins, the lowly Paiute, who don't even have horses. They would have no more effect on our expedition, he said, than a fly who lands on the horn of an ox.

The past year has not been a good one for the Ute. Their stores are depleted and the new crops are green. As a consequence I've been disappointed in my attempts to renew to any great degree our provisions, although Mr. Lake has generously offered 300 lbs of flour. It will have to do.

You must not be alarmed by the Chicago papers, and when you read of the wreck owing to Ora's negligence, keep in mind that I softened the blame for the public's eyes; but remember as well that here you read the true story. Tomorrow or the next day, depending on the availability of Indian porters, we return to the river to reunite with our company. But I fear that Frank Goodman will not be with us. He has hinted as much. The mule train goes north next week for Fort Bridger, and he will probably be on it.

Here, we leave behind the last meager signs of civilization for nearly 800 miles. I often wonder what we'll find, and feel strangely torn between my thirst for adventure and the desire that springs up to make an end of it now and see you again and embrace you once more, my sweet sweet wife. But that will not happen for many months yet, until our voyage is finished, and for the time being you must be patient and trust in my star, as I trust in your steadfast constancy and draw strength from your love.

Your Loving Husband,
Wes

2

With Major Powell gone to the Uinta Agency, Jack Sumner was in charge, and since Hawkins and Hall had both gone with the Major, someone had to cook. The task fell to George Bradley.

They'd camped in the lee of some gray eroded bluffs on a rise above the river. Bill Dunn and Jack Sumner walked up to George, busy stirring a pot on the fire. "What's for supper?" asked Jack.

"Beans," said George.

"The hell was all that shooting then?"

"Saw a white pelican."

"Get him?"

"No. Filled him so full of lead he must have sunk and drowned. But those reeds are one big mud bath. Lord, the mosquitoes were beastly though." George scratched his neck.

"Don't I know," said Jack.

"Found some currants," said George.

"For what?"

"For what? To add to the beans."

"I wouldn't have thought you could mix beans and currants," Bill Dunn said. "Beans and onions. Beans and pork fat. Beans and grease, peppers, you name it. But currants is sweet."

"Not so. They're tart."

"So much the worse."

"Who's the cook here?"

"They're spilling over," said Jack.

George looked down. The beans had erupted in a frothing mass out of the pot into the fire. "I said who's the cook here."

"You are, you are."

He threw in the currants he'd gathered that morning, or rather uprooted, the mosquitoes being so thick he'd taken the whole bush. "They won't swell no more."

Jack sat on a log and watched as the beans, after a pause, continued to boil over. "What happened to the ducks?"

"You ate them this morning."

"That's all the meat we get?"

"'Less you shoot some more."

"Do I detect a saucy note?" asked Bill.

"It's just don't carp until you taste it."

"Fair enough. Can we carp then?"

"You can do what you damn well please," said George.

Oramel and Seneca Howland emerged from their tent, where the heat this late in the day had become intolerable. "What was all that shooting?" Ora asked.

"George missing a pelican."

"I didn't miss him."

"What's for supper?"

"Scorched beans."

The three tents had been pitched beside one another—the first time since the beginning of their voyage that George hadn't camped off by himself. He'd thought if he was going to cook he'd best stay with the others, but already regretted it. At least he had his own tent. Jack and Bill slept in the second one, the Howlands in the third.

"Saw some Indian lodges," said Jack.

"Where?"

"Scrub flats near the White River."

"Occupied?"

"Would have said so if they were."

"What sort of lodges?"

"Of the arbor type."

"How long ago abandoned?"

"A week or so I guess. Charred bones in the fire."

"Is this something we should worry about?" asked George.

"I think not," said Jack. "The Utes are pretty friendly. I've had my run-ins, but by and large they're straight."

"The Major and Hawkins could have met up with them."

"Could have."

"Hawkins knows shit about the redskins," said Seneca.

"That ain't true," said Bill Dunn. "I seen him one time chase a squaw who took his hammer."

"Did he get it back?"

"He got something back, but it wasn't a hammer."

"What's that supposed to mean?"

"He got paid for the hammer."

"That ain't worth no hammer."

Jack said, "You'd take it if she was dishing it out."

"I'm talking about he married her," said Bill.

"Oh. Where is she now?"

"Run off with a buck."

"What about the Major?"

"What about what about him?"

"Does he know shit about the Indians?"

"He knows their fucking language," said Bill.

"He thinks he does," said Jack.

"You know it, Jack, don't you?" Seneca sat on a log beside George, who'd taken the beans off the fire and was sniffing them.

"I do."

"How do you say 'Green River'?"

"Seedskadee."

"What about 'fuck'?"

"They just say fuck. They picked that up from us."

"You mean they never did it before we came along?"

"Very funny, Seneca."

"Well, the Major's bound to meet them at the agency anyway."

"He's bound to do that."

"He's bully enough."

"He is that."

"For a man with one arm."

"I first met him in the mountains, I thought, Good Lord," said Jack. He moved over on his log to let Ora sit. "I thought him and his crew was about as fit for roughing it as Hades is for a powder house. That was last year in Middle Park. Hot Sulphur Springs. Ever been there, George?"

"No."

"He come out to pick flowers on the mountain peaks with a bunch of schoolboys and Methodist parsons, excuse me, Ora. I guided him up to Long's Peak. I got to say he's obstinate. He looks at something square in the face, then goes ahead and does it. We were the first ones to climb that peak. No one done it before. He just wouldn't give it up, so it took a few days. But a man ought to have a better reason for climbing such a mountain than finding out if forget-me-nots grow on its top. On the way down we passed a monstrous snowfield and every inch of snow was covered with grasshoppers. You could have filled a dozen wagons. Two bears was there feeding on the hoppers but so slow it looked under water. Numbed by the cold they were. I wanted to shoot one but the Major forbade it."

"That was when you first met him?"

"That's what I said. He brought letters from Denver from my brother-in-law. William N. Byers, you probably heard of him."

George gave a shrug.

"He owns the newspaper there," Jack said, "where Oramel worked on it too, and anyway he requested me to show this Major Powell the country. I had my trading post then, which I gave it up for this picnic we're stuck on now. I saddled him up and took him about and we made some collections. I gave him some proper ideas about the habits of the elk and the mountain sheep and the marten and the beaver, as he had gotten all his information from books. He thought beavers used their tails as trowels, but I disabused him of that. I took him to a beaver village. He thought grizzly bears was gray and as a matter of fact they range from jet black all over to yellow to as gray as the gray wolf. Anyway, he seemed to get stuck on me and wanted me to leave Middle Park and go with him the next summer to the Badlands of Dakota on some sort of geological exploration trip. I declined the proposition and fired this one back: that we explore these here rivers and canyons. He jumped at the prospect. I couldn't back out. Now he might claim it was his own idea, but what he won't tell you is at first he thought it was foolish until I urged him on and explained what a feather it would be in his cap if we succeeded."

"I thought you said he jumped at the prospect."

"I did."

"Then you said he thought it was foolish."

"First he thought it was foolish, but after he considered it awhile he jumped at the prospect. We spent the winter up and down these parts, looking at the river. This was as far south as we got. Him and his wife and his brother Wallybird. You ought to thank your lucky stars Mrs. Powell didn't come on this trip. Mrs. Pick-That-Up and Go-Fetch-Wood and Watch-Your-Language. You think *he's* bossy? She's a handful, that one."

"Amen," said Ora.

"Was he always climbing mountains?" asked George.

"He was always climbing mountains, taking elevations, gauging this and that—width of a river, height of a cliff, weight of a pebble. Drop him in the desert the first thing he'll do is draw you a map. I used to call him the Professor. If the Professor could only study geology he'd be content to live without food or shelter."

"What I can't stand is he's so godawful cautious," said George. He was spooning the beans into bailing cups. Earlier that day, fishing through the supplies, he'd found some hardtack Hawkins must have been saving and now he passed it around.

"These beans is scorched," said Bill.

"It don't hurt."

"They taste awful."

"Sure he's cautious," said Jack, "but better safe than sorry."

"True enough," said George. "His way is safe. But it takes up all our time. Portage don't agree with my constitution. He sees a three-foot wave and he wants to line down. Sometimes I think a chained lion would scare him."

Bill Dunn raised his head. "That ain't true."

"He's afraid of spoiling more rations," Jack explained, "by getting them wet."

"He wastes his time climbing cliffs."

"Well, that's in keeping with his character. Only takes a short study to read it like a book. The Professor always wants to figure everything out."

Bill Dunn sprayed a mouthful of beans into the fire. "I'd as soon eat dirt."

"Go ahead then," said George.

Bill stood and threw his cup down. "This useless weary waiting. Waiting for the goddam cook to return."

"Shoot us some meat then."

"Not if you're the one to cook it." Bill walked away.

The others picked at the beans, ate the hardtack, and drank a lot of coffee. "Think something happened to them?" asked Seneca.

"They should be back by now," Ora said. "I don't like stopping this long either. We ought to get going."

Later on, Seneca posted himself outside the clump of willows where they'd dug their latrine. When Bill Dunn emerged, hitching up his britches, Seneca asked him, "Bill, are you Dunn?"

"Shut your damn fly trap."

"No, really. Are you Dunn? You gotta answer it."

"Sure I'm Dunn."

"Well, wipe yourself!"

That night, twelve thousand harvester ants in their underground nest near Ora's bed crawled across the vast talus slopes of seed they'd gathered during the day. In their excavated cave, dark as a bear's innards, they methodically coated the seeds with saliva to prevent them from spoiling, then went out to fight enemies.

The next morning, Ora showed his brother his arm. Five or six inflamed ant bites, some blistering already, ran between his elbow and wrist.

"Does it hurt?"

"Won't kill me."

Seneca sought out George Bradley to get some saleratus to make a paste for the bites, but George could not be found and his tent was taken down. Then he went to find Jack, to see if Major Powell had returned yet, but he hadn't. Standing by the river, Ora spat and shook his head at this news. It was the Fourth of July. They'd been here six days.

As for George, he'd gone on strike; they could cook their own food. He'd moved his tent downstream where the river widened to a crossing—the only ford on the Green River between Denver and Salt Lake. The Utes used this crossing and so had a regiment of California volunteers during the war, marching to Denver. They were said to have sunk a ferry in the river in case they ever came this way again, but George assumed it was just a raft and didn't bother to sound for it. Instead, he set an American flag up on a pole to celebrate the Fourth, and sat on a rock. In his shirt and drawers, he stared at the flag and at the river behind. For three successive Fourths he'd been in the wilderness—two years ago at Fort Sedgwick protecting the town of Julesburg from the Sioux, last year at Fort Bridger in Wyoming, now here. Alone. And where would he be the next Fourth of July? And why was he here suffering privations when he could have been home?

No, that wasn't true. The Major had obtained his release from the army in order to go on this expedition because he knew boats. If he hadn't come, where would he be now? Back at Fort Bridger. This trip, if he survived it, was his ticket home. He thought of Henry. Aunt Marsh. The graves on the hillside far away in Massachusetts with grass and flowers waving. How many of those he knew and loved would be under that hill by the time he returned?

George decided to examine his tintypes, ruined in all the rapids. Foolishly, he'd kept the album shut in an effort to preserve it, and now he saw the result: the album itself was falling to pieces and some of the pictures had been wet so long they were spoiled forever. He took a bitter pleasure in tormenting himself with the freaks the members of his family had become: Mother with one eye, Aunt Marsh with half a head, Eddie just a chin, Henry cut to pieces, Lucy noseless. He had other pictures of each one except Aunt Marsh, so he stared at her, trying to conjure her back. Would he ever see her again? See any of them? And did they think of him as he did of them?

Lucy in her ruined picture had a sad, weary look. O Father, he thought, direct me to thy mercy. He took out his journal and complained in pencil about the spoiled tintypes. *What shall the end be? God alone knows and wisely keeps it from us.* Despite their condition he carefully replaced the tintypes, his only ties to home, in his album. He thought of writing down squarely and frankly, *I am utterly alone and despondent,* but shook his head and clenched his teeth and brought his fist down on his right knee so hard the foot jumped. It was a physical effort to keep himself intact, not to grow apart from everything and everyone he'd known, never to lose them. Yet he knew what would happen if he walked through the door in Newbury right now: first argue with his father, then storm out, then head west again. He smiled to himself. It was good to complain. The more he complained the better he felt, and in his journal he wrote: "The weather is delightful and we are in excellent spirits."

Something odd was coming down the river, turning and bobbing. He walked down to the shore. It was meat, a pair of hams. Around them like foam floated uncooked beans and clumps of something brown. He stormed upstream to the others' camp.

"What the hell's going on?"

Stumpy Jack Sumner, standing in the beached *Maid,* tossed sacks of flour into the river. His shoulders looked rounded. "What's going on is I'm throwing this out."

"That's our flour."

"Gone moldy."

"I could have sifted it."

"Then you should of. The Professor will obtain fresh supplies. This flour went bad. Ditto the meat. Found two rancid hams and some wormy beans to boot. I settled to let the river have them. They'd only spoil the rest."

"Those hams were redeemable."

"I noticed your menus did not include ham."

"You should have consulted me."

"Off on your promontory? Brooding like Ulysses? Who put you in charge?"

3

That night at dusk, despite the heat, Jack Sumner, Bill Dunn, and the Howlands built a bonfire and shot off their guns in celebration. Seneca jogged down to invite George to join them, but he declined. They kept firing their guns — after all, it was the Fourth, to hell with saving ammunition. Around them in the darkening valley prairie dogs reared up and whistled in warning. Sharing their holes, burrowing owls mimicked the prairie dogs, nodding and chattering outside the tunnels. Bighorn sheep raised their snouts. Patches of hair stood up on the rumps of pronghorns. Jackrabbits rotated their ears toward the gunshots while up on their hind legs beside eight-foot-tall sunflowers.

Light drained from the valley. By the river, the smoke of the driftwood bonfire hung still and heavy in the cooling air.

Prodded by Seneca, the others told stories about Lo, the poor Indian. The green Seneca had come west just the year before and wasn't accustomed to Indians in the wild. "Ever kill a redskin?" he asked Jack.

"They're pretty hard to kill," said Jack. "Won't surrender, won't die. Put a ball through one buck who was coming for me, but the fellow continued at a considerable speed, reloading his rifle, so I said, 'Did I not tell you I don't wish to kill you? Surrender or die.' This was near Trapper Lake. Can't recall the provocation. There's no telling what goes on in their superstitious minds or what you did to offend them. He raised his gun and sent a ball past my head, so I loaded up again and put another one through him. He sat down, threw his rifle away, and pulled out his bow and arrows. He shot them all, then kept plucking the string when he run out of arrows, and then at this juncture my partner come up and sends a ball through his breast. It did not kill him either but distracted his attention. The only thing that did the trick is I loaded the muzzleloader with quartz crystals, having run out of balls. Gave him a bellyful. As he expires he beckons me over. '*Tu no vale nada,*' he told me. 'You are no good for nothing.'"

"Tell him about the keg of powder at the trading post," said Ora.

"Well. It begun a redskin stole my horse. This was two Utes at Middle Park. One seized my horse's bit and his partner tried to shoot me with an arrow. I slid off the horse and ran toward the lake, and they made the balls whistle past my head but I outrun them."

"But they had a horse!"

"Shut up, Seneca." Oramel was loading his pipe. "Let him tell the story."

"Well sir. I got behind a rock and picked one of them off as they was coming down the trail just as easy as that. His partner run away. Retrieved my horse and made it back to my store which it was a popular resort amongst the nomads. We outfitted hunting parties and grubstaked miners and traded with the redskins and made a good living—better than this unproductive expedition. That's where I first met the Major, as I mentioned. My store was the place the Utes normally thronged from morning to night asking a hundred questions a minute. One time this particular brave come in and looked at all the goods, and once he was finished you know what he wanted? He wanted the miniature I had on the wall of a certain amiable lady from

Iowa. I let him see it and hold it in his hand, which was a mistake. Didn't want to give it up, offered me everything for it. Offered his bow and arrow, a catamount skin, a peace pipe, and some silver nuggets. Where he got the silver I haven't a notion. Those offers being refused, he moved on to his clothes, his horse, and all his property, plus his wife and children, which prompted me to scold him severely. I had to pull out my weapon to get the picture back, and I banned him from the store from that day forward.

"Well. After I shot the Ute, who shows up at my store? It was this smitten brave and about a hundred of his fellows. Were they livid? You bet. They were bent on vengeance for the warrior I shot. It does no good to reason with a redskin with blood in his eye. I explained to them the facts but they were not appeased. I said to that brave, 'Did I not ban you from this here store?' No white men were about at the time, not for fifty miles. I had to proceed with determined coolness, so I drew my revolver and cocked the hammer and pointed it right at two boxes of powder only ten feet away. And I tell that clutch of savages the sooner they depart the better, for I will blow that place to kingdom come if they stay one more minute. This speech worked wonders. They seemed to be impressed. After that they treated me with greater respect."

"Would you have really done it, Jack?" asked Seneca. "Fired into that powder?"

"Damn right I would. Better than dying at their hands. Ask your brother, he was there."

"I thought you said no white man was about for fifty miles."

"Ora don't count. He was with me on this one. Better all of us die and go to hell together than be tortured all day and night for three or four days and then killed. The Utes have a scholarly interest in torture. They like to ponder its effects."

Oramel Howland sucked on his pipe and blew smoke into the white evening sky. In the light of the bonfire Seneca fixed his eyes on Bill Dunn. "What about you, Bill?"

"What about me what?"

"Ever kill a redskin?"

"A hundred or a thousand."

"No, really."

" 'No, really,' he says. I'm a loathsome scoundrel. I've done scurvy things. I'm no respecter of persons."

"But did you ever kill an Indian?"

"Take your eyeballs off me. I'm not comfortable being stared at like that."

"I'm just asking a question."

"You're looking at me like a half-starved dog."

"It's a free country."

"Then I'm free to shoot you. Turn around," said Bill. "I won't abide being stared at."

Seneca watched Bill for another moment. Then reluctantly he shifted on his log and turned his back. "There. Is that better?"

"I cannot tell you how much. The back of your head's a lot prettier than the front."

"Now will you answer me?"

"What's there to answer? My times with Lo don't bear repeating. We never had no special quarrel. I always got along with them untamed sons and daughters of nature. They treated me swell. Thought I was some sort of long-lost kin."

"Thought *you* were an Indian?"

"There's some that still do. This one jumped-up Ute used to call me his brother. I said to myself all right then, brothers share everything, I'll share his wife. I enjoyed her favors and two days later was walking through the fields when who should leap up right up beside me from the grass and grab onto my wrist? Greased all over and painted for a battle. I draws my dagger, he draws his, and the meantime each of us holds the other's wrist, like this."

Seneca turned around.

"Turn your fucking head!"

"You were showing me something."

"I wasn't showing *you*," said Bill. "You turn around once more I won't say another word."

Seneca turned back.

"So we tumbled about. It was more than a hugging match, be assured. I called him a heap of shit with eyes and he called me a wrinkled old cunt with tits, and it went on like that. Did I say he was considerable heavier than me? Buck naked too, save for a breechclout.

Oiled from head to foot, as I mentioned already. His keen knife made a plunge at my breast and I made a plunge at him and we jerked at each other, which our wrists were still locked. Then with a pass of my left foot I buckled his knee and brought him to the dirt, but he pulled me down too. In a wink he was on me. His knee was on my chest and he still held my arm and aloft he raises his knife, long and hard and sharp. And he says to my face, 'Die, piss-ant.' I believe it was the worst thing that ever happened to me. 'Pindah lickadee dee-dah doo-dah,' he says. Indian talk for 'Go cash in your chips.' And he holds the knife there, savoring the moment, the savage monster. Triumph and delight was glaring from his glittering black orbs. Or glittering from his glaring black orbs, I can't recall. I lived more in that minute than I done in a hundred years, howsomever all this transpired in a second. He cocks his meaty arm. Raises the knife. Down comes the blow of the deadly weapon."

Bill Dunn stopped. Seneca swung around. "What happened?"

"Didn't I say not to turn, Peach Fuzz? Now you spoiled the whole thing. Are you done, Bill? Yes, I'm done."

"You have to say what happened! Did he miss?"

Jack Sumner said, "I presume he must of."

"I'm not saying he missed and I'm not saying he didn't."

"That's the most amazing story I've ever heard."

"Ought to be," said Bill. "I read it in a book."

"What?"

"Just like him." Bill nodded at Jack.

Morning didn't look much different from dusk. White sky overhead, dark valley beneath. The willow frame so carefully constructed by Seneca to hold his mosquito net had collapsed in the night and the netting now lay across his cheek, affording the whining bugs easy access. His head lay near the open door of the tent, and soon the sun's rays struck his brow, but he kept his eyes closed. Behind the whine of the mosquitoes came the sound of the river rinsing its banks. He kept drifting off. Then he heard another sound—horse hooves in wet sand—and opened his eyes. He didn't see a thing until out of nowhere two enormous Indians stood before the sun outside his tent. The blinding nimbus around their continents of head threw their features into shadow, and Seneca grabbed whatever came loose—

mosquito bar, blankets—sprang to his knees, and huddled back in the tent, bedding clutched against his neck. The classic posture of bedroom terror, learned from a book.

He heard Andy Hall's voice: "Where shall we put these sacks of flour?"

Hawkins's too: "Roll out! Roll out! Chain up the gaps! Meet our guests, boys!"

The two Utes, as it happened, had hauled their new supplies from the Uinta Ute Agency. Seneca crawled out of his tent, followed by his brother. The Indians had already climbed back on their horses with three more in tow. Their long black hair hung in two tails braided with red cloth. The single part down the center of their scalps was painted with vermilion, as were their eyes. Their shirts and leggings were deerskin.

They looked around the camp. Looked right through Seneca, hardly noting he was there.

Andy formally shook each man's hand before they trotted off. Thirty sacks of flour lay on the ground, but Hawkins declared there wasn't much sense in packing them away until the Major arrived—he'd just order them unloaded and redistributed. Major Powell and Walter, he said, were hoofing it back and would not arrive till midday. Jack Sumner asked Hawkins, "He's bringing more?"

"This is all."

"Can't live on just flour."

"Might have to," said Hawkins.

4

Wes and his brother returned that afternoon without Frank Goodman. He'd had enough rapids and hand-me-down clothes, enough freezing when wet and burning when dry, enough mud in his hair and sand in his pants fraying his skin and exposing his nerves.

Jack Sumner asked Wes where Goodman was going.

"Fort Bridger. Chicago. New York. Merry England."

"Good riddance," said George, packing his boat. His step was lighter now, and it wasn't just George; everyone expressed relief that at long last the whiner was gone. Three boats now, each with three men—it made more sense.

Still, once they'd started off, something seemed missing. They'd been abandoned, they were one less today, and it made them feel vulnerable. Quitters could just tell a partial story, but sometimes that proved to be the only one.

In the *Emma Dean* Jack Sumner told Wes it felt different without Goodman.

"He'll be okay."

"I suppose we're better off. One less mouth to feed."

"Do I detect a note of envy?"

Jack shipped his oars. "You detect a note of caution. We're low on food. A lot of it was spoiled and I had to throw it out."

"They were low at the agency too."

"But *they* ain't venturing a thousand miles through unexplored wilderness. Don't they got braves sitting around all day with nothing else to do but hunt? I suppose they have gardens? And supply trains going back and forth all the time."

"You should have come with us, Jack. You could have played General Sherman to their Atlanta and requisitioned all the stores. Yes, they have all those things, but the gardens are scant. The Utes are reluctant to plant or farm, like many Indians. How much food did you throw out?"

"Just a smitch, really."

"Then what's the problem?"

Jack rowed again, pulling hard on the oars. "There's no problem," he said.

"We have hunters too."

"Fine. We do. All's we need is game."

Wes looked at Jack. How much *had* he thrown out? The *Emma Dean* went silent, save for the groan of oars in the tholepins, the click of blades slicing water. Through Wes's mind raced the usual anxieties, the unthinkable yet surely possible horrors: to starve, to drown, to plunge headlong from a precipice. The river was pulling them toward a great canyon rumored to be so deep in the earth they could conceivably find themselves trapped, unable to go ahead or climb out.

Starvation had seemed the least likely possibility until the wreck of the *No Name*. Wes had purchased enough provisions for a good ten months, not because the expedition would take that long—though who knew?—but to be on the safe side. One had to plan for the worst. But with the loss of the *No Name* and spoilage from water, the supplies were already cut in half. Thirty sacks of flour couldn't make up the difference. And Jack's pound-foolishness likely meant even less. And less food meant less time: diminished opportunities to explore and take readings and gather rocks and fossils and collect hypsometric data. "How much food did you say you threw out?"

Jack sighed. "A few sacks of flour. One or two rancid hams."

"You could have trimmed the hams."

"They'd been whittled down to nothing already, Professor."

Jack hadn't called him that since last winter. Things felt different now. The real problem was additional spoilage, from boats so battered and knocked about by the river they couldn't help but leak. They'd have to portage more—but that took more time. Every solution added to the problem, save one: stopping to hunt would extend their provisions and give Wes the chance to collect, to observe. Data are the characters in which the truth is written—the truth of their voyage. Without that truth, he thought, what purpose was there in continuing, except to hang on and survive?

Wes thought of George Crookham, his one-man prairie college, the man who'd taught him to puzzle out everything he learned, to boil things down to principles. Crookham's two-room log cabin in Ohio consisted of living quarters and a kitchen squeezed into one room—and library, workshop, classroom, wonder cabinet full of Indian relics, fossils, crayfish, dried plants, and articulated skeletons, organized on shelves and tables, in the other. Wes never did become a preacher as his father had intended; instead, infected with a passion for knowledge by Crookham (a friend of his father's!), he began pursuing it himself. At twenty-two, he rowed up the Mississippi River to St. Paul, Minnesota, then walked across the entire state of Wisconsin, taking notes and gathering specimens before walking back home to Illinois—they'd moved to Illinois by then. He did it again in succeeding summers, or rowed down to New Orleans, or up the Ohio, bagging knowledge all the way. In the Civil War, he enlisted as a private, purchased books on military science, and taught himself the principles of defensive engineering. He soon was made an officer, and scarcely four months after enlisting, Lieutenant Powell found himself in charge of constructing earthworks and forts at Cape Girardeau on the Mississippi. The loss of an arm at Shiloh didn't stop him. Six months after it was amputated he was mapping out tunnels at the siege of Vicksburg, erecting shields and fascines of bundled cane, digging saps to within seventy yards of the Confederate parapets, and meanwhile studying the nearby hills incised with creeks and rivers to understand the landforms. His men sapped the hills by night, and by day Captain Powell—he was Captain now— sifted the resulting excavations for rocks and fossil mollusks, which he wrapped in scraps of cotton and posted home to Illinois. After Vicksburg they resectioned his arm stump, to mitigate the pain, and made him a major.

According to Pascal's dictum—taught to him by Crookham—to understand something, you had to understand the principle from which it springs. Wes liked to break things down, find the root of each part, then assemble them again looking for the hidden connection. He let the unknown siren him, then worked to erase it. His men, both in the war and on this voyage, often found him preoccupied, sometimes troubled and moody, until out of nowhere his eyes struck a match and he seemed on the verge of a dozen eurekas.

Sometimes he thought the planet Earth could be as much as a billion years old. Of course it was inconceivably older than Bishop Ussher's date for the Creation, 4004 B.C., most likely even older than Lyell's and William Thompson's hundreds of millions of years. And Amos Eaton's diluvian deposits had not been laid down by Noah's flood, as that pioneering but misguided natural philosopher had claimed. Lyell's calculations, based on changes in species for the lapse of time between the Cambrian and Tertiary, and Darwin's ideas about evolution made it clear that the sedimentary rocks in the canyons of the West were so much older than human life that Noah's flood had to be a recent blink, a minor episode in Old World history. If it ever happened.

He and George Crookham, that bear of a man, had opened Indian mounds when Powell was a teen, and chiseled fossils from rocks, and with Crookham's friend William Mather studied the fundamentals of surveying and geology. They sliced birds and rats apart and examined the stinking contents of their stomachs. They analyzed soils and rocks, salts, coal, and other minerals, and blew up pumpkins with their own homemade powder of saltpeter, charcoal, and sulfur sifted through a cloth. Once, with Mather, Crookham took Powell down Salt Creek Gorge and showed him the runaway slaves hidden in rock shelters high above the river. Crookham was a stationmaster for the Underground Railroad; later, pro-slavers burned down his farm and museum.

To have Crookham on this voyage! Alas, he'd died years ago. To have a dozen Crookhams, though one Crookham alone was worth a dozen men. And weighed as much. Crookham in his prime knew as well as anyone that feeding the mind required a full stomach. Wes did have one expedient today: last year, he'd met a trapper who'd planned to winter in this valley and start a garden in the spring. Help yourself, he'd said; once past the Uinta River, start looking for an island.

Wes had been looking for a while now. They were leaving the marshes and cattails behind. As they floated down the river he felt the valley close in back of them—the blister beetles, prairie dogs, snakes and mosquitoes, the geese, herons, and deer, the pelicans and dragonflies, all knitting back together and shutting them out.

Ten minutes later they came to an island, and Wes told Jack to land there. The other boats followed. On a rise beyond a sandbank grew a garden in the wilderness, but nothing was ready. No corn, no potatoes, no beets of any size. Andy Hall declared that the tops made good greens—his mother used to cook them—so they gathered a kettleful of potato, beet, and turnip tops, and Hawkins boiled them and shouted, "Grub pile!" Beastly stuff, but it was a change of pace from dried apples and bacon, and it filled them up.

They lay on the sand beside the beached boats. This island afforded a final look at the Uinta Mountains, and Wes gazed at their broken profile while his stomach burbled. On a voyage like this, the country behind you abetted the river; it too dragged the unknown into view.

Wes called Hawkins over and asked about the flour—how much

of it was smutty? It was odd—instead of answering, Hawkins's eyes rolled up and he fell to the ground like someone slain by the Lord at a Methodist camp meeting. Andy Hall dropped, and Seneca Howland spun on his heels and ran into the brush. An icicle of fear entered Wes's heart. Then something in his stomach rippled and crawled and contracted to a fist. Soon he was heaving his guts into the river along with Jack and Walter. Some squatted in the brush, others rolled on the ground clutching their bellies and moaning like cows. All except George Bradley, who'd abstained from the greens. Hawkins insisted they hadn't been cooked enough and apologized profusely, but once he'd recovered Wes announced it was undoubtedly some emetic substance in those tops, or in the soil.

No, said Walter. They'd been poisoned somehow by Frank the Lime Juicer.

Andy, who'd disappeared into the willows, emerged holding up a trophy: a vine he claimed to have pulled from his throat, still mostly raw with a potato on its end. The latter was small and hard as a stone.

They recovered, and the next day when they started off, low cliffs appeared. Walter Powell sang "Flow Gently, Sweet Afton" just when the river began to pick up speed. Weird things started happening. A bighorn carcass lay beside the river, and they landed to see if the meat was any good. Lying there, it seemed to twitch. Jack pulled out his pistol. But Wes flipped it over and, as though mocking them, it turned out to be crawling with beetles.

Standing in the shallows, Ora took compass bearings and jotted down notes. Wes approached him. "How far have we come?"

Ora asked dryly, "From where?"

"From the Uintas."

"I haven't footed that up yet." He put the compass in his pocket. They stood beside the *Maid*, Wes on dry land, Ora in the water. The *Maid* was where Ora kept his instruments It was his boat now, not just the cook's.

"The water will fly into our boats again soon. I asked at the agency about the river ahead. Those who claimed to know said it descends into a canyon and the rapids there are violent."

"Something new."

"You'll have to be alert and watch for my signals."

"I understand that branch of the business pretty well."

"Good. We can't afford to lose another boat."

"I shouldn't think we could." Ora looked away.

"I'll pause at the mouth of the next canyon for your compass bearings."

"How far is that?"

"I'm not certain."

"Well, you say the word. You're the chief."

Wes turned away and made for his boat. Another piece of distasteful business out of the way: his daily conference with Ora.

They climbed back into the boats and floated downstream. The walls increased in height as the valley they'd been in for nearly two weeks finally evaporated. This canyon wasn't like the others. No dramatic entrance, no high gates or columns. And it was colorless, Wes saw. Even the sky wasn't blue anymore but white with a thin layer of haze. They stopped for compass bearings, started again, and the river swept in great curves and gouges. Terraces on its banks were bare of vegetation—deserts turned on their sides. As they rounded a bend, a half mile ahead a boulder rolled down a slope slower than a covered wagon—large as one too—end over end into the river, landing with a silent splash.

A persistent stink had begun to boil out of the men by midday, Wes had noticed.

He named this place Desolation Canyon, to the silent accord of the men. They ran some rapids. No one had much to say. He sent out the hunters, and he and his brother climbed to the rim and saw goblins of stone and distant forests and, on the horizon, great ships of rock. They found fossil teeth of fish high on the cliffs. There were no water pockets, and now when they stopped they learned to carry water lest their mouths fill with cotton.

The hunters had no luck. A starving land, said Hawkins. The canyon steadily deepened, but Bill Dunn obtained some strange elevations suggesting that the river was flowing uphill. Wes saw why: two of the barometers in the box were leaking. At the same time, distinct strata began to appear in the canyon walls. He remembered a system of measuring strata devised by George Crookham for just this contingency, and when they landed he explained it to the men by holding a little seminar in the sand.

Suppose none of the barometers were accurate, he proposed. One had cracked and they'd repaired it with a spare glass tube, but now the others were leaking and would have to be repaired at their next layover. Meanwhile, without knowing the true atmospheric pressure they could get a good sense of relative pressure by using all three barometers, the chronometer, and their best watch. He and a partner would climb the canyon wall with one of the barometers and the chronometer to record at half-hour intervals the atmospheric pressure, first at the base and then at the top of a stratum. Two men below with the watch and the other two barometers would also record the atmospheric pressure at each half hour. If those barometers differed, they'd average the readings. And the Major would continue his climb, taking readings every half hour precisely at the bottoms and tops of strata until they reached the top. This meant hastening to get to the next one on time, or, alternatively, waiting. In this way they'd determine the relative pressure, giving them differences of altitude—and from that they could measure each stratum's thickness.

Following this system, Wes and Ora climbed the canyon wall while Bill Dunn and George Bradley took the readings below. Ora tired easily. The walls were steep and ragged and the cliffs ran through a maze of crags and slopes, forcing them to scramble up gulches of loose rock and pull themselves onto ledges. So after the first time, George swapped with Ora and the latter stayed below to complain to Bill Dunn about the Major's new hobbyhorse, this endless carting of fancy equipment up and down dismal walls, and when could a man have time to make the maps he was expected to make? Bill said nothing. He averaged the readings and pulled out his notebook and recorded their putative pressure each half hour on the minute.

By day three, this canyon was deeper than the others and still barren and dry. A melancholy man might with satisfaction choose it for his final hours, Jack Sumner remarked. Wes pointed out that it was the depth of Hades—three to four thousand feet from river to rim. And to himself he wondered if the Utes at the agency weren't right after all—the ones who'd warned him that the river kept descending and descending until it vanished underground.

One dreary afternoon Wes and George Bradley climbed up the canyon wall to measure the strata, and Wes stormed ahead, up a rock slide then across a bench with George in tow. Both men wore shirts and drawers. The bench led to a slope at the base of a stratum where they waited for the moment to take their first reading. Then they trudged across sliding plates of rock. They angled to the left and the edge of a cliff appeared below them; their slope began to narrow. Reaching a crevice, they sat and waited to take the second reading where a sandstone wall rose. Then Wes handed the barometer and chronometer to George and squeezed into the crevice and wormed his body up. George passed the equipment back when he slithered past Wes, and in this manner they leapfrogged each other toward the top.

At one point the crevice pinched out and Wes leapt for a foothold. He grabbed a projection—a thin flake of rock—then found he couldn't let go with his one hand and couldn't climb up or down without letting go.

Weathered gray columns guarded gullies and gulches. Below his broken buttress the cliff plunged straight down past pedestals and minarets to a slope of fallen rock, then fanned out to terraces that led to more cliffs and deep ragged gorges. He could conceivably fall all the way to the river, the brown-green ribbon far below his feet snaking in and out around the roots of canyon walls. He spotted their toy boats strewn on a sandbank. Across the river the walls were broken apart by lateral canyons as far south as he could see. He gripped his flake of rock for balance but tried not to pull it; all the rock here was friable. One knee wobbled like a broken spring.

"Up here, Major." George had found a bench above him and lay across a rock. He reached down with his arm. Wes stood on his toes, hugged the rock, strained his muscles. Yet he could not let go. He might do it quickly—release his grip and simultaneously with one sudden lunge grab Bradley's hand. But when he played it in his mind he was already falling, swinging out and down like a toppled ladder.

Bradley tried the barometer. It reached, but Wes thought it might break. He had the oddest sensation: concern for his precious instrument constraining the instinct for self-preservation. At last George pulled off his boots and flannel drawers and lowered the drawers down on top of Wes's hand. One finger snagged the cloth, then his thumb hooked around it. His desperate hand gathered the flannel until he had a good grip. George pulled him up by his one arm and his feet churned the wall, ripping rocks from its face, until he lay beside his rescuer.

"You're trembling."

"Yes. Muscular reaction."

He was breathing hard too and sat there for a minute, averting his eyes from the white legs and hairy privates of the man beside him. George arched his back, brushed off his bottom, and pulled on the drawers. "I'm thankful they held," he said. "What if they'd ripped?"

"You'd be out a pair of drawers," said the Major.

"Could have taken yours."

Wes tried to smile. "Yes. You could have." He looked him in the eye. "I don't know how long I could have lasted," he said.

George scowled. "You were fine. You weren't exactly hanging by your fingertips."

"It's not that. It's something else. Not being able to move or let go. Nothing but emptiness below. You almost want to say be done with it. Let go with your one blasted arm and drop."

"Well, it does that to a man."

"I felt a tug. As though my plunge had been scripted." He shook his head and shuddered. "It was fate."

"That's not fate, Major Powell, it's a strong imagination. You wouldn't be here right now if it was fate."

"I know," said Wes. He felt calmer now, the trembling had stopped. He stood and extended the one arm to George. "Thank you. How can I thank you enough?"

"You can shut up about it. Sir."

They took more readings and arrived at the top and looked around at the plateau stretched high across the river. Gulches and valleys cracked the yellow land running into the canyon, which plowed directly south. This high plateau was forested with pines. Not far off, a stand of piñons had burned and the blackened remains with elevated arms looked to Wes like tarnished candelabra—grotesque reminders of home. A haze in the air obscured distant landmarks. He did not have the means, nor did Oramel below, of linking their proximate geography with the greater land around it. It seemed a massive slippage had occurred; they were following a river utterly ripped from earth. The river and its course together were an island unmoored by any link or earthly membrane to the continent, though

Wes did run through possible connections in his mind. To the east was the Grand River, which they would meet somewhere ahead, where it became the Colorado. To the west might have been the Wasatch Mountains, or just clouds. Utah Lake was somewhere west too, the Great Salt Lake north of that—but how far west and north?

The following day, in running some rapids the *Emma* broke an oar, then lost another. Now only one of Wes's boatmates could row, Bill or Jack, and the rapids grew worse and Bill couldn't land before they reached a fall, which whipped them past a rock whose reflex wave, a huge S, filled the boat with water. Wes stood to flag the others to shore. Another wave hit, rolling the boat, and he was thrown into the river.

The water was nearly as warm as a bath and the life preserver kept him afloat, but the speed of his passage downriver was shocking—it seemed like falling through air. Though one arm could tread, he still felt helpless. Waves tossed him up and troughs pulled him under. Twenty feet ahead he made out Bill and Jack clinging to the overturned boat. They rode the river like sticks—or the river rode them—and Wes soon caught up. In slower water they flipped the boat back and urged it to shore. But the river rebraided and Bill got sucked under till Jack caught him by the collar and jerked him to the boat, which had found a new line rolling toward more rapids before they could climb in.

They tobogganed toward a trough and shot out of the water, still clinging to the boat. They went under so deep their feet grazed the bottom. A blanket roll sped past. At last the river bent left and swung the boat and men into a pile of driftwood. Wes grabbed the blanket roll and they were safe. But two rifles and one barometer had been lost in the river. And two other blanket rolls. And Wes's flag. From this point on he'd have to signal with his hat. And they were down to two barometers.

5

They built a big fire and spread their clothes out to dry. No one said much, and all Wes had to do was nod at the driftwood and the men got to work. From the logjammed wood they chose the best pieces and got the whipsaw from the *Maid*. Seneca and Bill propped a log on a rock and started cutting it lengthwise. Wes watched his brother keep the log steady.

When they were finished, Jack Sumner and Walter used an ax, then an adze, and finally their knives to shape the narrower slab into oars. Andy Hall and Oramel relieved Bill and Seneca and ripped another log. Wes felt useless—he couldn't help it. He walked around the camp. Meanwhile, Hawkins cooked a meal of coffee, biscuits, rice, and beans, but they were low on beans so each got just a pittance.

They were camped in some sand hills beside a gravel bar, not far from a stand of stunted cottonwoods, the only trees in sight. Everyone was exhausted. Hawkins split his blanket roll and Wes split his—now dried by the fire—and Sumner and Dunn each got a new blanket. Bill threw his on the sand, lay down, and fell asleep while the day was still light.

Soon all were asleep except Seneca Howland. He was staring at Bill, with his black hair and greasy buckskin pants and shirt and black beard and huge hairy nostrils, snoring like a bear. Seneca lay on his side, elbow propped up, while the canyon walls darkened. A bee landed on his blanket. But he stared at Bill. Seneca had always been good with his hands, quick and furtive. Last year in Denver he'd caught a mockingbird that had been keeping him awake outside his and Ora's house. It was the middle of the night and he didn't use a lantern because that would scare the bird off; he just followed its song. For no reason—pure deviltry, said Ora—he trapped it in the outhouse for his brother to find when he rose the next morning.

The bee hadn't moved. It wasn't a bee, he saw now, but a yellow jacket. Sniffing something on the blanket. Could yellow jackets sniff? Quick as a wink Seneca pinched it with his fingers, careful to grip each side of the body, and brought it to Bill and stuffed it in his nose. Then he ran back to his blanket and pretended to sleep.

After what seemed to be an age, Bill started making a monster catawampus and woke everyone in camp. He ran around screaming and jumped into the river holding his face, for the wasp had slithered right up into the sinuses. No one seemed to know what was happening except it involved his nose. Wes told him not to panic. But Bill's face was inflating. He stood ankle deep in the shallows of the river tearing at his hair, then looked at the clumps of black hair in his fists. Seneca told him to take a big swallow of the river and blow it through his nose. Bill did; it didn't work. Keep doing it, said Seneca, and at last the yellow jacket shot from his nose and landed in the river. It spiraled up and flew off.

"Got a bee in his nose!"

"Worse. A yellow jacket."

"Christ's sakes, Bill, were you wearing perfume? Is there pollen in them pits?"

"How could such a thing happen?"

"Bees are forever looking for holes."

"Correction. Yellow jacket."

Bill's face had swollen up on one side of the nose, closing that eye. Seneca made a paste of saleratus and applied it to the skin. He brewed some coffee and brought it to Bill, who was shaking on his blanket.

"Just my shitty luck."

"You'll be better in the morning."

"I could use a jug of whiskey."

"So could we all."

Seneca fed Bill the coffee as they talked. "Does it hurt very much?"

"Worse than being scalped."

"You ever been scalped?"

"What kind of question is that?" Bill's eyes were tearing. His cheeks looked like plums attacked by a blight.

"Will the redskins be dangerous up ahead, Bill?"

"No more than this country."

"They could shoot us from the rims."

"They got better things to do."

The next day George Bradley was knocked from his boat in the middle of a rapid, but his foot caught in the seat as he fell. Wes heard the shout and turned to watch but couldn't help—no one could.

George in the *Sister* got dragged through the river with his hea[d] shoulders submerged, but with great effort one hand grabbe[d] gunnel to lift his head enough to breathe. He let go and got dun[k]ed again and kept repeating the process. Meanwhile, the boat was hea[d]ing toward a cliff. Walter and Seneca pulled on the oars as hard [as] they could, and when the danger was past Walter caught hold o[f] George and hauled him into the boat. Later, when asked what ran through his mind while trapped underwater, George told Wes all he could think of was his tintypes being ruined.

That night gargantuan winds picked up water from the river and sand from the banks and blasted the camp they'd set up on a sandbank. It blew the fire into the river and started on the boats pulled up on the sandbank, so they had to run and grab them. But jumping up meant their blankets blew away, so for a while they were running back and forth from blankets to boats through curtains of sand. Blankets stuffed beneath their arms, they made deadmen with the oars. Standing half naked, backs to the wind, they were peppered by sand and water equally—it felt like grapeshot and blood. There were whitecaps on the river, some a foot or two high. Those who had shirts pulled them over their faces.

The wind declined a little, and with the boats secured Wes suggested they walk backward toward the camp. This they did, and wrapped themselves up and lay there all night while the sand piled like snow. In the morning, Bill and Seneca, clinging to each other, looked to Wes like a single colossus half buried in sand.

The water slowed and rapids ended. Walls receded from the river. The boats clumped together, drifting with the river, and nearby cliffs shrank, gray seamed with black, soft and broken and bare. Ora pointed out that they were passing through coal.

Andy Hall sang a song and Hawkins threatened to brain him if he persisted, but Andy knew only one verse anyway. So he sang it a second time, then stopped:

When he put his arm around her,
She bustified like a forty pounder.
Look away, look away, look away in Dixie's land.

"Watch what you sing, Jockie," said Hawkins. "You got half the Union Army in these boats."

s long over."

r over. And where the hell did you get them lyrics?
hat's no kind of word."

nma, Wes stared at a maze of gullied cliffs with broken
g down. He knew why things had begun to feel differ-
r since they'd entered this canyon the world had cut its
m and his men: this was their first truly unexplored
Vith Emma he'd scouted the Green as far south as the
, staring down at the river from widely spaced sites on cliffs
med with snow. But this barren land with its grudging vegetation
and no game at all—no deer, sheep, or coyotes, not even a beaver—
this place was unknown territory on their maps, and it didn't seem
human. They'd cast their nets, of course; they'd taken compass bearings, found latitude and longitude, measured elevations. And like a
great mammoth, the land had shrugged them off, and still held its
back to them. They hadn't even roused it.

Into a valley of dry rolling tableland the water bugs floated. With
no eminences to climb, Wes couldn't take the hawk's point of view,
but as they slid through this valley he looked back at that labyrinth of
terraced gray cliffs, with their river lost within it like Daedalus's
thread, and wondered what were *they* if the river were a thread? It
dwarfed the capacity to imagine, this landscape.

Part Four

1

Toab sees them again in the thick stand of piñons across the clearing: three white men huddled together, one with raven-black hair and black beard. Light pours through their bodies, and shadows of trees drag frayed ropes and strings across their pale flesh spotted with blood.

Rivers and water are older than the sun, and blood older still, here when all was dark. A hawk shrieks overhead. From her tilted plane, she draws the men deep into her yellow-red pupils, netting their remains. In his dream Toab has to kill them again, but he can't string his bow, the cord won't reach. He can't shoot the arrow, his weak arm collapses. The arrows fall short, fading in air.

He picks up a rock and throws it at the men, but thick waves of wind seem to swallow it whole. And when he flies across the clearing, feeling his limbs stretch, the knife he's carrying won't penetrate. It's like stabbing smoke.

2

Kwits saw his uncle Toab cresting the ridge with a deer across his shoulders, blood drooling from its nostrils. Face painted red, feet firmly planted, blue sky behind him, piñons below. Toab triumphant.

From his crouch above a wind hole, Kwits watched. Away from

their camp in the yellow-brown dirt among piñons and sage, the boy had found this hole in the earth. Hold a feather at its mouth and it shoots straight up.

When Toab told Kwits go hang yourself, he meant go get sticks for arrows; when he said jump off a cliff, he meant fetch water—it was their private code. Kwits tried to go where Toab went, tried, like a dog, to piss where he pissed. Once when he was younger—just a puppy, said his mother—Kwits pissed on his own legs and stood on his head and wet the rest of his body so he'd smell bad and no one would eat him. Pooeechuts scrubbed his skin with dirt and yucca suds until it was raw. Little coyote, you listen to too many stories.

Now his mother's arm had swollen yet shriveled, a mushroom filled with dust.

Toab disappeared across the ridge.

Kwits uprooted a bush and crept on hands and knees toward a cautious deer, stopping when it turned to look in his direction. A rock-laugher laughed—a wren perched on a boulder. Two jays quarreled in a tree. One said, When I get mad the land fills with fog. The other said, When I get mad the mountains turn to dust and everything becomes flat.

They thought a lot of themselves.

Kwits jumped at the deer and the deer jumped too, but it was Soxor, who snatched the bush away.

She ran to the wind hole and thrust her face in its mouth. The black flood of her hair rose into the sky.

Let's turn ourselves into hawks, she said.

Let's turn ourselves into mice, he said, and they did. They were hundreds of mice under Iron Clothes's lodge, running in and out of walls.

Let's turn ourselves into rats, she said, and they gnawed everything around them to pieces.

He chased his sister and tackled her, handing her some bark: Patch these moccasins for me! They practiced lying on each other like husband and wife. He stood and made her watch while he pulled aside his breechclout and pissed on the ground.

Let's find Chookwadum, he said, and they hunted in the brush. They killed all the Navajo, rescued the girl, brought her back home, showed her the wind hole.

They spotted some rabbitbrush. Uprooting one plant, they peeled the bark off the roots and chewed the tangy, gumlike inner flesh. Their mouths filled with juice. They broke branches off the plant, removed the stems, and turned them over and had skoomer dolls—a row of stick figures with twirling green skirts.

Soxor wore a bark skirt she'd made from cliff rose, and as they walked back to camp Kwits taunted her with singing:

Bark aprons bounce up and down,
Up and down, up and down.

Their camp consisted of piñons and junipers augmented by brush propped against branches. They hadn't built a morning fire because it might attract Navajo—not those they were searching for but others, witches, the kind who become coyotes at will and dig up the dead and tear apart the living.

Or maybe those were the ones they were searching for.

Already Toab was butchering the deer. He thought they'd risk a fire. Mara blew on the smoking twist of cedar bark they'd carried from home while Onchok dumped a load of wood beside her, and Soxor went for water. Not even the fear of Navajo witches could keep hungry people from eating fresh deer meat.

Kwits's mother lay in a brush shelter. Their burro was hobbled over in some bunchgrass. The camp was somewhere in the midst of Black Mesa, well away from the trail they'd followed yesterday through washes and ravines. Toab had found this place below a ridge and thought it looked safe, so they'd slept here last night. After several days of walking, the trail would fade, he'd been told back at Walpi, but by then they'd see Paiute Mountain to the north and all they had to do was go in that direction. Two or three more days would bring them to the People from the Other Side.

The deer lay on its side. Toab had already cut off the forelegs and sliced the neck, leaving the head attached by a flap of skin. Now he was slitting the belly, throat to crotch. Kwits sat in the dirt, chin in hand, and watched him work. He watched the new metal knife, one they'd gotten in trade for a basket at Oraibi, as Toab sliced. Onchok and Toab pulled the opened deer apart and the guts slumped forward and they tugged them out. Mara gathered up the slimy red and gray confusion and took it aside to squeeze the contents from the entrails.

Arms, hands, and clothing were soon smeared with blood and grease.

If his sister was out getting water with the jug, then what was this warmth gently landing next to Kwits? The dirt hardly wrinkled, no dust rose. Kwits took advantage of his mother's jutting knee to braid his fingers on it as a platform for his chin.

The two men skinned the deer. Onchok pulled and ripped and Toab reached inside to slice the stretching fabric of tissue, fat, and blood. Little by little the animal gave up its shape and lay there, a congealed mass of white and red rawness.

The stomach fat and the fat above the hips had come off with the skin. Toab removed the head and Pooeechuts took it and handed it to Mara. Then Pooeechuts draped the heavy skin across one arm and dragged it away.

The fire was going now. Mara threw the head and emptied entrails beside the burning wood. When the coals got hot enough she'd push them closer. On the other side of camp Pooeechuts used a hoof to scrape hair off the deerskin. With just one good arm she was having trouble, so Kwits ran up with his own hoof, but she shooed him away. Children shouldn't do that, she told him. They shouldn't even watch. Still, his chin was smeared with blood from sharing the raw liver with the men. Someday he'd be a man. Now he was an acorn.

Mara took the deer hoof from Kwits.

Soxor returned from the spring they'd found. She poured the water from her jug into a basket hanging from a tripod, then went back for more.

Mara went to get the knife and a shoulder blade, and the two sisters turned the deerskin over and scraped the fat and blood vessels off the inside of the skin. Pooeechuts's useless arm hung at her side. The burro honked and snorted—he smelled the fat and blood. With two sticks Mara fished a stone from the fire and carried it over. She dumped it in the water, then together the sisters lay the deerskin in a hole Pooeechuts had made and lined with leaves. They poured the hot water over the skin.

Chunks of meat skewered on branches spat and sizzled. On coals underneath, the head, entrails, heart, and kidneys roasted. Onchok turned the skewers and made sure the heart and entrails didn't burn.

He kept turning the head, whose eyeballs steamed, and under gray coals he put the blood roast—a paunch filled with fresh blood that would cook all day.

Soxor returned with another jug of water.

It wasn't even midday but they ate all they could and rested in the shade. Jays came and watched from the branches, and flies laid eggs in the uncooked meat. Kwits lay in the dirt with a prosperous belly, and his mother fell asleep to a scraping sound: Mara kicking a stick Onchok poked at her ankles.

Mara stood and woke her sister. Together they dragged the deerskin from its hole and heaved it over a pole planted in the ground. Mara found a stick to use for rinsing, and they slowly twisted the skin around the stick, wringing it out. Pooeechuts told Soxor to get some more water, but she was lying half asleep. She groaned and rolled over. So Toab told Kwits to go jump off a cliff, and the boy hopped up and found the water jug.

Would you like a basket cap? asked his mother. The others laughed at the joke: Kwits doing women's work. He strapped the tumpline across his unprotected head and marched off with the jug hanging down his back.

3

Toab built a small fire beneath a rack of drying meat to keep off the flies. He looked at the meat, the racks, the fire, and thought about the Navajo. How long could his family stay here? If the Navajo spotted their smoke, they'd be in trouble. They were looking for Navajo, for a certain one, but not for roving bands out raiding the countryside. He knew the Navajo were strong, dangerous, and arrogant, and this was part of their range. They could be anywhere.

He announced to everyone, those awake and those asleep, that they'd stay here for two days while the hide cured and the meat dried, then would have to move on.

Toab's the boss now, Onchok said. He tells us what to do. We ought to get going to look for my daughter, but no, he wants to stay here two days.

Toab said nothing. He decided Onchok was just feeling surly. His brother, reluctant to come on this journey, now was eager to resume it.

They'd saved the best parts of the deer—the soft meat beside the backbone, the heart, the kidneys, the blood roast, and the head, which was soft and juicy after roasting all day—and that evening after dark they feasted again, stuffing stomachs and intestines, blood vessels and muscles, every spare inch of body. Toab didn't have to say take your time and eat a lot. Who knew when they'd get fresh meat again? They had to be strong for the journey and the search, despite Onchok's impatience.

They lay by the fire as though floating on earth. Onchok took a long drink from the water jug and handed it around. He lay back and teased Mara's ankles with a stick and she pushed it away, but he persisted.

Toab fed the fire, watching his brother. He felt a story coming on. Because this one was true, he knew he could safely tell it in the summer. Listen, he said, here's a story, pay attention. It happened to people like us, to Shivwits. Like us, they left home for a long time and walked a long distance. These people walked south. Twelve went and two returned.

Onchok continued to tease Mara's ankles.

These people camped as they traveled, continued Toab. They came to a house in the middle of a valley equally distant from the mountains east and west. This house was the place dead spirits went, who entered it as butterflies. Inside lived a man who swayed back and forth capturing the butterflies. He buried them in rows in the dirt floor, and after a while they rose as little dolls that looked like real people—Paiute dolls in rabbitskin blankets, Navajo and Mookweech and Havasupai dolls. The man liked to take them and stand them in rows and move them around and make them fight with each other. Among them were some bad-smelling white dolls. When the man left the house the twelve Shivwits sneaked in and took the Indian dolls and started back north, but the white dolls chased them and a white horse tracked them down. The Shivwits hid in a wagon filled with branded cowhides, but someone soon threw the cowhides in the river. Before long the cowhides started moving, and out of the water came a herd of living cows that trampled the men—all except two brothers. They'd managed to find a hole in the ground where the cattle's sharp hooves couldn't reach.

One said to the other, What have you ever dreamed? The other said he dreamed of bullets raining down, but none of them struck the horse he was riding. Only if someone shot it in the forehead would his horse be killed.

They crawled out of their hole and the white dolls, now grown to the size of men, chased them on horses, shooting their guns. The first brother's horse was shot out from beneath him, and his brother turned back on his horse to help. At that moment a bullet sped toward the second brother's heart, but his medicine horse lifted its head and caught the bullet in the brow and fell down dead.

The brothers ran off. They kept moving north but could still smell the white dolls, their white breath chasing them, their foul armpit odor. The brothers knew those smells would make the Shivwits sick.

Sick? said Onchok. I have a wife who eats too much. She'll be sick all right. He looked over at Pooeechuts reclining in their shelter.

Mara looked too. He doesn't want you to get fat, she told her sister.

I don't care if she gets fat, said Onchok.

He wants you to get better, said Mara.

Pooeechuts said nothing.

Onchok raised his voice. Saliva flew from his mouth. I ought to have my head chopped off for marrying a woman who's always getting sick. It's her fault she was shot.

Pooeechuts looked down. No one spoke.

Toab put all the leftover meat, cooked and uncooked, in a buckskin sack and hung it from a tree.

Onchok continued poking his stick at Mara's ankles until she moved away. Toab watched him throw bark at his sister-in-law, trying to catch her eye and gesturing with his head. Mara joined her sister and soon the two were asleep in the shelter. Toab and the children walked to the other shelter. Owls began to hoot and coyotes to howl. Onchok squatted next to the fire, clearing his throat. Toab watched him from the shelter. Onchok stood and fed the fire and plucked a burning stick and scratched the dirt. He sang,

Your little old rabbit
Sits under a bush.

He walked around the dying fire, and the smoke perversely followed him. He threw bark chips toward Mara inside her shelter, but nothing moved in there. Onchok sang,

Underneath the tree
She sleeps, she dreams.

He lay down in the dirt and sang about the land unsatisfied and hungry. The ants were starving, the children dying, rivers dry. Toab watched him fall asleep.

The next day the sisters staked out the deerskin and Toab turned the jerked meat on the rack. A haze hovered in the air. The day seemed paralyzed. Toab and Onchok climbed up the ridge every now and then to scan the plateau but never spotted Navajo. The two did find new grass for the burro.

That evening when Onchok teased Mara's ankles she walked over to Toab, squatted before him, and asked him to louse her. He ran his hands through her hair, pinched out the lice, and cracked them with his nails then threw them in the fire. There's one on your neck, he said, chasing it with his finger down her throat.

Then it was his turn to squat and be loused. If it wasn't for me, she said, the bugs would eat you up.

Darkness came again. Toab lingered by the fire with his brother, but at last Onchok joined his wife in their arbor. After a while Mara came out and sat next to Toab. Let's do something, she said. Let's go into the woods.

They climbed a ridge and descended to a hollow. The moon with a frog clinging to its face had risen in the south and threw shadows in the grass. Let's lie down, said Mara. Let's play with each other. He lay in the grass at the edge of a shadow and she kneeled beside him. She reached inside his breechclout and pulled out his prick, pushed back the foreskin, and examined it closely. She swayed from side to side, fingers underneath it, watching it grow. She leaned down and licked the tip, grinning up at Toab.

Turning away, she lay on her belly, fists balled beneath her. She rose on her knees and extended her buttocks and he lifted her dress. Already she was rocking back and forth when he entered. He couldn't do it fast enough, nothing could. Faster, she said, and he did it in motion. She grunted like a man and he whimpered like a girl. Her cheek was in the dirt and she was looking at the moon while he reached around and cupped their sliding groins. She felt him push deeper, ungraining her flesh, and she slid back to meet him and wove her trap tighter and suddenly it sprung and they burst inside each other. He pulled up her shoulders and their backbones cracked together.

He held her like that and they fell on their sides like two empty sacks back in the human world. They were still plugged together. Mara raised her head and felt a breeze—that wind hole in the earth. Her face lay beside it.

Pay me, said Toab. Pay me with feathers.

She plucked a pubic hair and placed it in his hand.

4

Back there in Oraibi, Pooeechuts had thought about it and decided not to die. Dying was easy—too easy, she thought now. The soul wanders west to the shore of a river, and if the person crosses the river, the soul becomes a ghost and the sleeping body dies. She believed she'd left her body and looked at the river then turned back. At the banks of the river she'd seen her sister Mara washing bloody clothes.

Her children would be motherless if she died. She couldn't die, they had to find Chookwadum—that's why she'd turned back from the river. First the pain was a hot coal burning her arm. As the pain dulled, however, the warmth spread through her body, and she slept all the time. Soon she could move the arm a little and dreamed a small twig was hanging in her mind. That twig was her arm. The wound leaked clear liquid and swelled like a rattlesnake choking on a rabbit. Eventually, she couldn't bend the arm completely as its skin had pulled tight. A waking dream haunted her: when she tried to turn the arm, the bone inside it moved, parting from the flesh like a bone in cooked meat.

The pain came in waves but fatigue blossomed out of it, which comforted the pain. It was a kind of medicine. Her injury had profited her, it appeared, by giving her some rest.

She could raise the arm a little, but it had the feel of an empty sleeve stitched on. The skin turned gray and the swelling went down, and when she touched around the wound the arm felt like a soft pouch of sand. She'd adjusted somehow and didn't feel as weak anymore. With her arm curled against her body she went about her business.

When her own mother died, her face was painted red and her body, wrapped in cliff rose bark, was left inside the wickiup while all the women wailed. They slammed her grinding stones against a boulder, breaking them in half. They tore up her clothes and baskets and moccasins, carried her body and possessions on a litter of lashed-together poles, and placed her on a ledge, covering everything with rocks. Back in camp, they broke apart the wickiup. An aunt approached Pooeechuts, who was cowering by a boulder. The woman gripped the girl's hair and with a flint knife severed lock after lock. She was just a child then, and Mara only a baby. Her beautiful long hair—that's what she remembered. They moved somewhere else and never went back, and life for a while felt as it did now, like walking blindly in a cave. They wandered in darkness, lost.

Her aunts had to teach her how to weave baskets because her mother never had. When Pooeechuts was a girl a half-finished basket always looked like a spider. Though her name meant Mouse, she'd loved watching spiders pull threads from their abdomens and stitch their bodies back and forth, lifting their long legs across elastic pathways to weave their webs or wrap their eggs or bundle caught flies. She'd seen them spit on prey or loosen a trapline to collapse a tent of threads around a struggling moth. When she was Chookwadum's age she didn't play with boys. She wandered off and watched the spiders, who became her friends, who gave her clues for making baskets. Their webs became her models.

Now, would she ever weave another basket? She decided to look for a spider and find out, and started walking from their camp, trying to find a web. The light struggled through the trees, then blazed across the sky as she threaded rocks and cacti, crossing a plateau.

Soon she forgot where she was going. This land of shrubs tilted toward a cliff and the sky was so blue it crushed the horizon. Her purpose seemed to vanish.

She wandered around, making sudden turns underneath the blazing sun.

She sat down and there it was. At a prickly pear's base, the web spiraled into earth. Protected by a spiked pad, the tubular web resembled twisted hair, and its gray and white strands were strewn with debris—bits of leaf, brown needles—yet no trees were in sight. Inside, the curling tunnel of the web grew smaller and smaller until it vanished from sight. You're it, she thought. You are what I've been looking for.

The web held a mass of completely still spiderlings. She couldn't see the mother inside, but she had to be there. Then, as Pooeechuts withdrew her shadow she saw the spiderlings were skins—black chitins left behind. Had the web been abandoned? No, something moved inside it. She touched it with a twig.

Onchok sometimes collected certain spiders and crushed them to a pulp to make poison for his arrows. Back in Oraibi, Pooeechuts had allowed one of those to bite her. She'd pinched it with her fingers, put it on her arm, and provoked it by blowing on its back. Its belly grew red, it bit her withered arm, and for a moment the arm flared back to life.

The moment passed. The red spot on her skin grew white, then disappeared.

This web looked like hair gone gray and fine as dust yet strong as metal. A small blue feather caught in the outer lip had probably been placed there by a spirit. She'd heard of parrot feathers, and though she'd never seen a parrot, she thought this could have been one. She reached to pull it off but realized she'd done so with her bad arm. The arm shriveled and curled, snapping back against her side, where she tried to forget it.

But she could never forget it. In the days since she'd been shot her posture had changed because of her arm. That side of her body wouldn't move, wouldn't pour forward naturally, not even while walking. She leaned in that direction, especially when alone. With someone else around she made the effort to correct it, but alone she didn't care, and besides, it didn't hurt, just felt extra, left over, a dried-up umbilicus.

She crouched before the prickly pear, reached with her good arm, and tugged at the feather. Carrion beetles scratched over to watch, death flies descended. Pulling at this feather she began to tear the web, and she thought of gray coals in a dying fire that split apart red. She pictured an unupits spurting from a stick in a blazing fire, a stream of flaming gas: a spirit escaping. The spider shot out and spit a gluey venom directly in her face and she fell back terrified.

5

Is that a good berry?

Tastes sour.

They were traveling again, Onchok ahead as though in charge. Then came the burro, lame but steady. A burden basket on either side, he hadn't balked yet. Behind him Pooeechuts dragged herself along, and behind her came the children. Last, Mara and Toab eating serviceberries he'd found after breaking camp.

The sky was white with clouds and the mesa green and yellow. No trees here, just grass, sage, and rabbitbrush. It wasn't their land; it felt different from home. It ran into gullies or rose toward low ridges and as they walked it tilted up or maybe down, Toab couldn't tell. He felt as if they were fish in the channel of a river that stayed in one spot as the water ran past them.

Soxor squatted in the dirt, then caught up with her mother. Don't do it in the trail, said Pooeechuts. Don't leave any urine or hair on the trail for the Navajo to find—they'll use it to witch you.

Toab watched Kwits pick up a long stick and tease his sister's ankles, as his father had done to Mara. It didn't work in either case, didn't make the other love him. Kwits was smart enough to know when he was being perverse—it only made his sister angry. But the angrier she got, the more she ignored him, so he kept on doing it.

Kwits stopped on the trail and refused to go farther.

Good, said his mother. The Navajo can have you.

So he sat. Toab and Mara stepped around him, and no one looked back. After a while he raced past them on the trail and caught up with his mother, shouting Noneku nonee! Noneku nonee!—Carry me! Carry me! She ignored him.

Raindrops fell in the dust. They seemed to make more dust. One drop, Toab knew, for every bush and for each human being, no more and no less. Then a ceiling of water collapsed around the Shivwits and poured off their heads and shoulders and made the trail a brown stream. Five minutes after that everything was dry again.

Hawks circled in the sky.

They camped in whatever hollows they could find. Kwits still had his stick, and Toab showed the boy how to catch a rabbit with it, by reaching as far as he could into a hole, hooking its fur and twisting the stick, then dragging it out. According to tradition, his mother and father couldn't eat the meat because he wasn't old enough to marry. They made a small fire and the others had the rabbit. Kwits ate the best parts, but not the liver, his father wouldn't let him. Onchok said the blue lump on the liver's tip was poison—sometimes he even used it on arrowheads.

Each morning Toab sweetened his breath by rubbing sage on his teeth and chewing piñon pitch. Each night he and Mara went into the brush and lay down together.

At last they came to the edge of Black Mesa. Below them the ground fell into a valley and on the other side began its slow rise across red and green hills to a distant horizon warped by the broad gray hump of one mountain. Toab asked Mara if that was Paiute Mountain, and she answered yes and wouldn't take her eyes off it. Pooeechuts stared too.

Above, rags of clouds shredded in the wind. Below, hot air blew up from the valley.

Left of Paiute Mountain, a broken range of hills ran along the horizon. Or maybe they were clouds, Toab couldn't tell. They were off in the distance, at the edge of the world.

They started down a trail but the burro wouldn't move. Toab and Onchok got behind and pushed him but had to watch his legs. They did not drop their shoulders and strain—that's when the kick would come.

Ahead, Mara simply whispered, Come. The mule lurched forward and walked down the trail.

The floor of the valley was blanketed with heat and filled with saltbush and bunchgrass. Toab spotted a prairie dog village between scattered boulders. He broke away from the others and crouched as he tiptoed to a boulder, and the dogs wormed up from their holes and whistled. After a minute he stepped away from the boulder, and while the dogs watched the others crossing the valley he fired arrows through two of them so fast they never turned. He ran to the bodies and as they lay there twitching he thanked them for dying then slit their bellies. With his finger he pulled the innards out and hung the bleeding dogs in his belt by their necks. He caught up with the group.

Climbing out of the valley on the other side, they passed between pink-red sandstone knobs and hills. Canyons opened in the rolling dunes and ridges with flat meadows on their floors, and snaking through the meadows were gulches and arroyos whose sides were dry mud. They were mounting a gradual ridge, they saw—soon the canyons lay below them. Slowly they threaded sparse piñons and sage and crossed bare rock. They stayed on the rock so as not to leave tracks and stopped at water pockets and found a shallow pool where water bugs swam.

They let the burro drink and eat the grama grass that grew in the folds between slopes of rock.

They slipped into a ceiling of new, cooler air. Paiute Mountain looked closer—broad, soft, and gray. The broken plateau stretched out beneath their feet toward the waiting horizon. They saw bursts of light inside the white clouds left of the mountain but couldn't hear thunder, not yet. To the east, their right, was an endless field of canyons and overlapping valleys in running formations, with red cliffs mounting in steps above each other and shadows at their bottoms.

The deepest canyon of all lay at their feet. Across it, the far wall swelled in the sun, red as blood. Toab saw them first: the cliff had been undercut by a deep alcove, and inside its shade were numerous houses, square piles of stone with square windows in their walls. From above they looked small and blended into the rock so were hard to make out. All at once the western clouds caught up with the sun. The cliff above the houses receded in the shade and the village of dwellings became more visible.

Toab stared. The Newe had always broken Navajo taboos without suffering any consequences, he thought. Those ancient cliff dwellings built by the Mookweech—some still stood at home—were taboo to the Navajo, who, fearing ghosts, never went near them. Toab checked with Onchok, who thought they'd be safe there. They scouted a route into the canyon before the storms came.

They picked their way down along sandy shelves and ledges. Great domes of sandstone swung into the canyon. Buffaloberry and mountain mahogany grew between boulders, and the rocks gave off heat, but the sky darkened and behind them in the west the thunder grew louder—bears mating in their dens.

On the canyon floor they turned into a forest of Douglas fir and aspen and found a faint trail. Hot air left over from the cloudless day rose toward the sky, and turkey vultures rode on its rising columns, swinging into the cliff and missing it by inches. The scrub oak was thick, and springs crossed the trail, oozing out of canyon walls. Toab saw poison ivy and turned and warned the others. Then, to their rehearsed amazement, he took a few leaves and rubbed them on his arms—they all knew he was immune. His power made him bullet-, lightning-, and fireproof, and poison ivy's fondness for blistering skin had no effect on him.

They rounded a spur of the canyon wall and saw the enormous arching overhang right above their heads. A row of stone houses rose inside the alcove from buttresses of rock, pink and brown in the shade. Wooden poles ran along the roof lines. Steps had been cut in the leaning cliffs below, and Toab hobbled the burro and they climbed into the alcove using fingers and toes. Standing in the dirt next to the dwellings, amid potshards and grinding stones, they watched the rain just beginning across the canyon. Lightning in the sky lit their darkened alcove.

Old poles lay around. With scraps of shredded bark Onchok started a fire and arranged the poles in radiating spokes meeting in a hub of flames. As they burned, the poles would be pushed into the fire. Kwits and Soxor ran from roof to roof and climbed broken walls of houses and squeezed through their windows. Kwits hurried back with something in his hands to give his mother: a human skull whose forehead had been bashed. She held it, stared into its empty sockets, then threw it as far as she could into the canyon.

Toab had collected some spiky fendlerbush twigs on their descent into the canyon, and with the green wood he laced up the bellies of his prairie dogs. He singed off their yellowish fur in the fire and placed them in the coals where they smoked and sizzled.

The heavy downpour began but they stayed dry beneath the overhang. Horsetails of rain swerved in solid air, and brown ropes of water hung down the canyon from the opposite rim. Canyons magnified the thunder, and as the afternoon darkened the strikes of lightning grew blinding, even next to their fire, making it seem like a spark in empty space.

They peeled the skins and ate the prairie dogs with pine nuts and agave. An owl hooted. Coyotes howled. The sound of water was everywhere. And when the rain stopped the flowing water persisted, coursing down the canyon walls and gouging channels through its floor.

The sky lightened overhead just before nightfall. Toab and Mara crawled through the low door of one of the houses and slept in the warmth of the plastered walls, with soot smudges on the ceiling five hundred years old and still smelling of smoke. Zigzagging lines and giant serpents had been painted along the base of the walls, and mazes above them. Toab knew there was power in this old place, and when he slept he had prophetic dreams. He saw a horde of babies screaming and sobbing, crawling toward him on their bellies to be comforted and held. Their noses and mouths poured out poison foam. He shouted, Blood! and the foam turned to blood. Wide-shouldered beings stood above the babies.

Mara shook his shoulder. He sat up, rubbed his eyes, and saw nothing in the darkness.

You shouted, she said.

He felt closed in by the four walls and ceiling. Far from home, inside darkness. She said, Come here. He couldn't see her.

They fumbled blindly, spinning each other, groping for limbs.

Let's do it like this.

No, like this.

The next morning Onchok found some good mahogany right inside the overhang, and the others waited while he carved digging sticks. They climbed out of the alcove and followed the trail through the canyon to a clearing where more canyons met. Mara and Pooeechuts led the way now, since they were entering their homeland. They found the largest canyon and hiked along its wide bottom, muddy in places from last night's rain.

6

Soxor sat inside their brush arbor weaving a seed beater. Children climbed nearby trees or fought around the spring, using sticks to throw mudballs. They wouldn't throw mud at her, she thought. Her blood would come soon, Pooeechuts had told her, then she'd no longer be a child. She'd be a woman any day and pictured the blood descending from the moon, entering her neck, and sinking through her body until it pooled between her hips and flowed out into the sand and no one could touch her.

This place was different too. It was hotter here and even older children didn't bother with breechclouts, just went naked all the time. Yesterday, Kwits had swung on a yucca rope hanging from a tree and been scolded by a woman. That rope was not for children, she said. It was for women to hang on to when giving birth.

They'd never had that at home, a rope for giving birth. Everything was different here. These were her mother's people, but they were unlike her mother and they didn't know that toothaches were caused by certain worms or that the number of warts on Soxor's hands predicted the number of children she would bear. In their arbors these people hung boughs of pine needles, not branches of sage, and they didn't put paint on a child's head as a charm. They thought that was crazy.

At home the land looked good; here it was strange. Up around Paiute Mountain everything was a chaos of red and yellow rocks.

Rock flattened in plains and rolled into hills with running cracks and overlapping plates that sounded loose and hollow when walked across. Greasewood and sage dotted runnels and folds in the red rock splashed with gray and black lichen. At least inside this canyon the people planted gardens. That was something the same. The spring kept their soil moist, and they'd dug a channel from its source below a cliff to their fields of corn, squash, and melon.

The children were running footraces now, that was the same too. They screamed and placed bets with pieces of bark and ran between a pair of trees. The canyon here was wide, the broken cliffs low, the bottom slung in a broad, sandy curve. Amid bunchgrass and saltweed Soxor spotted her mother and Mara and their relatives examining the corn. It was easy to recognize Pooeechuts down there. Her whole posture had changed: her body tilted, her shoulder slumped, her arm helpless at her side.

Soxor sat cross-legged beside her sleeping father and wove the seed beater. At home the huge canyons were obstacles to travel, but here all the obstacles were set on the plateaus. Here the land fought itself and prevented passage, with its walls and cliffs and knobby spires and domes. Soxor had been told she'd better start running. Her blood was coming soon, and when it did she'd have to run east every morning to gather wood from far away. But you couldn't run east here—the land was carved north and south. So for practice she ran through this canyon, which at least was flat and sandy in the middle.

The running felt good. The canyon continued all the way to the river, but she didn't go that far. She gathered wood and walked back to her family's camp, past the People from the Other Side, who watched from their arbors. They shouted, Run! You have to run back, too!

If your blood came, you ran. They did that the same way.

Above the far canyon wall Paiute Mountain rose, thick with trees and ravines. Ledges of sandstone protruded from its slopes and sheepskin clouds hung behind it. These people had sheep, or some of them did. That was something else different. Pangwits, her mother's brother, was said to be wealthy because he had a lot of sheep.

Down by the spring a badger followed Kwits around. In the sand beside some willows the boy walked zigzags and the badger followed.

Soxor wove her seed beater. She'd cut the willow rods to the right length beforehand. Now she turned the frame over and began a second row, and with each stitch added more warps. She patiently held the warps in place with her bottom fingers while threading the twine stripped from yucca leaves and tying it off with forefingers and thumbs.

The weaving calmed her. She wasn't as homesick. Your mother taught you how, then you taught your own children, and they taught theirs, and things would always be the same.

Her father groaned beside her, waking up. I'm hungry, he said. She put aside the seed beater and ran down to the gardens. Mara and her mother gave her a melon.

She walked back among children hopping like toads, playing games.

I'm starving in this place, her father said when she entered the arbor. My knees hurt, he said.

She sliced the melon for him. He tossed pieces into his mouth.

They laughed at our burro, he said.

I know, she answered, recalling their arrival. After entering this canyon ragged and tired, after Pooeechuts and Mara found their brother Pangwits and the people shrieked and cried, after things had settled down, someone remarked that they must have taken turns carrying that burro. Everyone laughed, including Soxor. Laughing was something you did with other people whether you actually meant to or not.

Pangwits was a large man. He appeared slow-eyed, lazy, fat, and careless but was always doing something. He liked to joke around and say shocking things. He looked at their burro and asked, Who deflowered him? He'd been to Shivwits country, Soxor's mother had told her. Before Soxor was born, when Pooeechuts crossed the river with her father to trade and found herself a husband, Pangwits had come and had met Onchok. This time when they met, Pangwits said: Well, Onchok, I am old and ugly now, but I'm sorry to see that you look even worse.

Onchok just laughed.

Soxor had learned something about these People from the Other Side. They called her family's band by the same name. To each side, the others were the People from the Other Side.

Pangwits turned out to be a prophet too. The smallest tribe of people would drive the largest one back from where they came, he said. In the future everyone would be branded or marked. He'd visited the underground country, he said, and everything was backward there. People hunted at night and slept in the day and copulated in full view. When he picked up some meat the people called out, Don't eat it, it's excrement. But he ate it anyway and found it tasted good. Yet when he defecated the underground people thought his excrement was meat. They picked it up and ate it.

When people heard these things, Pooeechuts told Soxor, they felt frightened inside.

Soxor wished he'd prophesy that they'd find Chookwadum. They hadn't yet asked about the Navajo Hashkay. First came hospitality, renewing old acquaintances, making new ones, harvesting seeds, hunting rabbits, holding feasts and dances—then they could ask.

I'm weak, I'm starving, said Onchok to his daughter. Has somebody witched me?

The melon was gone, so Soxor gave him a seedcake. He devoured it like an animal.

Come here, my baby. My firstborn, my baby. You were always my baby.

She sat down beside him. She let his head rest on her shoulder.

I'm old, I'm good for nothing.

She stroked his long hair.

I should never have let that Mormoni man take you children.

Pretty soon he fell asleep again. With care she cradled his head and lowered it to his parfleche. She picked up her weaving. If her father and mother both remained sick, she'd have to take care of them. She'd have to be a woman. Her blood could have come when she ran to get the melon—she thought she felt different. She looked at her father—he slept, eyes closed—then reached beneath her dress and examined herself.

Nothing.

When it came she wouldn't be allowed to touch herself. She'd be given a scratching stick. Her eyebrows would be plucked and her hair cut and dressed by Mara, her own special attendant.

If it came and she failed to tell someone, her elbows would turn black.

That afternoon every woman in the village went out to beat seeds. With their baskets and seed beaters, they traveled up the canyon to where it widened to a valley. Though Pooeechuts couldn't work, she went anyway, walking lopsided like a poorly made basket. Amid yellow sunbursts of ricegrass, Soxor fanned her beater right and left in long arcs and the seeds flew everywhere. Mara showed her how to keep the arc tight and with short sweeps and scoops direct the seeds into the basket. You did it with your forearm, not the whole arm. When the basket in her left hand had become nearly full, Soxor dumped the seeds in the burden basket resting on the ground.

The showers of seeds sounded like rain and the women sang, then talked about their husbands. Someone's husband was a good hunter but always hunted at night and ended up in other people's beds. Another was so lazy he leaned against a rock to bark his orders to the women. Waking him up was like trying to rouse a bear.

The seeds filled the smaller baskets then the burden baskets as though cascading pool to pool. The walk back was slow; the women were carrying rivers of seeds. The air was hot and still in the afternoon sun and Soxor poured sweat and her skin grew wet and clammy. The basket on her back became heavier as she walked. In her lashes, beads of water blurred the green and red land, the blue and white sky.

Back at the village the women cleaned ashes from the fire pits and started the fires and gossiped some more. They gathered piles of greasewood. They sprinkled cold ashes over seeds in large trays and tossed them in the air to winnow the chaff, which migrated to the edge and fanned out in the wind.

Mara advised her niece as she winnowed. When the chaff was mostly gone Soxor tossed the seeds higher and blew off the ashes, shaking seeds as they landed. Around the clean seeds ashes formed a semicircle which she brushed out with her fingers. Then Mara fetched a smaller tray.

Tired after hiking through the canyon, Pooeechuts lay now beside her husband in the arbor. Soxor watched her mother; she was doing this for her, acting in her place. She raked hot coals into the smaller tray, then gripped it with both hands and Mara poured the seeds on. Soxor tossed and rolled the tray, keeping coals and seeds moving without burning the basket, and Mara smiled and nodded.

As the seeds roasted, suspended in air, some swelled and burst until the coals slowly cooled. Soxor pivoted her wrists, sending cooked seeds to one side of the tray, dying coals to the other. She brushed out the coals and had a tray of roasted seeds.

When enough seeds were winnowed and parched and ready, she and Mara took turns grinding. Mara sat behind the slab, singing as she ground:

> *The wattle on my nose*
> *I am shaking up and down.*
> *What is it, what is it?*

She ground the seeds to fine powder. Then Soxor tried it. She sat with knees up, heels beside her hips, the bottom stone before her. Mara fed her the seeds and Soxor did it in motion, moving back and forth too fast at first. Mara said slow down. No, Soxor said, she liked doing it fast. She was sweating in the heat, hair in her eyes, and she rocked back and forth, gripping the stone and doing it fast, and still her blood wouldn't come.

They made a mush of the meal by mixing it with warm water and called everyone over. People scooped it from a pot and nodded their approval. Nobody hunkered over his food and glared at the others. They didn't do it that way.

Part Five

1

Wes thought they were floating back in time, eon by eon, through land unlike anything they'd yet seen. A thousand years was nothing in this place. You could see time itself sliced open and revealed like a mass of scar tissue.

No rapids. Calm. Flatwater forever, the river looping dreamily. Low red mounds ran beside the river, with isolated buttes, cliffs, and spires beyond them. They were grotesque monuments, some long, some blunt, all red as flames in the merciless sun. Like ships those stark formations glided slowly backward as their boats passed.

Their next landmark would be the San Raphael River approaching from the west, but that could be anywhere, around a bend or fifty miles downstream. Cakes of sand collapsed from high banks into the river. "Turkey vultures," said Jack Sumner.

Wes looked up and saw the feathered carp. Black floating garbage birds.

Here, the river swung in long pointless curves collapsing in sections generally southward.

Wes's eyes grew heavy watching Bill Dunn row. Some days this happened; the heat, the lack of sleep, the recurrent anxiety, all forged a fatigue heavy as chain mail. He'd foreseen this landscape as though in a dream, having read Darwin—envisioned a place so unpeopled and harsh that time couldn't unspool, so it piled up then washed away then piled up again, grain by grain, inch by inch. Now he pictured rivers cutting into the red land like liquid buzz saws. Land so old it began a thousand times across millions of centuries. It aged by growing backward, grew through deprivation. It built itself up out of what wore away, so became a land that wasn't there anymore—instead, its past was. Plateaus shrank to mesas when undermined cliffs fell away like riverbanks. Mesas in turn eroded into buttes then towers then fingers then mounds ground into sand dunes surrounded by more plateaus and mesas just beginning the cycle.

Plateaus, mesas, buttes. Gristmills for dreamscapes.

And water was the key. In this place with little water, water was the answer to the shapes the land assumed. If only Emma were here, he could sit her down and tell her how this world had evolved, how the land took on its features. She so loved being explained to. Talk and explanation had been their refuge ever since they'd first courted—against the wishes of their families. For they were cousins. Or almost so. Wes's mother and Emma's father were half sister and brother, and, the story went, had lost contact with each other after emigrating from England. They'd planned to cross on the same ship, but Joseph Dean had been late and it sailed without him, and for twenty-five years neither brother nor sister knew where the other was. Emma and Wes were full-grown adults by the time her father and his mother found each other. On his first visit to Detroit to meet his long-lost uncle and cousins, Wes had sensed, facing Emma, that *he* was the one being reunited with a missing sister. They agreed later on that each felt in retrospect like two halves of a whole. They thought alike, talked alike, finished each other's sentences. And once they'd grown fond of one another's company, separation made them feel incomplete.

The war came, and Wes enlisted. Seven months later he requested a furlough and traveled to Detroit and married his cousin. After he lost his arm at Shiloh, she nursed him in the hospital, helped him learn to write with his left hand. He could have been mustered out a hero, but Grant asked him to stay on. He agreed on condition that his wife of one year could be with him at the front, and Grant consented.

A year later, at the siege of Vicksburg, when the Blues commandeered farmhouses for their officers, Wes and Emma lived in one together. There, they collected rocks and fossils and studied the very land formations being sapped per his orders by his troops. Mornings he would stroll into the kitchen, bully and confident despite his missing arm. Emma made them coffee. Spring had already assaulted the mudflats created by war, mosquitoes were breeding in artillery craters, and in the warped light passing through the thick windows Wes explained his earthworks to Emma, describing the hills, ravines, and valleys, and how an entrenched meander of the Mississippi River had nearly isolated the town, like — like the buttes sliding past their boats right now on the Green River.

Her face would light up. She'd nod and pour them coffee and ask a few questions or request that he repeat the part about the meander. And when he repeated it, he'd understand it even more clearly. He'd see the bluffs on which the town sat, and the river below them, and the alluvial plain on the opposite bank. He would not grab her waist and waltz her around the oilclothed table, however; they would simply hold hands, his one in both of hers.

If she could be with him now! He'd lowered his head to his single arm, bone tired from the sun. The ticktock rhythm of Dunn's rowing calmed him. His spine slowly sank, his shoulders dissolved. Falling asleep, he saw dust devils flex and twist in the heat — ghosts tortured by the passage into matter. He saw puddles like disks fly across playa and beds of oil shale burning in caves, their blue light making craters in the night. Wes found himself floating through a land of solid ghosts: rocks caught in midboil, mountains shriveled by erosion. Deep in his mind, far back in time, mountains rose and basins sank. Swamps became deserts, deserts vast lakes, lakes enormous glaciers, glaciers inland seas. In the mudflats of a freshwater sea, avocets and sandpipers gleaned worms and slugs and beetles, and birds of rainbow color stood on stick legs. Above them, on moraines, giant ground sloths heaved themselves onto trees whose bark they raked off with pickax claws. A saber-toothed tiger pursued a grunting tapir and dragged him down by the snout, and — what happened next?

Wes felt this dream was under his control, so he could see what he wanted. And the colors were glorious! A part of his mind still heard the dull groan and repeated splash of Bill Dunn's oars. Another part was describing this to Emma, showing her the world as it once was. With a slow liquid lurch the tiger ate the tapir's face, and the world filled with red. He covered the carcass with leaves, twigs, and dirt to eat the rest later, but later never came. Instead, the earth rolled and shook. Boulders plunged down and the inland sea shrank. Mountains collapsed, their long languid jaws fallen open like bellows, and the land squeezed out from underneath itself, buckling and folding. The whole country pitched and careened toward the south.

He wasn't explaining to Emma anymore; she could see for herself. See a fault pull apart in the bowels of time, creating a depression larger than Italy: the Gulf of California. It acted as a siphon. Rivers left over from the freshwater sea began to splice together. Looping through deserts, braiding and unbraiding, changing courses on a whim—now they could drain. Now with a future toward which to burrow, one meandering river converged, dragging all its feeders. Its course became entrenched, converted to curves and gooseneck bends, and in its wake the unzipped earth poured out its colors. The plateau turned red as more sandstone was exposed, then green, yellow, white, but most of all red. And the river in the rock poured through his dream—

Wes snapped awake. Their boat had run aground. Watching him, Bill Dunn scowled. Beneath a merciless sun, Bill and Jack Sumner had to climb out and push the *Emma Dean* off a sandbar. Wes knew why Bill was scowling: their leader and pilot, unable to row, at least could warn of sandbars.

It had been right there. He'd been on the verge of learning the secret, learning it with Emma—how rivers sliced through mountains. It lay across a cleavage in his mind, and now, wide awake, he'd lost it.

Sluggish, he resumed scouting the river. The air was hot and dry and the sun a glowing drill. Clouds to the west looked oddly green on the horizon. Here, the river was wide and slow and shallow, and every bend held another hidden sandbar.

They passed some mudflats bordered with willows. Bill shot a beaver he dragged into the boat, where it bled and dried up and smelled as bad as Bill.

At last they came to the San Raphael River, twenty feet wide and six inches deep. Something in the soil had colored it white, and Hawkins said better not drink it. They landed and climbed the steep sandy bank and found evidence of Indians: wickiup poles and corn shucks and yucca sandals and arrowheads and flint chips in abundance. The men collected the arrowheads. Bill asked, "How come they left these here?"

"Discards," said Jack Sumner.

Wes resumed his authority. "Jack's right," he announced. "Put yourself in their place. You chip away, chip away. Then it chips wrong and you toss it in the pile."

"You could say they was perfectionists."

"So these here are worthless?"

"They have value as specimens," said Wes.

"Specimens of what?"

He'd filled his empty sleeve with arrowheads, then pinned it up.

"Of a passing world."

All except Hawkins, who stayed behind to cook, took a hike west toward sandstone pinnacles. The land was wholly naked: not a green thing in sight. All was rock and sand and the heat rose in italics. On the Green River the breeze skimmed the water's coolness and made the heat more or less bearable, but not here on bare rock. Here, thought Wes, reflected sunlight baked your brains.

Gullies and runnels containing rivers of red sand ran through the plated rock, which cracked as they crossed it. They were forced to avert their eyes from the sun sliding down the sky, and cheat north. Their legs hardly wanted to move, it seemed. Wes and his brother headed for a ridge of upended rock and found a treasury of fossils: ammonites, hamites, crinoids, and others.

From the relative eminence of this broken ridge, Wes looked around. Erosion caught frozen in the act, he thought. Words rinsed through his mind from a half-remembered poem: "We are columns left alone / Of a temple once complete." There were mountains in the distance, green and silver peaks. Beyond his men to the south, long shadows spilled across shipwrecks of rock and plunged into cavities.

All at once the light caved in and he thought the sun had set, though minutes ago it seemed several hours from setting. They turned back toward the river, growing smaller by the minute. Lost ants, he thought. Wes kept looking back to where the sun had disappeared, to great glowing clouds massed on the horizon rising over the mountains. Lightning lit up the thickest of the clouds and he stopped to watch the show. It was easy to imagine ancient volcanoes spewing out ash and showers of sparks and plumes of future rock.

In fact the sun hadn't set, just dropped behind the clouds. Then it found a gap between clouds and mountains and cast a flat cone across the red land. Wes turned back east and saw the sun had lit not just buttes and pinnacles, which flared up like bonfires, but odd half volumes and remnants and fragments that hadn't been there before. Gables, necks, escarpments, ragged ledges, tops of alcoves—all dragged from the shadows.

The fire went out again. A heavy blue light thick as ink fell around him. Laminae of sand slid over rock producing strange whispers, and sand in the wind needled Wes's eyes. By now his nostrils had grown so raw and dry that inhaling air felt like breathing matches.

Back at camp Hawkins shouted "Grub pile!" and washed the Major's hand. The men with bailing cups got to eat first; it seemed to be a soup. Andy Hall wondered out loud how many more campfires between here and the horizon dotted this land. Jack Sumner wagered none.

"What about them arrowheads?"

"Old. They use metal points now."

"They got rifles now. That's what they use."

"So this here camp—"

"Ain't been used since you were born."

"Since General Washington crushed the king."

Jack Sumner nodded. "Wonderful that such things as corn shucks and arrowheads should last longer than the history of a nation."

"What's this pottage?" Bill Dunn asked.

"Beavertail soup."

"Three cheers for the cook!" shouted Andy.

"You call this cooking?" Walter Powell barked. Wes looked at his brother. He was in a black mood, anyone could sense it. "Hawkins's cooking," Walter declared, "ain't fit for a skunk."

"It *is* skunk," said Bill. "Make your dick curl."

"No, you're the skunk for saying it."

Bill cocked his head. "For telling the truth?"

"You smell like one too."

"Have done with it," said Wes. "Walter, you're a flower, and Bill, you're a skunk. You're a pretty angel, and you're a dirty devil. It's a big enough world."

"Small enough crew."

"What did you call me?" asked Bill Dunn.

144

"Major Powell, sir, it ain't Bill's fault." They all looked at Seneca. "He didn't cook this poison."

Andy Hall said, "It's beavertail soup! A delicacy!"

Hawkins watched the others jaw about his food. Early in the trip he'd confided his general policy to Wes: don't respond to opprobrium, smile when men abuse your cooking. Now he positively grinned.

Walter stormed off to brood on a rock. Bill asked Wes again, "What did you call me?"

"Calm down, Bill."

"Am I a dirty devil?"

"You just need to take a bath."

"You got no call."

"Can't you see what I was doing? My brother is sometimes like a caged animal. He was damaged by the war."

"So was the rest of us. What's his excuse?"

"Give him some leeway. That's all I ask."

"You mean turn the other cheek?"

"If that's what you want to call it."

"Not interested." Bill's face looked red, almost lurid in the firelight. "If I turned the other cheek you'd just slap it yourself. Blood's thicker than water."

"Then don't turn the other cheek. What do I care? Just obey orders."

"You mean I haven't done that?"

"I mean my only interest is in maintaining order. We have a long way to go. We must learn to get along."

"I get along fine."

"We're all in this together."

"Whoever treats me white, I'm good to that person. That's how I am."

"Fine. Let's be done with it."

"Give me an order then."

"In due time."

"No, go ahead, give me an order. See if I obey it."

"Bill, you're a trooper. Let's wind this up."

"Go ahead. Just one order. Order me to take a bath."

"All right, then. Take a bath."

Without a word Bill spun on his heels, clambered over flint chips down the sandbank in the dark, and plunged into the river fully clothed. The men whooped and cheered. He came back soaking wet, boots and breeches coated with sand from climbing the bank. He picked up a biscuit and his bailing cup and finished the soup.

2

The next day the river entered a new canyon. Gradually they descended, the red walls grew higher, the water ran faster but stayed smooth and flat. They decided to lash the three boats together as long as the river remained free of rapids. That way only two men need row, each with one oar, in the outside boats.

"Maybe we seen the last of the rapids," George Bradley offered.

"I've heard that one before."

"Ora," asked George, "how much fall we got left?"

Ora dug out his calculations and thumbed through scraps of paper. "Let's see," he said, fishing pockets for his pencil. The *Emma Dean*, with Major Powell, Sumner, and Dunn, was outside on the left—the river's east side. Bill Dunn manned an oar. They'd lashed another oar across the starboard gunnel and tied the *Sister* to that, with Walter, George, and Seneca in it. Same with the *Maid*—they'd lashed it with an oar to the starboard of the *Sister*. In the *Maid's* bow, Ora scribbled columns of figures. "From the railway bridge to Black's Fork, a hundred and thirty-five feet."

"Christ almighty," Andy Hall said. Behind Ora in the *Maid*, he manned the other oar. "You going to go through the whole fucking journey?"

Hawkins, sprawled in the stern of the *Maid*, was smiling. "That's all right, Ora. Forget we asked the question."

"To Flaming Gorge, two hundred and sixty-two feet."

"Is that including the first figure or in addition to?"

"Well. You see, I'm adding it up."

"You haven't done it till now?"

"It's just a matter of footing up the figures. To the end of Red Canyon, four hundred feet, which makes six sixty-two."

"Will someone shut him off?"

Ora plugged on, oblivious. He made their entire fall in elevation from the starting point as two thousand and some odd feet. It was known to the men that the Colorado River met Callville, Nevada, at the Great Canyon's end—and the end of their voyage—at five hundred feet above sea level. In round numbers. More or less. Wes had obtained a rough map in Washington, drawn by Mormon pioneers, which offered that figure. And they weren't far from the Colorado River now—just fifty or a hundred miles ahead by Ora's reckoning. But they still had, before the expedition's end, three thousand feet to fall.

"Say again," said George.

"Three thousand feet to fall."

"We ain't even fallen half?"

"I could double-check."

Even their silence was no encouragement to that. At last George remarked, "Let's get this ride over with."

Jack Sumner considered it his duty to help. "Could be it's distributed in rapids and short falls."

"As opposed to a waterfall half a mile high?"

"You will find no waterfalls on this journey," said Wes. "None to speak of."

"Why is that? Professor." Jack sucked his teeth.

"Nature of erosion approaching base level. Waterfalls occur in the side canyons, not the main channel. The river itself fills as it scours. This is a land constantly eroding, with little vegetation to hold it in place. So the river carries tons of debris with it as it runs. Any waterfall would soon silt up and form a slope."

"Comforting words."

"Besides, it's not the fall that makes the rapids. It's the nature of the rock. Soft rock like this will not produce a lot of rapids. It's the hard rock you want to worry about. In hard rock canyons like Lodore, obstructions in the water, debris from side canyons, haven't found their level yet. They've not been worn down. That's the cause of your rapids. That, plus the fall." He glanced up at the deep red monolithic cliffs lifting from eroded terraces of sandstone.

"Will we get wet, teacher?" Andy Hall asked.

"There's bound to be dunkings."

"I melt if I'm too wet," said Bill Dunn. "Leave me in a pothole."

"You'll just dry up."

"Not me. I'm a sponge cake."

"You'll dry up like a frog lost in the desert," said Oramel. He'd surfaced from his figures.

"Nothing left but the smell," said Jack Sumner. "A glutinous puff, a gust of oily fumes. There goes Bill rising back into the sun."

The three boats lashed together ran aground on sunken sand and Bill had to step out and push them off. It was difficult for their unwieldy assembly to stay in the main channel, which crossed from rim to rim as the canyon swept in curves. The second time they ran aground Bill shouted "Shitfire!" and couldn't manage to push them off by himself. Jack and Walter had to help. After that they decided to unlash the oars and drift apart, allowing each craft to find its own way. Rowing was hardly a chore regardless. Once they caught the main current they moved along nicely, and Wes helped by alerting the rowers to it. He saw how the river slid inside itself. Inside the river was another river that did all the flowing, and with his arm he pointed it out. The rest of the flow hung behind in sluggish eddies, trailing in pools and scraps of shallow water.

Great blocks of sandstone fallen from cliffs lay on the banks. The red water mirrored red rock, Wes saw, because just as the rock held the river in its course, so the river contained the rock inside itself, as sediment and sand. The rock began as mud, and to mud it was returning.

The river slowed and coiled back on itself. At one place it swung back in two great bow-knot loops, taking, by Wes's and Ora's estimates, nine miles just to gain one half.

3

Wes spotted a tower evidently built by humans, not erosion, atop a galleon butte, and he told the men to land. They crossed a dry shelf of cracked plates flecked with greasewood, Mormon tea, and prickly pear. The high collar of this butte was conglomerate—gravel embedded in finer sandstone—and they climbed a faint trail leading up.

On the butte's flat top, the size of a playing field, the tower turned out to be two connecting towers, both of unmortared stone. Their broken ceilings were open to the sky, and judging from the stones strewn about their base had been lowered by the centuries.

"Who built this thing, Major?"

"An ancient race of people."

"Redskins?"

"Prince Madoc and his Welshmen," said Jack Sumner.

"That idea's hogwash."

"Could be ancestors of the Moqui in Oraibi," said Wes. "It's likely this tower at one time was part of a comprehensive network. You have an unobstructed view. A string of such watchtowers could unite a scattered people. Warn them enemies are coming."

"Didn't work. Here we are."

"How old is it?" asked Andy.

"Here we go again."

"I can ask, can't I?"

"Hard to tell," said Major Powell. "It may have lasted centuries. Could be older than Christ. Things endure in this landscape. No vines to grow around it, no roots to undermine it. No earthquakes. No floods would reach this height."

"Godforsaken spot just the same," said Jack.

They walked the butte's rim. Cliffs, terraces, benches, plateaus ascending the scale from brown to red to greenish gray, conspired to hide the river upstream. Its brown course showed below, though—it wrapped around their butte. Rock shelves appeared to plow across the river, and a yellow canyon at its bend swung to the west through tilted benches to a bandshell of rock.

Back in the boats they meandered with the river and passed other stone buildings squatting on ledges. They camped on a sandbank across from a tower perched inside an alcove high on a cliff with no apparent way to climb into its niche. Rockfalls close by suggested other structures could have been there once.

The sun dipped behind the canyon's western rim, but upstream the walls still burst into yellow-red flame. Then the light collapsed and a wind came down the canyon pulling color from its walls and piling folds of angry water against the river's current. "Mohammed don't go to no rapids," said Jack. "The rapids come to him."

The water calmed. The river mirrored the sky's remaining light, but broken and scattered pools of shadow—blots of shifting darkness—floated downstream.

Frogs and crickets sang all night.

Wes heard splashes in the morning and spotted a heron on the far bank diving for plunder.

When they launched again he felt the alien wonder of water in a desert. Their river was a ghost. A gargantuan butte looking like a fallen cross turned into two buttes as they floated past, but he'd already named it the Butte of the Cross, and that's what it became; two became one.

Shaped like a dart, another heron flew low, proceeding upriver a few feet above their heads.

Some walls beside them resembled mouths of pitchers, dipping to lips eroded by water, which surely poured over during times of heavy rain. Behind one Wes glimpsed a basin with a pool that mirrored the whirling wall behind it.

They floated through hatches of millions of gnats, and couldn't help but breathe them in.

The cliffs grew higher, to thirteen hundred feet. The river angled down, still perfectly flat, and became a slanted plane. This could have been the effect of the rock beside the river, of new strata sloping up— they'd seen such cliffs before.

No, it was a flume, a slide—the river plunging. They were picking up speed, though the water was smooth. Then the river slowed and they came around a bend and there it was, splitting the high earth in two: the Grand River met the Green and formed the Colorado. The sight was dramatic but hardly celestial, yet Wes's heart soared. No one had ever seen this place before, at least no white man. Walter shouted "Hurrah!" and Wes did something odd: he stood in the boat and all but embraced the confluence before him, with one arm and a stump. The Grand had appeared unannounced, it seemed, slipping in between walls of rock. And it was the mother river, that was clear to Wes. It was larger and coffee-colored and accepted the Green into its body, making, as it swung south, one reddish-brown muscle cleaving rock through unknown country.

He felt their depth in earth. All around were high cliffs, and up there was the world most people walked upon. The Grand River started four hundred miles away, high in Colorado near Long's Peak. He'd stood at its headwaters just last year with Emma; now he drifted toward its mouth. No one said a thing.

They rowed up the Grand and camped on its left side, on a sandbank backed up against a cliff. Hackberry trees provided sparse shade. Jack Sumner took the temperature of the Grand—six degrees colder than the Green. They measured the width of each river at the junction, and that night Wes unpacked the sextant and found their latitude to be 38°12′ and their longitude 109°54′. But those figures would have to be double- and triple- and quadruple-checked on this layover, he announced.

4

The sun had dropped behind the rim. On a rock a collared lizard pumped up and down, burning fat stored in its tail. A tree lizard jumped from a hackberry tree onto the sand, and nearby a pepsis wasp carrying a trap-door spider raced past like an old crone hauling a sack. The wasp scuttled over centuries of sand with the octopal spider dragging underneath her. She found her hole beside a piece of driftwood, stuffed the spider in, and deposited a single white egg on its belly. Then she crawled out and, jerking back and forth, kicked enough sand to fill the hole's entrance and flew off.

The larva would have hatched five days later and fed on the spider had not a whiptail lizard dug it out right away and swallowed everything at once, spider and egg. The meal filled him with pleasure. He ran off upright on powerful hind legs, swiveling his head madly left and right, casting out his tongue and snapping it back, fishing for more smells.

With the sun gone, crickets and frogs emerged from rocks and mud and began their evening racket. Near the base of the cliff above the Grand River, a giant desert centipede broke into a nest and ate the baby mice inside. A walnut-sized bat with ashen gray body and black ears and paws descended from the cliff in slow erratic loops amid a spiral of gnats, mouth wide open. Other bats, these pallid and larger and more numerous, flew low across the confluence. They broadcast a high electric buzz audible to humans, thus startling the men standing in the shallows, who'd been panning for gold.

Pallid bats smell like skunks. Bill Dunn swung at one. He saw them as sudden, fitful, and bodyless, motes in his eye, while they saw him as a mere obstacle. It took a spray of echoes to make the world solid, to knit a mesh around Bill, to dodge his swinging hand.

"You won't hit them things, Bill."

"They smell like dirty devils."

"They woke me up last night. Felt a wing brush my head."

"Must be a cave nearby."

Major Powell was gone, climbing cliffs with his brother. Hawkins and Andy had cleaned up after supper and made the gold pans available for anyone who'd grown restless. George was camped alone farther up the shore and Jack Sumner had built a small fire inside a shelter to repair the barometers. Seneca sat on an upended boat watching his brother and Bill pan for gold. "Any color?" he asked.

Bill looked up. "I got a number of colors."

"You could pan a hundred years and get yourself a stickpin."

Oramel said, "It runs all the way from several dollars to a few cents a yard. In places."

"Fine as dust," said Bill. "Son of a bitch to save."

"What'd you expect? There's no mountains nearby."

"Plenty of excavated earth. This is one jumbo quarry we're at the bottom of."

"Fat lot of good as far as that goes. Have you seen a hint of quartz since we launched on this voyage?"

"Useless piece of country."

"Why quartz?" asked Seneca.

"Where's your brother been?" Bill looked at Ora. They were wading back to shore, swatting at the bats. Bill actually struck one. It landed in the water, stunned, and floated off.

"Smell my hand," he said to Seneca.

"Christ! That's *worse* than skunk."

"Quartz is your sign of buried gold," said Ora. "It occurs in league with granite."

"Which there's granite ahead."

"Who says?"

"The Professor."

"Well, he's probably right. So what are we waiting for?"

"Let the fun commence."

They walked up to Jack, who'd built a little wickiup to keep out the sand while he worked on the barometers. He'd looped a wire around the glass tube's neck to hold it over a fire of dried willow twigs, and passed the tube across the flames, gently boiling the mercury. He slid another, thinner wire up and down inside the tube to encourage the bubbles. Beside him on a rock sat the cistern and leather bag, and beside that the brass case. "Busy?" said Ora.

"Busy as a one-armed paper hanger."

"We can help you with that."

"Don't touch a thing. Don't kick no sand neither." His brush shelter was snug and shaped like a pocket purse. The other three sat outside and watched him work. Daylight was declining but Jack's little fire lit up his red face.

"How long you been at this?" asked Bill.

"Long enough."

"It was a hundred four degrees out there before the sun set."

"I'm not surprised."

"When's the Major coming back?"

"When it suits him to come back."

"Did he take food?"

"None for him to take."

"Dried apples and such."

"His ideas nourish him." Jack held the tube up, seemingly satisfied. "No more bubbles." He poured more mercury from a flask into the tube and held it at a slant above the fire. He inserted the wire, moved it in and out, and soon the bubbles returned.

"Why don't you talk to him, Jack?" Ora asked.

"Talk about what?"

"About getting a move on."

"You ain't tongue-tied, are you?"

"He won't listen to me."

"What makes you think he listens to me?"

"I'll talk to him," said Bill.

"And what will you say?"

"Stop this dilly-dallying and stir your stumps pronto, you one-armed bag of pus."

"I'm sure that will do the trick."

"I'll say it nicely."

"And he'll say how come you wasted your time panning for gold when you could be out hunting?"

"Nothing to hunt! Bats and more bats."

"I saw some beaver lodges."

"Where?"

"Up the Green."

"Where?"

"A mile or two. Back at that canyon."

Bill looked at Jack then walked away, down to the boats. "Move your ass, Peach Fuzz!" Seneca ran down and they righted the *Maid* and dragged it into the river. The canyon walls had darkened but the river and sky held a little glow, enough to see by. They jumped into the boat and, hugging the shore, Bill rowed across the confluence and headed up the Green.

An hour later they returned with two fat beavers, shot through the head and bleeding in the boat. Bill was soaking wet; after killing them he'd jumped in to retrieve the bodies before they floated off. At least he'd cooled down—it was still over ninety degrees in the canyon. Wes and his brother had also returned, and as all stood around the fire—all but George Bradley—Hawkins looked over at Andy Hall and silently mouthed the words "Beavertail soup."

"Beavertail soup?" bellowed Walter Powell. "I *love* beavertail soup."

"We'll have some in the morning."

By now it was dark except for a wide strip of stars across the sky—nail holes in the universe.

In the middle of the night rain woke the men. They lay there half asleep thinking it would stop. Instead, it rained harder, and since they hadn't pitched the tents they were forced to unpack the wagon sheets in darkness and sleep underneath them, stewing in the heat.

Hawkins roused the crew at dawn. "Roll out! Plunder!" He washed the Major's hand and, as always, served him first. The others helped themselves. Hawkins's meaty soup was a success, all the more so since the morning was cool, relatively speaking. Their instruments said eighty-eight.

But the clouds had moved out and the sun struck the river before creeping to their sandbank. Wes and his brother had carried back pitch from trees on the canyon rim, so they put some in a pot to warm on the coals and prepared to recaulk the boats. Each boat, emptied, lay upended on the sand, and they spread the gear and food on wagon sheets to dry. George and Walter Powell worked on the *Sister*, Hawkins and Andy on the *Maid*, and Jack would have started on the *Emma Dean* except he had the other barometer to repair.

Wes, Bill Dunn, and the two Howland brothers inspected the food. What they found appalled Wes. The coffee and dried apples were fine, but the beans were sour and the bacon spotted with blue and green mold despite repeated boiling. They opened every sack of flour and found each a mess of green fermentation. "Hawkins should have told me," said Wes. They dumped all the flour on a wagon sheet and sorted through the pile, picking out the yellow-green crusts and lumps. They washed out the sacks and hung them on branches of hackberry trees to dry in the sun. That wouldn't take long. In the past few weeks, as their altitude had dropped—and the temperature risen —Wes had discovered he could wash in the river and find his hair and beard had dried by the time he made his way back to camp.

Everyone's skin was dry as paper. The sandy dust was everywhere. It got underneath toenails, causing them to loosen and flake off like rust on the joints of a stovepipe. Wes's thumbnail was cracked to the cuticle. All the men complained of sandpaper buttocks, cracked and swollen lips. Only eating and drinking gallons of water kept them greased enough to stave off mummification.

They worked on the beans. By scrutinizing each bean they managed to save about half a sack. They trimmed the bacon and boiled it once more and wrapped it in oilcloth.

As they sat in the sand waiting for the sacks to dry, Wes looked at the men. Oramel rested his arms on his knees and his head on his arms. Seneca dug in the sand with a stick. Every man had lost weight on this trip except Bill. Even bent over, Ora hardly cast a shadow. And all had grown beards except Seneca Howland, whose hollow cheeks flared. Bill was staring at Wes. So Wes looked at him, and Bill asked if he'd scouted the river ahead.

"Hardly any of it to speak of. Cliffs are too high. I've never seen such broken land. Rocks standing up, rocks lying down, everywhere rocks. I'll take another look today on the west side."

"So we won't be off today?"

"Nor tomorrow."

Seneca jumped in. "Why is that, Major?"

"You can see what we're up against. We have boats to caulk. Instruments to repair. Food to sort through."

"And you got your observations to make," said Bill.

"Yes, I do."

"How many is that?"

"What?"

"Observations."

"The latitude and longitude of this confluence hasn't been known to within a hundred miles before now. I intend to get it right. It will take a few days."

"Two? Three?"

"It depends on the clouds."

"And I suppose you also got your rocks to figure out."

"There's always that."

"There was talk you had concluded to stay here until the eclipse of the sun on August 7."

"That's nearly three weeks away. We shan't be here that long."

"Relieved to hear that. This here rate of travel is too pissin' slow for the food we got left."

"There's enough for two months."

"If nothing else happens."

"We shall have to rely on the hunters in that case."

"In this starving land? It's a wasteland of rock."

"But who knows what lies ahead?"

"I do," said Bill. "More of the same."

"So you're a prophet."

"More of the same only worse is my guess."

"Is there rapids ahead?" Seneca asked.

"Of course there's rapids ahead. There's bound to be rapids. If not around the next bend, surely soon enough. Ora, how far have we come on this voyage?"

Ora knew that one. "Five hundred and thirty-eight miles from Green River City."

"And by my estimate," said Wes, "we have that much to go. We've only begun the real work of exploration."

"If it's all falls and rapids, well hell," said Seneca.

"Well hell what?"

Seneca snapped his papery fingers. They sounded like raindrops plopping in the sand. "Just like that," he said.

"Just like that all right."

"What's that smell?" asked Wes. "Smells like skunk."

"Bat juice on my hand," said Bill.

"Ora, why don't you check on those sacks."

Ora stood, refreshed from his nap. He examined the canvas flour bags hanging in the sun. "Should have taken gutta-percha."

"A trip like this is full of should haves."

"Dry as bone," said Ora.

Wes walked down to the boats and found a mosquito net in their scattered equipment. Ora held a flour sack open and Wes placed the net across its mouth, pooching it down, and Bill shoveled flour into the net. Wes and Seneca raked it back and forth until just bits of smutty spoilage were left. They dumped it in the sand and shook out the net. Wes lay it back across the sack.

"We will have more rapids," he said. "We will have severe rapids. And to preserve our diminishing rations from spoiling we shall have to portage often. There's nothing else for it. And the hunters will have to redouble their efforts."

Ora shook the flour down. "Can't blame the hunters for your own failure to replenish our supplies at the Uinta Agency."

Wes looked at Ora. "You take command, then. You take the helm. You'll have to stay awake."

"How can you ignore the needs and wishes of your men?"

"I do not ignore them. Who tells you I ignore them? Are you their representative?"

"By God, they could use one."

"Ora, my friend." Wes's voice softened. He even raised a smile. "Ora, we're all in this together. I do not blame the hunters. I don't even blame those who sometimes nod off and fail to see my signals and wind up wrecking boats and shrinking our supplies before we've hardly gotten started."

"Well, I blame those whose signals never came."

Bill Dunn shoveled more flour into the net. "Hellfire, if there's blame to spread around, I blame this wasted country."

"That's enough from dirty devils."

Seneca's face was just inches from Wes's. "Don't call him that. He was burying the hatchet."

"I'll call him what I please."

"I got more," said Bill.

"Keep it to yourself."

"More than you got any idea."

Wes shook his head, looked down, and forced a laugh. "Simmer down, Bill. We've a long push ahead. Fine work we're doing here quarreling and complaining. Someone's got to be in charge. You can't have nine commanders. I conceived this expedition, I set it in motion, I had the boats built. You agreed when you came to submit to my orders."

They all looked at him. They'd been standing in the sun, each lowering his brow. Everyone was sweating, but the dry air and heat vaporized the sweat the moment it appeared. "I for one don't fancy starving in this wilderness," Ora Howland said.

"Then give me your support."

The sack started twitching. "Hold on," said Bill. He reached beneath the net into the sack and pulled out a lizard. "You never saw that, Ora?" The ghost of a lizard was powdered with flour from its head to its tail. Bill gripped it by the tail, and when he raised it the tail broke off and the lizard dropped down and raced across the sand. Bill still held the tail.

No one said a thing.

They discarded more than two hundred pounds of flour, a fourth of their supply. The six hundred pounds left would barely last two months for nine hungry men.

And more was bound to spoil, Wes knew. Despite repeated caulkings, all the boats leaked worse than before and more rapids were ahead. And another boat could smash. Wes looked at Ora, who, it seemed clear, was sizing him up—taking Major Powell's measure.

Coffee. Dried apples. Flour. Saleratus. Half a sack of beans. A moldy piece of bacon.

Part Six

1

Toab shook his head. What are you doing? Are you just lying there?

Alone in the arbor, staring into space, Onchok wouldn't look up. Yes, I'm just lying here.

Do you have to lie there?

Yes.

Why?

Because I'm tired. I'm tired and weak. I think my wife has witched me. She put her poison in my heart.

Why would she do that?

Because she hates me, that's why. She wants me to sicken and die like herself.

You're talking like a crazy man.

It's true. She knows she's dying and doesn't want me to live either. She's jealous of the living.

She's not dying, said Toab. I think she's getting stronger.

I think she's half dead.

No she's not. She'll get better.

I'd like to die before her. Then you could marry her. You are my brother. If I die, you should marry her.

No I shouldn't. Don't be crazy. You're not going to die.

Yes I am.

You're not dying, you're going to live a long life. You'll live long enough to be an old man and sit by the fire and pull things toward you with your cane. Right now you're acting stupid. You're just a little sick. Maybe you're homesick. Are you homesick, brother?

No.

There's nothing wrong with you. I came here to get you, to go hunting rabbits. Can you come? Are you well enough?

Of course not. Can't you see?

Then I'll send Pangwits. We'll go hunting and you can lie here and sleep as much as you want. But when we come back I'll send him to medicine you. He'll drive out the poison. Should I send him?

What you wish.

Toab walked off, and an hour or so later, when the shadows were just beginning to lengthen, joined Pangwits near the gardens. He summoned the hunters and they started down the canyon. Boys ran ahead with their hooked sticks that they thrust into rabbit holes, but had no success. Instead, they found chuckwallas in the rocks and tried to pull them out with their hands. The crafty lizards puffed up deep inside their cracks to hold themselves there, but the craftier boys stabbed them with their hooks, deflating their lungs, then pulled them out. Soon the boys marched ahead, each with one or two chuckwallas hanging from his belt.

They hiked through juniper and sage, up a broken gully onto the rim, then north into high desert and pygmy forests. On the plateau between their canyon and the next, Toab watched the hunters drive stakes into the ground and unroll the rabbit nets to make a corral. They hunted the same way the Shivwits did back home: everyone spread out and, gradually converging, drove rabbits from the brush into the corral. Some tried shooting the rabbits as they darted ahead, but Toab saved his arrows until they closed on the corral and he shot the rabbits there. Those who ran out of arrows climbed in to retrieve them and with their sticks clubbed the living rabbits tangled in the nets. Soon everyone was gathering rabbits and arrows and wiping bloody arrows on their breechclouts. They killed nearly forty rabbits plus the dozen or so chuckwallas and started back to have a feast.

The wind blew steadily over the plateau. Clouds shot across the sky. The sun flared up like a coal being blown on but the breeze relieved the heat. Low on the horizon, the sun was dropping toward the mountain. On days like this Toab sensed the invisible world inflating inside the visible one and leaking through rips in the membrane between them. Rocks hummed and spirits whistled. A face with hollow eyes peeled off the wind, snagged the light, tore open, and was gone.

Several times since they'd come to the Other Side Toab and Mara had gone off into the woods and Pangwits had stumbled across them in the dark. Don't mind me, her brother said. That's the way the world goes. He turned it into a joke: he tripped going off the way he'd come and howled like a child. Pangwits seemed to show up whenever anything happened. If a dog had puppies, before their eyes were open he picked them up and juggled them like balls. In this way, he kept track of the goings-on in his village. He knew everyone's business.

When Toab told him why they'd come here, he rubbed his chin and shook his head. Hashkay? he said. Never heard that name.

Something like that, said Toab. The people at Walpi said he lived around here. If you can't find Hashkay, ask around for some Navajo with a Paiute girl.

That's like searching for a skunk with a smell. They all have Paiute captives.

Ask for Chookwadum, said Toab.

Skinny One? That's like searching for every Paiute in the world. All of them are skinny.

Except you, said Toab.

Except me. But my soul is skinny. I have a Paiute soul.

Can you help us? asked Toab.

You came all the way here just to look for a girl? Simpler to make a new one, said Pangwits. But he sent out two men to ask around at the Navajo encampments for Chookwadum. If she was a captive, they could arrange for a meeting with her captors.

The two men had been gone three days.

Now, walking back from the hunt with Toab, Pangwits bragged about the Navajo. He knew all about them. When Kit Carson and his army were rounding up Navajo a group of them hid up behind Paiute Mountain. The army never got this far; they scoured Black Mesa, marched through Canyon de Chelly, but never came here. I was glad to help the Navajo, said Pangwits, but I didn't like the glint in their eyes when they began to look around. They commented on the grass here, how good it was for grazing, how we Paiute didn't even have sheep, how we didn't need all this land. And we were protecting them!

After that, Pangwits got sheep—he bought some from the Navajo for Paiute buckskins and baskets. Meanwhile, the army captured most of the Navajo, but not those at Paiute Mountain. Five or six years ago, the army marched the ones they'd caught south to a new home, where a lot of them died. Then last year the army let the Navajo come back. It's crazy, said Pangwits. The whites are as fickle as women.

When the Navajo returned, those at Paiute Mountain joined the rest of their tribe, and not long after that some Navajo brought their herds to this plateau, but Pangwits drove them off. In reprisal, they killed two of his people. So Pangwits got a war party together and made preparations. They painted their bodies and danced and sang a song to witch the Navajo. He repeated it for Toab:

Fall asleep, you weaklings, you aren't hard to beat.
Your women can shoot us better than you.
You're too tired to fight us, you who fall asleep.

The war party marched east toward Solid Rocks Upward, where the Navajo who'd killed the Paiute were living. A coyote crossed the warriors' path, so they captured it and took it with them. A little farther on, a Navajo crossed their path, so they took him also. When they camped for the night, they staked out the coyote and cut him open. They staked out the Navajo and did the same—cut him down the middle and pulled his chest apart. They ripped out the coyote's heart and the Navajo's and exchanged the two. This drove their enemy crazy. The Paiute beat them in the battle. Now the Navajo respected the Paiute, said Pangwits.

They didn't take revenge? asked Toab.

Too terrified, said Pangwits. We licked them good. We killed a lot of braves.

Toab asked how many.

A lot, he said. I can't remember exactly. We took care of them. They won't be coming here to herd sheep anymore.

By now they were descending back into the canyon and Toab asked Pangwits if the Navajo who took Chookwadum would really want to have a meeting. Or would they just stay away?

Don't worry about the Navajo, said Pangwits. I know what to do.

Will they want to fight us?

They know better than that.

Pangwits was either a fool or very powerful, either dangerous or harmless. Maybe both, thought Toab.

Back at camp they prepared for the feast. They built a big fire, cleaned the chuckwallas, and threw the rabbits on the flames without cleaning them. When their fur was burned off they raked the rabbits out and opened them up and snagged the entrails with their fingers, then buried the rabbits in the coals with the chuckwallas and threw the entrails on top.

Toab asked Pangwits to medicine Onchok while the meat was cooking. Everyone else held a round dance in which the People from the Other Side joined the People from the Other Side. There were so many dancers the circle was enormous and the song filled the canyon. They all held hands—all except Pooeechuts. No one would touch her withered gray hand, so she had to sit and watch.

The sun had descended behind Paiute Mountain, sending its last spokes of light into the sky. Colors deepened in the canyon. Birds sang, mice whispered. Crickets and frogs began their evening grind and ants stitched new paths in the scuffled dirt, bringing in the last harvest. The huge group faced the fire and circled left, raising their left feet, stepping with the beat, and dipping their knees while dragging their right feet. They were circling the earth, putting it to sleep.

Rocks are forever rolling off the mountain,
Rolling off the mountain, rolling off the mountain.
But the summit remains, the summit remains.

The rabbit chitlins were ready. The group ate the snacks, cracking them with their teeth. Toab looked up and saw Onchok walking with a cane toward the fire. He wobbled and swayed but with determination. He clearly looked stronger. Pangwits followed behind and Toab pulled him aside and asked what he'd done.

I fixed your brother.

The canyon grew darker. A few people started dancing again and soon everyone joined in. Even Onchok broke into the circle, moving like a corpse summoned back to life, struggling, it seemed, to reassemble himself, but embroidering the struggle, Toab could tell. Others instead showed no emotion as they moved left in perfect unison.

Crawling along, crawling along,
The twilight has a home, the mountains have a home,
Have a home, have a home.

Toab sang with the others while watching: watching Mara with her deer pipe necklace she'd gotten in trade at Oraibi; watching the children, Kwits and Soxor, training for adulthood; watching Pangwits, whose neck and arm flaps resembled vulture wattles. All seemed possessed by the dance, and Toab too stepped left and dragged his right foot and soon felt the wheel making slow revolutions at the center of things. Everyone moved left, left with the stars, whose secrets in the gathering dark began to whirl around them. This was how the world started, how it learned the first elemental power: to string things together.

When they finished, they dug into the coals and ate the lizards then the rabbits, breaking rabbit bones in half and sucking out the marrow. The rabbits' ears pulled off easily, and they passed them around for the elders and the leaders. There was seed mush too, with its sweet nutty flavor, and juice made from wolfberries mixed with squawbush berries, a bitter concoction unless sweetened with the sugar shaken from common reeds—the brown excrement of aphids.

They danced some more and Pangwits went into a trance. He fell down, breaking the circle, and two men rushed over and seized him by the arms, but he heaved to his feet and shook off their grip. Standing next to the fire, looking left and right, Pangwits sang in an eerie voice. He seemed ready to explode. The men reached out to restrain him again, but he ran through the fire, scattering its coals. He kept running, reached a boulder in the sand, and slammed back against its face. He fell on the ground and all was silent.

Toab and Mara stood by the fire watching. Onchok grabbed his cane and hobbled to a rock. Overhead, the stars stared down on their heads with the eyes of the dead.

Pangwits's voice grew high and low, two different voices talking to each other:

Prophet, speak! said the high voice. Why am I lame?

So that your spirit may walk, said the low one.

When will my blood come?

When your thoughts are pure.

Why does a little gnat have six legs and six wings whereas the mountain lion has only four legs?

It would be stupid of me to talk about these things when the love of all creatures is absent from your heart.

Why is my arm crippled?

Strength has crippled it.

He described voices inside wires and boxes made of iron rushing over the earth. Toab would admit to his grandchildren years later that Pangwits could have heard about the telegraph and the railroad from other Indians. Yet Toab himself hadn't heard of those things, not then at least, and he'd been to lots of places, more than this prophet. Pangwits talked about voices trapped inside boxes and shadows in boxes that have the power to hold whoever sees them as prisoner. No one will squat in the world of boxes, instead they'll sit, he said.

Sit on what, prophet?

On boxes with arms.

When Toab's grandson told his own sons and daughters these prophecies nearly a century later, he was seated on a crate in the kitchen of his house and his children were lined up on a car seat against a yellow wall watching Road Runner cartoons.

The next day Onchok felt so much stronger he didn't need a cane. You were right, brother, he said to Toab. That man's medicine is powerful. He did a lot for me.

What did he do?

He gave me strong medicine.

So now you won't die?

Someday I'll die. But not right away.

What about your wife? Toab asked. Will she get better too?

Onchok looked away. She already has, he said.

Will her arm be all right?

Onchok didn't answer.

In fact, Pooeechuts grew worse. Pangwits tried to medicine her. He chanted and blew smoke on the arm and sucked poisons from its wound—pebbles, a bullet, a bone, cactus spines. But to Toab, Pangwits's heart didn't seem to be in it. He'd given up on her, it appeared. And she couldn't bend her arm anymore.

The men who'd gone to search for Hashkay hadn't come back. Pangwits announced that he'd look for them himself, but as he was making preparations they came walking down the canyon.

The men squatted with Pangwits and Toab and talked. They'd found Hashkay, but Kwits had heard the name wrong. Hashkay turned out to be Hoskininni, a powerful Navajo. Pangwits knew him well; his band had hidden from Kit Carson's troops behind Paiute Mountain. Hoskininni had Onchok's daughter now, but he hadn't stolen her—his brother had, he said. If he and his brother returned her, they wanted something in exchange. They wanted guns. They were coming on horses and would meet them in two days in the same gorge at the base of the mountain where five years ago they'd taken refuge from the soldiers.

You go, Pangwits told Toab.

You'll have to come too, Toab replied.

Pangwits looked doubtful. But what choice did he have? He'd become part of the Shivwits' story.

2

What did you bring to give them for the girl?

Something they want, said Toab.

They want guns! said Pangwits.

Do you have any guns?

Of course not. This is crazy. I shouldn't have come.

I thought you knew all about these Navajo. I thought you said you knew how to deal with them.

I do, said Pangwits. But he looked edgy. He seemed uncomfortable dressed in antelope leggings decorated with feathers, snake skins, and squirrel tails. Toab wore just a breechclout and shirt. Still a little weak, Onchok rode the burro. The three crossed a plain through stunted piñon giving way to saltweed, blackbrush, and greasewood. A group of Pangwits's male relatives followed behind, herding sheep.

Directly in their path Paiute Mountain heaved its bulk across the spreading land. The rising sun behind them lit the fins and canyons rutting its sides and its broad green summit of tall pines and firs. The blue sky, immobile, was empty, omnivorous. At the horizon it was so intensely blue it almost looked black.

Toab knew how to act in most circumstances. Obey the rules and don't break the taboos, watch and be careful, hold back, don't flinch. But in dealing with the unpredictable Navajo, rules became uncertain. Tell them how strong and powerful they are? Give them what they want? Don't respond to their insults?

He'd never met a Navajo—only the one at Walpi, if he counted.

Which do you think is worse, he asked Pangwits, a Navajo or a Ute?

I don't see many Ute. Two came through here a year ago maybe and asked for some corn. They were running from the soldiers. I didn't like the way they looked and thought they'd start killing anything they saw. They said they were lost and didn't know where they were going. They didn't care if they died.

But which is worse?

I think the Navajo are worse.

Approaching Paiute Mountain, Toab felt its authority. Up and down its slopes were cracked seams and fissures. Climbing, the men circled low walls and domes, skirted rock slabs fallen between hefty piñons growing in the mountain's runoff. A box canyon ended at tall shafts of sandstone, broad-shouldered monoliths crowded together. Junipers, Gambel oaks, cliff rose, bunchgrass, and splashes of yucca grew at their base. Between seams of swollen rock, fragments of a stone wall ran outside the entrance to a cave.

Near the cave, coals, charred bones, flint chips, and smashed pots littered the ground. Five years ago, Hoskininni's band had hidden here from the Americans. Pangwits himself had shown them this place; they'll never find you, he'd said.

Wood still lay piled next to the cave. The Paiute started a fire on the broad flat slope outside the entrance and lit juniper branches and carried them into the cave. A few blankets and hides lay against a wall. Charred bones and old moccasins surrounded a fire ring, while farther back a stone pit lined with upright slabs held nut shells.

Their torches flared out and they exited the cave. It was late morning now. Toab hobbled the burro a few hundred feet down the canyon. Pangwits and his men built up the fire and started slaughtering the sheep they'd brought for food.

When the Navajo came, tall on their horses, they crossed the plateau below in plain sight, creating plumes of dust. They took their time and disappeared below the cliffs, then mounted the trail. Passing Toab's burro, one of them said something and laughed. Behind this brave on his horse, arms around his waist, sat Chookwadum. Toab's heart exulted—then he winced. Would they really surrender her? She didn't look any different: dark-eyed and skinny, head slumping forward when, apparently surprised, she saw her father and uncle. She rested her head on the brave's back and hugged him tighter, approaching the camp. He helped her dismount and she hung back behind him while he walked toward the fire.

Onchok jumped up and approached his daughter, but two of the Navajo blocked his way. They made him turn around and gave him a push and he hobbled to the fire, glancing back at the girl. Toab had never seen his brother look so small, not even when the Mormon boxed his ear.

But these confident Navajo could make anyone feel small. And they only numbered four, as if to say we're not afraid of you Paiute. You contemptible Paiute. All wore red headbands and loose cotton shirts and trousers and bright red moccasins coated with dust. The tallest and oldest walked up to Pangwits and embraced him, shouting Makewa—the Paiute greeting.

Makewa, mumbled Pangwits.

A thin mustache hung like string beside the wrinkled lips of this Navajo elder. I smell meat, he said in Paiute. The other Navajo stood around and looked blankly at the Paiute men. I hope you cooked a lot, Pangwits. A lot of good fat sheep. We're hungry after traveling so far.

He walked to the fire where the meat spat and bubbled. This looks good, he said. We'll eat first, then talk. We've come a long way.

Toab carved up the joints and ribs and chunks of meat and each Navajo brave shouted out what he wanted. For Chookwadum he cut a big piece of leg and handed it to a brave, nodding at her. She sat on a rock behind the Navajo, nibbling at the meat. The Paiute sat on one side of the fire, the Navajo on the other, some on rocks, some in the dirt.

Soon the fire died down, the sun climbed into the sky, and everyone ate and tossed bones into the bushes.

Thank you, said the tall one with the mustache. He stood to speak, and though it sounded slow and dry, like a fine powder, he spoke the Paiute language well. That was good, he said. How's your corn? he asked Pangwits. Have the crows been after it?

Not really.

Have the ears appeared?

Some.

Good, he said. You have good land.

It's all right, said Pangwits, sitting in the dirt. Toab watched this man who did all the talking; he had to be Hoskininni. Two of the Navajo climbed to their feet and went to look at the cave, but Hoskininni barked something in their language, causing them to turn and come back.

You can see I brought the child, he said.

I see.

I hope you brought something good in payment.

Pangwits looked at Toab, who walked to the burro and took some things out of the burden basket. He swaggered back with two long burlap bundles and placed them in the dirt in front of Hoskininni. The Navajo leader didn't look at them. Pangwits did, though. He looked at the bundles and looked at Toab and faintly smiled.

Onchok also gazed at the bundles and lowered his head.

I didn't steal her, Hoskininni said. I want you to know that. I wasn't even there. My brother found her, he said, nodding toward a younger man who sat expressionless beside him. You know what his name means? It means Walk Up in Anger. My name, as you know—Hoskininni—means Giving Out Anger. And that man there guarding your girl, he's Won't Do As He's Told. The one beside him is Stealing Cattle. Sometimes thieves cross the river and steal cattle from the Mormons. A relative of Stealing Cattle was killed by the Mormons who caught him stealing cattle. This man here named himself in his honor.

Sometimes the Paiute help, he continued. But sometimes the

Paiute betray our men and tell the Mormons when we're coming. Sometimes with the Paiute it's hard to really know what they're going to do.

Pangwits said nothing.

I want you to know no one kidnapped those children. They were taken because they were by themselves in the middle of nowhere with no one else around. They were all alone. Where was their family? Ask the girl if it's true they were completely alone. Ask her.

We don't have to, said Toab. The boy came back. We know it's true.

Are you their father?

I am, said Onchok.

Well, then. There you are. What did you expect? Their father wasn't anywhere around.

The children had just run away from some Mormonis.

How did the Mormons get them?

They bought them, said Toab.

Well, I see. I understand. Hoskininni sneered and looked away. They would have died there in the middle of nowhere if my brother hadn't found them, he snapped. What if the Ute had gotten them? You wouldn't see them again. The Ute would have sold them to the Spanish. Or maybe the children would have starved to death out there in the desert. It was for their own good my brother took them. What did you expect? If their own father doesn't want them, why can't we take them? We treat our children well. We know how to care for them. We don't sell them to the Mormons. We never hurt our children. Those children had been beaten.

Onchok and Toab both spoke at once:

I never beat them!

The Mormoni man beat them.

Hoskininni looked at Toab. If you say so. Are you one of those who made peace with the Mormons?

No. I hate the Mormonis.

Then why sell them your children?

Toab said nothing. Pangwits said, My relatives stayed away from the Mormonis.

Not so far away they couldn't sell them their children.

It was a terrible mistake. They know they shouldn't have done it.

I understand. You Paiute are poor, you have no horses, you had to do what you did. And now you've come all this way to correct your mistake. It takes a brave man to know he's done wrong and try to correct it. I'm glad you've come. He looked at Onchok and Toab. You are this man's relatives? He nodded at Pangwits.

Yes.

Pangwits used to be my friend. He protected us from Kit Carson and his soldiers and I'll always be grateful. Red Clothes and his men were cutting down our peach trees, burning our gardens, shooting our people, rounding them up to take to Hwééldi. He did it. He made the Diné go there. But some of us held out. I'm glad we did, too, because a lot of people died on the way, and more when they got there.

Hoskininni wasn't talking to Pangwits anymore, he was talking to Toab, who stared back at the man. Now they're back home, said Hoskininni. My people are back. But I'll always be grateful that we escaped their fate. I even returned with a herd of sheep last year to thank our friend Pangwits. These sheep we've just eaten—they might have been some of those I gave him then.

Pangwits looked away.

But not long ago I came back with more sheep and Pangwits got mad. He said it wasn't my place. What did I want to drive my sheep there for? That's what he said. That grass was his, he said. He didn't want us living in his canyon. He called it his canyon. Take your sheep back up on the rim and stay there, he said. Stay up there with your sheep. I said to him, Who do you think you are? You're just a Paiute. You don't scare me. You didn't make this canyon, that's what I said. You didn't make those rocks. You didn't plant those trees, bushes, weeds, and grasses. You don't have any business talking like that. If I want to stay someplace, why can't I?

Hoskininni opened his arms as though in appeal. He moved his stare from Toab and glanced around the fire at everyone else, then lowered his voice.

Not long ago I learned that friends of Pangwits had killed one of our people. After that we had a battle and killed a lot of Paiute and now we're enemies again. I know how these things happen. I've been through it all. I know all about killing and taking scalps. I don't want your scalps. If I were compelled to take them from you just because of your treachery, I wouldn't even keep them. I'd give them to our dogs and even they wouldn't want them. If they did, I'd shoot them. Even though they're good dogs. Good dogs who don't turn and bite you when you're friendly.

Why talk about that? blurted out Pangwits. Talk about something else.

All right then. I'll talk about people who treat their neighbors poorly. They accept your gifts, then, when you come to visit them, they tell you to leave. But if they want something from you, they ask you to come and they cook for you and act like people should.

I should have poisoned the meat! Pangwits shouted.

The other three Navajo jumped to their feet and started for their horses — to get their rifles, thought Toab — but Hoskininni stopped them. He laughed. Where is Keshtelee? he said to Pangwits. Or Machukats? Or Pakay? Did they come with you, Pangwits? What happened to them?

Pangwits stared at Hoskininni stone-faced.

Keep your canyon, said the Navajo. Keep all its precious grass. Its grass too good to be eaten by my sheep.

I've seen where you graze your sheep, said Pangwits. The land has been ruined.

Hoskininni smiled. Kill me, then. Go ahead. I don't care about dying. I'm an old man. There are plenty of people all over the world who are dying right now. I know I'm not alone. Go ahead, kill me. I'll let you, Pangwits. You killed my heart already, finish the job. I've eaten your pine nuts and hunted your rabbits. I've taken your women and children prisoner. I've killed your friends in battle. Now I've come here so you can kill me, so do it, go ahead. I'll let you do it.

I don't want to kill you.

Are you a coward?

No.

Hoskininni spit in the fire and looked down at the bundles. Let's see what you brought. He unwrapped the burlap and took out the rifles and held them up, one in each hand. Then he looked at Toab. So Pangwits is your relative. Did you know he's a witch?

He's not, said Toab. He's a good man.

Hoskininni sneered. He used to be a good man.

The old Navajo turned and said something to the one he called his brother. His brother barked at the brave guarding Chookwadum, who took her hand. She stood looking down and he led her to her father, already on his feet, face trembling and buckling as the child drew closer.

Onchok embraced her and wept. Welcome, my child. My own little baby. I'm so glad to see you, I'm glad you're back again.

Chookwadum stood stiffly, arms by her sides, submitting to Onchok's weepy embraces.

Thank you, Hoskininni said to Toab. These are nice guns. I'll take good care of them. Guns are what I wanted. We'll put them to good use—we'll kill some Mormons. Where did you get them?

From a Mormoni.

Good! I like that. I like turning their own weapons against them. It's a good idea. It's funny. Thank you. Now we're finished. We're all through. It's time to go home. I guess we'll start back now.

We have some blood roast, said Toab.

No, that's all right. We have to go home.

Without looking at Chookwadum, Hoskininni and his men walked back to the horses, removed the hobbles from their legs, mounted them, and left.

The girl watched them ride off, her face blank and distant—watched them snake down the canyon and march across the scrubland.

3

When Onchok brought his daughter back on the burro, he pointed out Pooeechuts's arbor. As the girl raced to her mother, Pooeechuts jumped up and started singing:

My feather was lost
At dusk on the hills.
Now she's come back.

She embraced Chookwadum with her good arm, sobbing and laughing, but the girl seemed afraid of her mother's other arm and kept to one side, weeping on her mother's neck. Chookwadum, only ten, skinny and tall, towered over her mother and had to bend down.

Pooeechuts stepped back and looked at her daughter, holding her elbow. She called everyone over to welcome her back, but the girl spotted Kwits and he ran off with her, dragging his sister by the hand. They found the other children down by the spring.

After a while, she wandered back alone. By then her mother was sleeping again inside her arbor. Chookwadum bent down, peering inside. She stayed close to the arbor looking puzzled and uncertain.

The village planned a feast and round dance that night to celebrate Chookwadum's reunion with her family. Late that afternoon Toab started a fire; when it burned down to coals, they'd roast all the grasshoppers the villagers had gathered and grind them into meal to make cakes for everyone. Mixed with squawberries and a little cornmeal and sandgrass seed, they would be delicious. He piled on the wood in the big fire pit. Chookwadum, back with the children by the spring, played on stilts. He watched her walk in circles and crash into the others then wander off blindly by herself. She wouldn't join their game and follow the leader. The stilts looked continuous with her legs. She resembled a skeleton.

Her strange, vacant manner could have come from the shock of seeing her mother. Toab realized that Chookwadum had returned to find her mother sick; she might be afraid that Pooeechuts was dying.

She hadn't yet been reunited with Soxor, now in seclusion with Mara. When the men had gone to meet with Hoskininni, Soxor's blood had come.

Toab walked off toward a clump of trees where a hand game was in progress. Onchok had joined it. After bringing home his daughter, he hadn't wasted any time in trying to make up for the loss of his guns. Toab saw now how much he'd succeeded. Behind the players were their winnings, and Onchok had a pile: blankets, buckskins, arrows, baskets.

Two rows of four men sat facing each other. On one team, those in the middle, singing, moved their arms beneath a blanket, which heaved up and down. One flipped a corner back, tossed up a wooden plug, snatched it back, and bucked the blanket, making the dust fly. Their partners beat a hollow log with sticks.

The four men facing them watched closely, motionless. Two leaned toward each other, muttering as they watched: Onchok and Pangwits. The song stopped abruptly and the men threw off the blanket and held out their fists. Facing them, Onchok slammed an arm across his chest and flung out the other, shouting Wuhkavee— "summit." His thumb and first finger made a claw. They opened their fists, and he'd guessed right: the unmarked wooden cylinders were in the outside hands. They had to give them up.

The cylindrical plugs had a groove in the middle and the two marked ones were wrapped with sinew in the grooves and glued with pitch.

Toab watched while leaning against a tree. Wives and children watched too, also other men placing bets on the side, one of whom tugged Toab's arm, but Toab shook his head. Now Onchok's team chanted and beat on their log. An old man and Pangwits sat in the middle, stirring their arms underneath a blanket that rippled and flapped and heaved with confusion. Six counters had been stuck in the dirt before Onchok—straight thin sticks. Four more and his team would win. Never before had Onchok been so lucky, and he lifted his head without changing his expression and gave Toab a look, slack lips almost smiling.

He was getting there, thought Toab, growing rich, winning things. His luck had changed; he must have had good medicine. But not everything was better. Chookwadum was acting like the dead brought back to life, and Pooeechuts was weaker. She slept all the time.

Farther down the canyon Toab saw Mara combing Soxor's hair in their secluded arbor. Mara had become the girl's attendant. She loused her and washed her. She made sure that Soxor stayed alone and used scraps of sheepskin between her legs and didn't touch herself. They'd miss the celebration.

He wandered through the canyon. He uprooted a yucca plant and walked back to the fire pit, scraping the outer skin off the roots. He put the roots on a rock and pounded them until they'd become soft and stringy. Adding water from a jug, he mixed the pounded roots in a basket lined with pitch that he carried down the canyon and left on a rock for Mara to fetch—shampoo for Soxor's hair.

Back up the canyon, Toab noticed Chookwadum sitting by herself on a rock. Something was in the air, something different. Onchok approached Toab and slapped his back. Well, brother, I was lucky.

What did you win?

Two buckskins, two blankets. Some pretty good baskets. I won some sheep.

What good are sheep? We're leaving here soon.

I'll give them to Pangwits. Onchok stood before him smiling.

Toab and Onchok walked to their arbors. It was afternoon. Hot. The village seemed lifeless. They needed new moccasins, but who would make them? Pooeechuts was sick and Mara in seclusion. They threw their deerskin on the ground—the one they'd brought from Black Mesa—and stepped on it lengthwise and with Toab's knife drew outlines for soles. After cutting them out, they took turns draping the hide across their feet to outline the uppers and cut them out too. They slashed the uppers down the middle to pass around their ankles and cut out the cuffs and the strips to make strings. Then they sat in Toab's arbor sewing the uppers to the soles with sinew they'd saved from the deer's legs.

We're just withered old women, Onchok said.

Let's gossip about our husbands, said Toab.

Let's not. Let's sew our mouths shut.

That wouldn't stop me.

Let's cut out our tongues.

That might work.

They watched Chookwadum in the middle of the canyon. She jumped up from her rock and climbed on her stilts and hobbled around in circles again.

When Onchok finished sewing, he held up a moccasin, placed it on a rock, and admired it. Smiling, he removed the medicine pouch from its cord around his waist and tossed it up and down. It made a satisfying clack. Toab wondered where he'd gotten it.

They trimmed the welts and punched holes in the uppers and threaded them with strips, then flattened the seams by holding a piece of wood inside the moccasin and pounding the outer surface with a rock. They tried them on and wrapped the strips around their ankles and walked back and forth admiring each other.

Very attractive, said Onchok. Will you marry me?

Let's go into the bushes.

They filled the moccasins with damp earth and put them on a boulder outside Toab's arbor where others could see them. Then Onchok took the rest of the hide to his wife's arbor to measure her feet.

He left the medicine pouch behind. Toab opened it and dumped its contents in his palm: bones. Human fingers, each one intact. Medicine bones, the most powerful kind, the kind that talked to you and told you what to do. Onchok must have gotten them from Pangwits. Toab looked over at Pooeechuts's arbor where Onchok was helping his wife to her feet. She stood on the hide so he could outline the soles.

There was balance in everything, he knew; if someone grew sick, someone else grew healthy. Medicine bones exploited this balance, twisted and misused it. A man recovered his health at the cost of someone else's. He gained power by sacrificing others, usually his loved ones. A man with bones like these paid with the lives of those who were weakest, his children and wife, in order to be strong.

He poured the bones back into the pouch, wrapped the cord around its mouth, and put it back where he'd found it.

That evening Pangwits slaughtered more of his sheep. The people feasted on mutton and grasshopper cakes and held a round dance with Pangwits calling out the songs. He recited the lines, then all sang together:

In the blue water
The trout wags its tail,
Wags its tail, wags its tail.

Chookwadum danced joining hands with the others, hopping as she stepped left, bending her knees and dragging sideways. She was painted yellow from her hairline to her neck, with red on her chin, under her eyes, and across her forehead. Pooeechuts didn't dance but watched from her arbor. Mara and Soxor stayed down the canyon in seclusion.

When the dancing was over, Toab walked down the canyon,

picked up some pebbles, and threw them at their arbor. Mara came out and walked toward him in the darkness. She put her hand between his legs. I'm ready too, she said.

4

The day before the Shivwits left, Pangwits, Toab, and Onchok built a sweat lodge. They stuck willow branches in the sand near a fire, bent them over to make a conical frame, and covered it with blankets. Each had tied up his hair and wore only a breechclout.

Back home, the Paiute didn't have sweat lodges. Toab and some others had learned about the practice from their friends across the river, the Havasupai, and Pangwits had learned it from the Navajo. It was a heat test, said Pangwits. It made you suffer in order to purify you and rid the body of evils, but it did destroy some people. It was expected to destroy you. He'd seen Navajo braves emerging from the sweat lodge shaking little arrows and other witch objects from their arms and legs.

Toab agreed. In a sweat lodge you suffered, and the suffering strengthened you.

With sticks Pangwits fished a hot stone from the fire and rolled it on the ground toward the sweat lodge. Toab held back the blankets around the opening and Pangwits said Paa and rolled it inside, bent over in a sweat, suffering already. When you entered a sweat lodge you had to say Paa, otherwise a ghost might seal up the entrance and those inside would die.

He went back for more and soon five or six hot rocks had been rolled inside the lodge and the three men crawled in. Pangwits came last with a water basket and a spray of sage branches. There was barely room for three to sit around the small pile of stones. Pangwits dipped the sage in the water and showered the stones, and the steam made a roar and seemed to rob the men of air. Toab felt his eyes sting and instinctively closed them.

In that nutshell space they could hear one another's breath and smell one another's smell. The steam burned their skin, and when it started to cool Pangwits threw on more water and the pain spread and thinned from the base of their necks down across their chests. It soon became a caustic pleasure; Toab felt the sheets of tightness peeling off his shoulders. He was dripping already but couldn't tell if the wetness was sweat or jelled steam.

He opened his eyes. Sage leaves had landed on the hot rocks and their odor filled the lodge. His hot face and head felt ready to burst. The Navajo, said Pangwits, liked to sing and yell during their sweats, but he'd never done that. He asked Toovuts—Wolf—to protect them and threw on more water and a bush of hot steam burst among the men. Toab's head spun. One time, said Pangwits, there were deer in this canyon, but medicine beings took them all away through mazes of canyons. Sometimes you can see them up beyond the mountain, but they don't come around here anymore.

Maybe it's the Navajo with their sheep, said Onchok.

It could be that, but maybe the deer don't come because of something we did—or didn't do. When birds and animals were humans like us, a long time ago, Pangwits said, they came together in hard times, like when somebody died, and they howled at each other. They knew how to suffer. Each had a special song. Later, they became the animals and we became the people and we forgot those songs. We can't sing them anymore. We can't whistle like a bird or howl like a coyote. Go ahead, try it. See if you can.

No one made a sound.

The animals can't speak, not anymore, but it's much worse for us, Pangwits said, that we humans can't sing. The Navajo think they can, but they can't. Only animals can sing.

Toab started making yelps, high-pitched yips and barks. Then he let out a wail that petered off to a string, a long frayed line hung with more barks and yips. Pangwits joined him in barking and yelping—even Onchok tried it, though his bark sounded much too human to Toab, who was enjoying this. He began to feel possessed. He growled and showed his teeth and snapped at his brother, clawing and ripping the air with his fingers. The others watched Toab barking like a dog, amazed at first. Then all howled together and broke into laughter. Their broad sweating faces grinned and Pangwits said they ought to leave now.

They crawled out and cooled off. After a while Pangwits fished more stones from the fire and rolled them into the sweat lodge. The three men crowded inside again, saying Paa. They tried other songs —bird songs and rabbit squeals and hawk calls and bear grunts—but they wouldn't have fooled either animals or humans. Threads of steam thick as wool absorbed the crazy sounds and held them in the air for the men to see, ripe and brightly colored.

Three more times they went back into the sweat lodge, until Onchok gave up. I'm not like you, he said to Pangwits. I don't have fat to spare.

I don't either. I'm down to skin and muscle.

That's pretty juicy muscle.

When they'd finished, Pangwits told the others he wanted to go with them tomorrow and visit their country. Take me with you, he said. I'd like to see that place again. I know the best route, not the way you came. It's the way we went when my father crossed the river and Pooeechuts met Onchok. We go west past Paiute Mountain, that's the way to go. Take me with you tomorrow, I'll show you the way.

Toab and Onchok looked at each other and Toab shrugged. The way they'd come here, through Havasupai and Oraibi, was tortuous and long, he knew. Pangwits's route would be more direct. Where do we cross the river? asked Toab.

At the ford, said Pangwits. We just walk across. At O'poment, where everyone crosses.

Part Seven

July 20–August 3, 1869

1

At the confluence of the Green and the Colorado, Bill Dunn held up the reconditioned barometer, cocked one eye, and inspected the scale. His lips moved so distinctly that watching from his tent Wes could understand the reading: 25.9. Bill stood ankle deep in the shallows and pulled out the watch, then returned it to his pocket, clamped the barometer under one arm, and jotted down the figures.

Wes exited the tent and, swinging his arm, walked toward Bill. He wished to explore the side canyon they'd passed coming down the Green while approaching this confluence, so he asked Bill to take him.

"Not interested," said Bill.

"Thought you could come along and hunt."

"You thought wrong."

"Suit yourself."

"I will."

He could order Bill to take him, but they'd had words. Might as well ease off. So he asked George Bradley. With the other good barometer they made their way upstream along the Green's west bank, where the current was slow, and landed at the mouth of an alluvial fan still running with water from last night's rain. The willows were thick at the bottom of this wash and a pungent smell—part lemon, part tobacco—rose from the wet rabbitbrush. They cut through this jungle and climbed up dirt slopes above the canyon's mouth and passed another ruin, the foundation and lower walls of a stone house. "More ancient temples," said George.

"Just a cottage. Ordinary people went about their daily lives."

"In romantic desolation."

"They didn't see it like that."

"How did they see it?"

Wes thought. "As home."

The dirt slopes became winding sandstone cliffs fifty feet above this side canyon's bottom. Cottonwood trees, piñons, and junipers grew at intervals below the two men. As they climbed the canyon pinched, and they passed a series of ledges or steps across which a string of water frayed and pooled. This rock, white as snow—a freshwater limestone—ran in overlapping plates with red sand collected in crevices and shallows on its broken surface.

Their climb angled up through sandstone cliffs with waterfalls and pools, up a steep trough of boulders and loose rock and sand. George carried biscuits and dried apples in a knapsack, Wes the barometer. They moved in silence and Wes thought about his men. Bill Dunn seemed to have turned against him, but why he couldn't fathom. The poor brute was a victim of his volatile emotions. A harmless man really, if somewhat shabby, and of course a dirty devil. Wes had commanded plenty of Bill Dunns at Shiloh and Vicksburg. It was for them he'd lost his arm! His job was to lead them, Bill's to follow. Nine leaders made for nine separate goals, and none would be successful—the war had taught him that. George understood—Jack Sumner too—but Ora did not. And Ora was far more bothersome than Bill, being moody and distracted and stubbornly cocksure, a bad mix in such a regiment. Whatever Ora did he did late, but always it was right, at least according to him. He plodded and fumbled and didn't pay attention, and if he made a mistake it was the fault of others. Nothing could shake him from that conviction. In Wes's mind, Ora unearthed the darkest memories of his father: the ungenerous zeal, the imperative complaints, the refusal to back down. And Ora never had a solution to offer, just ominous counsel.

By contrast, Wes thought of himself as an undeterable solver of problems. Intractable things could always be made to yield to success. Knowledge is the greatest good, it advances human prospects.

Knowledge, not faith.

Such thoughts led, by well-beaten paths, to thoughts of Wes's father. He pictured the Reverend Joseph Powell entering a room already longing to correct what he saw. Those sitting there hushed.

Wes's father was bedrock, predictable, consistent, whether removing a book left on a chair or preaching in a barn while the snow fell outside. In his son's mythic memory—though he knew not in fact—it was his father's unyielding opposition to slavery that split the American Methodist Church. Wes was twelve years old. The family had just moved to Wisconsin after mobs in Ohio had broken up his father's meetings with stones and shouts of "nigger lover." The new Wesleyan connection, the northern half of the split, forbade slavery and drink, and its conference was governed by a democracy of laymen, men and women whom Joseph Powell met riding horseback through southern Wisconsin, holding services at noon in village squares and farmers' fields. Only fifteen acres of the land he'd bought when they'd arrived had been cleared enough to farm—he left Wes the task of breaking the rest. The boy managed the farm while his father rode the circuit, preaching at every stop the identical message he'd preached in Ohio: faith in the people's God, Jesus Christ, a common man like them. In Wisconsin at least the people listened. Christ was not exactly a farmer, of course, but he worked with his hands and still managed to be strict, and he understood people's weaknesses.

Meanwhile, Wes single-handedly ran his father's farm.

Christ understood human weakness because he was a man himself, but did Reverend Powell? To Wes he'd always been the reed that wouldn't bend. Full godliness streamed from one person to another via piercing eyes, firm manly handshakes, strong and steady words, traits Wes had learned too. As a boy Wes had memorized the entire four Gospels. His father always assumed Wes would follow in his footsteps, but the older he became, the more Wes's mind wandered. George Crookham had infected it with his prairie college. And Reverend Powell had brought this about—he'd asked George to teach his son!

From Wisconsin the family moved to Illinois, where Wes planned to study science. His father promised him a year at Oberlin if he'd help break another farm, but when the year came Reverend Powell insisted he study for the clergy, and he refused.

He left home to teach school to earn money for college but kept coming back out of loyalty to family. Reverend Powell in time became a fading titan commanding his son to choose Jesus Christ.

That voice never left Wes; it guaranteed that choosing science would be an act of defiance. And science in fact was the mental occupation that resisted common sense. You disciplined yourself to fight stubborn ways of thinking, and if you succeeded, if you shone your light on the world from new angles, what wonders appeared!

Science was God turned inside out, Wes thought; it shaped God from mud and sticks and gave Him your voice and took away His name. Now His name was Science.

Still, Wes hadn't yet solved the riddle of rivers cutting right through mountains.

Now he changed his mind: Ora wasn't like his father. The physical resemblance was certainly there—the long gray prophetic beard, the thin and wiry body. But Ora was more a synthetic Reverend Powell, with spirit gone bitter and constricted. Ora could never have the effect Wes's father had on people, the power to move them by voice and example. The whole of Ora's eloquence consisted of whines and chastisements and complaints. He was a perfect example of those who came after the great age of titans.

Wes no longer had faith in his father's religion, or in anything sectarian. It was Ora's religion as well, as Ora reminded him at every opportunity. The world is too large for narrow minds, Ora! As for Wes, he believed in an all-embracing Spirit, a mind-soul expressed in evolutionary progress.

George had stopped ahead. Their canyon appeared to be boxed, Wes saw. A sweeping sandstone cliff, smoothly concave, with a single rope of water slung down its middle faced the two men. They were closer to the rim, and here everything whirled in horizontal layers whipped from solid rock of orange, white, and yellow. They could climb up here—up the same path the water came down—but the rock would be slick and they'd surely slip and fall. George found another route, up a steep gully to an overhang of sandstone, then across a narrow ledge, so narrow they crawled on hands and knees to traverse it. It grew wider toward the end and broadened to a hanging valley above the dead-end cliff. This valley turned out to be a little park tucked halfway up the canyon, containing piñons, junipers, yucca and bunchgrass, with a green thread of water running down the middle and cliffs on either side.

They stopped to watch a canyon wren pick spiders out of cracks in the huge boulders. It hopped, it tipped up, it flapped down, it stabbed.

Another slope led to another sheer cliff and they spotted a slot running up through rounded domes. Here, Wes handed the barometer to George, stuffed himself into the slot, and wormed up. George climbed too and pinched past Wes, handing him his pack and the instrument. They ascended overlapping ledges, squeezed between boulders up a final cranny, and gained the shelf above.

They were in an amphitheater of deep red sandstone, though the color right now seemed oddly bleached. Then Wes saw the sky had turned white with high clouds. When had that happened? The sun had become a constant torture of late, yet he hadn't noticed when it disappeared.

They made their way left over benches and tables and little pinched fissures in sandstone dunes. Their canyon had ended; they were climbing open rock sloping up along a cliff. Where it narrowed to a crevice, stones had been stacked by long-vanished humans making steps to the top. And there, on the rim, a polylithic ocean spread to the horizon, crest after crest of rocks caught in leaps, or squatting to leap, or carved apart in midleap. Red, white, and brown; yellow, gray, and green. Swirling beds of rock, knobs, points, and pinnacles, all uniformly sliced by horizontal layers whose bands joined across bowls of empty space.

They took elevations. Ate dried apples and biscuits. In craters on slickrock shaped like perfect lenses yesterday's rain had collected in pools, cool and delicious. They crossed the surface of the rock following shelves and the edge of a gulch and had to jump across fissures and skirt fat domes. At last they came to a spot where both rivers were visible, and a portion of their camp: toy boats and two-legged bugs.

Then they started back.

At the confluence, when they stepped from the boat Wes watched the two rivers for a while. Today it was the Green whose color was chocolate and the Grand that had cleared up. Where they met a straight line ran down the middle, joining the two rivers at the hip, one light and one dark.

Wes looked at the rock walls above the confluence with eyes still pulled by the flow of the water. The cliffs bent and moved, their base pulling right, their pinnacles left—the world ripping open at its seams.

Dark clouds rolled in and they pitched the tents. That night it rained hard and thunder shook the rivers and lightning lit the cliffs. It had cleared out by morning, but waterfalls poured in several places over canyon walls, some brown, some clear. In a small alcove behind their camp a clear stream of water plunged over a ledge into a little basin, and as the sun struck their side of the river the men took showers. Seneca and Jack dragged Bill Dunn there and, while the others held him down, stripped off his clothes and pushed him under the stream, where he danced on nimble toes. Black hairs covered every inch of his body. "Cold as ice!" he shouted.

Wes knew it wasn't. Warm as a mother's spit was more like it.

When everyone had finished and sat to eat breakfast, the sound of falling rocks came from the alcove where they'd showered. They turned to see a boulder the size of a hog slowly rolling in dreamtime over the ledge into their basin, instantly smashing into a pile of yellow powder. Unexposed sandstone, Wes observed, was yellow, and that heap of sand was the only yellow thing in this rockbound world of brown, gray, and red. He shrugged and shook his head. George observed out loud that *that* was good luck. Or maybe it was bad, he couldn't tell which.

2

The *Emma Dean* moved in five directions at once, and when it geed the passengers hawed. It rode up a mountain of water, slid back, rocked, and spun. The deafening roar consumed shouts and screams and crescendoed to a hiss, a needle in their ears. On all sides the river hung above their heads, for this pit was where it folded—where it slid into a trough—and they were going backward now. Broadside, the boat rolled on its axis, and the gentle way it slipped under the water seemed almost an afterthought. Like a nurse, the river immersed the little babies in their morning bath.

Then it swept them from that hole, but now the boat was swamped and they were clinging to its sides. Across the sunken boat Jack shouted at Wes.

"WHAT?"

"I SAID THIS IS GETTING OLD!"

They shot through some waves straight, rode up and down others. Bill Dunn let go and rode behind the boat. Jack later said he heard something like thunder deep inside the river and swore it was boulders being dragged along the bottom. They hit a clear chute and sledded down the river, which broke into steps and they struck every one like toys being dragged downstairs by a child. At last the river turned and a tongue of rock extending from the inner bend enabled a great centrifugal curve to whip them into an eddy. They spun in brown foam. Wes's feet struck bottom. Bill Dunn followed as though tethered to the boat—Wes saw he was clinging to an oar. But they'd lost the other three. They dragged the *Emma Dean* ashore, tipped the water out, and sat on the sand, watching the others fly past.

They'd been thrown in an instant from summer to winter, for the water was surely colder than the air and the canyon walls were dark. When would this voyage end? The broken canyon walls of hard sandstone and limestone were not sheer cliffs but high enough to block the sunlight. Wes said it made him think of Lodore, but Jack Sumner observed that this Colorado River held more water than the Green. It drained an enormous portion of the continent, from mountains in Wyoming to those in the east rising from the plains, combining the water of two river watersheds—so the rapids were worse.

The others landed downstream and made their way up the bank. They built a fire to dry themselves, unpacked the equipment, and spread it on bushes and rocks to dry. The river never ceased to roar.

Farther downstream was a large pile of driftwood, and from this they selected the straightest logs and spent the rest of the day whip-sawing oars.

They portaged and lined down repeatedly, numbly. One day, in eight hours, they managed a mere three fourths of a mile, and again the bow and stern compartments of the *Emma Dean* and the *Maid* were leaking. George Bradley's loving care of *his* boat, the *Sister*, meant it was tighter. Still, this new canyon, named Cataract by Wes, was merciless on boats. It sprung a plank in the *Emma* and nearly ripped the iron strip off the keel of the *Maid*.

And their camps were not pleasant. In most places they scarcely found room to spread their bedding.

The walls grew high again. It rained, then rained more, and long gouts of water poured from every cliff. In camp one evening an ominous rumble came from somewhere in the earth. Sitting on driftwood, they sensed it through their legs then felt it in their molars. Wes jumped up and screamed, "Move!"

"Take it easy, Professor."

"What seems to be the problem?"

"Hold your horses. Calm down."

Wes dragged someone's bedding to higher ground, ran back and seized a sack of precious flour. As the roar grew louder the others roused themselves and collected all they could. They untied the boats and pulled them upstream, and as they were retying them the riverbank exploded and a flood smashed into the river from a narrow side canyon. They watched it from a ledge. Full of branches and debris, white with foam and spray, the brown flood enlarged as it poured into the river. Andy Hall whooped. The rattle of cobbles wasn't too bad, but the sickening thud of rock striking rock reminded them of cannonballs landing in the war. It plowed underneath the beach where they'd been camped, scouring a channel, tossing up sand. For half an hour it gushed before shrinking to a trickle and leaving a six-foot gash in the earth. "Christ almighty," said Bill.

Next morning they launched into rapids again and flew around a bend where they spotted a herd of desert bighorns on a slope.

The lead boat floated past the sheep and landed in a cove. At Wes's signal the others pulled over just below and readied their weapons. Bill Dunn and Jack Sumner crept between rocks and around a large buttress to get a good shot. The sound of the explosions ripped through the sheep's spines, which buckled as they ran. One sheep fell and the rest clattered down on sharpened hooves over naked rock toward the men below, where Hawkins shot another.

At the sound of Hawkins's rifle the herd changed course and flowed back up the slope over ledges and talus. The other men fired again but didn't hit anything. They all chased the sheep and fired more shots, but their prey was soon gone. In the end they'd killed two fat rams and George Bradley hailed it as the greatest achievement of the trip. They lashed their trophies to the bows of the two larger boats and found a sandbar downstream with sufficient driftwood to build a large bonfire and slaughter the sheep. Gorging on the forequarters, ribs, and fat, on the tender meat along the backbone, even the flanks, they stuffed their stomachs and intestines, their blood vessels and cells, every spare inch of their bodies.

3

"Begin with *plateaus*," said Wes. "This entire region began as one vast plateau containing smaller plateaus, or *anticlinal upheavals*, which, though smaller, are nonetheless of great amplitude. They often possess steep escarpments facing the axis of the flexure. Sometimes the streams that head near the axis excavate valleys and divide the great block into *mesas*. This is especially the case where the streams near their upper courses follow the strike of the beds before turning to cross the more or less abrupt lines of maximum flexure. Then *mesas* result."

"Say again?" said Hawkins.

"Then *buttes*, smaller in dimension, yet their altitudes may reach several thousand feet. Often the gulches which form the deep, reentrant angles of a line of cliffs have lateral gulches, which by continued erosion coalesce, and the salient angles are gradually cut off from the escarpment, which is ever retreating. In this manner *buttes* occur as outliers of cliffs. Due to erosion, their sculpted escarpments, their buttresses and columns, produce what seem to be architectural effects. Many look like ancient temples."

"Egyptian piles," said Andy Hall.

"Some are indeed pyramidical in shape. Some continue eroding and become *spires* or *towers*. But don't confuse those with *volcanic necks*. There have been many volcanoes in this vast country, boys, created by molten matter rising through vents. On cooling, those vents, now filled with lava, become harder than the sandstones and marls and other rocks which they'd forced upward. Over time the softer rock erodes, revealing black chimneys which were once inside the mountains. *Volcanic necks*."

"So what's badlands, Professor?" Having torn the meat off a rib with his teeth, and chewed the rest bare, Jack flung his bone away. "We hear about them all the time. It's like puzzles and mazes. Twisted-up knots of land."

"Exactly," said Wes. "Hills carved from sandstones and shales, from other easily eroded stone. Sometimes when the channels of drainage inosculate and gorges form about their heads and degradation is increased by an undermining process—I call it *sapping*—the walls then are carried back in steps, the tread of each step being the summit of a harder bed, the rise the escarped edge of the bed above, underlaid by the softer, which continues to corrade."

"Well, that explains it." But Jack had no idea.

"In these cases, fantastic shapes result: *domes, pinnacles, minarets, alcoves,* bold cliffs with deep niches and cavities. Rows of sculpted columns and pediments, a vast forest of forms. All naked rock, the sediment of ancient lakes."

"Lakes in this here desert?"

"It wasn't always a desert. At one time it teemed with reptiles and mammals, some of them gigantic. You'll find preserved bones of fishes, birds, and dragons, fossilized shells, all embedded in these rocks."

"Dragons, Professor?"

"Monstrous ancient lizards. Erosion reveals bones of great antiquity preserved by hardened minerals which seeped into their cells."

"So erosion's the key?" Andy Hall asked. His large nose and jug ears, molded by firelight, struck Wes as the product of erosive forces too.

"The key to knowledge in arid country, yes."

"What about earthquakes?"

"Violent upheavals are the exception, not the rule. *Erosion* is constant."

"Goodness gracious, Major," Ora piped up, "erosion's not everything. It didn't split your Split Mountain back there. How could it?"

"Erosion accounts for a great deal," said Wes. "It answers many questions."

Across from Wes, Ora fed the fire; it made a barrier between them. Sitting on a log, Ora then leaned back and clasped his hands around a knee. "Sometimes it does, and sometimes we got to be content to do without answers except what the Lord provides."

"What the Lord provides is an intellect with which we may understand His creation."

"And when we understand it and sinners with second thoughts start foaming at the mouth and fall down in convulsions and roll around on the desert, what then? Is our sins eroded too? I'll repent my mistakes and you'll repent yours? When that day comes I hope we can stand it. I hope we'll embrace in full godliness, Major."

Sheep bones lay around the fire: a spine, a skull, the shipwreck of a rib cage. The men waited for more, but the lesson was over so they turned in, bloated and sated, and slept like the dead. And feasted again the following morning, then packed the remaining meat in ragged oilcloth.

The battered boats still leaked. "Ought to caulk them again," Wes announced.

Hawkins groaned and Ora mumbled, "Let's just push off."

Wes called for volunteers to gather pitch, and George and Walter each raised a finger. They followed him up a steep side canyon and across a terrace, looking for trees. Wes trooped ahead with starving strides and swinging arm, up a rock-strewn gully then across an esplanade to a bowl of broken cliffs. Somehow George and Walter got left behind.

On top he walked south and found a stand of piñons. He pulled out his knife, leaned into one, and reached up to cut the bark. For hundreds of miles south and east to the horizon, the red land surrounded him, broken and empty. Only on the ocean could a skyline hold more. Ahead of him lay a troubled mess of canyons, any one of which might have held the river. To the east, green mountains a hundred miles away rose from the horizon. Closer in the west, across the river canyon, five distinctive peaks stood without coordinates or altitudes or names—they weren't on any maps—but Wes felt that he'd run out of names. His store had been exhausted. He surveyed the nameless landscape. The empty sky dwarfed it.

He made another cut near the base of the trunk and ripped the bark down between the two incisions. With the flat of his knife he scraped the exposed wood up from below and watched the pitch thicken on the blade. The sweet smell made him hungry.

He realized he had nothing to store it in. He wiped the heavy knife on the bark slab he'd removed.

The solitude felt good, and he lingered, took his time. With the knife he cut the sleeve off his shirt, the one he didn't need, then tied off one end and picked up the slab and scraped the pitch into the sleeve. For the next two or three hours he walked from tree to tree, collecting pitch and filling the sleeve until he had almost a gallon.

Later, back in camp, they dragged the boats onto the sand. Walter and George had collected pitch too, and they heated it all and caulked the boats again—for the five hundredth time, Bill Dunn remarked. "If they leak, they leak," he said.

Wes shook his head. "If they leak, you starve, Bill."

That afternoon when they launched the boats, the canyon became a perfect flume with a limestone floor. The walls closed in, the river grew narrow, the water speeded up, the waves flew into the boats. Once more the river inclined like a slide and the cliff beds dipped and they swung around curves up against the rock. Here the river too rolled on its side, thus cushioning their passage, and they shot through unharmed.

At last the walls dropped away and the river slowed and before them the world seemed to fall open. Blue sky bruised their eyes and the red land rippled. Off to the right were those unknown mountains Wes had decided he could name some other day. Already he'd begun to toy with the idea of returning to these canyons. And the next time he'd bring men who knew about surveying and how to draw maps, men he could talk with, men who might even recognize *mesas* or *buttes* or an *anticlinal axis*.

They sailed past low bluffs of deep red sandstone. Flowing out of naked rock, a stream entered from the right, the west—no, a full-blown river completely unexpected. Thirty yards wide, maybe two feet deep. It couldn't have been the Paria, thought Wes. That was several weeks ahead. And their next major landmark was supposed to be the San Juan River, which would enter from the left. The *Emma Dean* turned up this unknown river but didn't get far. Sulfurous and muddy, the water stank like rotten eggs. Wes asked Bill, "Is this a trout stream?"

"It's a fucking sewer."

The Major leaned over the edge of the boat, scooped up some water, and held it to his nose. Then he threw it back. "I christen thee the Dirty Devil," he said, and Jack looked at Bill. That evening in camp Wes made sure Ora got it right for his maps: the Dirty Devil River, heretofore undiscovered. When all had bedded down, Seneca whispered to Bill in the darkness, "Such a lovely name. You ought to feel honored."

"Shut your damned piehole."

"Bill, are you Dunn?"

Downstream in the morning they spotted more ruins, practically a village. They landed and explored them. The rock houses, in an overhang a hundred feet above the river, had been intricately mortared and chinked, even plastered, though in most places the plaster was gone and the roofs were caved in. Steps had been carved in the sandstone below leading up to the houses. On a shelf below the dwellings, scattered on the ground were flint chips and arrowheads, fragments of pottery, tiny ears of corn, pieces of sandals, even a small section of ladder lying under a piñon.

Jack Sumner wished to know how anyone could contrive to live in such a place. Wes pointed out that on the floodplain below, on that raised table, if you cleared away the shrubs and cactus and willows you could have a little farm. Perhaps they irrigated. And for water they filled their vessels in the river and carried them up to their houses. Picture it, said Wes. Women walking in a line from the shore with clay pots balanced on their heads. Picture these houses with smooth plastered walls and tightly framed doors and windows. Naked urchins running up and down ladders and across the sturdy roofs. Their mothers grinding corn or sewing garments with needles of bone and threads made of sinew. See that circular excavation over there? he asked.

On the edge of the alcove, where the sandstone billowed out, was an underground chamber whose stone walls rose a few feet above the earth.

"The Spanish call that an *estufa*. A stove, a heated chamber, a gathering place. Picture half a dozen young fellows beating drums and smoking pipes as they bask there in the winter. It isn't always summer in these canyons, boys. It's not always this hot. You could picture these braves with togas—sheepskin robes thrown about their bodies. Their dusky red skin has a velvety gloss, their jet-black hair is tied back in a knot, and their small black eyes set off their Roman noses. One young buck, very tall and dark, emerges from the chamber through a hole in the roof—he climbs up a ladder—and a pretty girl with the easy carriage of womanhood that never saw a pair of corsets shouts something at him. Or throws a handful of mud, which strikes him on the neck. He slowly turns. He sees her."

Wes watched his men and smiled.

"Oh Major Powell sir it was just getting good," said Andy Hall. "Please don't stop there."

"We know what happens next."

"I'd still like to hear it."

Andy picked up a rock and threw it toward the river. But it fell short. "Why plunk a village here?"

"In all likelihood the nomadic tribes were sweeping down upon them and they resorted to these cliffs and canyons for safety. Or it could have been the Spanish."

"Destitute of vegetation as a city street," said Jack.

"Perhaps it wasn't at that time."

"I suppose it was an Eden?"

They had a good laugh at that one.

4

"Hawkins, how come you changed your name from Missouri?"

"You asked me that already."

"I did?"

"I never was Missouri. That was just a handle to my name."

"What about Rhodes? Missouri Rhodes?"

"Nosy, ain't you."

"Oh, sure. We've been on this river for over two months working like galley slaves, with our lives depending on each other and the way ahead full of unknown dangers and who knows if we'll survive, and you call me nosy."

"It ain't been that long."

"What?"

"Two months."

"Sure as hell has. We started May twenty-fourth. We're almost out of July."

"You bring a calendar?"

"Tick off the days inside my belt with my knife."

Andy rowed, Hawkins lounged. Back in the stern Ora fiddled with his maps, for the river once again had grown calm and still. The deep orange sandstone of the low walls stood in rounded shoulders streaked with black stains, or swept around a curve of the river convexly, like sails carved by wind. On straight runs the cliffs broke into columns, concealing moist recesses with springs and waterfalls. This was *almost* an Eden. Even the heat blooming from the canyon walls was solaced by a breeze. "How come you changed names?" Andy asked again. "Were you right with the law? Running from something?"

"No."

"To which?"

"To all your meddlesome questions."

"Well, if one's no, the other's got to be yes."

"I wasn't right with the law, but it wasn't my fault."

"So you were on the lam."

"I was making things right with the law. Still am."

"Jack said you wouldn't run if your pants was on fire."

"He said that, did he?"

"My guess is it had to be a woman."

"Your guess is wrong."

"What was it then?"

Hawkins's face had grown thinner since they'd started this voyage. Not exactly gaunt and haggard, more taut and foxy. His eyes sunk in shadow and his large shaggy mustache drew attention from his mouth, which was usually closed. Hardly room for a chin in that face, thought Andy, who had chin and nose to spare. Hawkins's trunk was thin too and would make a stringy meal, all muscle and wire. "I was new in town, that's all. Alls I wanted to know is what time it was."

"What town was that?"

"Boonville, Missouri. I never seen it before."

"So you accosted a stranger on the street and asked him for the time?"

"I knocked on someone's door."

"And what happened?"

"He tried to have me arrested."

"For asking the time?"

"It was the look in my eye is what he claimed. Plus the piece of wood in my hand."

"Piece of wood?"

"Well, it had my name on it. What could I do?"

"You mean you hit him with it?"

"Not exactly. He says I threatened him."

"How come your name was on it?"

"I was putting my name on things at the time. My mark. 'Missouri.' Carving it on trees. Wrote it on my rifle stock."

"Your rifle?"

"Which they gave me in the war."

"This was during the war?"

"Near the end. Anyway, I think he recognized that piece of wood."

"How could a man recognize a piece of wood?"

"Milled lumber. See, I had my eye on it. Stack of it down by the riverbank. I'd been watching it for days. Looked to me like it wasn't being used. I wanted to see who it belonged to. Don't tell this to a creature."

"I won't."

"They was only two houses down by that river. The road ended at the river."

"Which river was that?"

"Which else? The Missouri. And upstream the bridge was guarded, and far as I could see I didn't have much time to build my raft."

"Your raft?"

"To cross the fucking river!"

"This is getting confusing."

"All I wanted to know was what time it was! He acted like I was some sort of crazy lunatic."

"So you clubbed him with the wood?"

"I didn't get the chance to. He run off for the sheriff. If I was a bad person I could have ransacked his house. But did I do that? No. I ran back to the bank and finished cobbling together my raft, which he said it was his wood so I had to make it quick. But I didn't succeed. They come and arrested me right there and then. So I never got to see her."

"Who?"

"My sweetheart."

"Then it *was* a woman!"

"Except I never got to see her. She'd gone on to Kansas."

"She lived in Kansas?"

"That's what I been told. Used to live in Missouri, but then her family, see, they moved on after the war started up to Lawrence, Kansas. See, they was abolitionists and mine was pro-slave."

"So you fought for the Confederacy?"

"In a manner of speaking." Hawkins looked around. Oramel's arms were draped across the stern compartment and he'd laid his head down and fallen asleep. Andy shipped his oars. The red cliffs and bluffs spun slowly past. "Sure, I joined the Rebels, but it was hardly an army. Remember how divided Missouri was? I was just a squeaky farm boy. Price and his famous American Knights and his bloody guerrilla friends Anderson and Quantrill come marching through town and I saw my chance for glory, plus leaving the farm forever and for good. So we marched across Missouri pitching for St. Louis, but the Union troops headed us. We marched on to Columbia, but by then we were stove. We didn't have nothing left. You get tired of nailing farmers up against their barn doors and shooting their eyes out. I figured if I joined on my own I could discharge myself too, and anyway by then all hell had broke loose. It weren't an army then but a pack of jackals. They'd divvied into bands and scattered west and south, for Kansas City, for Indian territory. I headed west too, but by then the bridge was guarded and getting across the river was a quandary. So I sold my gun and crept off in the night and built a raft to cross the river. But the sheriff collared me. Just for asking the time."

"Did they throw you in jail?"

"They threw me in jail but they had a deal then. You want to get out of jail, join up. So that's what I did. I enlisted."

"In what?"

"The Union Army. Mustered in as a private in Company One, Ninth Regiment, Missouri State Militia."

"You mean you fought for the Confederacy and then fought for the Union?"

"That's what I did. More or less. Less more than more. Didn't have much choice. There were times I didn't know which side I was on. Just think of it. Me, who couldn't cross that bridge, wound up being one of the ones that guarded it. It's enough to make you think."

"But how could you do it? How could you shoot men you'd been fighting with?"

"I never shot no one. I shot above their heads."

"They might have shotten you."

"They was all gone by then. Scattered to the winds. The war was about over. It was a lost cause."

"Which cause was lost?"

"The other side's, of course. Something you should know about that war, Andy. It wasn't North versus South. It wasn't abolitionists fighting slavers. It was the officers against the common men. The real other side was us, including—I say *including*—the niggers. I might not have known which side I was fighting for, but I knew which side my bread was buttered on. I knew what it was to shoot and what it was to get shot at. I knew what is was to run and what it was to hunt down them that run. But what I didn't know was sitting on a fat horse on a hill watching a bunch of crazy farm boys acting out orders to butcher each other. I hadn't tasted that. I knew about pulling farmers out their doors and asking which side *they* was on and they look around shitting their pants trying to find a clue. In other words, trying to figure out who's asking. And I was just like them, see? I didn't know no more than them which side to be loyal to. What it finally come down to is I got across that river. After that, there was no more questions to be asked. I got out of Missouri fast as

I could and looked for my sweetheart in Lawrence, Kansas, but her and her family had moved on by then to Lord knows where. So I kept going west. Never did find her. Thought when I came west it was supposed to be full of bushwhackers and Rebels."

"That's Texas, Hawkins."

"So I managed to learn once I ended up in Denver, which was all of it Jayhawkers. Met Jack in Denver and joined him in the mountains where he built his trading post. Came on this voyage all stocked with men that fought for the Union."

"Except me."

"Except you. You didn't fight at all, did you? That's what we got in common. I fought for both sides, you didn't fight for neither. What's your excuse?"

"Too young."

"Well, hell, my friend. If you would've fought, you'd know in your bones it was a wash either way. You would've been an enlisted man, right? That's the only difference."

On the last day of July the San Juan River finally entered from the east between sandstone knobs. Their smooth slopes were tempting and Wes tried climbing them to make his observations, but they proved too steep. He backed down, disappointed. They started off again, but Ora pulled abreast of the *Emma Dean* and told Wes he had a problem and they ought to land. He hadn't taken any bearings at the San Juan and already they'd passed it a mile back. Wes wished to know why he hadn't taken bearings, but Ora's thin lips remained stubbornly closed. So they landed and Wes decided to explore. Let Ora row upstream in this heat if he could. The rocks were hissing hot and not once that day, not even at dawn, had the thermometer dropped below a hundred.

Wes and his brother found a shady grotto in a fissure in the cliffs, its sides scooped from solid rock, which opened to an arbor with redbuds and cottonwoods on a winding shelf above a string of water. Inside, the hollowed-out rock billowed to a coliseum two hundred feet up, whose ceiling was merely a narrow winding skylight between tall walls. The high sweep of rock was hard and streaked with black, the lower rock was friable, and the harmless pool of water at their feet had carved out this chamber in a previous existence, blasting through the sandstone. The walls were baked sunlight: yellow above, red below, also brown and black, even purple in places. Water from springs streaked down crannies through watercress, moss, and ivy, and collected at their feet in a pond on the sand. Only dripping water eclipsed the perfect silence until Walter tried a shout.

What an echo! It wasn't even an echo, more like music from inside a sound box. Walter sang "Laura Lee" and the walls embraced the sound and seemed to sing it themselves. So they called this place Music Temple and brought the crew in to camp. All tried a few choruses that night, including Ora, who'd returned flushed from head to foot with his maps clutched in his hand.

Here, the Howland brothers and Bill Dunn etched their names in the wall, and Andy watched Hawkins wash the Major's hand when supper was ready—sour beans and sour bacon, their sheep meat had spoiled—and thought it was the Confederacy and the Union reconciled at last. After they'd eaten there was another round of singing, and when Andy's turn came he croaked "The Battle Hymn of the Republic." Later, he told Hawkins he'd charge up Cemetery Ridge for Major Powell but for no one else. Hawkins pointed out that it was the Rebels who charged up that ridge and the Union soldiers that slaughtered them, but Andy said what difference did it make.

Jack Sumner and Bill Dunn tried panning in the river and found more color here than any other place on the voyage, though still nothing larger than a grain of sand. "Make note of this spot," Jack said to Bill, and the latter drew a cross in the mudflat with his finger.

When they were back in the boats Andy said to Hawkins, "Bill Dunn's as dumb as a box of rocks."

"What makes you say that?"

"He don't know shit from honey."

"I demur," said Hawkins.

Ora said, "He's nature's child."

"He's quick is what he is," Hawkins declared. "Say what you will, he is a species unto himself. And he's truer than a dog."

They explored more glens downstream: winding narrow passageways opening to cliffs where springs burst from rock. In the sand below them grew cottonwoods and willows, aspens and scrub oaks. In Glen Canyon—as Wes named this stretch—the vegetation took shelter and grew amid water springing from rocks, trying to reach the sun reflected down its grottoes.

To the left on the horizon, floating with the river, loomed a single, wide, dark, massive mountain. It moved, but not past them. It looked too lonely and remote to have a name, so Wes didn't bother bestowing one upon it.

Besides, it had one already. It was Paiute Mountain.

The river picked up speed.

Wes had read the description of Fathers Escalante and Domínguez, who in 1776, on their way to Santa Fe, had crossed the Colorado somewhere near this place. He alerted Jack and Bill to be on the lookout for a tall butte above the southwest bank where the river swung sharply east and a ford that began near the foot of a cliff crossed to a sandbar on the left bank.

They landed in order to climb a rocky spur and scout the river ahead. The red rock along the banks gave way to desolation—a broken desert filled with towers and monuments. Wes took observations and Jack and Bill spotted a small herd of sheep down a slope near a sand dune. Jack shot a ram. This one he lashed to the bow of the *Emma,* and with its curled horns it resembled a figurehead.

5

That afternoon Wes felt that he and his men were the only human beings left on earth. It wasn't just the world of stone, the solid red and yellow flood rising in waves up tiered walls beside them; it was the plastered heat, the smell of the river, the ceiling of sky and explosion of sun, the taste of his own ferrous teeth, the floating movement of the boat. No one said a thing. Glen Canyon had placed them in nine separate rooms, each room a trance.

Massive golden curls of rock pocked with swirling craters and petrified dunes containing untold secrets slipped past left and right.

After a while Jack said, "There's your crossing."

Wes looked up. A notched butte filled the sky while ahead the river crimped. All was remote and silent and oppressive. Their thermometers read one hundred and six.

They landed at mudflats rimmed by a broad alluvial meadow that pinched to a cliff on the right bank, and Wes tried to cross the river at what looked to be shallows, but the current was too strong. Was this in fact the crossing? According to the description, a river entered from the right, but all they could find was a muddy canyon upstream. Ora said it was the crossing, but Wes wasn't sure. If it was, El Vado de los Padres hadn't only been used by the fathers. Dead stars of leftover campfires littered the meadow below the cliff, and charred bones lay around. They looked like bones of cattle, not game, which the men couldn't fathom. But Wes informed them that Mormon settlers who lived west of here, perhaps within a hundred miles, had been raided by the Navajo for the past several years, and the Indians' route to the Mormon ranches must have crossed here.

"Shall I put it on the map?" asked Oramel Howland. "The Crossing of the Fathers?"

"Wait till we see what's up ahead."

"Is there more crossings?"

"This is it. If it *is* it. The only one for five hundred miles."

A well-beaten trail snaked through the intermittently muddy side canyon they'd found. They followed it to where it terminated at steps cut in the sandstone sloping up left. The steps were lined with logs and fill, and the sandy fill held cattle tracks. It must have been the crossing. But where, Wes wondered, was the tributary the Mormons called Ute Creek? Could it be this empty canyon?

He looked up at the steps and decided to try them. Placing his feet where the fathers might have placed them a hundred years ago, he climbed the cross-bedded sandstone over bald rock past saddles and cones and pinnacles and ribs. Then he looked down at Ute Creek, if that's what it was. Heaves of rock seemed to swallow it.

That evening Jack butchered his ram and skinned it with his knife, notched twice on its handle — to obtain a better grip, not to tabulate victims. Hawkins made a mutton stew with the last of the beans, and no one quite knew whether to celebrate the fresh meat or mourn the passing of the beans. Nor did they know what to do with the legs, the head, the stomach, heart, intestines, so they left them there. The meal had a last-supper mood to it.

The men bedded down when darkness slammed its door, then a full moon rose in the southeast and a lone coyote howled. They'd all thrown their blankets around the dying fire, all except George Bradley. "That's no coyote," said Jack. "It's a redskin."

The howl broke into high-pitched yips and yaps shading into barks and even something like whines. "Coyote," said Bill.

It didn't take long for beetles and screwworm flies to find the fresh bighorn carcass. Under the moon, in the warm air, they feasted and swarmed and laid eggs on the meat while the exhausted humans slept. Something padded toward their camp: the coyote. He walked on his toes, marking rocks and bushes, and stopped near some sagebrush, perfectly still, one paw cocked. He arched his back and pounced and with one quick snap killed a fat wood rat, tossed it in the air, and swallowed it whole.

He found the sheep's carcass and circled it, sniffing. He sniffed rocks splashed with blood, sniffed Jack Sumner's knife. In his haste to clean the sheep, Jack had left it on the ground.

The coyote licked the knife. It cut deep into his tongue. He jumped back and licked his paw, then did it again to taste the blood his tongue had left there. He trotted to the river and drank, then trotted back and rolled in the offal and jumped up and gorged himself, stripping the bones and devouring the organs until he couldn't tell if the blood he was tasting came from himself or the sheep. When he'd eaten his fill he left the head and skin but carried the rest of the carcass to the cliff, hid it under rocks, and covered it with dirt.

He loped off and wandered for a while, stopping to lick his paws with bleeding tongue. Eventually he made his way to his den, behind a stunted piñon up against a cliff. He crawled inside the tunnel and his pups yipped and whined and he brought up the food from his stomach in increments and fed them like a mother bird. But what they liked best was the blood on his tongue, and even as he fed them they were licking his muzzle and paws and tongue and teeth to get a good taste of it.

Part Eight

1

Toab and his family marched across a sandy plateau with Paiute Mountain on their right. Round and full, alone in the sky, it poured up from the horizon pulling everything toward it. Pangwits had guided them left of the mountain to avoid the maze of canyons between it and the river. They were following a trail and Onchok asked Pangwits who used this trail. He asked about the ford at O'poment. Isn't that where the Navajo cross the river when they raid the Mormons?

It's the only crossing, Pangwits answered. Everyone uses it.

What happens if we run into Navajo?

Don't worry. I know what to do.

Toab thought, I've heard that one before.

Now and then Pangwits inspected the trail but couldn't find footprints. The sandy earth held tracks until the rain erased them, and it hadn't rained in weeks. He'd taken a cane, not because he was lame but because he liked canes, and used it to poke at rocks and bushes to see what he could find. No one's been here for a long time, he said. And we have clouds today. A good day for traveling!

The clouds helped to shrink the distance from the sky and made the mountain look even larger.

Blackbrush. Sage. Mormon tea. Rabbitbrush. A few trees in folds where the dry washes ran. The evenly spaced bushes and trees left easy room for walking, but the sand made it tiresome. Toab and Pangwits led Pooeechuts on the burro, followed by Mara and Soxor, Chookwadum and Kwits, and Onchok in the dust twenty paces behind.

Pooeechuts gazed at the mountain, felt it rolling toward them. She'd come on this trail a long time ago with baskets to trade on the Other Side, and things looked familiar. They didn't call it Paiute Mountain then, they called it Mountain Sitting, Kaivakaret. She and her father had crossed the river at O'poment, climbed steps cut in the rock, and walked through a hash of canyons and cliffs, through forests and deserts, to get to their relatives. Her father vowed never to go there again—the way was too hard for such meager returns.

The burro stopped walking and Soxor had to slap it. The sharp sound made Pooeechuts think of being shot. The hot seed in her arm, the coal heating up her body, the bullet going rotten like a bean —it had ripped her life in two.

Looking down, she saw the white man sighting up along his rifle. He chose to aim at her, not one of the men. His left eye twitched, the one that sagged and squinted beneath raven-black hair. She'd been running up the slope without looking back, that was her mistake. She should have entered his tent. She would have done what he wanted. What difference did it make? Her husband didn't care. When the man grabbed her arm and pulled her toward the tent she gagged at the smell, but better that than this. Now she was hauling a dead thing around attached to her shoulder and soon its poison would enter her heart and the stream of moments always flickering by would slow down and stop, and then where could she hide?

If she could only be alone, she'd feel a lot better.

If she'd had a gun, she could have killed the white man. To kill someone, she'd heard, aim a little over his head—aim where his mind is.

The land grew more broken. Snaking through its folds, they entered a shallow canyon obstructed by low mounds and hills. Pangwits looked confused, flailing with his cane. They spotted water here so watered the burro and drank their fill and continued. After a while the canyon floor rose and they found themselves crossing trenches and troughs on gritty sand and hard mounds of sandstone. Sandstone knobs obscured the route ahead and they began to feel lost until they saw the coyote. He was climbing the slope of a gully to the right, looking over his shoulder. Coyote's leading us, said Pangwits.

He's led us before. Toab watched their shifty friend.

They climbed the same slope and crossed a rock terrace. They came to a mesa and mounted steep talus up benches and ledges through broken cliffs, following the coyote. When they reached the top he was gone, but Pangwits pointed them south across the mesa cropped by flaring canyons. Canyons snapped at their feet and the sinking land ahead looked torn up by swirling walls of rock. The mountain was behind them, at their right shoulders now.

They skirted the mesa's sharp edge, gradually descending as the light changed, as clouds lost their glow and darkness rose and spread. They climbed down through broken land and from the burro Pooee-chuts watched a scorpion scoot across a rock in the dying light. They stopped at a wash next to some willows, and those who wanted to ate seedcakes and nuts and the others fell asleep. Mara and Toab wandered away. Pangwits and Onchok sat next to a boulder, huddled over some bones. Tired and achy, Pooeechuts stared at them. She saw it all—saw death congealing.

When they started off the next day at dawn, Pangwits announced that he knew where they were. He knew the way now. The rising sun had illuminated enormous buttes and towers ahead on the horizon. Today would be hot; the blue sky contained just a single white smear. Onchok called out for frequent rests, and that was fine with his wife, since the stiff-legged burro jarred her bones with every step. The earth opened up and walled them in again and rolled boulders in their path and dampened more sand and planted thick willows to obstruct their progress. Pangwits said those who didn't know the way could wander in circles forever in this country. Ahead the land bulged, and broken domes of rutted sandstone, white, yellow, red, rose from below. A faint path threaded this confusion, coiling downward through its folds. They stopped at water pockets still cooled by shadows.

They crossed the shattered country and descended bald rock to where the river was hiding inside the knotted earth. The last heave of rock made a bulging ramp down to the riverbank.

They followed the river the rest of the morning and arrived at O'poment. Toab saw right away that the water was high. The tail of a sandbar fanning into the river seemed to dissolve as they approached; it became a crease of water. On the opposite bank solid red cliffs rose above the river and caught its moving light. Pangwits waded in to inspect the ford, probing with his cane, and two nooses of water at his calves pulled harder by the minute.

He turned back to shore. It's too high, he said.

What can we do? asked Onchok.

Wait.

How long?

Until it goes down.

Onchok looked around. I can cross, he said. I have strong medicine.

You'll need it, said Pangwits.

We'll need more than that if the Navajo find us here. I'd rather take my chances with the river.

Onchok walked to a stand of willows, cut a long shoot at its base, and trimmed it. He said to Toab, You come behind. Toab grabbed one end of the willow and followed his brother onto the ford. The sound the water made pulling at their legs became louder as they moved, and in a moment Onchok just stood there, looking as though he might turn back. Instead, he took another step. The reddish water climbed his waist. His right arm stretched back, clutching the willow, and Toab's left arm gripped the other end. Both faced upstream so their knees wouldn't buckle. Onchok leaned forward then floundered in the water, struggling against it. Toab swung around to hold the branch with both hands and shouted at Onchok, It's better this way.

What?

Turn your side to the water.

I can't stand up!

Onchok too held the branch with both hands but had sunk to his chest where the water piled against him. He spat and coughed, fighting the river. Toab held on, inching back the way they'd come, and Onchok went under. Toab pulled back, heaving him to his knees; his hair spread on the water. As Onchok emerged Toab continued to backtrack across the ford but was skidding downstream. Pangwits waded in from the shore and inched forward, bracing his legs, and grabbed Toab's breechclout.

In a chain the three men lurched back to shore.

We can try again tomorrow, said Onchok.

Toab looked at him.

They built arbors from the willows, gathered driftwood downstream, and were about to build a fire when Onchok stopped them. It would announce their presence, he said. At least it was hot, at least the river cooled them off, at least they were already dry. Soxor brought her mother the best food they had, one of their agave cakes wrapped in corn shucks. Like a child, Pooeechuts left the food in her mouth, staring at nothing, then remembered it and chewed.

A coyote howled that night three times in a row. Bad sign, thought Toab.

They slept in the sand under a moon that crawled through the water beside them all night.

2

In the morning Pooeechuts spotted Mara and Toab farther down the river, where they'd slept. She ate seedcakes and jerky while her husband paced the shore, inspecting the water. It's lower, he said.

It doesn't look lower.

That sand crescent's back.

Onchok gazed at the other bank. Pangwits joined him and shook his head. It doesn't look good.

Toab walked up. Let's build a raft, he said.

We could do that, said Onchok. Let's try the ford first.

Pangwits pinched cornmeal from his medicine bundle and threw it to the east. He mumbled a request to Toovuts to protect them while they crossed this river and protect the burro and the food. He scattered the cornmeal in the six directions, turning as he did so.

Toab and Onchok went first again, clutching a long willow shoot. This time Toab led, walking straight ahead with his side to the current, taking care to brace himself before each step. Onchok did the same, and with the river at their hips they made it across without stumbling.

Toab went back for the children. They dispensed with the willow branches and held hands in a chain, but Toab carried Kwits. Soxor and Chookwadum waded between Toab and Pangwits. The river rose almost to their armpits and Chookwadum slipped, but Pangwits yanked her to her feet and they finished the crossing. Then Toab and Pangwits went back and strapped on the two burden baskets carried there by the burro and crossed again, leading Mara.

They returned to help Pooeechuts mount the burro and lead it across, but she didn't feel strong and could hardly hold on. In the middle of the river the burro stopped. Pangwits slapped its haunches and pushed from behind. Toab tugged the hair rope but the creature wouldn't budge. Seated on the burro, slumped and faintly smiling, Pooeechuts watched Toab. The burro stood firm but was skidding downriver inch by inch as its hooves were undermined. When it slowly fell it didn't keel over; instead, it leaned back and its legs swung up and Pooeechuts spilled off, relaxing her knees. As the burro slipped away then shot down the river, Toab grabbed her arm. That's when the pain flashed behind her eyes and everything turned white and she heard herself scream. Releasing the arm, Toab gripped her dress and Pangwits labored forward and helped pull her to her feet. Almost dragging her now they struggled toward shore and emerged from the river.

She sat on the bank, her vision coming back little by little. The burro rolled over and over downriver. It washed toward the cliffs where it struck bottom and lay motionless in the shallows, feet sticking up. Dead, said Pangwits. But in a moment its legs started kicking. The burro rolled to its feet and reached shore.

Between the base of the cliffs and the edge of the river ran a narrow slope of red dirt and scree. Onchok and Kwits raced down this strip, and when they got to the burro it was standing, watching them. They led the animal upstream along the bank.

The sun had risen above the eastern shore and was low in the sky but already burning. Poking around, Onchok found a fire pit. These ashes are still warm, he said.

Sometimes people come here, said Pangwits.

Pooeechuts was shivering so they gathered some driftwood and built a fire in the pit despite Onchok's objection. They'll see our smoke! he said.

Huddled in the sand, his wife held her arm.

Fresh bones of an animal were strewn in the grass. And Kwits had found the head and skin of a bighorn tossed on the shore. It looked pretty good. When the fire had burned awhile they cut off the skin and threw the head on the coals.

Not far from the bones Onchok spotted a knife with a notched handle. Testing it on his thumbnail he found it was sharp, much sharper than the one they'd traded for at Oraibi. Despite the loss of his guns he'd begun to grow wealthy in Pangwits's village from playing the hand game, and a good knife was something a wealthy man owned. Yet the wealth just fed his worry; he had more to lose now. Let's not stay, he said. We ought to go on. Someone's just been here and could come back.

Let's cook the head first, Pangwits said. I'm hungry.

Cook it, then go.

Your wife doesn't feel well.

She can ride the burro.

I think she needs rest.

Meat will make her stronger.

But Pooeechuts wouldn't eat. When the head was cooked they offered her the tongue but she didn't want it. She huddled by the fire saying nothing. At least she'd stopped shivering.

Toab began building her an arbor using driftwood poles and willow branches. Onchok ran up and asked what he was doing.

We'll have to stay here a few days. Your wife is feeling bad.

We can't stay here, said Onchok. The Navajo and Ute use this crossing all the time.

We don't have much choice. Your wife can't go on.

Let's leave her here then. She's dying anyway.

We shouldn't do that. She's not an old lady. Her time hasn't come.

She's dying. Leave her here.

I don't want to, said Toab.

Onchok hurried from Toab to Pangwits, insisting they go. Pangwits shrugged, looking down. Mara and Soxor built more shelters and helped Pooeechuts to her feet. Holding her good arm they walked her across the alluvial meadow toward the cliff with the arbors at its base. Onchok ran up and grabbed his daughter by the arm and jerked her away. He shook her and shouted in her face to get ready. We're going now! he screamed. Toab took Soxor's place and led Pooeechuts to the cliff, laid her in a shelter, and covered her with a blanket. Onchok stormed off looking for a way to climb the cliff and scout the land around them.

At the base of the cliff, Toab found more remains of the sheep, offal covered with dirt. He looked around, thinking Coyote was near. Often Coyote hid his kill like that if he couldn't eat it all. Once, he found a bear killed by his brother Wolf and burrowed inside it, eating all he could, and left the skin behind, filled with sticks and dirt. He was always hungry, always lustful, Coyote. He stole food, tricked friends, often bungled things. Had he tricked them yesterday in leading them here? One time as Coyote walked through the woods he saw some birds juggling their eyes and thought he'd try it too. He plucked out his eyes and tossed them in the air, but they caught on branches. He couldn't get them back.

Another time Coyote thought he'd try to fly and took some goose feathers and glued them to his arms. But he fell from the sky and broke his head open and ate his own brains from a fragment of his skull, thinking it was mush in a bowl. When the top of his head began to feel cold he realized what he'd done.

He discovered sewing. He invented menstruation. He made the world the way it is, Toab thought. But he fucked his own daughters and stole his brother's wife and killed Bear's children and took Owl's eyes. He schemed to correct the accidents he'd caused and only made things worse. He was always glancing back, looking over his shoulder, and Toab sensed his presence now. A wind blew through his soul. He felt a sudden chill. Something would happen, some catastrophe, he thought. Something or someone was coming toward them, or had already been here, or was here now. Coyote, what's this story? I don't like the looks of it.

3

As the sun rose and the day grew hotter, Pooeechuts drifted off. Her tongue had swollen up and she couldn't hold a thought and her heart raced. She'd gone from cold to hot in a wink, sunk into fire. Her eyes felt ready to burst like hot coals. The more they hurt, the more she clamped them shut. Shadows passed. She squeezed out the light.

A plunge inside her body unnerved her, made her flail. Her eyes flew open and saw Chookwadum beside her, face wrung with anxiety. She thrust her burning hand toward her daughter's frown, making her jump.

Mama, I'm hungry! A sizzling hand print grinned across the girl's face.

Get yourself a seedcake, said Pooeechuts.

Chookwadum spun around and raced back toward the river.

Pooeechuts watched her Skinny One run off, remembering how weak and frail she'd been at birth. Some seeds hold bones finer than hairs that never grow strong. By contrast, Pooeechuts was vigorous as a child. She'd walked around on earth changing her shape and switching her movements with the mountains and canyons, becoming herself with each step, each breath. Because she'd been small, small but strong, and quick on her feet, they'd named her Mouse. Now when she walked it was on the earth's hardness with stiff brittle legs, all strength drained out. They ought to go and leave her here, let her die by herself, as her husband had said.

The sun had dropped behind the cliffs, throwing her into shade. She sank into herself and tried to understand. We all have the same death, the same for everyone, and always it drags you out of your body. It pulls you in a circle, Pooeechuts thought, and one end of the circle meets the other end. It's death from one direction, birth from the other, and either way you're torn apart. There are no ends and no beginnings, she thought, and when the time comes to die you go on a journey completing the circle, but you do it alone. You almost feel better, or you don't feel anything, don't feel like a rabbit skewered on a stick and boiling in the flames. You just feel alone, and she was happier alone. Except for one thing.

From her arbor in the brown and blue glow of late afternoon, she watched Kwits and Soxor play in the river, watched Chookwadum eat a seedcake, Onchok and Pangwits huddle together, Mara and Toab walk upstream. Soon they disappeared.

She heard snatches of talk between Onchok and Pangwits, the same old thing. Maybe no one will find us here, said her brother. Maybe she'll die soon, said her husband. They looked toward her arbor and, seeing her watching them, stood and approached. Onchok reached for his medicine pouch and bounced it in his palm.

Pangwits asked her how she felt. Lying there, she said nothing. He said he thought he'd try another healing ceremony.

Don't bother, she said. I won't get well.

We'll have to go tomorrow, said her husband. We can't stay here forever. He tied the pouch to his breechclout.

Don't worry about me. You can just leave me here. I'm going to die soon. Worry about yourselves, not me.

How do you feel? Pangwits asked again.

I don't think I'll get better. I won't live very long, that's how I feel. I'm just skin and bones. I think I'm not going to live very much longer. I think I'll die any time. I feel hot. My tongue feels dry. Bring me some water.

She was sweating and her face flushed again. She'd begun to breathe quickly. Pangwits went to fetch their water jug, and while he was gone her husband hissed, I know what happened. You tried to witch someone and you witched yourself instead. You tried to witch me. Now you're killing yourself. Your own witchcraft is doing it.

She just looked at him. Take good care of our children.

Why do you say that?

Pangwits returned and she drank half the jug. I'm burning up, she said. Leave the jug here.

Pangwits said, Let me sing over you.

No, she said. Thank you for the water.

He walked away and left the jug behind.

Onchok asked, Should I bring you some food?

I'm not hungry.

If you're burning up, let me take off this blanket. He pulled the blanket off, one they'd gotten at Oraibi, and looked at the arm lying there like a stick. He touched it.

What are you doing?

Does it hurt?

I can't feel it.

To him the gray skin felt crackly, lifeless. The wound itself had healed but left a ragged black crease, and it smelled bad. Onchok looked away. I shouldn't have said that about the witchcraft, he said. It's the fault of the man who shot you.

It's my fault, she said. I shouldn't have run.

No, it's mine. I haven't been good.

She looked at him. How so?

Never mind.

They fell silent.

Toab and Mara reappeared below, walking by the river. He held her hand. Pooeechuts said, I want to talk with my sister. Onchok went down and sent Mara up.

By the time Mara got there Pooeechuts was shivering. Mara pulled up the blanket Onchok had pulled down. Pooeechuts had begun panting like a dog and tried to get up but couldn't and felt desperate.

All at once she went blind. Her eyes were wide open but things were blazing white. This time it was for good. She'd never see again, she knew. She saw inside, though. She pictured white foam spilling out of her soul, eating the world, and understood: she herself was death.

She said to Mara, Listen to me.

What?

I have something to tell you. It's about you and Toab.

4

They moved on the next morning and left Pooeechuts there to die. The children cried and so did Mara, but Chookwadum was the unconsolable one. The others had to drag her away. They pulled her through sand upriver to the trail in a side canyon while she screamed,

Mama! Mama! They put her on the burro and held her there. She fell forward on its neck and howled.

Pooeechuts had told them all what she'd told Onchok, that she wouldn't get better. After talking with Mara, she summoned the others and they gathered around her, leaning in close. In a hoarse, faint whisper, she urged them to go. She was almost dead, she said. They couldn't wait there; the Navajo might come. She didn't want to put them in any kind of danger.

What about burning your arbor and clothes and saying the prayers? asked Toab.

Those things aren't important. Pray in your hearts.

They did paint her face red and wrap her in a blanket. Pooeechuts lay there in the arbor as they left. She didn't move or call out. Her face grew smaller until they couldn't tell if her eyes were open or if she could see or whether she was conscious or even alive. They turned left into a canyon and never saw her again.

They hiked up the canyon through willows and bulrushes over broken land, muddy in places. Pangwits found the steps cut in sandstone to the left and they climbed past the logs and sandy fill. The burro didn't slip—he was slow but surefooted. Before long, Chookwadum stopped crying, got off, and walked.

But later, when they trudged up a sandy spur toward a notch of stone, she started howling again. They let her shriek. Mara draped her arm across the girl's shoulders, but she threw it off. Their dusty path passed rabbitbrush and sage, and when they stopped to rest and looked back where they'd come from, waves and waves of red and white rock rose toward Paiute Mountain. They couldn't see the river. The sun had been slurred across half the sky by a high white haze. Their sandy slope was hot and Chookwadum still shrieked, so Mara gave her a good shake. She quieted down. Then Mara joined Onchok.

Pooeechuts had told them something else too. Toab had watched her talking with Mara in that arbor alone. Pooeechuts talked and Mara listened, shaking her head, but at last the younger sister hung her head and nodded, then summoned the others. After she urged them to leave her there to die, Pooeechuts looked at Toab, then Mara, and whispered that Onchok had a new wife: Mara. Now Mara's your mother, she told each of the children.

So now Mara walked beside Onchok, not Toab. Toab hung back, trying not to feel anything. The sister married the widowed husband, that's the way they'd always done it. That kept a family together.

They passed the notch, made by two pinnacles just wide enough for the burro to fit, and descended through an alkaline desert toward a rocky plateau with more buttes and mesas and spires all around.

Now Pooeechuts's children had a new mother, that's the way it should be. Now Onchok wouldn't be lonely, thought Toab. Now everything was right, even if everything felt dead. Toab slowed and let a distance grow between himself and the others. Crossing the slickrock, he didn't know what to do. His chest felt pulled open, heart filled with sand, and the sand was leaking out; he felt it trickle through a hole. He stopped walking and stood there and looked at the sky. Steal Onchok's medicine and bury it, he thought. Those human fingers in his pouch were the poison, the witchcraft—they'd killed Pooeechuts. The dead want things around them to be dead, and they'd gotten their way. He could stay away from Onchok. He could kill him, run off, and go back home alone. But he couldn't kill Onchok—Onchok was his brother. They'd have to have a talk. It wouldn't do any good. And now Mara was his wife.

As though sensing his thoughts, Mara looked back and saw Toab standing there. After that she avoided his eyes. She looked away or down.

Toward late afternoon the light seemed to fracture. Clouds rolled in and covered the sun. Things right beside them seemed distant and watery. No one knew what to think.

Then the sun broke through the clouds and it was half a sun. They'd heard about this, about the sun disappearing and bad things to come, and the children started crying. Pangwits led them around, aimless and uncertain, ducking from the wounded light. Then more clouds came, the light went flat and hollow, and the air itself seemed to cast a blank shadow. What were they supposed to do? Onchok found a water hole in the rock floor at the base of a fractured cliff and they camped. They went about their business as though everything were normal. Every day and night should turn out the same as the one that came before it, that's how the world lasts. But this day wasn't normal. They couldn't look at each other.

Mara stayed with Onchok and the children slept nearby. Toab camped alone.

The next day fissures marked the land, deep thin cracks they had to avoid once the sun rose and they could see. The sun was whole again and its light filled the sky. Crossing this landscape they stepped over cracks but others fanned open and they detoured around them. Later on, once again clouds filled the sky. The temperature dropped, a wind whipped through the sand, and it began to rain.

No one mentioned Pooeechuts. The Newe never talked about the dead, and she must be dead by now. The wind blew sand and rain in their faces but they slogged on.

Crimson cliffs sat on the horizon, shading to purple, and gusts of wind whistled. Red and brown puddles rippled on the rock. The group descended a steep sand-choked ridge to a leaden stream below, which they followed past a few cottonwoods and red eroded cliffs back to the Pawhaw—the Colorado. They were downstream now from O'poment, the ford, where they'd left Pooeechuts, below that impassable canyon with its high cliffs. Here were stands of willows and alluvial flats and benches and tables and a wide valley. The clouds began to lift. The sun emerged again, and just before it set, it lit up the standing rock. On one side, brown plateaus and rocky ledges, on the other, wet cliffs red as blood in the sun. They stayed here but didn't build a fire—Onchok wouldn't let them. Again Toab slept away from the others. He hadn't spoken to anyone since leaving O'poment.

The next day was hot, but the wind still held moisture and soon the clouds returned. They hiked south along the river in this broken valley, then southwest beside the cliffs and gullied brown ledges bare of growth. The ledges buttressed higher pink parapets rising to the west. Between the river and the cliffs a plateau widened into a flat desert valley. This brown skin of land contained the river canyon, running south through the earth like a scar from a lightning bolt, and as it receded their steps began to lighten because they were drawing closer to Paiute land. But Toab hung back, alone with his thoughts.

On the horizon the first familiar landmark began to appear: Mountain Lying Down, the Kaibab Plateau. The cliffs on their right had become a long mesa whose shoulders and spurs ran out into the desert, while on the ground ahead, strewn across the parched land, were massive brown boulders some fifty feet high: House Rock Valley.

Three or four hours ahead was a spring — they were making for that.

Toab had lost sight of the others and didn't care. He said to himself, I'm walking like a burro. Head down, haunches stiff, stringy tail hanging. In the winter my tail will freeze and break off and I won't even notice. Burros eat each other's tails when there's nothing else to eat. When there's nothing else to eat, people eat burros. For a burro there's no sense in going on or stopping, either one's the same. The burro doesn't care about anything, thought Toab, and no one cares about burros. They carry things for people and sometimes carry people and walk until they drop. You wouldn't leave a burro in a pasture to eat whatever he wants and smell the other burros — that would be foolish — you'd tie him to a tree. You'd kick him if you had to. The burro doesn't care. He's stupid. He's our slave. That's how we made him. We made him to have something stupider than us. More stubborn too, Toab decided. Burros do what they want unless you kick them hard. They're pretty good kickers themselves, which is why they appreciate kicks so well. I better stop thinking so much about burros. I'll stop when I want and just stand here like a burro. I'll stand here all day, leaking sand, waiting, waiting for my kick.

A gunshot broke the quiet. Dust rose ahead and Toab started running but couldn't see past all the boulders.

Drunken gray clouds raced across the sky. He rounded a boulder and stood face to face with three men on horses, each gripping a child. The closest one stopped and scowled down at Toab. Black hair painted with vermilion at the part, eyes ringed with vermilion, vermilion stripes down his legs. He held Soxor against his earth-colored torso, seated on the horse. The horse shook its mane and snorted. Soxor's wild eyes pleaded with Toab.

The second man, holding Kwits in one arm, held a rifle with the other, its stock braced against his shoulder. He pointed it between Toab's eyes. The last one had locked the squirming Chookwadum against his chest with a cane — Pangwits's cane. Each child was gagged and bound at the wrists, each wide-eyed and gaping at Toab.

The horses clopped slowly past. The three Ute stared down and Toab stared back. Another Payuche, said the man holding Chook-wadum. The rifle leaked blue smoke.

They broke into a gallop.

Then they were gone and Toab raced ahead between towering boulders. He came to a necklace of blood on brown rock beneath which Pangwits lay, face down. One shoulder had exploded. The burro stood about a hundred feet away, eating weeds. Onchok and Mara squatted next to the body. Toab's brother looked up.

It wasn't Navajo, Onchok said. It was three Ute.

I know.

Part Nine

We are now ready to start on our way down the Great Unknown. Our boats, tied to a common stake, chafe each other as they are tossed by the fretful river. They ride high and buoyant, for their loads are lighter than we could desire. We have but a month's rations remaining. The flour has been resifted through the mosquito-net sieve; the spoiled bacon has been dried and the worst of it boiled; the few pounds of dried apples have been spread in the sun and reshrunken to their normal bulk. The sugar has all melted and gone on its way down the river. But we have a large sack of coffee. The lightening of the boats has this advantage: they will ride the waves better and we shall have but little to carry when we make a portage.

We are three quarters of a mile in the depths of the earth, and the great river shrinks into insignificance as it dashes its angry waves against the walls and cliffs that rise to the world above; the waves are but puny ripples, and we but pigmies, running up and down the sands or lost among the boulders.

We have an unknown distance yet to run, an unknown river to explore. What falls there are, we know not; what rocks beset the channel, we know not; what walls rise over the river, we know not. Ah, well! we may conjecture many things. The men talk as cheerfully as ever; jests are bandied about freely this morning; but to me the cheer is somber and the jests are ghastly.

— JOHN WESLEY POWELL

1

"Where's Ora?" asked Bill.

"Off somewheres pulling his pud."

"Loan me your knife, Jack."

"What for?"

"Pry the face off this watch."

"I lost my knife. What happened to the watch?"

"Got dunked in the river."

"Is it running?"

"No. Can't read the numbers neither."

"Aha."

"It's just another watch."

"Worth something to the Major. Worth a lot of money."

"The fuck do I care?"

"He won't like it, Bill."

"There ain't much he likes."

Jack was right, though. Bill decided the best he could do was to fess up, get rid of the watch, and take his medicine. So he walked up to Wes and handed it to him.

"What's this?"

"That's your watch." They were in another canyon, this one with sheer cliffs of polished red limestone growing higher by the mile, prompting Jack to observe there was enough marble here to build four hundred Babylons. They'd already run half a dozen rapids and lined down twice and stove a hole in the *Maid* while trying to lift her over rocks. With George Bradley's help, Andy was repairing it. Seneca Howland and Walter Powell were dipping their shirts in pails and wringing them gingerly lest they become a wet mess of threads. The day had been one endless cycle of soaking and drying in the hot sun, which didn't stop at parching clothes and skin. It also rooted out moisture from blood vessels, brains, and organs.

Walter Powell was singing "John Anderson, My Jo." They'd camped on a sandbank beneath a wall with a cleft above their heads, a pour-over in times of heavy rain. But that day the sun had cauterized the sky and not a cloud was in sight.

Their second time lining down had occurred at a rapid with a vicious tail that swung the *Sister* back upstream. Its rope went slack then taut as a bowstring, caught Bill Dunn's armpit, and pitched him into the river. It dragged him under and he'd been forced to climb hand over hand up the rope to get out. When they camped two hours later and Bill realized the watch was still in his pocket, his first reaction was at least he didn't lose it. But water had gotten under the glass and penetrated the case and now sloshed around inside. The glass was so clouded the watch's face was obscured.

"You careless ape. What on earth did you do to it?"

"I got pulled into the water and the watch was in my pocket."

Jack walked up. He'd seen Wes's scarlet face. "Dunn came damn near being drowned," he told the Major.

"Little loss there. Why was the watch in your pocket?"

"I was taking elevations."

"You didn't put it away?"

"Didn't have no chance to."

"That watch cost thirty-five dollars."

"Ain't worth a peanut shell now."

"Is that your attitude? You sound proud of what you've done."

"I ain't proud. What's done is done. No sense in crying about it."

"By God, I'll make you cry."

"You don't need to. Boo-hoo."

"I'll teach you a lesson."

"You couldn't teach me how to shit in a hole."

Jack wasn't sure whom to pull away, Bill or Major Powell. He hooked Bill's arm and led him stumbling backward. "That ain't the right spirit," he hissed to Bill. "You should have said you're sorry."

"I'm sorry!" Bill shouted. "Boo-hoo!"

Jack swung him around. "What the hell are you doing? What's wrong with you?"

"What's wrong with me is how do you fight with a cripple?"

"You don't."

"Well, don't make me. That's what I was doing, not fighting with a cripple. Next time you can tie one hand behind my back."

"It better not come to that."

"If it don't, it won't be any thanks to him. He's been that way to me from scratch."

"Learn to stand it, Bill."

"I can stand it. What I can't stand is him taking observations every five minutes and latitude this and longitude that and the thickness of the strata and writing down the fucking time and I forget what-all. Him and Wallybird." All had stopped what they were doing to watch the fracas except Walter Powell, still booming out his song. He pulled his shirt from the bucket, held it up dripping, then looked at the rest of the crew.

"Maybe I can't stomach certain things neither," said Jack, "but I got to. Most men can stand what they got to stand if there ain't any choice."

"Well, I got a choice."

"No you don't."

"I can throw his fucking chronometer off a cliff."

"You do that. He'll throw you off after it."

"With one arm?"

As for Wes, he stood in the same spot looking at the watch and even thought he caught the second hand moving. But it wasn't. This is what he got for subjecting his expedition and its valuable equipment to the influence of uneducated egotists and so-called mountain men. Since they'd launched back in May, every time Bill had touched one of the instruments Wes had felt himself stiffen. He'd tried to teach him their value, the care they required. But when Bill took elevations, one urge dominated Wes: to remove the precious barometer as quickly as possible from his grasp when he was finished.

And now this watch. The Bill Dunns of the world wrecked whatever they touched.

One hazard of being self-made, thought Wes, was having to

do everything yourself. But what choice did you have? It was you against the world.

The next morning started off bright and sunny, which lifted Wes's spirits for a while until the sun hit the water. By ten A.M. their thermometers read one hundred six. Wes had christened this Marble Canyon; reddish-brown cliffs gleaming black in the sun loomed up behind other reddish-brown cliffs unfolding from walls standing next to the river. The men struck a string of rapids that battered them to numbness, each worse than its precursor, and at last decided they'd better line down. Four hours later, having gained five miles, all fell asleep in broad daylight, too exhausted to do anything, even eat.

In the middle of the night Hawkins made a fire and cooked biscuits. A few men, awakened by the smell, gobbled them down and plunged into sleep again.

They woke to a day Wes had envisioned since the expedition's start: August 7, the solar eclipse. No one complained about delaying the journey, since they could rest. With Seneca's help George Bradley put four new ribs in his boat and caulked her. Jack Sumner, Bill Dunn, and Andy Hall made a stab at going hunting but didn't climb very far and saw nothing so gave up. Wes and his brother took observations and after noon packed up the best of the remaining barometers, the sextant, and the chronometer. They crossed the river, searched out a side canyon, and began the long hike to the rim to witness the eclipse and measure its duration. Wes had read James Cook's account in the Royal Society's *Transactions* of observing the 1766 eclipse off the coast of Newfoundland. A solar eclipse, Wes had decided, was the best means of finding longitudes, and their map in progress needed this one reliable reading as a reference point around which to adjust. The newspapers being saved for him by Emma would be full of exact observations of the same eclipse at known longitudes, and back home he could calculate their longitude here with utmost precision simply by comparing his readings for time with those in the papers. His job today would be to find the latitude, sight on the sun with the sextant, then with Walter's help time the eclipse to the second with their chronometer. A double check would not be possible, though, without the watch destroyed by Bill, and at this thought Wes clenched his fist and felt his mood turn black.

Their knapsacks bulged with the surveying equipment and canteens and biscuits. Up a steep side canyon they found an S-shaped gully that cut through red, yellow, and brown layers. They reached a sloping terrace and the sun crushed them into earth, but on they climbed, up a titan's staircase, searching out a break in the soaring cliffs above. Walter announced the temperature as one hundred ten and they slogged on. Their canteens were Civil War issue, made of laminated wood, which sweetened the water. The river, behind and below, fell out of sight. Clouds began to pour across the sky—the first they'd seen in days—and now and then the sun disappeared. No, thought Wes, not clouds, not now. He searched the unused corners of his mind for means to supplicate the gods.

He would offer a human sacrifice to the sun. He would rip out Bill Dunn's heart.

It took them all afternoon, nearly four hours, to reach the rim, where they pulled out the equipment and built a platform of rocks, hurrying now, racing the clouds. Thankfully the temperature had dropped. The clouds came from the west, where they'd massed into a mountain range, and those that broke off and shot across the canyon and over this platform had grown progressively larger. The two men stood on a flat sagebrush plain that kept changing color in the shadows of the clouds, green to brown to yellow. To the east it led to a single low mesa, and behind that to sketchy mountains in the distance.

The eclipse began with the wink of a shadow, the merest nibble at the sun's blazing edge, and Wes jotted down the time. But a continent of clouds overtook the sun and covered the sky and that was that, the end of their eclipse. On a darkening plain they stood feeling powerless. Walter grew bitter, infected by his brother's mood. "Typical," he said. "By God, I'm sick of it. This blow was timed perfectly, Wes. Give the devil his due. He has to be grinning. Sometimes there's a tinge to how things turn out that makes you realize someone must be laughing. It's deliberate."

"Walter, I'm afraid it's pure coincidence."

"You would think that. The devil's a precisian."

Wes knew it was chance, yet Walter was right. It *had* been so perfectly timed! In his heart—he couldn't help it—he blamed Bill Dunn.

They packed and walked west across the plain but couldn't find where they'd climbed up. At crucial junctures Wes liked to build cairns, but they'd come here in a rush. They searched along the rim and the dry air tightened. Across the canyon and up on the far rim it was raining already. The light had caved in, gone gray and faint, and they were inside a shadow unlike any normal shadow because the eclipse was still taking place beyond the clouds even if they couldn't see it. All at once they were soaked and could smell the sage and creosote around them.

Halfway down a steep ravine the rain became a downpour and they had to seek shelter. The imitation dark got replaced by a real one: this eclipse was timed to end just before sunset. They picked their way over rocks on the side of a slope, unable to see what lay below them, and found an overhang at the base of a cliff. They sat inside it, shivering, and stayed there all night.

The first time it occurred to Wes that they hadn't heard gunshots during the night was the next morning, after they finally made it down. The usual practice for parties out after dark was for those in the camp to fire guns to guide them. No cheers greeted the Powell brothers either. The men were somberly eating. Hawkins threw on more coffee and cooked up more biscuits. The Major felt certain the men had been discussing him. At last Ora said, "How was that eclipse?"

"Obscured by clouds."

Jack asked, "When will the fun commence?"

"When we're done eating."

They finished, cleaned up, packed the boats, and pushed off.

2

"When are you going to pay me for that watch?"

"You mean apart from when I get paid for my labors?"

"Watch your mouth, my friend. I've had enough back talk."

"Well, I apologize, Major. I thought you said 'pay me.'"

"After your carelessness with my equipment you have the gall to complain about not collecting wages? You, Mr. Dunn, were a volunteer."

"You said you'd pay the hunters."

"I said I'd pay the hunters in lieu of bacon rations. That was assuming the hunters would hunt. Do you call yourself a hunter? If you are, where's the meat? All you've done is consume provisions and equipment and abuse the instruments. Everything you touch, you sully."

"Get off my back. You ain't half the man I am."

They stared at each other in the *Emma Dean*—Bill pulling on the oars, Wes giving him his Elijah look, enhanced by the quantity of wool on his cheeks and his pinprick pupils in this land full of light. He bore a hole through the man as he had a year ago when they'd first met and he'd recruited him for this voyage, but Bill did not shrivel.

Wes's gaze caught something odd: Bill Dunn did not have earlobes. The ears just swung in and adhered to his neck. They were loathsome, he felt—offensive, disgusting—and why had he never noticed it before? An impulse to smash Bill's wretched face nearly overwhelmed him.

He looked up at the sky, the canyon, the cliffs. The sun struck the red water and the red walls and exploded in air, nearly blinding him.

Yesterday, they'd hit a stretch that forced them to portage five separate times in little more than three miles. It had rained again, and where they camped driftwood was so scarce it took the crew a good hour to find enough for a fire. Wes announced they'd have to go on half rations for the rest of the voyage and no one said a word. Supper was coffee and biscuits and more coffee. It swelled in their stomachs and helped them forget how hungry they were.

Today was hot again. That morning they'd run more than twenty rapids in thirteen miles and made four long portages. At least the river had since calmed. The red walls of the canyon rose so high and bright no one could see what lay above them, and their enormous buttressed columns conjured ancient kingdoms. Wes thought of Egyptian landscapes he'd seen in chromolithographs. Some columns had collapsed and burst across the terraced slope between cliff and river, the tumbled-down pieces larger than ships. "My name is Ozymandias . . . ," he thought, then realized he'd said it out loud.

"That's not any kind of name," said Bill.

"When will you pay me?"

"I can give you a complete rundown on that subject. I'll pay you when I'm a millionaire."

"So you're a joker. A madcap. You may be interested to know I don't find you very funny."

"Nor me you."

"You don't play by the rules."

"What rules is that?"

"Do your work well and don't whine or complain."

"Oh, that's our task? I wasn't sure. I thought it was starve and get knocked about by raging torrents and sing happy songs."

Wes exhaled and his rigid posture softened. He leaned forward on one knee and grew conscious of Jack listening behind him. "Bill, please," he said in a gentler voice. "Listen to me. I harbor no ill will. Just cooperate and be a member of the team."

"That's what this is about? That's all you got to say?"

"We can settle on the watch at the end of the voyage."

"We can settle on it now."

"There's hard work ahead. Things will get worse before they get better. The food is running low. We're all in this together."

Bill said nothing.

"Can I count on your support?"

"You can count on I'll work without bitching about it. Which I've always done."

"That's all I'm asking."

Bill cocked an eye at Wes and kept mum. Wes looked around and pulled out a slip of paper. He thought for a minute, wringing Bill from his consciousness, and wrote down in pencil for his future journal: "Scenery on a grand scale."

They rounded a bend and Wes said to no one, "Look at that!" Bill turned around. Halfway up the red wall on their right a spring burst from the vertical rock and shot out and gushed down the cliff— white water pouring over mauve marble. Below, in its path, green vegetation cascaded toward the river, fanning into thickets. Watercress in lush beds, maidenhair ferns, monkey flower, poison ivy.

A half mile downstream the river made another turn, and on its outer bend a cave had been scooped out of the limestone by high water. Here they stopped and climbed a hill of sand into the cave, tucked underneath a huge overhang of rock. The cave was just a wink in the cliff's enormous brow, yet inside it was forty feet high and several hundred feet deep, pinching back to a five-foot ceiling in the rear. Its floor was pure sand. From the cave's shadow they watched, across the river, enormous rock walls of red, blue, and yellow shift in and out of sunlight. The sun even leaked along the cave's upper lip, painting it red.

Here, Hawkins cooked a meager dinner and they sat in the sand behind the shadow line, feeling radiated heat five feet away.

They pushed off again. The canyon walls rose. On the right bank four mergansers flew upstream toward the boats, low along the cliffs a few feet above the water. Ten minutes later they were flying downstream along the opposite bank.

A canyon wren practiced its descending fluting scale.

High on the wall a raven flew south, her shadow rising and falling across polished stone. Two ravens, equally black, shadow and bird, united in the niche where she slowed and landed. Below this niche where seams of limestone met, one blue-red, one brown, the yellowish profile of a boat appeared—curved bottom, flat top. This, in cross-section, was an ancient riverbed. The exposed earth here spilled unexpected secrets, and the rattleboned men were going back in time, sliding deep into the past. Wes felt it more than knew it, sensed all of them devolving. They'd lost weight, their clothes drooped like rags, some had no shoes, their nerves had been frayed, the leaky boats were lighter and felt ready to collapse at the flick of a wave into piles of clattering wood. And every foot forward stripped off more human padding.

They floated nearly motionless under the sun.

The clouds rolled in and it rained that afternoon. Rills and streams ran down the canyon walls and scrolls of mud curled over the rims. In the gloom of side canyons hung curtains of rain. Mud and sand polished walls, the rain washed them off, the sun exploding from clouds dried them to a luster. Beneath the boats the river grew red and rose a few feet. More rapids began and they had to portage. Then the canyon widened and the river calmed. Broken ridges led to cliffs terraced on their brows, thence to great volumes of rock stacked against peaks and rising through fractured planes and shadows. In the distance they glimpsed purple and gray timbered slopes, the highest they'd seen since leaving Wyoming.

Deeper and deeper they went into the earth—Wes hadn't thought it possible. For the last four days he'd been watching for the Paria River on their right. Now his mind shifted, revising the landscape. They were past the Paria, inside a new canyon. Back where this canyon so modestly began, what he'd called Ute Creek must have been the Paria. He'd have to tell Ora. By his reckoning they'd already traveled a good fifty miles through Marble Canyon. If that puny stream was in fact the Paria, they were now on the verge of the last canyon, the greatest of all: the two hundred plus miles of nameless oblivion Lieutenant Ives had tried to travel up in 1857. He didn't get very far. Instead, he and his party crossed overland to the Little Colorado River, circumventing the Great Canyon, then tried unsuccessfully to reach the spot ahead—it had to be close—where the Little Colorado met the Colorado.

In camp that night, to Ora's irritation, Wes argued these corrections. "You mean that wasn't Ute Creek back there?" Ora asked.

"Couldn't have been."

"Then where on earth was the Crossing of the Fathers?"

"Back where we thought so the first time. Where we found the carved steps."

"Where *I* thought so. You thought it wasn't."

"I couldn't be certain."

"Does this mean we're lost?"

"Don't be foolish, Ora. We're on the Colorado River. We know where it comes out."

"I'll be running out of paper with all these corrections."

"No need to redraw them. You can make final copies when the trip's over."

"That's not the way I do things. I like to get it right the first time. It saves a lot of trouble and headache later on."

"Well, my friend, that's the wrong attitude. Mapmaking is an imperfect business. A map is never finished."

"Mine are."

"I doubt it. How far do you make it we've come through this canyon?"

"Sixty-five miles."

"That far?"

"That far."

"I make it less than that. We should meet the Colorado Chiquito sometime tomorrow, if I'm right."

"If you're right."

Wes heard chants in the earth that night. He knew what they were: a trick of the mind and of the sounds of wind and water persisting in the canyon. Still, they were chants, not unlike plainsong. They were voices in his ear rising from the depths, rising and falling, keeping him awake.

The next day, as usual, a broad band of sunlight struck the tops of the walls across the river to the west. Directly overhead the sky above the eastern rim was imminent with light. The air below the rim, overexposed, seemed to volatize, then the sun erupted and it was already hot. They ate in silence, packed, started off, and ran a whole string of rapids on slackened boats whose frames had repeatedly been knocked out of true. In the middle of the day a foul-smelling stream, brown as a rotten orange, entered from the left: the Little Colorado.

3

George threw an old wagon sheet on the ground and commenced cutting new moccasins while listening to Jack grouse about this spot. It was the end of the earth, a miserable lonely hole where the only living things were lizards, bats, and scorpions, said Jack. Snakes too, added Bill Dunn, who'd plinked a rattler that morning—shot off its head. Bill claimed that in shooting a rattler you didn't have to aim, just hold out your arm and move the gun around. The snake did the aiming; it followed the gun and lined itself up. But that didn't work for Jack, nothing did. This dismal pit was hell's first circle, Jack was declaring, and George cocked his ear and kept quiet as Jack talked. He knew what Jack was saying: eight more circles to go.

"I don't know, Jack. Least it's peaceful," said Ora.

Jack, the Howlands, and Bill Dunn were once again smearing pitch on the boats. Major Powell was off taking observations. Down by the river Andy Hall and Hawkins washed the pots in filthy water. By the fire Walter Powell was refilling a barometer and singing something frazzled: "Yaaah yaa ya dum." George decided he'd been here before: it was the army times a hundred. Maybe Jack was right, maybe this was hell, because hell's nothing more or less than the same thing over and over. That plus the heat. One hundred nine degrees in the shade.

Today Hawkins had cooked the last of their bacon, a stringy tasteless mess. Only three things were left now: flour, coffee, and dried apples. And they were on half rations, and half of little equals next to nothing. The dried apples were wet and moldy, so they'd spread them in the sun knowing each time they dried they lost more flavor and gained more toughness.

A quail called and a canyon wren fluted down the scale. The wren sounded apt to George—music for creatures descending into depths and never finding bottom.

Seneca Howland did not agree with Jack that this was a worthless hole. It had a certain grandeur, he thought, but he wanted to know why they'd come here in the first place. "Once you come in here what can you do? Alls you can do is go out again."

"Why am I laughing?"

"Get on with it, I say," Ora announced. "I'd just as soon be in hell if they had such a commodity as a running start there."

"How long's he plan to stay here?"

"Two or three days."

"Imagine my surprise."

George knew his little domestic project was futile. The wagon sheet was rotten and fell apart as he cut it. He wrapped the sorry canvas pieces around his poor feet without bothering to sew them—just tied them up with cords—and the left one split after several dozen steps. He absolutely had to save his one pair of boots for portaging, since they were all he had left. In camp he'd taken to going barefoot, and his feet showed the consequences: yellow, scaly, cracked skin; toenails ground to powder by gravel and sand.

As more men had lost their clothes to the elements George had given his away, until all he had left was a single pair of drawers and a shirt. His rubber poncho had decomposed. And the boats! Scarred and gouged, they'd shed all their paint and the so-called oars were clumsy lengths of driftwood. The frames of the boats might as well be made of rope. George knew boats. For the past two months he'd kept the *Sister* tight as a cup, but now she was catching up. Maybe that was good. Maybe, he thought, the boats now had enough flexibility to slither through whatever rapids lay ahead. Maybe pigs will fly and the world grow honest too.

That morning he'd woken forgetting how to breathe, as though he'd been wrapped in wool. His eyes had crusted over, his tongue had swollen up, his skin felt as if crawling with bugs. A dead weight of terror lay on his heart, the certain conviction that disaster lay ahead —starvation, drowning, insanity, self-murder.

Since waking he'd managed to calm down. Morning terrors were the worst. Mornings you shook it out of your clothes, because it was forever there—the fear—like the scorpions so chronic in this canyon.

The Little Colorado rolled sluggishly below. To go easy on his boots George hadn't crossed it, but the others had. You could pick your away across the foul soup on rocks and on travertine dams just under the surface. Yesterday on the other side Seneca had found a chuckwalla in a crevice of the stratified sandstone bordering the river. He'd reached inside the broken plates of rock, yanked it out by the tail, and carried it back, but Hawkins refused to cook the smelly beast. No one knew what to do with it. As hungry as they were, they couldn't picture eating such a creature. So Seneca tossed it high in the air and it landed with a splat. Jack pulled out his pistol but Major Powell ordered him to save his ammunition. Anyway, it lay there and never moved again.

Over their heads the broken cliffs climbed. This was dragon country; its proportions weren't human. Brown scaly slopes, enormous red monoliths shading to green, falling back to forever. They'd never escape.

Jack Sumner felt the same way as George, but instead of terror his reaction was disgust. Around him the men had grown suddenly silent, and looking up the Colorado Chiquito he understood why: the Major was returning. Jack thought he'd be able to recognize that walk a hundred miles away. The long stiff-backed stride, the single swing of arm. No one said a thing as Major Powell walked up, ignoring them, and kept on going past. "Where the hell's he off to now?" muttered Jack. The Major walked toward the bend where the two rivers met, the little brown stink trap and the greenish-red Colorado. A small sandbar island occupied the juncture. Powell squatted down and looked at the island, stood and looked some more, then turned, peered downstream, and disappeared around the bend.

Jack spit in the dirt. "Can't sit still, can he?"

The heat seemed to sing. It hissed like a cracked boiler.

At Jack's feet was the snake shot by Bill Dunn. Jack poked it with his toe. He'd heard stories, though he'd never seen it happen, of rattlers striking after they were dead. One had been cut in two by a shovel and its upper half still bit a man's leg, which swelled up to twice its normal size.

Jack tossed the headless snake away from the boats and it landed beside the dead chuckwalla. Ora had killed a scorpion that morning after shaking out his boots and also tossed it away. Maybe they could pile up a lot of reptiles and vermin and make a bonfire. It would cleanse their souls. Still, reptiles were full of a substance that made for greasy fires, and scorpions repeatedly snapped like little firecrackers.

That night it rained and they unpacked the tents for the first time in weeks. They were stuck in time, thought Jack, like flies in fresh amber. They'd be here forever and no one seemed to care.

Seneca Howland dropped a frog in Bill's coffee. "You little shit," said Bill, and threw both frog and coffee in his face.

Wes had found an Indian trail up the Little Colorado, and the next morning decided to explore it. He walked upstream along the tributary, crossing from bank to bank. He didn't know that this foul-smelling water had been bluer than turquoise just two months ago, with a smooth silky texture and the odor of flowers—the way one might imagine water in the afterlife. The source of the blue was calcium carbonate that issued from a spring several miles upstream, but Wes missed the spring, hidden by willows at the base of a cliff. He missed the green-gray mound of travertine deposits and the hole on top that led to the third world, and missed the rock upon which Masauwu had sat when the first humans emerged.

He did find the faint trail leading up broken rocks and shelves, seven hundred feet high with, in places, steps cut in the rock. Then he hiked across a sloping terrace to a steep winding gulch slung like a loose rope between massive buttresses casting slanted shadows. Another terrace led to still another cliff of brown and red rock, tan and purple too, eroded here and there into pinnacles and buttes. The trail snaked back and forth, now toward the main river and canyon, now deep into the Little Colorado gorge, before petering out. Two thousand feet above the two rivers Wes had yet to reach the rim. He gazed east up the chasm of the Little Colorado, marveling at the power of that puny stream to cut such sheer walls plunging into nothingness. And the stream was not the result of the canyon, but rather its cause. How could such a thing be? At one time the river must have been enormous, and must be so in flood stage, but still . . .

He doubled back west toward the main canyon, looking for a route up. The barometer revealed that the rim above must have been over three thousand feet, the highest yet on their voyage since Desolation Canyon. Rounding a cliff he looked off to the west and saw the edge of a great plateau in the distance, even higher than the rim above his head—more than a mile high, surely—its towering escarpment abruptly scooped open as though by a great paw. Deep gulches ran up and down its sides, ragged flaring canyons set with great pinnacles mounting toward the horizon. The land rose and rose, tumbled into the sky, and the river ran through it, although it wasn't visible. He could see only a portion of this gulf, cut off by his cliff, but enough to suggest the immensity of the rest.

The Great Canyon, of course.

He clung to a flake of rock leaning out. He'd never dreamed a canyon could cut so deep a gorge or so wide a swath. Water sought the lowest ground until it came to the ocean or died in the desert, and in doing so found the path of least resistance. That was common sense. But to cut through a thickness a mile or more deep? Rivers made canyons, not vice versa, and canyons, you could say, were mountains in reverse. The deeper the canyon, the higher the land mass, by definition. For a river to cut through such a rising mass of land it would have to run uphill as well as down, which was impossible. Nor would an ancient lake be able to drain with such relentless force, unless—

Unless. He tried imagining this but couldn't.

Hiking back, he passed a rattler mostly buried in sand. Just its head was exposed and its yellow-brown eyes capped by two horny brows. Wes brushed it with his gaze and registered *rodent.*

As for the rattler, it sensed a passing breeze of meat, a meal inside a threat, but didn't bother to rattle, just flicked its tongue in and out, testing the Major's shower of chemicals. In fact, it didn't see so much as taste and smell the human, feel his radiating warmth with its facial pits, catching in the nerve ends of each one a sort of heat shadow, a living picture of a large, moist body.

Wes spotted a second rattler farther down, slithering off the trail toward a mesquite bush. Picking up a rock, he smashed its pointed head. He heard castanets behind him, spun around, and saw another. This time he jumped aside and threw the rock, which bounced off the snake, causing it to flex and writhe. Wes, heart in mouth, found a larger rock and smashed that one's head too. This is what you do to snakes in the wilderness, he reflected, out of breath, marching off, arm and shoulders still trembling. He never carried a weapon. It wasn't exactly a rational act, but who could be rational in a land harsh as this, which stripped you down to basics? His hand continued shaking and his stump hurt. He was hot, exhausted, filmed with sweat and dust. An hour or so later he arrived back in camp when just Hawkins was there, starting his fire. "Where're the others?" asked the Major.

"Found some more ruins."

"Where?"

"Across the crick."

That evening at twilight they huddled together under an overhang while a steady rain descended and their fire sputtered, half in and half out of their alcove. The rain wasn't heavy but already a rope of red water had lowered itself in the air before their shelter, illuminated by the fire. Beyond it the colors of river and canyon were siphoning from deep red to gray. "Some desert," said Andy.

"Rainy season," said Wes.

They talked about the ancient people who'd once lived in this canyon. Jack and Ora had brought in more arrowheads and shards, and described the foundations and walls of the houses in a little pinched ravine up the smaller river. Major Powell lectured the men on brute instincts, on the patience of the savage, on civilized man's advancement in culture by reason, not impulse. "Our method of evolution," he said, "is not instinct. It's based on those things that distinguish us from the brute. *Planning. Logical thought.* Mutual help, cooperation, *the rule of law.*"

"Exactly why God sent his son to us."

"And not to the savages? You have a point, Ora. Yet I've often thought: why condemn those people to ignorance for centuries, or even worse, arrange to show them the truth by means of other nations so appalled by their ignorance as to slaughter them instead?"

No one had an answer for that one. "The ways of God are not the ways of men," George Bradley said at last.

"You try telling them savages about Jesus Christ. I tried once," said Jack. "They think he's a Manitou."

"What's that?"

"It's basically your bogeyman. A monstrous scarecrow. Some hokey-pokey idea."

"Bill, tell the Major about the redskin you fought, the one who called you his brother," Seneca gushed.

"Shut your head," said Bill.

"Bill don't have much to say."

Jack Sumner grinned. "Poor Bill don't know beans about redskins."

"Nor anything else," said Wes.

Bill sat stone-faced. No one spoke. Then Jack perked up. "Well now, Professor. What lies ahead?"

"The end of our voyage. The Great Canyon, boys. Unknown country, unknown water. Ora, you tell them. By our calculations our latitude now is the same as Callville's."

"What's that portend?"

"It means that what we run goes west now, not south."

"How far west?"

"I could not find our longitude. Too many clouds. But Ora estimates we are approximately a hundred and thirty miles east of Callville."

"That's all?"

"But the river twists and turns. In river miles that could easily be two hundred and thirty. And we don't know what rocks beset the channel. What falls there are, what cliffs, what dangers. Nobody's ever been through here before."

" 'Cept the redskins," said Seneca.

"He means nobody civilized," Jack said. "Like us."

4

"What the hell is that?"

"A volcanic neck." Wes grew excited. They'd run about five miles after launching that morning in air washed by rain but heating up rapidly. Ahead on their left a black neck of rock rose from the bank five hundred feet high, and perched on its top was a parapet of sandstone—the same reddish sandstone as beside them on the river. Here, the rocks tilted upstream; beyond the neck they tilted down. It looked as though a giant plow had bisected the river, wedging rock to either side. Wes pictured the fault their boats were sliding over: how in ancient times lava had poured through a fissure in bedrock and stayed there in a wall, hard as steel, while on this side over the centuries—over eons and eons—the softer rock beneath got undermined by erosion. So the earth had slipped here and shifted and slid down five hundred feet.

"You plan to run this mess?" asked Jack.

Wes saw rocks in the river ripping up the water and realized he'd been hearing its roar for some time now. Squeezing past Bill, he stood on the bow and took a quick look. He signaled them right.

Beyond this fall the canyon widened. They portaged down a sandy bank, carrying the boats, since the rocks were thick as cattle in the river channel. In this large hot valley, eroded gentle slopes, rusty and green, swept up to the feet of distant terraced cliffs. They launched the boats again and the river slowed, spreading its banks. The sky was so broad it threatened to blind them. A few snowball clouds hung behind the cliffs.

The walls closed in again. The river picked up speed and rolled them like logs. They swept down past ledges and prows of rock and stopped when they heard a roar and had to line. George said sometimes lining down was worse on the boats than running the rapids, but no one responded. Only Wes suspected he was right. Often the water ripped at the boats as the men let them down hanging on for dear life, and the empty boats violently smashed into rocks. But what choice did they have? They lined down three more times and the canyon grew darker as the walls began to change. They lost their red gloss and grew high and humped, looming over the river—they were regular mountains, saw-toothed and black. A long rapid without end approached them like a runaway train, and they landed and camped at its head on the right bank. Jack counted out loud about a hundred large boulders exposed at its beginning, then a fall of fifty feet for as much as a mile through Alps of water. Camping here wasn't the best choice, but the light had grown anemic as evening fell and they were exhausted. Wes decided they could live inside that roar if they really had to, but it scraped his nerves. He knew it put them all on edge. He walked down the bank to scout the river ahead and came back and announced they were entering the granite: the roots of great mountains ground to bedrock long ago by the slow ship of time. Granite ropes in fact ran up and down the cliffs, embedded in the schist, but the black rock was schist—their source of murk and gloom.

The roar, as they ate and found their places to sleep, was not a lullaby.

The next morning, over coffee, Wes said to Bill, "I've decided you can pay me a dollar a day for the rest of the voyage, for your room and board. We have three or four weeks. About twenty-five dollars."

"What the fuck are you talking about?"

"Your payment for the watch."

"You're pulling my leg, right?"

"Most assuredly not."

"Bull is what I say. I'm not listening to this."

"I don't choose to care about what you listen to."

"You don't? That suits me."

"You think you're hard as nails, don't you? As far as I'm concerned you're just another mouth to feed. Why should I pay for it?"

" 'Mouth to feed,' he says. Cracker dust and peelings."

"If you don't like it, you can leave."

"I might just do that."

"You've opposed every step I've made to succeed. It was you who smuggled that whiskey on the *No Name*. By God, I won't feed you one more day. Pay me or leave."

Seneca jumped in. "Major Powell, sir, a bird couldn't fly out of this canyon."

"Shut your trap, Seneca."

The rest of the men had gathered around to listen, or try to, above the roar of the rapids. "In case you forgot, I'm in charge of this journey," Wes snapped.

"How could anyone forget?"

"You've refused to cooperate."

"Don't drive me, Major Powell. Dirty devils won't be driven."

"You'll never make a teammate."

"I'm as good as any cripple."

"By God," said Walter Powell.

Bill wasn't finished. "I can go down the river with a ding-dong like you, I can go with anyone. Basically what you want is for a bunch of men to agree with your notions. Whatever you do, you want us to do it, even if it's wrong."

"Don't make me do it, Bill. Don't make me send you packing."

"Plus you got a short fuse. I thought mine was short. You're just a little guy and you got a lot of balls, but you love to wind up your mouth and you're always the hero. Some of us thought you was the best in the world because you said you was, and we believed you. I'll show you short fuse."

"He's always taking observations!" Seneca said.

"Stay out of this, Peach Fuzz."

"Bill, you take and take but what do you give? You've been worthless on this trip. You never carried your weight."

"Pigshit," said Bill. "If you weren't such a cripple—"

"*I* ain't crippled," said Walter Powell, lunging at Bill, but Andy and Hawkins held him back. In the struggle they fell in the shallows and Walter thrashed around trying to free his arms. Then he just sat in the water. Bill and Wes stared at each other, the dark bearded recruit and the diminutive muttonchopped expedition leader. Downstream the river roared, but Jack coughed and Ora spat and suddenly it seemed it wouldn't take much to hear an ant cross a coffin.

"Come now," said Jack. "We got work to do." Walter, Hawkins, and Andy sat in water to their waists. "You men are wet, you can guide the boats down. Come now, Major Powell. Be done with it, Professor. Which one first?"

Red-faced, Wes gave each man a stare and walked to the *Emma Dean*. So she was first. Andy, Hawkins, and Walter waded in the shallows and lifted and kicked the boat off the rocks while Ora and Jack let it down on the rope. Seneca and George carried the bow rope downstream on the bank over cursed ground—a wilderness of rock. Wes followed. When the *Emma Dean* reached the end of its stern rope the men upstream let go of one end and pulled the rope through the ring while the men in the water clung to the gunnels. Then Seneca and George snugged their rope around a rock. Wes gave the signal, the boat was released, and it sailed across a plane of water with the boiling pit beside it. The water it ran on was flat as a belt but faster than bat squeal; beside it in the middle of the river the waves leapt and swelled and smashed into each other.

They lined down the other boats with the same results. They worked like machines set to run on their own and hardly looked at one another.

But the rapids were only halfway done, and now where they were the river shifted its bulk and swung against the right bank. So they had to portage. They carried the boats over more talus, walking on the rocks or wading between them. Still, no one said a thing. It was grueling work, and the sun hit the river and sucked out all their strength, and when they were finished they stopped to eat dinner in what shade they could find, though it wasn't yet noon. The river here was fast and welled up inside itself in spreading eddies and whirl-pools and disappearing tails, but at least it wasn't rapids. They could run it from this point.

Hawkins boiled coffee and cooked apples and biscuits and said, "Here's food." Wes sat down apart from the others. Hawkins didn't wash the Major's hand. He poured coffee, spooned apples, and passed out biscuits to the men lined up but did not carry a plate to Major Powell. Instead, Walter Powell served his brother his meal.

The men ate without speaking.

They launched the boats again. A few miles downriver they heard a loud roar. As they moved toward it, like a huge bubble the noise seemed to swell. Their long, straight approach, cautious and slow, carried them toward black walls of schist a thousand feet high and forming a V inside which the river pinched. Wes briefly thought it might be a waterfall, despite his conviction that none existed on this river. A smooth plane of water connecting the walls appeared to drop into nothing. He signaled the men right, where they tied up on rocks, but the sharp cliffs here made a portage impossible.

Wes climbed the cliff. Beyond a line of water, the river poured into a cauldron with great muddy waves, the largest he'd seen. It wasn't a waterfall, no, it was worse. Between mountains of water all was brown foam. It went on forever — he couldn't see the end.

He looked up the cliff and saw a line they could climb. Clouds had rolled in, which cooled the air, but the longer he looked the more certain it became that they couldn't carry boats up that cliff. Nor could they line down such a violent stretch of water with no shallows or banks on either side.

He, Jack, and Walter ascended the schist and felt the thunder of the rapids in solid rock even two or three hundred feet up. They climbed down where they could, found a ledge and promontory, scrambled up a shelf, descended some talus, and after several hours of clambering and scouting as far ahead as possible, they still saw no end to it. They had to run this monster or abandon the voyage, that much was clear. Back at the boats, Jack found the life preserver and handed it to Bill, who tossed it to the Major without inflating it; Wes himself had to do the honors. They boarded the boats and pulled away from the cliff as Andy Hall shouted, "What ho! She bumps!"

The *Emma* went first. The river poured ahead, they hit a sudden drop, and while Jack and Bill pulled on the oars they dove straight down. They were sliding sideways but by working the oars they barely straightened for the next wave. Meanwhile, Wes held his strap tightly and with the rubber collar looked like a Pilgrim in the stocks. Riding the next wave — it was twenty feet high — he braced himself and ducked, convinced they'd just keep going in a circle and flip over backward, but they didn't. They shot straight up, hung suspended for a moment, and plunged down again, shot up and plunged down, going up and down it seemed without going forward until, riding down the back of one large wave, the rhythm exploded and they slammed against a wall. They'd struck a double wave, he saw—the downside of the first smashing into a colossus curling back above their heads—and it felt as if the whole Colorado River poured into their boat, shaking it with such force it should have burst apart.

It didn't.

The *Emma Dean* was swamped but still wouldn't sink. Wes spotted Jack, who'd been pitched out, shooting like a rocket from the water. The boat slung down sideways into a long trough and Jack grabbed its stern. Wes and Bill sat in water to their waists and Bill shipped his useless oars and held on. They shot past enormous rocks, hit an eddy in the river—the eye of its storm—spun around and heard shouting, dwarfed inside the roar as the other boats passed. Neither was swamped. Wes watched the *Sister* jump the logs and the river snatch an oar from Walter's grasp, tossing it like a pencil into omnipresent foam, where it got swallowed whole.

The danger wasn't over. With Jack Sumner in the water, still clinging to the stern, the *Emma Dean* swung around, snagged a moving floor of water, and tore off again. The bow and stern compartments were just watertight enough to keep it from sinking, but that wouldn't last. Wes felt the river falling, collapsing down a staircase with repeated concussions. Every high and ragged wave, every low one too, broke over the boat. They struck a narrow trench and slammed from side to side, bouncing from one collared rock to the next, and this seemed to take forever. Still, someone sitting on the canyon's rim and timing their progress from beginning to end would have found it lasted no more than a minute. And this endless rapid was the longest on the river.

The water was cool and flew into their faces, scorched by the sun. At last Wes saw the other boats ahead, waiting in an eddy at the foot of the fall. The boats pulled out as the *Emma Dean* approached, and Walter in the *Sister* caught its bow post, tied on a rope, and hauled it to shore. Jack staggered to the beach and flopped in the sand.

They emptied out the *Emma Dean,* built a big fire, and dried off as they stood shivering. The sun came out and wrinkled them like raisins. Airing out the equipment Ora discovered a barometer was smashed. That left just one. Bill Dunn said that one was useless too, and Wes asked him what was wrong with it.

"Leaky bag."

Bill sat in the shade of the overturned *Emma* and Wes stood before him, looking down at the man. "When did this occur?"

"Somewheres upriver I began to notice it."

"Yesterday? Last week?"

"How should I know?"

"Was it packed away properly?"

"Yes and hell yes."

"Sand wreaks havoc on scientific instruments."

"Blame it on sand. Blame it on me. You're the world's living expert on my mistakes."

"I have a right to know what happened."

"Sure you do."

"Tell me the true story."

"You think if I knew it I'd waste it on you?"

Bill just sat while the Major stared him down. The river roared. Scattered ruins of afternoon sunlight fell around them. Wes spun on his heels and on a wagon sheet found the box with the remaining barometer. He saw that in fact half the mercury had leaked out. They were out of cement so he couldn't refasten the bag. They'd used up all their mercury too. So much for the barometers.

They ran more rapids and order broke down; it was every boat for itself. At a nasty-looking stretch Wes signaled all to land, but the other two boats shot through anyway. He fumed but Jack said what the hell, let them go. It was a shitload faster than portaging, he said. And fast water's all the meat we got left. So the *Emma Dean* shoved off and followed.

Clouds rolled in bringing rain that afternoon and there was no place to stop. They wound up sleeping in niches and clefts in the rocks above the rising river. Roll over and you drown. The rain continued all night, keeping them awake, and their ponchos by now were useless scraps of rubber. The weather broke in the morning, but they were still cold and wet in the shade in their shirts and drawers.

Then Ora announced he'd lost his notes and sketches from the Little Colorado to this spot. Wes said they'd find someplace ahead to lay over and take new observations, and he could foot up some estimates and restore the maps, but Ora said what good would that do? It would only be guesswork. Wes turned red, felt himself sinking—their whole trip a failure, no map, no barometers—and in his mind he grabbed Ora with two hands, not one, and slammed him up against a cliff. But in his body he simply stood there volcanic.

The sun hit their camp and all at once it was hot. This was torture, Wes thought: to freeze then burn then freeze again then burn. The crew's sun-blistered faces, untrimmed beards, and split lips no doubt reflected his. Like theirs, his shrunken skin seemed to clamp around his skull.

They started again, hit a stretch of calm water, and came upon a stream that entered from their right. Here were flowers and ferns and springs of fresh water, also willows and cottonwoods, even birches. Another wave of clouds threatened more rain, but the clouds turned to ashes and the rain didn't reach them. The hot air transformed it first to steam, then nothing.

They landed, caulked the boats once more, and took observations. Wes tried to talk Ora into mending his maps by making estimates for the portion he'd lost, but the sourpuss Methodist's heart wasn't in it, Wes could see. Ora'd long ago given up taking compass bearings at every bend of the river.

Wes shook his head. It was out of his hands. He felt almost relieved; he'd go solo from now on, get them through the canyon to the very end—it couldn't be that far—then each could depart for wherever he wished, for hell or Timbuktu. And next year he'd come back with more competent men, with surveyors and sailors and a geologist or two.

They camped for the night.

5

An immense side canyon sloped up from this spot, and the next morning Jack and Ora climbed it and found a log to cut for oars. They discovered more ruins and collected more shards. The hunters went hunting and fired at some ravens, missing them all, then wondered if what they'd seen were only shadows. Clouds blew in again, but they were high and held no rain.

Wes waited until they were working on the oars to hike up the same canyon. The creek beside it was clear and reflected the clouds so he called it Silver Creek—although later the name that stuck was Bright Angel, the Dirty Devil's good twin. He climbed and climbed, having nothing else to do. He ascended past roots of long extinct mountains toward Precambrian rock in which the world's first record of plant life had been scribbled. Above that was shale, then sandstone, then quartzite in regular pulses, then the same redwall limestone they'd already floated through, with gastropods and corals and trilobites and algae locked inside its pages.

This side canyon rose to a far rim as much as seven or eight thousand feet above sea level. Wes wished he'd brought his pencil. Six thousand feet of earth—maybe much more—had vanished here, washed down to the ocean, and the process was endless. It was still going on. Say three and a half cubic miles to each square mile of surface. Hopkins and Babbage had shown, he remembered, that the power to transport loads of given particles increased with the sixth power of the velocity of water. Once again Wes rehearsed describing this—what? this paradise of loss—to Emma. And picturing himself alone in the wilderness, he began to choke up.

The river here clearly had cut down, not up. It and its tributaries had sliced into this immensity as though into a cake, revealing its layers. It was not only deep but as wide as an ocean and flayed open like a titan's fallen carcass.

Wes thought for a moment, lost in vacancy. What if the river hadn't cut down? Suppose the land rose around it instead? He felt a little tremor, felt his mind shift. Around him, the land seemed to rise now, and he saw that for every inch it uplifted, erosion had removed an equivalent amount, or even more, which the river slurried off. His thinking worked backward, against the current, upstream. Before he fully understood it he knew he had the key, and saw how rivers cut through mountains, how the Colorado had opened this plateau. The river came first. *Of course,* he hissed. The river was there before the land began to rise. Its course had been established by the time the land uplifted. The river had already inlaid that land, entrenching its channel, incising its course. Then, as the land slowly climbed itself, as it upheaved warping all around it, the river continued cutting its channel as a buzz saw slices a log raised against it.

It was almost a letdown. Where was the mystery? The answer now seemed so obvious to Wes he couldn't fathom how he'd missed it. The Green River forswore nearby valleys and sliced through Split Mountain or Lodore Canyon for only one reason: it came first. Its course had been established long before those valleys and mountains had formed. A river cuts through land that then rises underneath it, and the river keeps on cutting. In other words, Emma, the water maintains the level it is at while the land ascends around it, and only when the land stops uplifting can you say the river is truly cutting down. Its tributary streams, in regular pulses, occupy mediating slopes and terraces, and *their* tributaries fan up still higher, being intermittent and seasonal and therefore not as unrelenting. With mathematical order, this rhythm of buttes cleft by ravines climbed in tiers to Wes's very feet, where he floated like a feather. He didn't just see it but felt it in his bones: how uplift and erosion worked inseparably, how all was contained in the first grain of dirt dislodged on a plain by the first drop of water. That was the seed that sprang with perfect logic in radiating patterns, regular pulses, although to be sure the logic was elastic and stretched across anomalies, such as bands of harder rock. Such stammers got woven into the design. Violence and confusion, turbulence and loss, all poured into one great maw of the Same.

Whom could he tell? Surely not the men below. What did they care about the formation of canyons via the antecedence of rivers? He decided to keep his discovery to himself and save it for Emma. She might object at first and say everyone knew mountains and clouds together made rivers, yet she'd be only partially right, since those were earlier mountains and clouds. Those were mountains from a previous uplift now worn to nothing, and once the rivers existed and the land rose again, the rivers made canyons, and eventually the canyons wore down the new mountains. Mountains rose and fell — there'd been many uplifts, Emma. It will be shown by this theory that with upheaval, degradation progresses, and with downthrow, sedimentation, and consequently all existing mountains are recent. The ancient mountains are gone. Nature abhors an elevation; she wears it down, carts it off, unloads it into the most convenient ocean. And movements of geology are slow, not catastrophic, because we see from the results that mountains uplifted no faster or slower than the rivers cut through them. I might venture to say, if we weren't in mixed company, that the ponderous upheavals of geological history are like tortoises mating. So much for earthquakes splitting mountains in two. So much for catastrophic upheavals resulting in peaks forty thousand feet high! If my gentle opponent would provide for me the mechanism of such a stupendous catastrophe —

In his mind he embraced his gentle opponent and forgave her her doubts and ran his lips through her curls. Her mountains of curls.

On his way down he passed the flute buzz of sage hens, the popping and snapping of tall agave plants shedding their seeds, and the sharp tang of rabbitbrush. He passed a horned toad ejecting blood from its eye and earthstar mushrooms scooting over the dust emitting clouds of spores, and he never saw a thing. The sun broke through the clouds and the afternoon grew hot and the world ran through Wes without leaving a trace. Approaching the river amid willows and cottonwoods, he walked into a moribund camp of sullen silence. The faces of the men reminded him of his soldiers on the night before a battle.

He pulled Jack aside to find out what was eating them. Jack said Hawkins had set the last of their saleratus on the riverbank and a boat swung around and its rope caught the box, pulling it into the water. "Wasn't nothing he could do." Now they'd have to eat sinkers: unleavened biscuits made from rotten flour and river water the color of baby shit.

But Jack knew it wasn't just the saleratus. One by one they'd all come around to his own way of thinking: this hole they were in, the so-called Great Canyon, was the worst hell on earth. It drove the spirit right out of you.

6

For Wes, their trip was effectively over. He'd made his discovery, he saw things differently now. They started off again and it rained off and on. Jack sucked his teeth and Bill pulled with all his strength on the makeshift oars, trying to finish this canyon before it finished them, but Wes just stared at the walls with new eyes, face streaming with rain. He saw through the camouflage, saw the river wasn't sinking into the canyon; rather, the land was rising around it. Their tents had rotted, their store of blankets had diminished to six for ten men, the men had lost weight—but Wes saw none of this, nor did he think about it. Instead, he perceived every fragment of the canyon, every piece of desolation, as part of the whole. And he saw that the whole was contained in each part.

Ora grew sick and neglected his maps, and hearing him cough increased everyone's misery—all except Wes. Wes pictured the river wearing its channel, sawing its way through a rising plateau. To him it was dramatic, unique, majestic to see clouds fill the canyon, clouds belonging to the sky, which thus increased the height of the cliffs on either side to something like infinity. To his men it was merely cheerless and desolate. It rained all one day then all the next, and flash floods shot from every side canyon. Thunder multiplied off the canyon walls, waterfalls poured over cliffs and down terraces, and each last bit of clothing and equipment and bedding wound up sopping wet, but Wes kept mum. In his mind he was testing turns of phrase for his monograph on the antecedence of rivers.

Hawkins announced they had nine days of food left.

"You call that food?" said Bill Dunn.

They struck a great succession of rapids, lining down some, running others, and losing more oars. The boats were so rattled and loosened at their joints they had to be caulked every day now.

The days blurred together. Once again the expedition entered schist. The slow sandstorm of time took a thousand years to pass and they moved inch by inch and seemed to get nowhere, even though the boats flew. Each morning Wes thought this would be the day they left the Great Canyon and reached the Virgin River, and each evening he thought it had to be the next one.

He looked around and thought, What once was solid rock had completely vanished.

Andy Hall tried a song, and Hawkins informed him he'd better shut his damned gash or he'd shut it for him. Andy asked Hawkins how come he didn't wash the Major's hand no more. Hawkins just shrugged. "He ain't worth it."

One evening Wes confided to Jack that he was thinking of giving up the expedition and looking for a side canyon to climb out of and reach the Mormon settlements to the north. "How far would such a walk be?" Jack asked.

"About a hundred miles."

Jack surprised the Major: "We're that close," he said, holding up forefinger and thumb. "We might just as well go the whole hog." Wes looked at Jack, holding his gaze, but said nothing yet. Their barometers were useless, Ora's maps pure guesswork, and even Wes's observations with the sextant had pretty much been abandoned. But when Hawkins announced that night that the flour was down to thirty pounds, Wes told Jack he supposed he agreed—they ought not to stop. But how could he be sure?

The men hardly spoke, hypnotized by their routine. By running every rapid they risked spoiling the remaining precious supplies or wrecking the boats, but by portaging they risked retarding their progress and using up the food. So they portaged some rapids and lined down others and ran others with boats held together by pitch. Logic ceased to guide them. They ad-libbed on the run. They entered rapids with tongues of smooth water down the middle and rapids whose ridges aped the canyon's walls. They hovered on brims of deep craters of water and dropped into some and shot up the other side and got hung up on rocks. They found the river didn't always flow downstream but moved from side to side. In a canyon whose walls were pure monuments of lava they rode over rolling barrels of water slowly turning on a pivot, then were slung beneath a wave and emerged downstream, intact but shaken, yet also dulled by unfruitful repetition. Even terror gets old. If the river was an ever-turning mill wheel grinding the earth down to a nub, it was grinding them too. Still, was it not the only way out?

It wasn't. One night Wes discovered that others had thought of leaving too. They were camped on a sandbank, exhausted and silent, when beyond some willows Ora began complaining out loud that to go on like this required a bunch of men who were stupid as pumps. Wes lay on his blanket and listened. "If I was you," Ora said—to whomever, maybe no one, or maybe this apparently careless trumpeting was for the Major's benefit—"If I was you, I'd get out fast." As for himself, Ora went on, he wasn't dead yet and did not intend to starve in this prison. "What are we," he asked, "plain dumb or just crazy? Go ahead, change my mind."

That did it. Wes conceived at that moment an absolute determination to finish the voyage and tell the world about it. We were running out of food, he imagined announcing at a lecture to the Young Men's Society in Detroit. The men were growing surly, the boats on their last legs, the instruments in disrepair, Ora's maps a lost cause. But we persevered. We stiffened our spines.

Then a moment later he thought Ora was right.

A small miracle happened. At a bend of the river they discovered a garden. Corn, melons, and squash grew in a clutter irrigated by springs running from the walls, and though the melons and corn were green, nine or ten of the squashes looked just right. Nearby were arbors covered with brush, and scraps of baskets, and deep fire pits filled with black coals. Sharpened sticks lay around, and in one of the shelters hung rabbitskin robes. Wes announced these were Ute or Paiute who must be close by, maybe hunting in the mountains while their garden grew. Surely they wouldn't begrudge starving men a few of their squashes. They loaded them in the boats as quickly as they could and ran down the river until they were certain no Indian could follow. Hawkins cooked up a mess of squash and sang out, "Grub pile!" For the first time in weeks they could fill their bellies. And Hawkins washed the Major's hand.

The following morning, August 27, the river swung west and they were back in the schist. Around noon they came to the ugliest rapids they'd seen since entering the Great Canyon. It was like hitting a wall. Spray from the rapids rose above the river, drifting back toward the boats. Wes signaled them right and they landed and clambered up pinnacles of schist but could see no safe way to let down the boats. A lateral stream from the opposite bank had washed enough rocks into the river to make a rough dam, and across them the water fell for twenty-five feet. Then a washboard of waves interrupted by rocks made the first rapid of three hundred yards, then came a second fall, difficult to see, then a thousand-foot rapid with armies of waves smashing into each other, this one formed by boulders from a side canyon, far more vicious than the first. A granite reef reached one third of the way across the river, giving this rapid a zigzag course that crashed into the left bank then rushed back against the right.

Wes was appalled. And at the bottom one boulder larger than a barn slanted out of the river, and across its flat top, water rolled uphill and poured left. Around three sides of this enormous rock the river made a collar and sucked itself straight down. Where the water reemerged was impossible to tell.

They returned to the boats and Hawkins cooked dinner. Wes and some others climbed the schist again and came down to the mouth of the side canyon. Beyond a field of boulders in a flat wash of sand a thread of water trickled, then the canyon ran north through wide gates of rock without seeming to climb. Its winding bottom was flat. The Howlands and Bill Dunn continued trudging up it as Wes and the others made their way back to camp in the main canyon. There, they jumped into the *Sister* and crossed the river in stubborn, glum silence. They climbed high above the river to the top of the schist but couldn't see below. The only view they managed was farther downstream where two more rapids waited.

They crossed back to the north bank. If they could let the boats down across the first fall, Wes announced, and run near the north wall to a spot above the second, it looked as if a chute might carry them through. But at that point they'd have to pull like hell to cross to the left and get around that final boulder and its suck, which blocked the river's middle. And the river zigged right where they had to zag left.

"Another bang-up plan," said Ora Howland. He, Bill, and Seneca had just returned to camp.

They tried lining down the *Emma Dean,* but the river drew it toward the middle, where the rocks were so thick it got hung up. With a bank on the right they could have used another rope to pull it to shore, but the river filled its channel to the wall. The boat wedged in the rocks and they couldn't haul it back. George had to climb a cliff and repeatedly jerk sharply on his rope and he almost fell, and the *Emma Dean* was getting damaged. By the time they got it back the sun had dipped below the cliffs farther downriver and everyone was exhausted.

Wes brooded on a rock. A small group of men held a meeting by the fire as daylight deflated. One broke off, approached Major Powell, and asked to have a talk. It was Ora with his jaw set. He came right to the point. "We won't do this anymore. It's time we parted company."

"Who's we?"

"Bill Dunn and myself. Seneca's thinking about it too. He's my brother, he'll come. I'll see to it he comes. We are not like you, Major. This rapid here's the last straw. You want to complete this journey so bad you can do it yourself."

"You're mistaken about me, old man. I've thought of quitting too. I've thought of hiking out north and finding the Mormons."

"I noticed you haven't said a thing about that subject except for rag-chewing Bill. You wanted him to leave. Well, now you got your wish."

"I did discuss abandoning the expedition with Jack."

"And what did Jack say?"

"That we should go the whole hog."

"That's not what he told me."

"What did he tell you?"

"He said you boys ought to do what you got to do. I might just join you, he said."

"I suppose he changed his mind," said Wes.

"What about you? Is that your thinking too?"

"My thinking shifts from day to day. I think we should leave, then I think we're so close and the country to the north is an unknown desert and the food is so low that the prudent course would be to stay on the river until the very end."

"Prudent? That rapid out there took lessons from the devil."

"I think we can run it."

"There you go, Major. You got no judgment on these matters."

"We've run some just as bad."

"Not half as bad as that." Ora shook his head and looked downstream where the river exploded beneath a last strip of sky and ran into darkness. His voice dropped in tone to a careful compromise between a question and a statement. "We could hunt for our food while walking out. God forbid we tax your provisions. I thought you'd let us take some rifles."

"I wouldn't begrudge you them, Ora. But we need to talk this out. It's not good to split up."

"Is it good the whole party gets dashed against the rocks? How I feel about that subject is it happened to me once and I'll never forget it. The *No Name* got smashed like a bunch of matchsticks and I was sitting in the bow. You haven't been privy to my dreams or waking terrors since then, have you, Major? The fact is you have no real feelings. No wonder Goodman left. I should have gone with him. Talk is cheap. Me and the boys, we've had enough of it. We're leaving tomorrow."

"What do your maps say?"

"My maps? They say what they've always said, that we're inside a hole deep in the earth and there's no way out. But that there canyon to the north looks promising, Major. It could be our last chance and we ought to take it."

"Have you footed up the distance? We could be through tomorrow."

"That's what I told myself every blessed night for the last two weeks."

"What's the distance to Callville?"

"How I get that information is from depending on you."

"Are the maps up to date?"

"I've not touched them for days."

"Bring them to me. I'll plot our course. Get some sleep. Think about it. Don't do anything hasty."

"We've done all our thinking and we're not inclined to put up with yours anymore. It's that simple, Mr. Powell. This here ain't the war. You can't court-martial us. It's time we parted company, and the three of us—me, my brother, and Bill—we aim to do just that. I wouldn't be surprised if the rest came too." Ora went to the *Maid* and got the maps anyway. He brought them to Wes. In the deepening dusk he walked back to his blanket, turned on his side and said something to Bill, then lay completely still.

Wes lit a candle, opened Ora's maps, and plotted their course for the previous week by dead reckoning. The night was clear and the stars sharp as tacks. With the sextant he made observations for latitude and found that the 35°45′ reading conformed pretty much to his plot. This put them a little south of Callville and forty-five miles due west of the Virgin River. Forty-five miles could be eighty or ninety by the winding twists and snares of an unknown river. And ninety miles could be three or four days, but it might be less. His reckoning of their course up to this point was deliberately stingy, and of the course ahead overly generous, since he wanted a worst case. It could have been half that. They could be out tomorrow. And twenty miles up the Virgin were several Mormon towns; they could reach them in a day.

The worst case gave them just enough food.

He walked over to Ora, sleeping on his side, and shook him, surprised by the man's bony shoulder blade. He felt, through his palm, the depth of Ora's sleep, the buried spring reluctant to snap him awake. At last it did. Ora rolled on his back and stared at Wes with sunken eyes, then smacked his sunken mouth, looking like a corpse. His beard laced with gray reached to his chest. Wes set the candle down and held the map above it and patiently explained the distance left to run. Ora feigned interest, then grew impatient, turned on his side, and said, "We leave tomorrow."

"Don't," entreated Wes.

"We've made up our minds."

Wes carried his threadbare blanket to the river and lay on the bank staring up at the stars. To come a thousand miles and spend three entire months and be this close to victory and end it all like this. He ran the numbers through his mind. Eighty or ninety miles but surely less. Almost definitely less. Their latitude put them anywhere between seventy-five and a hundred miles south of the Mormon settlements in Utah Territory, but he couldn't be certain. And the country was undoubtedly broken and slow. Running eighty river miles was eighty times faster than climbing out of canyons and crossing endless deserts, unless the rapids smashed your boats and snapped your toothpick legs and cracked your eggshell skull.

Wouldn't it be just dandy, he thought, if his grand discovery died with him on the river? He'd be tempting fate by going on.

He drifted in and out of sleep. Spotted a shooting star. Dark canyon walls with their sharp skylines rising and falling, black against black, framed a river of stars. This night was cooler than their recent nights—a first taste of fall—though he didn't need a covering. Downriver the noise of the rapids never ceased.

Once again his stump hurt, as if tasting danger. The day the ball hit his arm came back all at once, the single slice of time that had sectioned his life into before and after. Years ago he'd decided that losing an arm would never define him. He'd simply ignore it. But now worry exhumed it, gave it a shape. The missing thing was present, but as something forever irretrievably missing.

He lay there half asleep, eyes wide open.

At Shiloh he'd commanded one hundred and fifty-six men: Battery F of the Second Illinois Light Artillery, Captain Powell in charge. He was Captain Powell then, though in time the wounded arm, and his earthworks at Vicksburg, meant promotion to Major. Just before Shiloh Walter joined the battery as a second lieutenant, having reenlisted. No one saw it coming. They woke one Sunday in rolling tableland with forests and fields, peach and apple orchards, and heard distant drums, tinny bugle calls, then the roar of artillery. Then a thousand screaming Rebels came bursting from the woods.

Nor had anyone assigned Captain Powell's battery. On his own initiative he galloped with his men first to McClernand's front, but McClernand was retreating, so he took them to Sherman's amid a stand of hickories. Finally he went to help Prentiss at a crossing of two country lanes. His battery was placed before the Eighth Iowa and ordered to hold its position to the last. Here were swirling peach blossoms near a sunken road, and bees and sunny skies on a Sunday morning. And here they soon realized their army was cut off, its wings having fallen back, so they had to fight like a mad nest of hornets, and to what end? The battle was too large for any one man. Its dozen separate flashpoints were unconnected to one another, and this was the first time half the men had seen the elephant, including Wes himself.

He raised his right arm to signal fire, then found himself sitting on the ground while the minié balls hissed past. Walter hurried over. The future Major Powell sat there grasping fingers that were no longer his. He tried to pinch the wound together, but it ran up his arm and blood was pouring out and he knew the bones were smashed. Walter tied a tourniquet on and twisted it tight. He lifted his brother to his feet and dragged him to a peach tree and helped him sit down.

The wound seemed to glare in Wes's mind like sheet lightning. He couldn't quite remember the ball having struck. The pain unripped itself and ran up his arm heading straight for the heart, where he feared it would kill him. Wires of nerve melted, chips of bone flew. His shoulder slowly grew numb yet his mind began to sharpen. General Wallace offered Wes his horse, since he, the general, knew they were surrounded and soon would be captured with the remaining men. The Rebels would not want a wounded prisoner impeaching their movement, not even an officer, and Wes would be shot if they found him like this, propped against a tree. His only chance was to ride out.

So he did. He rode past mangled bodies, past the dead with eyes open, past the wounded on litters and the wounded trying to walk and the wounded sitting down and waiting for help.

He made it to the landing and was helped onto a boat. Emma met him in Savannah. Two days later his arm had swollen up to twice its normal size and they filled him with laudanum and administered chloroform. They held him down—he was still conscious— and sawed it off above the elbow in ten brutal strokes, separating the Major forever from his right arm. They threw it in a pile of other amputated limbs, and only then did he pass out, with the stench of blood and chloroform strung like a foul taffy between his nose and lungs. Two months later they resectioned the stump, since the nerves had regenerated. And they'd continued to regenerate in the seven years since. Through unsifted lumps and clusters of tissue they stabbed toward empty air, searching for their lost arm.

7

August 28. Three months and four days on the river. Three boats and nine men left. Fifty pounds of coffee, twenty-five of dried apples, about ten of flour. Sufficient powder and balls for a few days' hunting. Barometers useless, maps a wet pulp, boats a mess of boards.

George Bradley woke to a predawn light the color of used bathwater and saw Major Powell talking with Ora and Bill in low tones. Something was up. "Are you running these rapids or not?" George called.

No one answered.

George had woken with an idea. They could try carrying the boats across the first part; the water wasn't that deep and right beside the wall the current looked weaker. No one else had stirred except Hawkins, who was beginning his fire. The Major broke off his conference, walked up to Hawkins, and asked him a question. The cook held up a half-empty flour sack.

George got to his feet and asked what was going on. Hawkins said the Major had ordered him to cook half the remaining flour into biscuits. Major Powell had wanted to know how the apples were holding out too, and Hawkins told him. Should he cook them up as well? No, said the Major, just the biscuits for now, and a pot of coffee.

George helped Hawkins shape the biscuits and they baked them in the gold pans. Andy threw on the coffee, and Ora, Seneca, and Bill stayed apart in their cluster while Jack, the Major, and Walter conferred. "What the hell's going on?" asked George.

"Damned if I know."

No one said a thing at breakfast except Andy Hall, who asked Bill Dunn, "You got wood ticks on your johnny?" Bill fixed his eyes on the ground. The Major told Hawkins to divvy up the biscuits and he made nine piles. Each man had twelve biscuits but three were left over, which Hawkins attempted to give to the Major. He refused them; his share, he said, would have to do for him.

Jack and Major Powell conferred with Ora Howland down by the river. All at once George guessed what was happening, and—he couldn't hold back—he burst into tears, couldn't stop sobbing. Hawkins touched his shoulder. The Major walked up and explained that Bill Dunn and the Howlands had given up the expedition. They planned to leave. George felt bitter and sad, yet relieved. With three fewer mouths to feed at least the rest wouldn't starve.

Or he could join them. It made more sense to go.

Because the food was running out, Major Powell went on, and the rapids were severe, the three planned to hike up that canyon they'd explored and find the Mormon settlements a hundred miles away. Did anyone wish to join them?

"Major Powell," said Hawkins, "I propose to finish."

"We'll follow you to hell," Andy Hall sputtered.

Jack Sumner walked over, followed by the three schismatics. Only Walter was missing, off examining the boats. "These here madmen want to finish?" asked Jack.

The Major looked at him. "Who else is leaving?"

Jack said, "Not me. I'm a madman myself."

No one else said a word.

Now that he'd decided, Jack acted scornful. "Jesus Christ, Ora, we're almost at the end."

"That's what our bully Major said ten days ago."

"I was ordered to leave, now I'm leaving," said Bill.

"We've made up our minds."

Seneca nodded firmly in agreement but kept his mouth shut. He didn't look happy. "You too, Seneca?" said Jack. "You'd do this to Major Powell?"

Seneca stared at him. "Since when have you given a shit about the Major?"

George felt this could be his last chance but just stood there. They divvied up supplies; each of the three took a blanket and his share of biscuits. Though they were leaving the river, they were given only one of the expedition's three remaining canteens, with the understanding that the main party might meet with disaster and have to hike out too. The Major offered them coffee and apples, but Bill said, "We don't want your damn savories." They did accept two rifles and one shotgun, also ammunition and matches, and Major Powell requested they take the chronometer. Jack gave them his watch to deliver to his sister Mrs. Byers in Denver. As many of Ora's maps and the expedition's records as they could copy were divided into sets, each party taking one.

At the last minute George had the feeling he'd picked the wrong side. The Howlands and Bill were the sensible ones, and those staying on the river would surely come to grief. Why otherwise would Jack give his watch to those leaving? And why would the Major send his precious chronometer back with those three if he thought the boats would make it? Fear in the shape of a hook caught his heart. But he said nothing.

They decided to abandon the *Emma Dean,* as she was the leakiest craft—the six men left could go in the other two boats—and now everyone pitched in. Bill, Ora, and Seneca helped unload the *Emma* and helped them cache in some rocks the busted barometers, the rock samples and fossils, the arrow points and potshards, all of which, as George knew, would likely be scattered by the first high water. George piped up and suggested carrying the boats over the first fall. The nine men, working together in fast water to their waists, found it was easier done than they'd thought.

The Major told Bill to ask for Jacob Hamblin when they arrived at the Mormon settlements. Hamblin was their leader in the southern colonies.

All stood at the mouth of that canyon going north in a mudfield of rocks—the road to freedom, it seemed. Hawkins and Andy took turns hugging Bill, and George and Jack shook hands with each of the three while the Major and his brother stood beside the boats and watched. Seneca Howland wept. "Come with us, Bill!" Andy hollered at the end, and Bill said, "My ass." Ora and Seneca looked as though they wondered why Andy didn't supplicate *them.* Ora said, "You're mad to go on, the whole pack of you," but he was looking at George.

The boats pulled out and both groups waved as the six shot down the river. In his boat George rowed and threaded the river. He'd con-

vinced himself he was of the doomed party, though the rapids, surprisingly, weren't that calamitous. As they flew through the water he
glanced back at the three sitting on crags, motionless and grim. Walter and Andy fired their rifles in the air and gestured and shouted for
them to come on—it wasn't so bad, they could take the *Emma Dean*
—but they waved back for the boats to continue.

George's boat swept around a bend and the exiles vanished from
sight.

Part Ten

1

Mara rode the burro, Onchok walked beside her, Toab came behind. Slowly, they crossed Mountain Lying Down—the Kaibab Plateau. Air sharp and cool, trees tall and thick, blood-red sun slashing through trees, trail hacked by sunlight. The tall ponderosas smelled like home, but they weren't home yet. Having come this way before, when she was young, Mara remembered the dense green forest, so different from the canyons below Paiute Mountain. She remembered the excitement of leaving home and going someplace new.

What a plaything, excitement! It was for other people now. She'd watched her sister dying, witnessed her sister's children being stolen. Pangwits had raised his cane to charge the Ute and she'd seen him shot. She'd had enough excitement. The wound had two sides: a little hole in the chest, a bloody canyon in back. When the three Ute rode off, each with a gagged child, the three remaining Shivwits wrapped Pangwits in a blanket, lay him in a rock shelter, walled it up with stones, and burned his clothes.

All things have a reason. There are no accidents, she thought. Everything that had happened to them was Onchok's fault for selling his children, Toab's fault for searching for the girl, and the miner's fault for shooting Pooeechuts. It was the fault of the Americans and the Mormons and of course the Navajo and certainly their wealthy relatives the Ute. It was her fault for letting Toab fuck her and the fault of the river for being hard to cross and of the land for making travel difficult. As a girl she'd been taught that the land opened up for the people's benefit. It gave them warmth and water and good soil in their canyon to plant squash and corn. It protected and concealed them. They shouldn't have taken this journey in the first place, that's why everything had happened. Long ago her father should not have crossed the river to trade his daughters' baskets, and she and her sister should not have gone with him, and her sister should not have sneaked into the bushes to lie down with Onchok. Then the children would not have been born and Pooeechuts and Pangwits would not have been shot and Soxor's blood would never have come and Toab wouldn't have stood in the fire and she and Toab would never have met and she wouldn't feel hollow. Her life wouldn't be over. Mara and her sister would have stayed where they were, back near Paiute Mountain, and nothing would have changed. Each day would have passed the same as the one before.

She could think about her sister but not say her name out loud. Pooeechuts might hear and believe they were calling her. And if they called her, her ghost would come and haunt them with her wailing and upbraid them with all the things they'd done wrong.

The trail grew steeper and the trees stopped. They came to the edge and saw the world spread before them: green slopes rolling down to miles of smaller trees, piñons and cedars that bled into desert valleys. Their route down would cross the brown desert west to Rabbitbrush Water, then skirt a canyon and cross another desert to the mountain that marked the start of Shivwits land, Yuwinkadud, Ponderosa Sitting. There it was, low on the skyline to the west, a swelling hump, half in shadow already. It looked like Paiute Mountain. The sun hung to its right and the blue of the sky thinned to white between the mountain and the sun. Beyond that horizon was their plateau with its forests and clearings, its volcanic scablands, its canyons on all sides. Soon they'd be home. Soon she and Onchok would make their own children. And soon, when the children started to grow, they'd get stolen too.

That night after dark Onchok rolled on top of her. He looked off to the side so all she could see was his mouth's slack corner. After, she felt a stinging numbness and thought that was good, that was how she ought to feel.

The next day they descended a winding canyon and halfway down the pygmy forest reappeared—the piñon and juniper—but the trees thinned out quickly and a broad flat brown plain rose to meet them and the morning grew hot. The sun had risen in a haze that filled half the sky. What's this? asked Mara. She ran her hand along a wire, touching sharp metal thorns. The wire was attached to upright posts. Onchok called it a kweeup, a fence, and they climbed between the wires but couldn't get the burro through, so they climbed out again, drawing blood this time, and walked beside the fence. It obstructed their passage and they couldn't see the end, couldn't tell what it fenced in or what out. When they came to a place where the wires were ripped back, they passed through and resumed their direction, aiming for a low line of cliffs.

Toab spotted something that looked like a pile of rocks ahead, and caught up with Onchok. The rocks turned into four or five large figures out on the plain, but without horses, so they couldn't have been Ute or Navajo. Nevertheless, Onchok told Mara to wait. He and Toab crossed the brown land and the heat rose in waves. As they approached, the group of seeming titans shrank to normal size. Some ran off but came scurrying back when they saw who it was. They were Kaibab Paiute, neighbors of the Shivwits, and they stood around a butchered steer. Toab recognized their leader, Nankapeea, from dances and trades. He said Makewa and they answered Makewa. Nankapeea explained that they wanted to cook some meat but there wasn't any wood. The Kaibab Paiute looked at the burro, and Toab looked too. We could unload him and get some wood, he said. He waved at Mara to approach.

The Kaibab leader nodded, smiling. He was covered with dust and blood from the butchering. Or we could load the meat on the burro and bring it to the wood, he said. That way we wouldn't have to come back here.

Toab nodded. They wouldn't get caught, in other words.

The Kaibab wore breechclouts and sandals and Mormon shirts. What's your news? Nankapeea asked Toab.

Toab explained they'd gone a long way searching for Onchok's daughter. American miners shot Pooeechuts, and three Ute shot her brother in House Rock Valley and stole her children.

The Kaibab shook their heads, groaning in sympathy, and looked around, concerned about the Ute. When was this?

Two days ago. They weren't coming this way. They rode off to the north.

The Kaibab turned away and smiled in relief.

What about you? Toab asked.

We killed this steer. We were hungry. You can share it.

We're on our way to Rabbitbrush Water.

Let's cook some of this meat, then we'll go with you. Our families are there.

What about the Mormonis?

They won't bother us, Nankapeea said. But they cut up the steer as quickly as they could and hung the quarters on the burro, tying them with yucca cord. The burro balked at first with this new weight, though they'd removed the burden baskets. The smell of blood made him jumpy, and they slapped his haunches and pushed him with their shoulders. Toab and Onchok carried the baskets—women's work. At least both were doing it.

Five Kaibab, including Nankapeea, led the way back to the hole in the fence, then all headed north toward low cliffs and hills, and angled east toward a break between two plateaus.

Here they found piñons, cedar, and sage against a broken ridge and built a fire and cooked the meat. They ate as much as they could, because who knew when meat would come their way again?

Nankapeea talked about the Mormons, owners of the steer. He called them two-hearts. They baptized the Kaibab and gave them shirts and at the same time took away their water. When the Navajo killed some Mormons last year the Mormons caught two Paiute, his relatives, and hung them by their heels, twisted their thumbs, and made them tell where the Navajo were hidden. Then they captured the Navajo and shot them.

Mormon steer and sheep had destroyed all the grass the Paiute used to eat. When Nankapeea's family gathered pine nuts last year, a Mormon showed up and said the trees were his. They give us food and clothes, said Nankapeea, but their sheep and cattle scare off the deer. Some Paiute liked their leader, Jacob Hamblin, because one of his many wives was Paiute, but others accused him of bringing infected blankets to the Newe. He'd moved in up there next to Willow Water, where they were building a town, and now the water was theirs.

Nankapeea shrugged and grabbed his own shirt, saying, Look at this old shirt. It's falling apart. Time to get baptized again! He laughed.

Why allow them to baptize you if they're bad? Toab asked.

Not all of them are bad. They take away the things we need, take away the grass and water. But they give us new things like beef and shirts. They give us flour.

And crackers, someone said.

Nankapeea laughed. At Point of Hill Water, he said to the Shivwits, the Mormonis built a house for their soldiers and a corral for their horses. That's where our wives can earn a lot of crackers to bring home to us, in the house of the soldiers.

What do they do? Toab asked.

Nankapeea slid a finger into and out of his other hand's palm.

Toab looked away, disgusted.

It's not Point of Hill Water anymore, Nankapeea said. The water's theirs now and the Mormonis call it Pipe Spring. He said the name in English.

Three quarters of meat were left and Nankapeea proposed they cut out the best parts and hide the meat inside the Shivwits' burden baskets. They cut out some steaks, wrapped them in buckskin, and put them in the baskets, which they loaded on the burro. They headed west again toward Rabbitbrush Water, where Nankapeea's band had built their summer shelters. There, below the cliffs, amid sage and mesquite and a few scattered piñons, they dug a deep pit and roasted the rest of the meat under coals covered with dirt so it wouldn't be discovered.

On one side of their camp they'd planted a garden the likes of which the Shivwits had never seen. The crops grew in rows, and each row held only one crop, corn, squash, or melon. There were two rows of something Toab hadn't heard of—potatoes.

That night they boiled squash and ate the roasted meat and held a round dance. Nankapeea sang a song about the Mormon spirit Jesus, who suffered the children to come unto him.

Toab suggested they build a sweat lodge and Nankapeea agreed. He'd never had a sweat before. The next day they stuck willows in the earth and bent them in an arch. They threw blankets and buckskins over the top, leaving a crawl hole at the bottom. They built a fire and heated rocks and rolled them inside. Toab taught Nankapeea to say Paa when they entered and Onchok cut sage to sprinkle water on the rocks. Nankapeea wore his head ornament: a tin disk on his forehead, held in place by a tin strip curving over his head.

The lodge barely had room for three males: Nankapeea, Onchok, and Toab. As soon as they entered, Toab felt the heat. The stones were much hotter than those in Pangwits's sweat, and the day was already blazing outside. Onchok asked Toovuts to protect them on this last part of their journey, then threw water on the stones. The steam exploded and the men could hardly breathe. Thank you, dear Lord, for coming to the Lamanites, in Jesus' name, amen, said Nankapeea as steam filled the air. It rippled across the surface of their skin, and Toab held both hands over his nose in order to breathe, and his hands were burning up, but Onchok wouldn't stop; he threw on more water and more steam exploded. Toab's hot head felt ready to burst.

Toab was someplace else. All was brown and purple. His legs were paralyzed but a medicine man made a slit behind his knee and pulled out some bull snakes, which allowed him to walk. He saw the three white men huddled in their bower, the one with raven-black hair eating rocks. Toab fired at them and nothing happened. He tried to stab them but his knife wouldn't penetrate. He picked up a rock and pounded and pounded their heads with no result.

He jumped on a horse but suddenly felt made out of rags and couldn't sit upright.

He remembered how the Newe used to hunt. They would want a particular animal to die and so it would die and even butcher itself. Now he saw a lot of animals, but his bullets couldn't hurt them and his arrows fell short. They looked sick—the bighorns and deer and antelope and rabbits. Their jaws dribbled foam from eating blue loco. They ran across the horizon and never came back. Rock rovers did too, wrinkled ugly creatures who liked to catch people and throw them off cliffs. Water babies and witches, unupits and the kunishuv —snow-white beings who lived on the mountains and walked inside clouds—all ran over the horizon and disappeared and never returned. Last went Coyote, looking over his shoulder.

Toab lay on the ground. Coyote, he said, what's going on? What's going to happen?

I'm not Coyote, said Onchok.

Toab had fainted in the sweat lodge. Onchok and Nankapeea had had to drag him out, though they'd felt weak too. Onchok was feeding him water from a jug, cold, clear, and pure.

Nankapeea decided the sweat lodge was too dangerous.

Later that day the three Shivwits loaded up their burro and headed for home. Across a rise to the south was the house erected by the Mormons for their soldiers at Point of Hill Water, and they made a wide circle around it. When the Shivwits descended to a plain, Toab looked back and saw a split cedar fence running behind the compound and the scrawny new trees and the stone house with its massive stone chimney sending up smoke, and he felt sick inside. Point of Hill Water used to be owned by a Kaibab named Patchakwi; he'd let everyone use it. Where was he now? What had they done to him?

Under the sun they marched across the desert toward Ponderosa Sitting, their mountain low on the horizon. The yellow-brown desert grew dry and flat and the bunchgrass thinned, eaten by cattle. The valley grew larger, more level and barren. Endless, Toab thought. They'd never get home. Low ridges appeared, then isolated hills dotted with pines. They camped at the last running spring in the desert, Cave Water, under Shinarump Cliffs.

The next day the burro refused to go farther. They kicked and pushed him but he wouldn't move. They drank from the spring and ate seedcakes and only in midmorning did the burro move, and then only slowly. Mara didn't ride him—he seemed too weak. Over broad rolling hills they marched toward the mountain. More piñons appeared and they examined the branches and counted the cones. Toab said to Onchok, These trees look good. When the rabbitbrush flowers they'll have a lot of nuts.

Onchok didn't seem interested.

While climbing a rise just before the sun set the burro stopped again. He sank to his knees and seemed to rest on his neck. They took off the baskets and he keeled over. He died, so they butchered him and made themselves eat the meat, which was stringy and tasteless although faintly sour. They ate more the next morning, then Toab and Onchok carried the baskets. They left the carcass behind and marched on toward home.

Beside Ponderosa Sitting, above the lava flows, they visited a village of their neighbors and relatives, exchanged gifts and news, feasted together, and held a round dance. From this place they could just make out their land, the remote plateau where even Mormons seldom ventured. Walking there they'd have to skirt Parashont Canyon. They might meet more neighbors, and visit with them, so it could take a few days to get home.

They parted from their friends and started west toward their plateau. To the south, volcanic cones rose amid vast beds of cinder and flows of lava. Straggling junipers, piñons, and brush migrated toward the river, the same river they'd crossed after leaving home, the same one they'd crossed again before wrapping up Pooeechuts, painting her face, and leaving her in her arbor to die. They'd almost completed a circle, Toab thought. Of the five who'd started out and the two who joined them, only three were left to finish it.

It didn't feel like a circle. Things were different now. Because the three of them had changed they wouldn't end where they began. Instead, they'd reach home and find it wasn't the same. From now on, he knew, the effort to make each day alike would grow more futile. You examined the pine nuts as you always had and meanwhile you wanted more attractive things—guns, needles, mirrors. Onchok in particular wanted novelties, and Toab wondered how that felt. Wanting new things must have helped his brother forget his children, the ones who'd been stolen. He could get along without them because so much had changed, because nothing was the same. And when nothing was the same, the Same became a story told to kill the cries of absent children in the night.

2

"Go ahead and scratch a big arrow on that rock, Sen."

"How come?"

"In case they got swamped and the boats went bust."

"That's my suspicion too," said Bill. "They'll come running after us with their little tails tucked between their little legs."

At the mouth of the canyon forking left, Seneca stood on tiptoe on a rock leaning into the tall flat-faced boulder. With a piece of hard obsidian he scratched a four-foot-long arrow pointing right. The arrow showed pink through the dark patina.

"They'll see that a mile away," said Oramel.

"You sound pretty confident they're coming."

"Alls you have to do is think what they're up against."

"They're bound to follow."

"If they survive. And that's if."

Earlier Seneca had meekly suggested they might want to go back and try their luck with the abandoned *Emma Dean,* and ever since then Oramel and Bill had made sure he understood their decision was the right one. But this labyrinth of canyons couldn't help but cause them doubt. They did have a compass and they knew which way to go, knew they had to find a way to the northern rim. Exactly how to get there was the question. Each side canyon offered a choice, and should they try every one? They decided to reject those with dry floors, but this tortured Ora, who felt in his bones that the one they passed up would be the very one they wanted.

"You're good for something, ain't you," said Bill, nodding at Seneca's arrow. They'd just come back from exploring this fork running left—to the west—which, like the others, rose through broken cliffs before it boxed out. The plateau's rim looked to be a mile up, if that was in fact the rim. It could have been an intervening terrace. They'd resisted many smaller canyons but not this major fork, and the hike took most of the morning, in heat, past pink and black walls of granite and gneiss. At last the canyon pinched and a waterfall stopped them, a high narrow rope of clear blue water hanging so still you'd swear you could climb it.

Scrambling back over talus and gravel Seneca was mum. The other two sensed his misery, knew he was on the verge of tears again. Hunger like theirs did not affect only the belly; it filled the heart with dust, a dark powder of despair. It weakened you with hopelessness. They had to allow Seneca to exceed his three-biscuit quota that afternoon, and to make him think it wasn't just him—they exceeded theirs too.

Game in these canyons appeared to be nonexistent. All the more reason to find the best route. Up on the rim there'd be rabbits and deer, though Bill claimed he'd seen deer shit back near the canyon's mouth.

"Where's the deer then?"

"Could be a park ahead."

"Not in this waste."

They kept Seneca busy, gave him tasks to perform: looking out for game, scouting their route, scratching that arrow. The chronometer was their only heavy item and now that they were ready to start up the main canyon, Bill squawked and moaned about the instrument's weight. Seneca said, "My turn," took it with both hands, and packed it inside the blanket in his knapsack.

They trudged up the canyon in a slash of blazing air. The puny stream beside them frayed and unfrayed and did not relieve the heat. Though the sun sucked the air right out of their lungs, they had to keep going because that's what they'd chosen. The flat canyon bottom gradually mounted. Bill was intrigued by the quantities of gravel outwashed from somewhere on its floor, and kept looking for float. He kicked little holes but couldn't see any sponge, let alone solid quartz. And they didn't have their gold pans.

The high granite walls radiated heat and the canyon grew narrow. They could wander forever in the earth's bowels and starve to death, thought Seneca. He recalled what he'd said when Bill was told to leave: A bird couldn't fly out of this canyon, Major Powell.

"If they swamp," said Ora, still dwelling on the subject, "he'll just come running."

"Them boats are held together by spit and a prayer."

"Who designed them anyway?"

"He did, of course. George says they was designed by an ignoramus."

"What I'd like to know," Seneca said, "is why the hell we come on this trip in the first place."

Bill Dunn thought. "Adventure and science."

"Then it's a failure?"

"It was from the jump."

"I'll say this," said Ora. "We've seen places no white man has ever laid eyes on."

Seneca exclaimed, "Then how come we quit!"

"We took the prudent course. That's not any kind of life—bailing out boats and smearing them with pitch and smashing into rocks and who knows when you'll drown. Besides, that man won't ever get off his throne. He's the living expert on every blessed thing."

"He thinks his shit don't stink."

"You hear me, Seneca?" Ora continued. "In two or three days we'll be out of this maze and on our way to Denver."

"We could go to California and hunt for gold."

"Them goldfields is exhausted," said Bill.

"A nice tame life reading proof in Denver."

They came to a place where three canyons branched off, each with an intermittent stream and pools from the recent rain. Ora took compass bearings. The first ran northwest, the middle one north, and the third east but curving back south, the direction they'd come from. "Best to split up," said Bill. "Leave our bundles here. Meet back at this juncture."

"Good plan," said Ora. "Save us some time."

"I'll take that one there." Bill nodded to the right.

"It just runs back to the river," said Ora.

"How do you know?"

"The compass don't lie."

"I happen to have a suspicion it's the one."

"Suit yourself, then. I'll take the middle."

"I'll take the other," said Seneca.

"You ought to come with one of us," said his brother. "Alls we have to do is check out two canyons. If one of them goes, then we follow that one. If both of them are boxed, then we have to take the third."

"Ain't we smart eggs?"

"I'll go with Bill, then."

Ora said, "You can come with me, Seneca."

They decided to carry their guns but dug a hole and cached their knapsacks and marked the spot with rocks. The Howlands hiked little more than a mile before their middle branch opened into a bowl that rose to a cliff, then a terrace, then another cliff. The upper terrace, spined vertically with rock and dotted with piñon, swept all the way up to what must have been the rim. But the broken cliffs didn't

hold much promise. They might contain a few chimneys that a con-
tortionist like Powell might be able to slither up. Then again they
might not. There had to be a better way.

The brothers walked back to the main canyon, dug up their
things, and found some terraced ledges just east of the juncture.
They climbed a ship's prow affording them a view of the third canyon and perched there on its side in the shade of the rim, waiting for
Bill. After a while they heard a shot down his canyon followed by a
string of echoes, each distinct and sharp. "Think he's calling us?"
asked Seneca. "Or is there game in there?"

"If it goes to the rim, there's game in there," said Ora. "If it don't,
he's signaling."

"He could of shot a wolf about to make him a meal. A bear or
a wolf."

"I ought to go see."

"Me too, I'm coming."

"You stay here."

"Jesus Christ, Ora, don't treat me like a child!"

"Watch your smart mouth. You're still my little brother. The prudent course here is one of us goes in case there's any danger. Long as
you don't leave this here spot. I haven't noticed no one else here to
guard our things and listen."

"Listen for what?"

"Redskins."

"Redskins?"

"You heard what I said. All you got to do is get behind that rock
and keep your powder dry. Easy as rolling off a log, little brother."

"Don't call me that."

"Watch my back. Keep your eyes peeled."

Seneca scooped up their biscuits and packs and climbed to a
higher ledge. He sat behind a boulder and watched Ora scramble
down. Rifle ready, Ora glanced left and right as he hopped boulders
to the canyon floor below, and in the cross breeze from the mouths of
the canyons his beard forked and curled and his hair stood on end.
To Seneca he looked like the mountain men of yore — those who ate
raw liver and scalped unfriendly braves and married child squaws,
and wound up as human pincushions.

Then again, no. Not Ora.

He sat behind the rock, shotgun loaded and ready. Ora disappeared up the third canyon and soon all inside this gorge was excavated silence. The shadows slowly lengthened. Beneath some prickly pears below his perch, as indifferent to Seneca as he was to them, two bark scorpions had locked their front legs and were dancing back and forth, tails waving in the air.

Seneca listened, waited, and watched. The gun in his hands made him think of Vermont — of shooting red-winged blackbirds in the cornfields at home. There, fields were full of grass, tree stumps, and ferns, and the massed clouds with white veiny seams glowed within. Sunlight made the land green and the crabapples red and the shucked corn yellow. Before his older brother had departed, they'd gone out into the fields and bordering woods and fought with crabapples, threw them at each other from behind trunks of beeches, practicing for the war they both knew was coming.

Here, however, there was not a tree in sight. Scant shrubs and willows along the stream below, plus sage and yucca scattered on the canyon walls, supplied the only green. Otherwise all was red, gray, and brown. The sky was deep blue and some cottonball clouds had appeared above his head ignited by the sun, which had passed behind this cliff. But even in shade the heat had to be in the hundreds.

Another shot came from inside the first canyon and the echoes detonated, growing steadily louder, or so it seemed to Seneca, who continued hearing them long after they stopped. Whose gun it was he couldn't tell. He could wait here and see what else happened, then hike up the canyon himself, though the sun would set soon — he couldn't wait long. He could go right now, he thought. But he didn't. The fear creased his heart, shortened his breath. When minutes passed and nothing else happened an odd peace descended and he ate a biscuit. Eating occupied not just his stomach but his mind — it made things proximate, staved off worry. Anything could have happened, of course, and given such uncertainty, why not eat? He allowed himself another. They'd never tasted so good! If he didn't go now and, God forbid, Bill and Ora never came back, he knew what would happen: he wouldn't move from this spot. He'd stay right here ensconced behind his rock and never venture down. Eventually he'd run out of biscuits and wind up a skeleton in exactly this posture.

Something unnerving happened. Between his legs he felt himself growing hard.

Meanwhile, the dirt seemed to be alive. On the canyon's other side it absorbed the sun's heat and sent it back in shimmers. The cliffs appeared to shift and everything moved. Somewhere behind him grains of dirt slid. He turned and saw a tarantula scuttling down the bare slope.

He looked around but didn't see any others. He checked his feet and legs but found nothing.

Yet they were everywhere. This was their active season. Females waited inside their silky tubes in burrows in the earth, and males roamed the canyon, the cliffs, the terraces, and the plateau up on top, in a world apart from Seneca. And when the male found a female he bent her back and up, hooking his front legs over her fangs, and deposited his sperm in the furrow of her belly, then let go and fled before she could eat him.

Only when he spotted Ora and Bill emerging from the canyon did Seneca realize he'd finished all their biscuits. He tried not to care but felt afraid of Ora. Then he noticed Bill carried something on his back, and as they got closer he saw it was a deer. He burst from his perch in the rocks and ran down. Ora waved and Seneca fired his shotgun in the air, but when he got to the men Ora's face was red, his brow pinched. "I suppose you never heard of conserving ammunition."

"Who shot the deer?"

"I did," said Bill. It was slung across his shoulders and bleeding from the nose. For a horrid moment Seneca was tempted to tear it apart with his nails and teeth and eat the meat raw.

There wasn't much wood, just sage and willows, but enough to start a fire and cook the best parts of the deer, the liver and a haunch. Seneca said to Bill that if a deer was in that canyon it must be the way out. Bill agreed.

Each had a knife; they ate the deer with that and their fingers, destitute of forks and cooking gear. Later, Bill wandered back up the canyon and returned barechested carrying a load of wood inside his shirt, tied on the gun resting on his shoulder. Where the canyon swung north there were trees in its folds, Bill reported, scrub oak and cedars. He'd found plenty of deadwood and he'd found something else.

They asked what.

A trail. When the rocks and gravel on the canyon bottom ran out and the land began to climb, a faint trail appeared snaking up between boulders, rabbitbrush, and junipers. You could see sometimes it vanished, but it always reappeared. It wasn't a game trail or maybe it was, but people used it too. He'd noticed some fire pits. It headed straight north. Had to be the way out.

They gorged on the deer the rest of that day and built a frame of green willows and laid strips of meat across it hanging in the smoke. They kept the fire going as they ate, hiked up the canyon to gather more wood and look at the trail, then hiked back and ate more. They set the strips flat on rocks to dry in the sun. No one asked Seneca about the biscuits.

The next day they ate the ribs—the last of the fresh meat. They laid them on the coals and after they were cooked pulled them apart, using their teeth to strip off the meat. Each bone when they finished was white and polished. The jerked meat hadn't thoroughly dried, but they packed it up anyway and started up the canyon, clinging to the south wall to stay in the shade. When the canyon swung north amid cliff rose and juniper they came to an overhang, followed the trail up a short side canyon, gained a ridge above, then followed it down into the main gorge. The vegetation thickened, especially in folds. In places the trail had been shored up with rocks. It led to some cliffs and an esplanade where the land fell open in bands of green and red scalloped with gullies and scattered with piñons and junipers and sage. The trail disappeared at the foot of some talus fanning down beside a cliff, but they climbed the rocks and found it again, traversing a narrow ledge below the highest cliffs, where their path abruptly ended at a gap-toothed wall.

Here, they had to chimney up ten feet. Ora went first and the others handed up their packs and guns. As Ora climbed, Bill examined the white and brown rock, looking for quartz, a harbinger of gold. He tried the tongue test—broke off a chunk, wiped it on his sleeve, applied his wet tongue to the surface of the rock to dissolve the dust and highlight its color. He declared it was promising. He tossed it up to Ora.

Seneca climbed, then Bill, who had trouble squirming up the chimney, being squat and short-legged. Seneca had to give him a hand.

They'd gained a plateau almost as thickly forested as Vermont, Seneca thought when he saw it. Brush grew between the pines and they bushwhacked through it while the sun rose in the sky. But the air was cooler here. They found another faint trail and headed for a hill blue with ponderosas, past manzanita, cholla, yucca, cliff rose, and agave growing in the dry and crusty dirt. On top of the hill Bill continued to tongue-test the rocks, and Seneca and Ora scouted the view of their thickly wooded tableland and saw where it pinched directly to the north, eaten on either side by canyons. They'd have to go there, into the hourglass waist of this plateau, in order to arrive at a high volcanic cone that dominated the horizon. From there they'd see the lay—their passage back to civilization.

On top of their hill were some ruins of a dwelling, just a low wall. Potshards and arrowheads lay in the dirt.

Water was a problem when they resumed walking. They'd rejoined the faint trail threading the plateau, but all here was dry. Soon their canteen was empty. "If this here's an Indian trail," said Bill, "it's bound to lead to water." But it didn't, or if it did they missed it. They walked for several hours toward that volcanic cone, their stomachs cramping, eyeballs pinched, mouths full of strings. At the edge of a clearing they spotted some wickiups and hustled toward them, thinking they meant people, and people meant water.

But the dwellings were empty. There were four wickiups covered with brush and no one in sight. Hanging from each parabolic entrance was a large branch of brown sage.

They hiked north toward the cone. Except for a coyote looking over his shoulder they saw no more game, and the coyote took care to stay too far ahead for them to get a good shot. He disappeared in the trees and reemerged later from thick trunks and bushes. The land was long and hot and grew longer as they walked. The stands of ponderosa held few clearings, but now and then the rocks attracted Bill's notice, despite his raging thirst. His mouth was too dry to test them with his tongue, but he did take samples.

No water—not a sign. They tried to suck juice from the jerky that was left, but after taking one bite and looking at his piece Seneca spit the whole mouthful in the dirt.

"What's your fucking problem now?"

"This meat has worms!"

The others looked at the jerky in their hands—chunks the size of wood chips—and sure enough little white seeds of worms had hatched in its crevices. "Don't be hasty," said Bill. "Alls we got to do is cook it a little."

"I'm not eating wormy meat, cooked or uncooked."

"Suit yourself."

Bill started a fire at the edge of the trail while clouds rolled in. For a moment it sprinkled. But the rain disappeared somewhere in the air and hardly wet the ground and couldn't quench their thirst. When the fire was down to coals, he lay green sticks across it and spread the jerked meat on top of the sticks. He flipped it with a stick every now and then.

He picked out the largest coal and pushed it to the side with his shoe to let it cool. Meanwhile, he and Ora sucked on cooked jerky but Seneca declined. "Fine with me," said Bill.

"And what will I eat? I'm starved and I'm thirsty."

"Not my problem."

Ora said, "Biscuits."

When Bill's coal had cooled he took out his knife and cut a cavity in it, then crumbled ore samples into the cavity, sprinkled on a pinch of gunpowder, and pushed it in the fire. As it started heating up he made a tunnel with his fist and blew into the cavity, then shook out his hand and watched the ore begin to glow. He kept doing this, alternating hands, but the rock did not reduce. It only turned brown.

He kicked the little makeshift smelter. "Fucking waste of time."

"What seems to be the problem?"

"Not enough heat. Still can't tell if it's shit or honey."

"All that glitters," said Ora.

Just below the summit of the basaltic cone-shaped peak they arrived at hours later, Bill cut an inscription in a flat boulder: *Dunn*

1869. Above him, Ora and his brother scouted the land. Ahead lay fields with greenish pockets and folds in yellow grass. Beyond them, the land stretched endlessly north, a wide tree-covered plain.

They spotted something else too: a thin thread of smoke rising in the air beside a small clearing. Its source was hidden in the trees.

Seneca, who'd grown proficient at arrows, drew one beneath Bill's inscription, pointing toward the smoke, and added the word *Water* beside it.

It took an hour or so to reach the clearing, and the people there were waiting. They were half naked, in ragged dishabille, smeared with dust and grease. From their brush shelters they calmly watched the men approach. "Seneca, shlang that shotgun, why don't you."

"How come?"

"Give them something to think about."

Bill approached with his rifle held prominently in front. Behind him the Howlands also carried their weapons across their crooked elbows. Seneca stopped and broke his shotgun open over one knee, examined the breech, then slammed it shut. A man with skinny legs, squatting like a grasshopper, his body slung between his knees, looked up from a fire. Conical baskets lay on the ground, also grinding stones and water jugs. Bill handed his rifle and blanket to Ora and made straight for a water jug and, without asking, held it to his lips. The water streamed down his chin and pulsing throat and he stopped, gasped for air, then drank more. He offered it to Ora, who shook his head and pointed his bearded chin at Seneca. Bill retrieved his rifle and Seneca drank, then Ora drank last.

The people watched them. Parfleches and bows and quivers holding arrows hung in the trees along with shirts and squares of cloth. Rabbitskin robes, seed beaters, horn spoons, basket trays, and hats were wedged in the branches. Jerked meat lay draped across a frame in the sun. Brush shelters merged with the trees.

This flat land covered with bunchgrass and sage was hemmed in by ponderosas. At their backs stood the black cone they'd descended to get here—the only mountain in sight. Bill slowly approached the old man at the fire, who looked up half smiling. His face, a loose glove, and his wild mop of hair both drooped about his eyes. He set down his implements and pushed his hair aside. Like the other men, he wore only a breechclout.

Bill lay his rifle down. The man grinned and nodded, grunting something in Neanderthal—or so it seemed to Seneca—and Bill said, "Makewa."

Seneca asked Ora, "What'd he say?"

"Hello."

"Bill knows their lingo?"

"He knows a little Ute from up in Hot Sulphur Springs."

"So these here are Ute."

"Ought to could be Paiute."

"What's the difference?"

"Beats me."

The rest of the band had gathered around—men dressed in breechclouts, women in bark skirts, some bare-breasted. The children were naked. Old and young, male and female, all had matted black hair to their shoulders.

Bill said "Tu-kai" and made a scooping gesture into his mouth. The old man did something odd. He picked up a rock and offered it to Bill, and everyone laughed. "Merry bunch," said Seneca.

"Saucy as devils."

"They seen you tongue-testing that ore," said Oramel. "They been watching us," he said.

Bill brought his hand to his mouth once again, mimed eating something, rubbed his belly, and, smiling, ran his tongue over his lips. But the old man got to his feet and started talking up a storm and pointed south toward the canyon. He kept waving south, then gestured at Bill. "He's asking where we come from," Ora said.

"I say stop the fucking jabbering and feed us. Then we talk."

"You tell him that."

"They yell scandalous, don't they?" All the Indians were talking, some shouting to be heard, and pointing south toward the river canyon. Bill held up his hands and said, "Shut your damned fly traps." The old man scowled. Bill pointed to the river and gestured toward the east and made a waving motion with one arm, then pointed separately at himself and the Howlands.

The old man shook his head.

Bill did it again, saying loudly in English, "WE COME DOWN THE RIVER." He made a motion like rowing and swept his arms from the east down to the south, snaking one hand up and down.

The man seemed to catch on. He shook his head at Bill and mimed falling in the water. He smashed his head against the earth, then lay there motionless, eyes closed, lips gulping like a fish's. He stood and waved his hands to negate what Bill had said and even, it seemed, wagged a finger like a schoolmarm. He shrugged his shoulders, talking away, and said something sharply to the woman behind him.

Grim-faced, skin taut as a drumhead, with an inverted basket on her head and a well-ventilated deerskin dress, she walked to a tree, pulled down a parfleche, and fished around inside.

The man pointed at Bill, then the others. "Mericats?" he asked.

"Damned right. Americans."

The cry of a baby came from a brush shelter. A girl broke from the group and ran toward it in the trees. Smoke billowed up as the fire began to die and the man threw on wood. The sun to the west burst from the clouds, then retreated just as quickly. Then it came out again. Shadows stretched across the clearing. Two more women pulled down parfleches and handed out seedcakes and cakes of agave and jerked meat and nuts. One poured water from a basket hung on a tripod and with forked sticks lifted hot stones out of the fire and threw them in the water. Soon they had a sweet mush, and Seneca said it was the most delicious meal he'd ever sat to in his life, bar none. It rivaled Ma's hot chicken pie, he told Ora.

"You're just starved."

All squatted around the fire to eat. The Paiute nibbled at the food too, although Seneca guessed it was out of politeness. "This tastes like peaches." He held up the agave.

Chewing some jerked meat, Bill gestured to the north and said "Mormons?" to the old man.

"Mormoni?"

"Jacob Hamblin," said Bill.

The old man nodded and smiled, pointing north.

Bill gestured to this man and at the Howlands and himself and waved north again, nodding his head. The man's head bobbed, and with his arms he swept all of them north in a trice. Seneca understood: he would show them the way.

That night the Paiute held a round dance. The white men joined in, intoxicated with food and giddy with relief at having departed from the river and chosen the best course and met these friendly savages—friendly if squalid—and found out the way to the Mormon settlements. The round dance was lit by the light of the moon and a fire to one side. Everyone held hands, the Mericats included, and they slowly circled left. But the Howlands and Dunn took awhile to catch the rhythm. They collided with their neighbors and the song leader yelled at them. The leader, a young brave dressed only in a breechclout and red headband, paced back and forth, shouting out the songs and keeping everyone in line. When one song was in progress and Bill substituted a Stephen Foster ditty for the words, this man was not amused. He shouted and glared. But Bill persisted:

> *Katy Bell is in the dell*
> *How I love her none can tell.*

The song leader stopped the dance and barked at the whites. Then he and the old man held a confab. Meanwhile, a girl tugged on Bill's sleeve and hand in hand they walked off into the bushes. The song leader fumed and made to follow, but the old man restrained him and he stormed off. Another young girl grabbed Seneca's sleeve and was leading him off by the right arm when Ora caught the left one. Briefly they conducted a fierce tug of war that made Seneca laugh hysterically with embarrassment. He shouted at his brother, and some of the watching Paiute laughed while others turned away in disgust. Finally the girl gave up and walked off, chagrined.

Seneca was livid. "Rid me of you," he said to his brother. "Stop interfering with my private business!"

"It's not a good idea to fellowship them," Ora dryly responded.

"Why not!"

"They're heathens."

After Bill had been gone for a while, the old man went over to his knapsack underneath a tree. He'd opened the top and was removing the ore samples when Bill returned. He hadn't touched Bill's gun, just the ore; the gun still leaned against the tree. Bill picked it up and aimed the barrel at the man. "Put them rocks back."

Ora walked up. "He don't understand you."

"The thieving redskin understands. Put them back," he said.

"Is this worth a fracas?"

"Damn right it is. No one steals my ore."

"It's probably worthless."

"Must be worth something, he wants it that bad."

The old man wasn't smiling. He held out the rocks, spewed a stream of words, then threw them back into the open pack. Bill closed it, picked it up, and walked off.

The next morning the old man was nowhere to be seen, nor was the song leader with the red headband. But the rest of the people held another feast and this time they produced a pair of fat rabbits that they cut up and boiled into a stew. But Seneca, either from the rich food or from the night's excitement, felt an incipient rebellion in his guts and had to run into the trees. Ora pulled out Jack Sumner's watch and told Bill to try to trade it for food they could take on their way to the Mormons.

"That ought to buy their whole fucking tribe," Bill said.

It bought seedcakes, agave, jerked meat, nuts, and a burden basket to carry it all. Bill took the honors; his paramour from the night before wrapped the tumpline across his chest and he strutted around while the women shook with laughter, clapping their hands over their mouths. The men spat in the dust.

Through gestures and signs and a map drawn in the dirt, a young Paiute indicated where to find their next water. It wasn't far.

Seneca felt disappointed the old man wasn't leading them. What had happened to him?

Their departure was delayed by Seneca's recent infirmity, which, as he told Ora, disgorged from both ends. When at last they started off in the direction they'd been shown, accompanied by several urchins, Bill turned and shouted to the Paiute, "Give my love to Aunt Tilly," and Seneca joined in, "Hug babies for me," and Bill added, "Give old Uncle Josh a good kick in the ass for old times' sake, hey."

3

George Bradley stood in the bow of the *Sister* trying to open his knife and hang on to the gunnels and keep his balance simultaneously. He shouted up to Jack, "SHOULD I CUT LOOSE?" but the hellish rapids swallowed all sounds and he couldn't even hear himself. The men on the cliff had snubbed the rope around a rock and now leaned out shouting something down at George, clearly at a loss.

The *Sister* swung back into the wall again. George braced himself and she crashed against the cliff, then swung out into the rapids once more, straining on the rope. The boat, it seemed to George, was racing upstream, but in reality the river flew beneath her, rippling the boards. By now Major Powell had scrambled over to the men and shouted something at George, then yelled at the men. Andy Hall ran back to the *Maid,* no doubt to retrieve the other rope. They would tie it to this one, which had proven too short, and maybe then they'd attempt to let George down this flying hump of river. But how long could his boat last? Once again the *Sister* trembled, taxing the rope. Once again she swung into the cliff and George had to palm the knife, open now, while gripping the gunnels and bracing for the crash.

When she swung back out he knew if he didn't cut the rope, the boat would smash apart upon its next collision.

They'd made it through the first rapids, waving at the boys—the Howlands and Dunn—to come on, it wasn't bad, and Walter and Andy had fired their rifles for emphasis. The three in turn waved the six downriver, and once the river swung around a bend, Ora, Bill, and Seneca disappeared and that was that.

They'd struck more rapids but none they couldn't run. They'd raced downriver and that afternoon entered the lava again, black blistered cliffs knobbing up from the river, and came to another rapid —another hell, said Jack. After landing on the right the Major climbed the cliffs and said he thought they could line this one down, but he went ahead to make sure. Shit, said George, let's get it over with, so he and the others climbed back into the boats and he stepped into the *Sister.* They tied the shorter rope onto the bow post and lowered George down before realizing they should have used the longer one. The boat struck some vicious water—a humpbacked curl diving underneath the river—then perched there on its edge. Those on the cliff couldn't go any farther on their thinning ledge without being jerked off, so they snubbed the taut rope around a rock and watched George swing out then back into the cliff, uncertain what to do.

From the cliff above George, Wes felt himself praying it wasn't the end. "Oh God," he began. And left it there. George's face and posture—the way he crouched in the bow, holding up the knife, the glance over his shoulder at the boiling rapids—expressed absolute fear, the descent into paralysis. How many times had Wes seen it in the war? As though to trump God, George seemed to stand there for an eternity, looking frantically around. But once he'd decided—and Wes had also seen this—a calm seemed to unfold, the eye of the storm. He turned to check the river and, Wes knew, was appraising his options, choosing the best route through the turmoil, then turned back to cut the rope.

The *Sister* jumped the gun. Her bow post ripped loose and the rope, post, and cutwater shot into the air with such velocity Wes felt himself duck. The boat leapt ahead and George lost his balance. He almost fell out before scooting toward the stern, grabbing the great scull oar, standing up, and pulling to swing the boat around so her bow pointed downstream. Once turned, she dove straight into the water. But she flew up again on a high wave and commenced to jump the logs, up and down, up and down, and George somehow managed to stay on his feet.

Wes found himself writhing, making George's maneuvers for him. With George in the stern hanging on to the oar, the boat went completely under, and Wes's heart flew out of his mouth. George held on, though when she resurfaced the *Sister* was swamped, and now he stood in water to his knees. But the river had slowed. He waved and shouted at Wes—a war cry, Wes realized, knowing he'd made it. The boat got caught in a swirling eddy and began to swing around, another hell of repetition, but the rapids were over. He took off his hat and waved again at Wes, and the others on the cliff ran back and forth shouting. Two of them, Walter and Jack, scrambled ahead to find a way downstream.

Wes did something he'd been careful to resist the entire voyage: he dispensed with caution, scrambled down to the *Maid*, and never even bothered to scout the river. He, Hawkins, and Andy piled in, pushed off, tore out, and let the rapids take them. He gripped his seat with his hand and half stood in the boat, trying to see George. They shot across the humpbacked curl, dove down, and jumped the logs. They might have made it all right if they could have straightened out, but instead they ran the river going backward, sideways, crooked, straight, rolling with the waves. The *Maid* flipped on her side, half sunk in the foam, and held that position. They hit the trough that had sucked George down, shot beneath the surface like a dead stick, and came up, all three clinging to the bottom. Wading through fast water, George grabbed the overturned boat by the bow and pulled her into his eddy and against the low shore. Walter and Jack came running up the banks. In water to his waist, Wes grappled George and seized him with his arm, saying nothing ever gave him more joy in his life than to see him waving that hat. He managed half a bear hug and George answered with a whole one.

It was their last rapid. Later that day they ran out of the lava, granite, and schist, and camped beside a sleeping river. The following morning they swung to the north and ran out of the canyon, whose walls fell away to a wide valley with a spine of mountains descending from the right—the Grand Wash Cliffs. Here the land stretched like a fabric drawn tight on distant rollers but wrinkled by the river slung across its middle. To the west all was flat. In the *Sister*, Walter Powell took a deep breath and discharged a full six-verse performance of "Sweet Afton," doubling the volume for the finale:

Flow gently, sweet Afton, among thy green braes!
Flow gently, sweet river, the theme of my lays!
My Mary's asleep by thy murmuring stream —
Flow gently, sweet Afton, disturb not her dream!

Then he shipped his oars and let Jack row and lay back in the stern with his hands behind his head, satisfied—his brother judged—to have finished the voyage.

But they hadn't finished. Three men had left and they didn't know their fate. Wes ticked off in his mind the remaining shoulds: get to the Virgin River somewhere up ahead, find the Mormon communities, inquire about his men. Wire Detroit that he was safe; send love to Emma Dean. The longer the list grew, the more elated he felt and the less he could prevent the intruding sense of vindication. He would not even charge Bill for that watch! Poor volatile Bill, who'd made the wrong choice, who'd fled, as it turned out, just two days before they emerged from the canyon. Wes couldn't unravel—he didn't bother to try—his sense of triumph from the knowledge that those three had been misguided. When they caught up with one another, he'd be generous, magnanimous. He'd even shake Ora's hand.

Reeds and willows grew beside the river, egrets stood in the shallows. They camped that night on a bank where the current was gentle and kind, though Wes knew this water had just emerged from an endless vicious gauntlet. Overhead, the stars filled a sky contained by the whole bowl of the horizon rather than a narrow slot. After a month in creation's deepest canyon, it felt like sawing off the ceiling of a house. They built a fire of driftwood. For the first time since the Uinta Valley the mosquitoes were thick. "Surprise," said Hawkins. "Apple stew and coffee."

"I was hoping we'd have some biscuits for a change."

"We got those too."

Before eating, George offered a prayer in thanks for their safe delivery, and Wes solemnly listened. It was the beginning of Psalm 24: "The earth is the Lord's, and the fulness thereof; the world, and they that dwell therein. For he hath founded it upon the seas, and established it upon the floods. Who shall ascend into the hill of the Lord? or who shall stand in his holy place?"

All gave three cheers, ate their meager feast, and basked in the knowledge that they'd accomplished a hard and dangerous thing. "Boys," said Wes, "you ought to feel proud. You stuck like glue. There's plenty of men wouldn't have lasted."

"Like Frank the Lime Juicer," Andy said.

But Wes knew whom everyone was thinking of.

Jack looked puzzled. "That's it?" he said. "It's over?"

"I ain't saying it's over," Walter Powell said.

Wes agreed. "We have to reach the Virgin River."

"The *rapids* is over," Hawkins pointed out.

"And the canyon."

"The granite pisshouse."

"How far's the Virgin?"

"Thirty miles or so."

"Then what?"

"Then it's over," Wes said.

They fell silent and looked up at the stars, which seemed to hang ten feet above their heads. Hawkins said he thought he'd keep going to the Pacific, Andy was so intoxicated with joy he gave an Indian whoop, and Walter announced he already missed their death-defying rapids. But Jack still looked puzzled and Wes asked what was eating him. "I was just wondering," Jack said, "what we got out of this—except blisters on our calluses."

Andy said, "That ain't no way to think. We done something nobody ever done before."

"Nobody ever drove a paddlewheel over Niagara Falls either," said Jack.

"You're talking apples and oranges."

"Think them boys made it out?" Hawkins asked Jack.

"Damned if I know."

"Must be in Salt Lake City by now."

"Ain't even out of the canyon, I'd say."

"Major Powell, sir, you think they're okay?"

"I'm not too concerned. Bill Dunn's an experienced mountain man. He's a good shot—food shouldn't be a problem. Their worst worry will be water, I imagine. But with all the recent rain they'll find water pockets."

"Think we'll see them?"

"I'm hoping I'll hear some news about them in the Mormon settlements. We could even see them there—I suppose that's possible. It depends on their route and how they find their way out. I told Bill to mention Jacob Hamblin's name. They should be fine, but who knows where they are? Each day drives a greater wedge between us."

"Who's Jacob Hamblin?"

"Mormon leader."

"They'll wind up Mormons themselves," said Andy.

"Not Bill," said Hawkins. "He's got his own notions and he don't tergiversate."

4

You ought to throw away those bones, said Toab.

What bones?

The ones in your medicine pouch. You ought to get rid of them.

I don't have any bones.

Yes you do. I saw them. You were taking them out all the time back there.

Back where?

Across the river.

I don't have any bones.

Toab reached for the pouch and Onchok grabbed his wrist and held it for a minute, squeezing hard, then let go. The men had dropped back while Mara walked ahead. Toab and Onchok each carried burden baskets, and each felt a little foolish. They'd finally reached their country, their homeland, and Toab for one couldn't shake a strange feeling. Around them, every stone and tree, every faint trail, every clearing and meadow, the plateau running out to the edge of gaping canyons—the way the sky fit onto the broken horizon, the way sunlight struck cliffs and shadows filled fissures, the perfect cone of their lone mountain, the clouds, the roar of wind, the raven's wooden croak, the rock laugher's laugh, laughing at them —the place over there where they'd gathered rice grass, and right here where they'd thrown buckskins under piñons and with sticks knocked the cones, gathering pine nuts—all looked familiar, all said *home*. But something had changed. They'd been gone too long. The birds sounded different and the animals were hiding. They couldn't find their relatives and Toab felt anxious, unsure of what to do. He said, Where is everyone?

We just got here, said Onchok.

You should throw away those bones.

Why talk about that? Who wants to talk about bones? asked Onchok.

You tell me how it works. How you grow strong and powerful and wealthy and at the same time lose your wife and children. Tell me how that works.

You're talking like a crazy man.

They're the bones of a dead man's fingers, said Toab.

Don't be stupid.

Everything that happened is the fault of those bones.

That's not true. You're talking crazy. If you want to know the truth, it's all your fault. You're the one who wanted to search for the girl.

You're the one who sold his children for guns.

Why bring that up? You're just making things worse. You're jealous, I can tell. Now I understand. That's it, you're jealous.

Jealous of what?

Of my new wife.

Toab searched the ground for a rock with which to hit his brother, but nothing looked as if it belonged; it wasn't anyone's earth. I'm not jealous of your wife, he said.

What are you looking for? You want to kill me, don't you? I can tell you want to kill me. You've been witched, I can tell. Something's poisoned your mind.

You're the one, said Toab. You're the one who's a witch.

Kill me, then. Go ahead. If I'm a witch you ought to kill me.

Toab set down his basket and took a few steps toward Onchok. Onchok lowered his basket too and they faced each other. Toab said, That's right, I ought to kill you.

You've been witched. You're not yourself.

I'll be myself if you throw away those bones.

Onchok seemed to relent. I'll bury them, he said.

You'll just dig them up again.

I'll bury them tomorrow.

Bury them now.

I thought you said I'd dig them up.

I can see where you bury them. I can check if they're dug up. I'll check every day.

Onchok's brows rose and his slack mouth smirked. He grew a few inches and looked down at Toab and his voice changed. I know, he said. You want them for yourself.

Toab tasted gall. He didn't know what to do. Rage seemed to empty his arms, and like a rock in a sling his mind began to whirl, growing smaller and smaller, thinking Onchok was right. He felt bitter and ashamed. I don't want them, he said.

You do. I can tell. If you want them you can have them. You can bury them yourself. If you think they should be buried, bury them yourself.

All right then, I'll bury them. Hand them over. I'll bury them.

Each stood there waiting, Toab with his hand out. But Onchok didn't move.

They heard Mara shout and turned to see her running back. She gestured for them to come. They picked up the baskets and followed her up the trail, smelling smoke. At the edge of a clearing they spotted the shelters and lay their baskets down. They walked into camp and greeted the band of fellow Shivwits, all relatives and friends. Everyone rejoiced. But the three had to tell their news: they hadn't all returned. Onchok explained what had happened, how they'd walked a long way and been gone a long time and coming back had crossed the river at the ford to the east. Near there, some Ute shot Mara's brother and stole the three children. Earlier, miners near Havasupai had shot Pooeechuts and later on she died. He'd grown angry describing it. Everyone fell silent. And the people began to act more subdued as they set out their food. Some secretly thought, That's what you get for leaving.

Onchok told Mara to get the baskets and one at a time she brought them into camp. He pulled out their blankets and knives and baskets and ornaments. The others were impressed. Onchok had lost one wife but gained another and in the process had grown more wealthy. So perhaps, they thought now, it was good to leave.

Everyone ate while the shadows grew longer and the sun began to set. They built up the fire. Paantung, the old man's son, had news too. Three Mericats had been here and left that afternoon but went only as far as Log Water. They were going to the Mormonis.

Where did they come from? Onchok asked.

From the river. He pointed.

Onchok studied the young man with the breechclout and aquiline nose and thick hair and red headband. What did they look like?

They were miners, said Paantung. They were testing the rocks.

They ate rocks, said his father, but no one was laughing. Dirty white thieves, the old man added, trying to take our rocks. The one with the black hair had them in a parfleche.

They collected rocks and wouldn't give them back. They were looking for more, said Paantung. One went into the bushes with my sister.

His old father added, One threatened me with a gun.

Three men, said Paantung. Each one had a gun.

Three guns? said Onchok.

Standing next to Onchok, Mara spoke up and said they must have been the miners who'd shot her sister. First they tried to rape her.

Everyone began talking at once. One of Toab's uncles stood, held up his hand, and tried to make a speech. He grew so excited he was gumming his words and spraying spittle and they couldn't understand him. He slowed down and explained, clapping as he spoke, that these three men had come down the river. They hadn't crossed from Havasupai. They'd come in boats through the canyon.

Paantung's father ridiculed that notion. No one could come down the river, he said. Why would anyone try it? The idea was stupid. All nodded.

Onchok sneered and shook his head and coughed a laugh. He spoke with a low voice. They could have *crossed* the river.

Yes, of course. They could have crossed it.

But they never came down it. They're lying about that.

Yes, that's clear, they're lying. They must be the miners.

Paantung said, We should kill the Mericats.

People started shouting and Toab looked around, unsure of what to do, what to say, or how to say it. It was clear where this was going. He watched Mara talking, heard her raise her voice, and felt angry too. She wouldn't look in his direction.

Paantung raised his hands and everyone fell silent. If people kill us or steal our children, he said, the only way to stop it is to kill them. These Mericats have come between our fingers and legs and now they even want to take away our rocks. I know all there is to know about these things and what we need to do now. I know how these things start and how they happen and why we always lose. I've been through it all. That's all I have to say.

Toab's uncle spoke up. We shouldn't kill them, he said. If we kill them, more Mericats will come and kill us. He held up three fingers and said, Three for one — three of us for one of them. The Mormonis do that, they kill three for one, and so will the Mericats. I'm finished talking.

But Paantung's father said, We ought to kill them. That's the only way to stop them. Someone has to kill them.

They all began speaking. Onchok looked around and raised his hands and everyone fell silent. His voice when he began was hypnotic and deep and revealed no emotion. I'm just the same, he said, looking at Paantung. I'm feeling like you are. I'm glad you said what you did. He paused and scanned the crowd. But I'm not sure about killing them. Should we? I don't know. I don't like to hurt people. But those who shoot people and try to rape women ought to be punished. These men want to take our rocks and grass from under our feet, and they think it's all right to kill us to get them. If that's the kind of people these Mericats are, then I agree, they deserve to die. If that's the way they are, they're not people, they're lizards. They eat their own kind. They can't be happy where they are, no, they have to come here. They think they can take our things and kill us. They're cannibals. Bloodsuckers.

He stopped, glanced around, and looked at Toab's uncle. Some people say if we kill those three men more Mericats will come and kill us. They'll kill three for one. I say if we *don't* kill them right now they'll kill more of us. We have to teach them a lesson. They don't know the right ways. These people come here and get us into trouble and make us forget the way we used to do things. People get shot and everyone gets sick and people start dying and there's nothing we can do. My wife died and my children were stolen and no one can bring them back. We should kill those Mericats. Let them die, I say. I've just come back home and I ought to be happy but everything looks funny. I feel bad about it. Everything's different and I don't like it. What do you say, brother?

Toab shook his head.

Onchok said, And those Mericats have guns. You can't get a gun anywhere. It's good to have a gun. We could take theirs. If some of us had guns the Ute would stop coming to steal our children and the Mericats wouldn't shoot our wives. The way things are now a man ought to have a gun and have it with him all the time. When the others have guns, if they want to kill someone they'll just do it, just like that. But they won't kill you if you have a gun. That's all I have to say.

Paantung spoke up. Let's not talk about it over and over. If we want to get it done let's do it quickly.

Onchok took charge. Paantung, Toab, and I will do it. The rest of you stay here. We shouldn't have a war dance—they might hear. Listen in case you hear any shots, then you can come. There shouldn't be shots. I agree with Paantung, let's get it done quickly. An arrow in the back is best. If they keep running, the arrow works in. But if they're asleep I think we'll find it even easier.

The others backed off and the evening grew dark. Paantung and Onchok got their bows and arrows and stood by the fire. Toab joined them but didn't have a bow. What about you? Aren't you coming, brother?

Toab shook his head. It's not a good idea. If we kill them the Mericats will kill more of us.

If we don't kill them they'll kill more of us. We have to teach them a lesson.

How do you know it's the same men?

It has to be. One had black hair.

But how can you be sure?

Who else would it be?

Toab shook his head. This wasn't his story. This was the one he didn't want to have, the one where things grew worse and worse.

What difference does it make anyway, said Onchok. They threaten us with guns. They go off into the bushes with our women. They take our rocks. What will they take next? The trees? The river?

They can't take a river.

Oh no? They're pretty crafty.

It's a bad idea, said Toab. I'm not going.

Are you becoming a coward? his brother asked. You've never been a coward.

Toab didn't answer and Onchok felt strong. He was in charge now. He'd grown more confident and firm and determined, and didn't press Toab. Instead, he turned his back. It was better, he thought, that Toab wasn't coming. Onchok was thinking of the guns. This way he'd wind up with two of them, not one.

5

"I heard something, Bill. Out there in the woods."

"Most likely a deer."

Night. Thick stands of piñon and juniper, some hung with vines, surrounding a spring. Late-risen moon three quarters full. Frayed strings of light in the branches, on the ground, on their blankets and hands.

"I got to go again," Seneca said, and he was gone. When he came back he said, "It's them worms."

"It's that redskin food for sure."

"It's the worms in your jerky."

"You wouldn't even eat it."

"I think I ate one."

Ora was snoring a few feet off, and once again Seneca heard something in the woods, a soft snap of twig. "There. You hear that?"

"Some critter on the prowl."

Seneca listened but no other sounds came. He thought about the other men; were they still on the river? A roar came from the woods and the sky and distant canyons—the never-ending godforsaken rapids, he thought. But it was just the wind. "You think they're okay?"

"Who?"

"Andy, George, Jack. The Major."

"You didn't say Walter."

"Who cares about Walter?"

"Here's what I think, then shut your damned piehole. If their bellies and lungs ain't filled with water they're probably fine. If their food ain't run out they're just dandy, I'm sure. Making allowances for if the boats weren't smashed on rocks where the cliffs can't be climbed, they must be hunky-dory. They could shoot Major Powell and eat him for supper. Then Hawkins can say plunder truly, and Walter can grouse about the meat which he says tastes like skunk, and George can go gnaw on a portion by himself. Now for Christ's sake, please to shut your fucking gash, you little shit. I need some sleep." And Bill rolled over.

His arms behind his head, Seneca stared at the moon and let his thoughts drift back to Vermont. He remembered, growing up, catching animals on their farm. He'd once told his mother birds were in fact small people with wings, and spiders when you saw them marching through the air were riding fine grains of dust. He'd figured it out. Once he'd fed a field mouse to a stupid dray horse, who swallowed it whole. He'd seen oxen yawn and sigh when they were tired and even pine for dead companions. Oxen were smart as whips, thought Seneca. One at their farm could open all the fences leading down to the cornfield.

It was so green at home! Completely different from here. When he got back home he'd never leave again, he promised himself. He'd —

Ora groaned sharply and something whizzed by and Bill's cry was cut off. Seneca sat up quick as a bolt and a feather brushed his ear. Reaching to touch it, he felt something wet. Then with shocking force something kicked his thigh and his hand shot down and felt the stiff arrow. Men ran and whispered and bowstrings plucked, and as the noise increased and shapes rushed through the trees a horrible knowledge in Seneca's heart sank to freezing point. The next arrow pinned his arm to the ground and both wounds spread with a rippling pain — hot coals in his bloodstream — and his blood smelled like fresh beef. He felt extra bones when he tried to move and volumes of dead weight shifting inside but at least he could lie back, dizzy as he was. Sweat poured out of him and he found himself slurring, "I *did* hear something, Bill." The sweat ran off his skin into the earth, but it wasn't sweat, he knew. Flashes of pain burst in unexpected places, like his heel, with sledgehammer blows. Something smashed a rib and he felt short of breath. He wished he could lie back, then realized he had. "Bill. Hey, Bill."

Bill did not answer.

"Bill, are you Dunn?"

Then he thought what a time to say a thing like that, and he clung to the thought as the life leaked out. What a time, what a time.

6

The *Sister* and the *Maid* passed through three short canyons, low and tame, and when the third was behind them Wes spotted some Indians in a valley ahead who ran off and hid as the boats approached. Farther downriver, around a bend, Jack said, "Here's more," and there on the bank, climbing to their feet, was a large camp of mostly naked Indians. With just five pounds of flour left the expedition's crew began hollering for food. They pulled into shore and Wes took charge, cautioning the men not to leave the boats until he'd parlayed with these people. "What are they?" asked Andy, and Wes answered, "I'm not certain. Most likely Paiute."

He stepped onto shore, raised his hand, and shouted the Ute words for "friend" and "hungry," as he'd learned them at the Uinta Agency—"Tu-gu-vwun!" "Tu-gi-nur-oh-we!"—then pointed to his belly. The people looked at him puzzled. A large extended family, it appeared, they'd been sitting in shelters built of brush in the sand beside the river when the two boats floated up. Now they started running for the nearby willows. Wes shouted "Jacob Hamblin," and Andy observed, "It don't make no difference."

But four came back—a man, a woman, and two children. The woman wore just a basket on her head and the man wore only beads.

"Tu-gu-vwun," Wes said again. The man brushed off his buttocks. "Ka-ni-va? Town?" Wes inquired, and the man and the woman looked at each other. "Nu-ints?" asked Wes, pointing downstream. At last the man said "Kwop?" and Wes said "Kwap?" while Andy, Hawkins, Walter, and Jack, sitting in the boats, looked at the woman. "As disgusting a hag as ever rode a broomstick," said Jack.

It was as though she understood him. She gathered the children and ran for the willows. "Wait!" shouted Wes. "Kai-you-gay," he said, waving her back with his hand. As she stood watching them, shielding her eyes, her nakedness in the sun looked suddenly miraculous. To Wes, who hadn't seen any human beings other than his crew in more than two months, her burnished skin was freakishly dignified, even happily insolent, if also slack and lumpy. "There's your sweet Mary, Walter," said Jack, but nobody laughed. Wes felt naked himself, his clothes hanging like strings, and privately decided that nothing in that land was ever truly shielded. The sun hammered the earth then burned off the dust; the air went empty and even shadows glared. The place itself was naked.

Her skin was caked with sand and ropy black hair erupted from her hat and fell to her shoulders. Her strong wide nose and flared upper lip made her face seem almost mannish. The black hair of her pubis looked like a crow in flight.

Wes told Jack to fetch her a present, and Jack fished around in the *Sister*'s stern compartment and found a piece of colored soap. He climbed out of the boat and approached the woman, moving slowly, embarrassed. Man approaches deer, thought Wes. Jack stumbled through sand extending his arm. Her hand, palm up, received the colored soap and Jack stumbled back. The man walked up, looked at the soap, and held it to his nose, saying, "A-ni?"

Wes made motions of washing his face and splashing it with water.

"Kwop," said the man. Andy asked what that was.

"Tobacco," said Wes.

"Ain't got none!" shouted Andy.

The Paiute seemed to understand and stood there for a moment looking from one crew member to the next. Wes said again, "Jacob Hamblin," and the man nodded knowingly. Wes pointed downstream, then pointed up, barking Ute words all the while. At last the man shook his head and pointed back toward the cliffs and Wes smiled. The rest of the crew couldn't fathom this discussion. All at once the man and his family scrambled for the willows, where they disappeared. Wes said, "Let's go. Downstream," he added.

"I didn't figure up," said Hawkins.

"What did you ask them?"

"I asked if the Mormon towns were further down and if the other river met this one pretty soon."

"You said all that?"

"And what was the answer?"

"Go back the way we came. Cross Grand Wash Cliffs."

"Bullshit on that."

"That's what I say."

"I think," said Wes, "that he misunderstood."

They stopped for coffee and biscuits at noon, then started off again through land that steadily opened and spread. Saguaro cactuses grew on the brown slopes. Jack said, "More redskins," pointing ahead, and they rowed hard. "In the river," added Jack, and indeed several figures stood in the river, but it turned out to be three white men and one Paiute boy, all dragging a net. The shallows they stood in were at the spot where a wide, muddy river entered from the north.

They pulled hard on the oars. "Hello," Wes shouted.

"Hallo yourself."

"Is this the Virgin River?"

"That's what we call it."

"You fishing?" said Andy.

"No, we ain't fishing. Brigham Young ordered us to search for the remains of some damned fool named Powell and his river expedition."

"Looks like you found him," said Jack.

The man was a Mormon named Joseph Asey, the other two his sons, and the Paiute boy his "servant." The first thing Andy asked was if they'd heard about the three who'd walked out of the canyon, but they said they hadn't.

Joseph Asey looked them up and down and told them, "You bunch are as skinny as broomsticks." Word had gone out weeks ago that they must have perished in the depths of the canyon, he said. They were dragging the river to find any effects to send back to surviving loved ones.

Or to keep for yourselves, thought Wes.

They beached the boats and Asey led them to his shack. On the way he looked around and sniffed the air. "You Gentiles ever bathe?"

"We're just a passel of dirty devils," said Jack.

"What we need is shoes," said George.

At the shack Asey cooked up a mess of squashes and fish for which Wes's crew assumed the manners of hogs. Asey dispatched the Paiute boy to walk upriver to the town of St. Thomas, notify the bishop, and bring back food and news—and shoes—the next day. Then they ate again, fell asleep satisfied, and the next morning woke up so hungry they had to eat more. Wes talked about the three men who'd left the canyon and the burden they carried—the maps and letters, watches and guns, and the chronometer—and hoped it hadn't slowed them down.

Bishop Leithead himself returned with the boy, bearing melons, bread, butter, and cheese, but no news of the three. He offered the men a ride in his wagon back to civilization; Wes and Walter accepted. Wes told the others that the river from this point to the Pacific had been charted and explored thoroughly by steamboat, and in his opinion the voyage was over. Andy asked, "Is there rapids?"

"Not one," Wes said.

Then Jack, George, Andy, and Hawkins recessed to the bunkroom. The shack had two rooms, a kitchen and bunkroom, both made of slabwood nailed across studs. Wes wondered what sort of surprise they were planning, and thought of the other confab, held just four nights ago, among Bill and the Howlands. When they emerged their spokesman, Hawkins, told Wes they felt incomplete without going all the way to the Pacific Ocean. Jack asked the Major, "What about the boats?"

"You boys can have them."

Wes and Walter had already inquired if they could hire horses at St. Thomas, in answer to which Bishop Leithead confided *he* owned the stables that gave the best prices. Their plan was to ride to Salt Lake City and ask along the way about Dunn and the Howlands.

Then came an awkward moment. After exactly one hundred days and nearly one thousand miles and more than five hundred rapids and a hundred portages and the wreck of the *No Name* and the loss of food and clothing and three broken barometers and cold horrors at times worse than the war—after floating through a desolate moonscape more starkly beautiful than a thousand Niagaras—after losing collectively more than a hundred pounds and losing Frank Goodman and losing the three boys and not knowing what became of them and abandoning the *Emma* and their fossils and collections—they shook hands meekly and mumbled "Good luck" and said goodbye to each other. Even the man who'd once saved Wes's life with his drawers—who'd run the final rapids by himself, clinging to the *Sister*'s scull oar, an act of consummate bravery, thought Wes, involuntary to be sure, but executed with skill and aplomb—even George Bradley merely pressed the Major's fingers and never looked at Walter. Then Wes and Walter climbed into Bishop Leithead's wagon and started up the rough road beside the Virgin River. The other four men returned to the boats with replenished supplies and continued the journey.

Hawkins and Hall rode in the *Maid*, Bradley and Sumner in the *Sister*. In his journal Jack Sumner observed that once the river swung south after meeting the Virgin, it passed through a land of general desolation, useless on the whole and burnt to cinders. He never wanted to see it again, no more than the canyons they'd already conquered, all dull as wallpaper. They came to a canyon eighty miles downriver where a quartz mill was set up, but if it paid or not Jack couldn't find out from the canny Dutch boss. What they saw of Arizona was not worth settling, he wrote. A disgusted woodcutter who couldn't find employment—most of the land being destitute of wood—told him the whole damned territory was a bilk. In Mojave Valley they found some good land, but it needed irrigation to produce any crops. And the country below there was nothing to brag of, in Jack's opinion. The Chemehuevi Indians—a superior breed of redskins, he averred—made a living supplying fuel for the steamers plying the river between Forts Mojave and Yuma.

He and George managed to sell their boat at Fort Yuma. George continued overland to San Diego, while Andy and Hawkins finished the trip all the way to the Pacific in the Gulf of California. But Jack had had enough. He wound up sitting underneath a mesquite bush next to Fort Yuma, out of work and penniless after nearly two years of exploration, disgusted with the whole thing. "If anyone disbelieves any of this or wants to know more of the cañons of the Colorado," he wrote in his journal's final passage, "go and see it." And: "There has been many men long since that have proved that there was nothing to go for."

As for Walter and Wes, they went on with their Mormon hosts to St. Thomas and asked about Dunn and the Howlands there. No news. From St. Thomas they rode on horseback across the Beaver Dam Mountains, bypassing the Virgin River Gorge, and arrived in St. George and made fruitless inquiries. It took another ten days for the Powell brothers to make Salt Lake City, where they arrived on September 15—nearly three weeks after parting from Bill, Ora, and Seneca. And there the news had finally arrived that three members of Major Powell's expedition had been killed by a band of Paiute.

Wired from St. George, the report was based on Indian accounts that the men had killed a squaw and been murdered in retaliation.

Wes wasn't buying it, at least not publicly. The murdered men couldn't be his, he told the papers, for Dunn and the Howlands were honorable men and would not have hurt a soul. "I have no hesitation," he was quoted as saying, "in pronouncing this part of the story as libel." In private, however, he couldn't help wondering where his men were if they weren't the ones killed. They should have turned up by now. He found himself mourning poor Ora, Bill, and Seneca, though with reservations. They had only themselves to blame, after all. They were the ones who'd abandoned the voyage. And the accolades Wes received in Salt Lake—the numerous interviews, the invitations to lecture, the overflow crowd and thunderous applause at the Thirteenth Ward Assembly Rooms, where he spoke off the cuff about the expedition—served to confirm that he'd made the right choice in persevering to the end. By the time he and Walter returned to the States, he found he'd become a national hero. And the three missing men were never heard from again. And the news of their murder was never disputed.

Epilogue

One Year Later: September 1870

Dearest Emma,

How are you, my darling, and how are Charlie and your father, and how is the unexplored wilderness of Detroit? I'm afraid if my absence continues any longer you'll become a Penelope besieged by suitors. This will be the last season we are separated, I haven't wavered from that resolve—and why should you be less firm than a man? Be patient and forgive my protracted silence while I rant and make amends with mountains of paper and barrels of ink. (Brother Hamblin's recipe for ink: lampblack mixed in a round copper bowl with the glue reduced from ox-skin.)

You will reply that I informed you weeks in advance of this scheduled silence. Undoubtedly true.

But I've been here, believe it or not, for five hours, and should have written my wife the instant I discovered this secretary and chair! Dread of rudeness prevented me. Even Mormons value breeding—or especially, I should say.

Setting levity aside: not a day went by when I didn't long for you —on horseback, under a merciless sun, on the cold earth beneath a multitude of stars, squatting by a campfire amid a clutch of savages. I did succeed in finding those who murdered our men and will tell you about it. But in good time.

Received yours of the 10th inst. which with this I propose to eclipse, in length if not ardor. To answer your questions: no, the Mormons do not practice unspeakable debauches and blood sacrifices and devil worship, and the doctrine of plural marriage does not appear to have loosened their morals, which are neither more nor less degenerate than those of other pioneers in the wilderness—nor those of savages. Captain Bishop demurs on this point. He claims that the moral status of the Saints (as they call themselves) falls considerably beneath that of our civilized States and with few exceptions they are miserable sinners. They race horses, play cards, dance, smoke, and use intoxicating liquors of various stamps, and the Kanab belles, uncouth and void of grace, throw themselves at any man's feet. He exaggerates. As everyone knows, they do practice polygamy, which our countrymen think of as barbarous, but Montaigne's words apply in this case: most men think anything barbarous that is not their own custom. Brother Hamblin (I mean Jacob—most of the men here call him "Brother"; the preponderance of the women call him "Husband"), Brother Hamblin in fact may be a saint, in the general sense. He is not disposed to spout anti-Gentile nonsense as are many of his fellows, and he appears to have performed some actual miracles, such as going unarmed amongst the Indians—amongst the Navajos, no less—and never having been shot. I too believe that human trust and good will, not arms, are the way to win over the savages, but in Jacob's case this conviction came about by divine revelation. An angel of the Lord appeared to him, he says, and told him that if he never shed the blood of a Lamanite (a cursed race described in the Book of Mormon, whom they identify with the Indians), then no Lamanite would ever shed his.

According to his friends, he has since been in some tight spots but always survived without so much as a scratch. Over the years this has won the respect of sylvan men hereabouts.

This man Hamblin is six foot two inches, hook-nosed, squinting, slack-jawed, and slow of speech. He knows all the languages of the tribes in the vicinity. He never rises to anger nor descends to toadying, but conducts himself with dignity and tireless application. When I first met him at our camp he wore the ubiquitous blue overalls that all the Saints wear and, as a badge, a red bandanna neckerchief. But on our trek to search out the Shivwits Paiute, he exchanged his overalls for split-legged navvies, a fringed buckskin shirt, and Paiute moccasins. In other words, he went Indian, leaving me in my boots. I think he sees it as a mark of respect, inviting hospitality, to dress as they do, although in this scorching heat it also qualifies as practical.

It is his desk I write at and his ink I use and his food I eat. I paid him his retainer (the figure mentioned in my last) and he's been enough of a gentleman not to raise the issue of money again. He has given me a bed in his house, or fort, and extended every mark of hospitality to our little group of Gentiles. In addition to the principal wives, Louisa and Priscilla, who cook for us unceasingly, one of his many brides is a Paiute, which undoubtedly contributes to his good odor with the Indians.

When our retinue first arrived at this place we found two little houses described as a "fort" with horses and pack animals and buggies everywhere. By the time we returned, cellars had been dug and lots staked out and tents erected, or in some instances covered wagons, with fences and corrals and an abundance of stock, orchards and fruit trees, and even some barns raised. First buggies, then stock, then barns, lastly houses. Did I mention good roads? Actually, Kanab was first settled years ago, then abandoned due to Navajo raids, and only in the last year has it begun to recrudesce, under Hamblin's direction.

On the whole I've received kind treatment and straight talk from these strange people. Next year, dearest, you will see what I mean when you accompany me here. Please let me know when you've received a reply from Thompson regarding the maps I left with him. The work of surveying the canyon and river, tributaries, etc., may go on for two years and I need men like him—hardy men of talent. What else, you may ask, can one do with a gorge one mile deep, not much wider than a Chicago boulevard, and as long as the distance from Maine to Chicago, but survey and map it? Oramel's work was woefully inadequate, may he rest in peace.

When we left Kanab in search of the Shivwits, I did find an ideal location for a baseline—a flat desert plain six miles south of the settlement, large enough to lay out a line of nine or so miles for the work of triangulation. Brother Hamblin has no objection, of course, since his little community stands to profit from outfitting and feeding our party. By then Kanab will be a buzzing beehive, I'm sure.

We departed on the 13th inst., riding generally south on horses furnished by Hamblin. Walter Graves performed an ungentlemanly trick in carrying off Captain Bishop's spurs the evening before and all the time stoutly denying any knowledge of them, but Brother Hamblin set him right with a new pair—for a price, of course. Our trail followed an ancient Indian path through a forest of dwarf cedars and pines and came out at the foot of the Vermilion Cliffs. Several springs sit embosomed by the cliffs, one with an Indian village and garden, presently abandoned. The inhabitants, I was told, were out gathering pine nuts somewhere in this vast country.

The other, further south, called Pipe Spring, is where troops of the Utah militia are sometimes quartered. Outside the stone cabin, quarried rock lay around beside piles of freshly-sawed timbers, awaiting the construction of a fort on this site. Brother Hamblin told us the story of the name Pipe Spring. A number of years ago, he, his brother William, and Dudley Leavitt made a halt there, and Gunlock Bill Hamblin claimed he could shoot the bottom out of Leavitt's pipe at twenty-five yards without breaking the bowl, and proceeded to do so. He drilled a single clean hole. In telling this story, Jacob didn't make it clear if the pipe was in the man's mouth, so whether we have a Mormon William Tell or no I shall leave it to the historians to determine. We camped here for the night.

Southwest of Pipe Spring lies the forty-mile desert, where water is scarce, and beyond that the outer reaches of the Great Canyon, where the earth rends apart. Jacob had employed two Paiute Indians to help us find water in this scorching wasteland—Chuar'ruumpeak, the wizened chief, seated on a spare horse, and Shunts, his assistant, a one-eyed, bare-legged, merry-faced pygmy, who ran ahead to scout the way and came back to confer with his ancient chief and point us the right way—always ready with a jest, his broad open face a rich mine of sunny smiles.

Departing from Pipe Spring, we left behind a long line of orange and vermilion cliffs many hundred feet high. As we looked back at dawn, the sun shone in splendor on their painted faces and lit up the salient angles, while thrusting the retreating angles into shade, and I watched until my eyes fell into dream and the cliffs became a long bank of purple clouds piling up from the horizon into the heavens. Ahead, beyond the desert, was a mountain I recognized as one seen last summer on our expedition. With the help of our guides, it was there, beyond the mountain, that I planned to confer with the Indians said to have ambushed my men.

Dearest, you know how I pride myself on being able to grasp and retain in my mind the topological features of a country, but these Indians put me to shame. My knowledge is only a general sketch, theirs a particular and ever-vivid picture. After several days of scorching heat on a wide and empty desert, the land began to roll and the mountain to approach. The yellow land was merciless, and every gulch looked the same. Near one of the springs unearthed by our guides the bleached skeleton and skull of an ill-starred burro lay, and I wondered at the cruelty of the land and its indifference to those who venture across its great expanse unprepared.

The mountain, we saw, was of volcanic origin, and we soon arrived at ground considerably spread over with cinders, basalt, and fragments of lava.

Near dusk of our fourth day we reached a deep gorge on the flank of this mountain, where there was a water pocket. How can I describe my feelings in this place? I climbed a short rise of volcanic scoria and looking southeast once more saw the gorges, the deep and broken labyrinths, that flanked the Great Canyon. And everywhere I looked I saw evidence of my discovery that the rivers were here long before the mountains. East and west of this spot I counted four great lines of cliffs, all presenting their faces, or escarpments, southward. Going north from the Great Canyon, each plateau or terrace dipped gently upward until it met with another line of cliffs, which would have to be ascended to reach another plateau. What I am describing, of course, is the complex pattern of fracturing and erosion that occurred when this land was uplifted. Over the entire region in my circle of sight, limestones, shales, and sandstones were deposited through long periods of geologic time to the thickness of many thousands of feet; then the country was upheaved and tilted toward the north. But the Colorado River was already flowing when the tilting commenced, and the upheaval was excruciatingly slow, so that the river cleared away the obstruction to its channel as fast as it was presented. Furthermore, the rocks above were carried away by rains and rivers, but not evenly all over the country; nor by washing out valleys and leaving hills, but by carving the country into the aforementioned terraces, which in turn are intersected by lateral canyons. And all of this orchestrated immensity unites under the direction of a single Kapellmeister, the Colorado River.

As I stood there and watched, clouds drifted up and rolled tumultuously toward the foot of cliffs beneath me, and soon all the country below was one sea of vapor, a billowy, raging, noiseless flood, whose great waves dashed at the foot of the cliffs and rolled back once more and lashed the walls again. The sun at my shoulder was low to the west and caught the tops of those clouds and set them on fire.

After a short ride across deep ravines and scarred flows of lava the following morning, we descended to a valley where a village appeared and the ladies, paying taxes in the manner of Godiva, gathered seeds into a basket. Were these the Indians we sought? No, came Hamblin's answer—no, not yet. These were a band he called Uinkarets, meaning Region of the Pines, and were neighbors to the Shivwits. He suggested that they send a runner to the west, where the Shivwits lived another thirty miles away, and request them to come here.

We spent a day or so in this high desert fastness surrounded by lofty peaks and canyon cliffs, far from the comforts and cares of the world. Save for that first fiery cauldron when I gazed into the canyon, clouds rarely masked the air, and the sun as it circled overhead in the heavens changed the visage of the land from green to gray to gold, then at last to crimson—then gorgeous purple. Our Indian hosts showed me how they roasted seeds in basket trays filled with hot coals, by tossing and rolling the contents in such a manner that the seeds migrated, perfectly parched, in a pile to one side, and the spent coals to the other. I could converse a little bit with them in Ute, which appeared to amaze them. Old women laughed when I asked them to show me how they ground seeds—it was as if they should ask me how I walk on two feet—and children covered in rabbitskin robes hopped about madly, or simply stared from monkish cowls. The men of the tribe demonstrated a rabbit hunt, setting up two V-shaped wings of a net and then beating the brush, although few rabbits came. They said it wasn't the season.

The nights were cold and the days hot and dry but with cool distant winds—harbingers of winter. I induced the men to tell me one of their myths (tho' it wasn't, they informed me, the proper time to do so) which purport to give a history of an ancient race of animal gods. I'm afraid it won't do to recount it for you here, since the story seemed longer than our Old Testament, and the pauses interlacing it, allowing Jacob to translate, elongated it further, until by the time the withered specimen who was telling it finished and fell helplessly asleep I alone was awake. But I did write it down and will share it anon—when I see your shining face and we're together once again.

At last the news came that the long-looked-for Shivwits would come the next day, sometime before dusk.

Brother Hamblin warned me they were different from these villagers—they seldom saw Mormons or any outsiders, nor ventured from their isolated country, and in general had been judged an unfriendly lot.

The next day at supper time our hosts grew excited and several jumped up and went into the woods. They came back with twelve or fourteen frightened creatures, the sorriest specimens of humanity ever seen. Brother Hamblin had not prepared me for this; I expected ferocity and found poor and hungry wretches little more than brutes. The men had bare bodies, breechclouts, and no leggings. The women wore only rabbitskin blankets, tied across the right shoulder and hanging down the right side, and for skirts they sported doeskins, or skins of mountain sheep, with the hair left on. All were caked with mud or smeared with dust, all scratched their filthy heads, wild with black hair. They carried no weapons, but in truth the only weapons I could picture such specimens as these carrying were clubs.

Was it, my darling, my mind's fever pitch, my anxiety at meeting the murderers of our men, that made me see them as sub-human? I pictured them as having just emerged from smoky caves. If you had been here it might have stretched your belief to conclude that they love and regret and love again—suffer joy and dashed hopes, have dreams and disappointments—in the same manner we do. It stretched mine, as you shall see, but when all was said and done, well, you be the judge.

We shared with them our food—or the Uinkarets did—and after supper as shadows grew long these Shivwits held a pow-wow off by themselves in a patch of bare sand where they squatted and scratched. Then the seance began. We formed a semi-circle two or three deep, with Hamblin, Bishop, and myself at the head, the Uinkarets on one side, the Shivwits on the other, and a bonfire in the middle. But before we could start, the pipe had to be passed, and I began with my own—lit it and drew deeply on the bowl and passed it to my left. But when, from my right, the Shivwits pipe arrived, and when I saw the stem was broken off, and a well-chewed, saliva-soaked buckskin rag had been wrapped around the end and tied with sinew, I shrank from it, repulsed. I'm afraid, my darling, that I acted the coward and, to gain time, refilled the filthy pipe, all the time engaging in earnest conversation with Bishop to my left; then, all unawares, I passed it on unlit. No one seemed to notice.

A big cloud of smoke was blown, the tobacco was shared, and a long and profound silence fell around us as the air became amber and shadows spread to darkness. In the light from the bonfire, each lurid face blended into the next, until all of us were devils, whites and Indians alike.

At last Brother Hamblin stood up to speak, and my knowledge of Ute enabled me to understand some of what he said; he summarized the rest later. He introduced me by name and explained to the Indians in a creditable and awe-inspiring manner who I was and why I was there. He tried to make them understand that I was visiting their country because white men are eager to know many things, and he who knows the most is honored as the best. My object, said Jacob, was to learn about their country and their people, in order to tell other men at home; and he explained that I wished to come back and visit them again next year and take pictures and write down their language and stories.

Whether he defined these things for them—taking pictures and writing—I neglected to ask.

He made them understand that my purpose was not to work any evil upon them. That I was not hunting gold or other metals; that I would be along the river sometime next season with a party of men; and that if they found any of the party away from the river, in the hills, they must not be alarmed but regard them as friends and show them watering holes and give them whatever assistance they required. He reminded them that last year this had not happened; that with a group of men I had come down the river, and some of my men had wandered off and been murdered by their people, and this filled us with sadness. Why had it occurred?

The poor devils stirred and looked at each other and spoke among themselves until one of them stood and all grew silent again. This man, in a breechclout and with face painted red, tho' some had rubbed off, spoke with artful subtlety, I thought, but his hypnotic carping and thick reiterations grew frequently annoying. Once again I understood some words here and there; others, punctuated by a variety of gestures, the context made clear; and Brother Hamblin interrupted when he could to translate the rest. I listened with distrust and perverse fascination. His name, I later learned, was Toav, or Toab, meaning Rabbit Tick—an appropriate eponym if there ever was one.

Your talk is to-wich-wana, good, he said to Jacob, but looking at me. Ou-wick-er-am, very good indeed. We believe in Jacob and regard him as a father, he told me with a smile. I didn't trust the smile. When you are hungry, you may have our game, he said. You may gather our fruits and nuts if you need to, and we will show you the springs and you can drink our water. That's the way we've always done things. And the water tastes good. It's the best-tasting water around here, he said, and he ballyhooed the water until I grew restless and could scarcely resist the urge to shout, "We didn't come here to learn about the water!"

He dropped the smile. We will be friends, he said. We will tell all our people that Ka'purats is their friend. Later Brother Hamblin told me Ka'purats means Arm Off. We will tell them he is Jacob's friend, he said, and he went on about friends just like the water, then his voice dropped and he glanced around the group until, when he returned to my gaze, his eyes were round and black. I stared at him intently but his face betrayed nothing, as is the case with so many of these stoics. Did he see me as I saw him, that is, with the same mixture of curiosity, mistrust, and revulsion? I couldn't take my eyes off him. Look at us, he said. Look at our women and our children seated here. You can see that we are poor. We don't have horses. We climb the rocks and our feet become sore. We live among the rocks and all we have to eat is thorns. We have not much to give and you musn't think us mean. You are wise and smart; we are ignorant children.

And his subtle smile returned, as though he couldn't help it, and he said that last year some of his people had killed three men because bad people told them they were enemies. They told lies, he said. They claimed they were bad and we thought it was true and so we grew angry. We acted like children. We are very sorry. It's over now, done. Don't think of it again. We should be friends, he said. We're sorry we did it. When we do wrong, don't you be like us. Don't be children too and grow angry and kill us.

When white men kill our people, we kill them, he said. Then they kill more of us. It's no good. We love our country. We're poor, but we're honest. You have a good heart, he said, looking at me. You have horses and guns and many other things. We hear that the white men have a great number, and when you stop killing us, there won't be any Indians left to bury the dead. You are very wise. You have a good heart. That's all I have to say.

He sat down all at once.

As for me, I believed little of this rant. His remark that they were children was self-serving, Emma—he merely said what we wanted to hear. Still, in moments of horror I ask myself what sort of cosmic compass brought them together, these squalid primitives and my three men. Was it blind chance? If so, chance is devilish and cruel. Sometimes I fancy its fiendish laughter echoes through these mountains and canyons.

Our exercises concluded with a general hand-shaking and expressions of good will, and after that Brother Hamblin fell into conversation with another man, holding him while the others walked off. This man, Paantung, related more particulars about the deaths of our men. They came on the village of Shivwits almost starved and nearly dropping from exhaustion, he said. The villagers fed them and put them on their way toward the Mormon settlements, describing where to find water. But after they had left some other Indians arrived, having crossed from the east side of the Colorado. And they said those white men must have been the same miners who'd shot and killed one of their squaws. No, said the villagers, they'd come down the river. But these bad people pointed out that no one had ever come down the big canyon, that that was impossible, and that by telling such a lie they were trying to hide their guilt. In this manner this newly arrived group worked the whole village into a great rage. Three of them decided to follow the white men and surround them in ambush, but which three Jacob couldn't learn. They filled the men with arrows.

I requested Jacob to ask this man what became of their remains and the things they carried with them—their papers and instruments—and even tried to describe the chronometer, through Jacob. The man looked puzzled, or feigned the same, and I never had an answer.

Later on we all bedded down, the Uinkarets in their brush shelters, we in our tents, and the Shivwits in the sand. They cleared a small, circular space of ground, banked it around with dead brush and sand, and slept in a pile of human flesh—men, women, and children; buckskin, lice, and sand.

I slept well that night, in perfect peace, despite the fact that the murderers of my men were just five hundred feet away. It must have been Hamblin's presence. For one thing, neither the Uinkarets nor the Shivwits had attempted to steal a jot of our provisions, not even a lump of sugar. Altogether, my dearest, tho' I'm still haunted by that brave at our seance, and see him in my mind making his speech with the light of the fire guttering his face, with his black eyes shining and the corners of his mouth ever so lightly curled, I never felt in any danger. They were crafty little people, too enamored of dirt for my tastes, yet clinging to a life they've always known. I ought to add that I'm convinced this one Toab led the killings himself.

Nor did we entertain thoughts of revenge, you'll be pleased to know. I despise that so-called code. Like Jacob, I come unarmed among these people. Not guns and ammunition—pencil and notebook. Did I mention in my last that I've been taking vocabularies of every Indian I meet? This, in addition to collecting implements, such as baskets, robes, bows, etc. If these people are doomed to vanish from the earth, at least their language and culture will be preserved forever. Bring your sketchpad and pencils next year, dearest Emma, and you can contribute to the task of preservation.

As the Shivwits filed out the following morning, bedraggled and filthy—returning to their country—Captain Bishop remarked, "They're just animals with speech." He rebuked me for my answer: "So are we." The vanity of those who see through all illusions! One rebukes oneself too.

Over the following days, we scouted a route to the floor of the canyon by which supplies could be carried to the river next year via Mormon wagon trains. The promise I made to a certain loved one was foremost in my mind: never again to venture down the river without pre-determined points of rendezvous and supply—and of escape, if need be.

We returned to Kanab by the same route. Bishop stays with a family of pioneers and helps them build a fruit cellar, roofed at ground level. They haven't yet built a house—first things first—and he sleeps in their wagon. I've not dared ask him where he finds room amidst a family of seven. In the greater comfort of Jacob's little cabin, the Saint and I have had some discussions concerning the landscape, including the relative merits of several names for those mountains and forests we visited. I settled on Trumbull for the larger of the two mountains, and Logan for the smaller, after the senators, both influential with Congressional appropriations. For the region as a whole, it seemed to us that the Indian name Uinkarets would be most appropriate, and so we adopted it.

As we spoke, I stood up, then glanced back at the chair—the very one in which I am seated now, concluding this letter. It is an ordinary chair, ready-made and undoubtedly shipped here from the east, with the usual spokes and arms and splayed legs. And Emma, you will credit me with an inspiration—or with more of what you call so affectionately my madness. I imagined this chair, or one very like it, nailed on a boat for my next river trip. Can you picture it? I've often confessed to you (and no other) my feelings of helplessness in the work of river travel, being unable to row or assist very much with lining down and portages. But with such a chair, how much more could I contribute! From its eminence I would have an unobstructed view of the river ahead, and could guide us through the rapids—or, conversely, signal us ashore—and the men in other boats wouldn't fail to see my signal, since my head and shoulders would be raised above the others. I think the new boats should be decked in the middle—one of them, at least—and there I'll nail my chair.

Staring at this chair I fell into a revery while Jacob Hamblin watched. I wonder what he thought. The entire expedition on the two rivers washed over me like a flood. There I was, back on our voyage again, with an unknown distance yet to run, an unknown river to explore, and I felt the heavy load of all the cares and anxieties of that pilgrimage once more: the worry over food and the rapids ahead and the condition of the boats, and whether Jack would agree we ought to line down these falls instead of run them, and whether Ora would remember to take compass bearings, and whether Seneca would stop teasing Bill Dunn. No one had died yet; still, for all that, the feeling of doom was so overwhelming it unmanned me completely. But so was the feeling of exhilaration, for I've never lived so intensely as during those months, not even in the war. Fear and beauty together, the philosophers say, constitute the sublime, and the sublime was all our meat. Once again I ran through the Canyon of Lodore, and Andy Hall recited Southey's poem. His bronzed, hardy face came before me once more. What brave and good men, I thought, staring at that chair, overwhelmed with a joy that seemed almost a grief. Once again through Labyrinth and Stillwater Canyons, through Glen and Marble Canyons, and of course the Great Canyon, our swift boats flew. Through deep gorges, rushing waters, bottomless silences, tall and craggy cliffs built by artists celestial. And, seated on that chair, what a concept of sublimity would thereby be obtained, what a view of that stairway from gloom to heaven—unequaled on the hither side of Paradise!

Your Loving Husband,
Wes

Afterword

Readers interested in enjoying the ride should not read this Afterword first. It discloses the novel's climax.

John Wesley Powell did in fact organize a second exploration of the Green and Colorado Rivers, in 1871—with an entirely different crew—and did ride on a wooden chair nailed to a platform on the lead boat, which was, as in the first expedition, named the *Emma Dean*. He later became a prominent geologist and ethnologist, the first director of the Smithsonian's Bureau of Ethnology and the second director of the U.S. Geological Survey, which he helped to found. His *Exploration of the Colorado River of the West* contains a "journal" of his 1869 expedition that was written five years after the voyage and that combines events and observations from both the 1869 and the 1871 explorations. He and **Emma Dean Powell** had one child, Mary Dean, and lived in Washington, D.C., for the last thirty years of his life; he died in 1902.

After the 1869 expedition, **Jack Sumner** continued trapping and hunting, then married and settled in Rawlins, Wyoming; he later moved to Grand Junction, Colorado, and superintended a placer mine on the Dolores River. In his later years, he lived with his son in Vernal, Utah, and nursed an implacable resentment against Powell, whom he accused of failing to pay him for his work on the 1869 voyage and of ordering Bill Dunn to leave the expedition. His accusations were printed in a book titled *Colorado River Controversies*, published in 1907, thirty-eight years after the expedition. He died in Utah in 1907.

William Rhodes "Missouri" Hawkins became an Arizona farmer after the Powell expedition and served as justice of the peace in Graham County, Arizona. He also nursed a lasting resentment against Powell and described what he considered to be Powell's failures of leadership and character in both *Colorado River Controversies* and a 1920 booklet, *Adventures in the Canyons of the Colorado*. He died in 1919.

George Bradley settled in San Diego after the expedition and for fifteen years owned a fruit farm there. In 1885, his declining health caused him to return to Massachusetts, where he died in his sister's home in North Andover.

Walter Powell's mental health steadily declined after the 1869 voyage. He suffered severe headaches and long bouts of depression. His sister and brother-in-law cared for him until her death, when he entered a military hospital in Washington, D.C. He died there in 1915.

Andy Hall worked as a mule driver and a stagecoach guard after the expedition. In 1882, robbers near Globe, Arizona, held up the stage he was guarding, shot him, and left him for dead. He regained consciousness and managed to follow them, but they spotted him and shot him five times, and he died. He was thirty-one years old.

Frank Goodman was never heard from again after he left the expedition at the Uinta Ute Reservation in early June of 1869.

The remains of **Bill Dunn, Oramel Howland,** and **Seneca Howland** have never been found. This mystery has encouraged alternate theories as to their fate, the most recent of which holds that Mormons killed the three men and enlisted the Paiute to help them cover up the murders. This idea is intriguing but almost entirely lacking in evidence. The Shivwits who met with Powell in September of 1870, as described in my Epilogue, did indeed confess to the murder—unless one judges as plausible the contention that Jacob Hamblin either coached them to admit to murders they did not commit or mistranslated their words in order to deceive Powell. The former is unlikely because of all the Paiute bands in Utah, the Shivwits had the least contact with Mormons and other whites, including Hamblin; the latter is unlikely because even Powell's imperfect knowledge of Ute, of which Paiute is a dialect, would have enabled him to detect such a ruse.

The individual Paiute who participated in the killings have remained anonymous, with these exceptions: a Shivwits named **Toab** is sometimes mentioned in reminiscences of Mormon ranchers as having had something to do with the murders. Toab was in fact a nearly legendary figure for later generations of Paiute. He was said to have supernatural powers, to be bulletproof, and once to have stood in a burning bonfire without being harmed. To the degree that he was a hero to the Paiute he was a villain to whites, who jailed him for five days in 1907 for stealing a horse. Another Shivwits, **Paantung,** was also subsequently connected with the murders, principally in Frederick Dellenbaugh's account of Powell's second expedition.

The other Paiute characters in my novel are fictional. Their story is an extrapolation of statements made by the Shivwits during that meeting with Powell in September of 1870, as reported by both Powell and Jacob Hamblin. They said that Powell's three men came upon their village and were hospitably fed and shown the way to the Mormon settlements near present-day St. George, Utah. But after they left, more Indians came from the east side of the river who, when they were told about the white men, said they must have been the miners who'd shot one of their women.

The fate of both the Shivwits and the San Juan Paiute after 1869 is tragically typical of most western tribes. In 1903, when Toab was still alive, a Mormon rancher bought a small tract of land outside St. George and obtained permission from the federal government to move the Shivwits onto it; it has since been their reservation. The remote Shivwits Plateau, more than fifty miles away, became rangeland for ranchers. The San Juan Paiute (the "People from the Other Side") briefly had their own reservation near Navajo Mountain (Paiute Mountain in my novel)—until 1922 when the Paradise Oil and Refining Company persuaded the U.S. Bureau of Indian Affairs to return it to the public domain so drilling rights could be obtained. Later, after drilling proved fruitless, the area occupied by the San Juan Paiute was added to the growing Navajo Reservation. The San Juan Paiute are, in a sense, the forgotten Paiute; they were not officially recognized as a tribe by the federal government until 1989.

The canyon country of the Green and Colorado Rivers is also a major character in this novel, one whose subsequent fate likewise deserves consideration. In 1936, the Hoover Dam was finished, creating Lake Mead at the place where the Powell expedition emerged from the Grand Canyon. In 1962, Flaming Gorge Reservoir, made possible by the Flaming Gorge Dam, began filling the valleys and canyons of the Green River just below the town of Green River, Wyoming, where Powell's expedition launched. And in 1963, the Glen Canyon Dam was completed, and for the next seventeen years backed up the waters of the Colorado River along the heart of Powell's voyage until its spawn, Lake Powell, reached full depth. Lake Powell now stretches for one hundred and eighty-six miles and contains more than twenty-six million acre-feet of water. Beneath it lies the canyon that John Wesley Powell named for its "curious, narrow glens" amid great curves of sandstone, glens that once contained waterfalls, streams, cottonwoods, willows, oaks, ferns, moss, and hanging gardens, all sprung from naked rock. Glen Canyon also contained thousands of archeological sites, including numerous stone structures and cliff dwellings built eight hundred years ago by the so-called Anasazi, or Pueblo ancestors. Today, conservationists and conservation groups such as the Glen Canyon Institute advocate breaching the dam and draining the lake named for John Wesley Powell—and allowing the forces of wind, sun, rain, and river to restore Glen Canyon.

The chief sources for Powell's 1869 expedition are his *Exploration of the Colorado River of the West*, the journals kept by Jack Sumner and George Bradley, and the later controversial reminiscences of William "Missouri" Hawkins and Jack Sumner in *Colorado River Controversies*. For information about Powell's life and subsequent career, I consulted the two biographies of Powell published in the 1950s: William Culp Darrah's *Powell of the Colorado* and Wallace Stegner's classic *Beyond the Hundredth Meridian*. Donald Worster's more recent book on Powell, *A River Running West*, was unfortunately not yet published when I was writing this novel.

One of my main sources for Paiute oral history and culture was La Van Martineau's *The Southern Paiute*. Powell's own work on the Paiute was helpful too, as was Edward Sapir's and, more recently, Pamela Bunte and Robert Franklin's books on the Paiute in general and the San Juan Paiute in particular. Benn Pikyavit helped me with matters of language and pronunciation and with Paiute lore and stories. One source for rendering Navajo speech into English was the Navajo autobiography *Son of Old Man Hat*.

For the record: none of the historical John Wesley Powell's letters to his wife, Emma Dean, have survived. The letters in Parts One and Three and in the Epilogue of my novel are fictional constructions.

Thanks to Frank and Holly Bergon, Janet Silver, and especially Heidi Pitlor, whose suggestions for revising this novel were invaluable. Thanks to George Kocur for helping me to understand Powell's surveying methods, and to Donald Worster for his information about Emma Dean Powell. Special thanks to Mike and Mollie Willborn for letting me use their cabin to work on this book. And Scott Thybony and Tony Williams have my deepest gratitude for showing a stranger out of the blue—me—the nearly inaccessible Shivwits Plateau and the inscription on top of Mount Dellenbaugh that may or may not have been left by Bill Dunn.

John Vernon is the author of ten books, including the novels *All for Love: Baby Doe and Silver Dollar, Peter Doyle,* and *La Salle.* His acclaimed memoir, *A Book of Reasons,* was selected as a New York Times Notable Book and a Publishers Weekly Book of the Year. The recipient of two National Endowment for the Arts fellowships, Vernon teaches at the State University of New York at Binghamton. He lives in Little Meadows, Pennsylvania, and Estes Park, Colorado.

ALSO BY JOHN VERNON

A Book of Reasons

A NEW YORK TIMES NOTABLE BOOK

"Vernon's writing is so agile, and his grasp of history so absorbing . . . Paul Vernon left a deep mark on his brother's consciousness, and John Vernon has passed it on to his readers." — *New York Times Book Review*

In this "powerful, moving personal history" (*Entertainment Weekly*), John Vernon examines the everyday objects and activities that spark memories. When his reclusive brother, Paul, died and Vernon was charged with settling Paul's affairs, he came face to face with a house in a state of chaotic disrepair, decrepit and full of trash. As he sorts through Paul's belongings, Vernon explores the themes of brotherly love, loss, and self-discovery, making connections between his brother's odd, individual life and all our lives and the things that clutter them.

ISBN 0-618-08235-2